"Now that we're on a first name basis,"
I said, "what's this problem you mentioned?"

She frowned, black brows pulling down over the dark eyes. Then she lifted a leather handbag from the seat beside her, placed it on the tabletop, and opened its clasp. She reached inside and pulled out an envelope, took something from the envelope, and extended it toward me. I barely got a glimpse of what appeared to be several photographs, about four-by-five-inch color shots, then she jerked them away, stuffed them into the envelope and stuck it back in the leather bag, placed the bag in her lap.

Maybe I'd gotten only a glimpse, but the top photo had unquestionably been of a woman, nude, facing the camera and with her arms raised, hands holding a fluffy pink towel atop her head, the cloth covering her hair and falling down along one side of her face.

Look for these Tor books by Richard S. Prather

THE AMBER EFFECT
THE CHEIM MANUSCRIPT
THE KUBLA KHAN CAPER
SHELLSHOCK
TAKE A MURDER, DARLING

RICHARD S. PRATHER
SHELLSHOCK

TOR

A TOM DOHERTY ASSOCIATES BOOK
NEW YORK

SHELLSHOCK

Copyright © 1987 by Richard S. Prather

A TOR Book
Published by Tom Doherty Associates, Inc.
49 West 24 Street
New York, NY 10010

Cover art by Maren
Jacket Design by Joe Curcio

ISBN: 0-812-50783-5   Can. ISBN: 0-812-50784-3

Library of Congress Catalog Card Number: 87-50479

First edition: November 1987
First Mass Market edition: September 1988

Printed in the United States of America

0 9 8 7 6 5 4 3 2 1

For the two men without whose efforts this book would not have been published, and probably would never have been written:

RICHARD CURTIS, authors' representative (of his many virtues, not least is persistence,

and

MICHAEL SEIDMAN (everything a brilliant and caring editor should be).

Chapter One

It was the kind of summery Southern California morning when kids play hooky and lie on green-softened hillsides watching clouds make friendly faces. A day when men are stronger and more bold than they were yesterday, when lissome ladies are lovelier, more wanton, more willing.

It was a day when I felt as though one more deep breath of L.A.'s for-a-change-smog-free air would let me float right up off the pavement; when, no matter what might come my way, I could handle it in a breeze. On a morning like this, when the very air was laden with Fortune, Luck, Invincibility, and even Oxygen—and I was breathing in more than my share of those good things—no matter *what* came down the pike it would be a piece of cake, it would be a lark.

Or so I thought.

So I thought then . . .

I'm Shell Scott.

My six feet two inches and two hundred plus a few pounds were not floating above the pavement this splendid Monday morning in October. Instead, I was striding energetically up Broadway in downtown Los Angeles, toward the Hamilton Building where, up one flight and a hop down the hall, is *Sheldon Scott, Investigations*. It was not yet nine o'clock in the A.M., at least an hour, maybe two, earlier than I usually reported to myself for work, if indeed I reported at all.

1

Hazel would be surprised. She would be astonished.

Hazel is the cute and curvy, also bright, bubbly, efficient, indispensable, invaluable, and sometimes very-damn-smart-mouthed little lovely who mans, or womans—or, in this day of idiot language, persons—the PBX switchboard and computer corner at the end of the hallway outside my one-man office door.

I zipped through the Hamilton's lobby, disdained the elevators, took the stairs three at a time, and thundered down the hallway to Hazel's cubicle.

"Hello, hello, and good morning, and *great* morning to you," I cried, beaming at Hazel's back. "Isn't it grand?"

She was rapidly punching instructions into the IBM PC's keyboard before her, while rows of letters formed dancing word-graph patterns on the monitor's amber face, her compact but dandy derriere planted on the padded leather seat of a four-wheeled stool.

"Isn't what grand?"

"Everything!"

She spun around on the stool's swivel seat, patted both hands on the tops of her thighs, looked intently at me. "For a moment I thought the raucous individual yelling at the top of his lungs behind me might be an acquaintance of mine named Shell Scott. But, no, this can't be he."

"This be him."

"Not a chance. Him, it, is home asleep." She moved her legs, pulling with one foot and then the other to scoot her stool closer to me. "It is groaning as it awakens, smacking its gummy lips, suffering the terrible but well-deserved effects of all that womanizing and carousing last night—"

"What woman—"

"—preparing to get up and then go back to bed—"

"—and *what* carou—"

"—until tomorrow, or the next day, or whenever his hibernation ends." She peered up at me. "That coarse springy white hair, cut nearly as short as the Buddha's; those strange badly bent brows like cotton from vitamin bottles; that brutally savaged face, ravished and burned by the noonday sun . . . You do look a little like him even in this good light. But you cannot be the absentee owner of

Sheldon Scott, Sometime Investigations. Not at . . ." She glanced at a tiny and glittery watch on her slender wrist. ". . . eight fifty-eight in the *morning*."

"I'm all of those guys," I growled, disgruntled. "And then some. At least, I was until you started destroying my self-image again. How come you never fling yourself at me and bite my ears?"

She smiled. "There's an interesting letter waiting for you, Shell."

"Letter?"

"Must be important. It was delivered by special messenger half an hour ago. I put it on your desk—maybe it's a bomb."

"Bomb? What happened to our fight?"

"Time to get to work. Go! Get cracking!"

She spun, pulling with her legs and digging in her heels, scooting back to the humming PC.

"O.K., boss," I said. And got cracking.

I saw the letter, centered on the top of my solid-mahogany desk, as soon as I stepped inside my office. The letter, more accurately a large padded manila envelope, was from Bentley X. Worthington, Esquire, Attorney-at-Law, senior partner in the law firm of Worthington, Kamen, Fisher, Wu, & Hugh, of Phoenix, Arizona.

Interesting indeed. Bentley was a high-powered and very high-priced attorney heading one of the most prestigious law firms in Arizona. Short in stature but tall in spirit and integrity, he was a hair-splitter and i-dotter, but warm and likable nonetheless. I had worked for him twice in the past, first on a missing-person case and later on a missing-million job. I found the missing person in a little town called Quartzsite, which is almost indistinguishable from all of the unpopulated desert surrounding it that isn't called Quartzsite, and shortly thereafter recovered the eighty-seven dollars—all that was left of the embezzled thousand grand. I worked diligently, but also got lucky in both cases, and wrapped them up with such speed that Bentley bestowed seldom-given praise for "jobs well done, old boy."

Quite possibly, then, this was another case Bentley

wanted wrapped up in a jiffy, another quickie producing an embarrassingly fat fee for me. However, before opening the envelope to find out what might be cooking, besides cactus, in Arizona on this first day of October, I fed the guppies banging their noses at me on the glass front of their aquarium.

The ten-gallon tank is against the wall to the right of my office door; and guppies, less familiarly *Poecilia reticulata,* are marvelous little fishes about an inch to an inch and a half long, with spectacular gracefully flowing caudal and dorsal fins. They are among the most colorful little beasties in the world, displaying every kaleidoscopic color of a psychedelic rainbow, and after giving them the treat of some special ground crab meal, I watched them for a minute, delighting as always in their eye-dazzling friskiness.

Incidentally, if you were listening a little while ago, to Hazel, I feel it is important that we not get off on the wrong foot here. In weighing her slanders, I ask you to consider, first, that she is a woman, which explains many otherwise impenetrable mysteries. Second, that nothing she said about me was true. Third, even if a little bit of it was approximately true, Hazel practices exaggeration exceeding hyperbole and on occasion deliberately lies. And, finally, if you want to know the truth about someone, you would be wise to consult that individual best informed about the someone in question, aware not only of his faults but also of his virtues. And in this case, that's me, right? Listen to me, then:

I am a tall, well-muscled, bronzed fellow, one with the appearance of tremendous health and vitality, both of which virtues I in fact possess to a wondrous degree. I am thirty years old. And expect never to get much older, even if I live to be a hundred and fifty. While it is true that my hair is so blond and sun-bleached it might be called white, and tastefully barbered so it attains a length—measured straight up into the air—of only an inch, and the upslanting and then down-bending brows over my healthily sparkling, or piercing, or dynamic, or maybe steely gray eyes *are* white, and *are* maybe the approximate shade of cotton, they are *not* anything whatever like Hazel's dumb description.

True, my nose has been broken twice and set correctly the first time. And there is a fine scar over my right eye. And a little hunk was shot from the top of my left ear; but it was an insignificant hunk, from only one ear, and there was no real use for it so far as I can tell. Also true, I have been known to go out on the town and eat a bunch of rare prime ribs, and drink a bunch of bourbon, and hugely enjoy a bunch of girl; and I confess to a keen and appreciative eye for all the lovelinesses of the fair sex, and I have never pretended to be a monk or a hermit or eunuch. O.K.? So? What's wrong with that?

As for the faults—well, we *all* have some of those don't we?

I climbed into the big swivel chair behind my desk and opened the envelope from Bentley X. Worthington. Took out: a two-page letter on the law firm's stationery, neatly typed with carbon-paper ribbon and signed "Bentley" in a heavy flowing script; a single sheet of heavy white bond paper with some names and dates and other information typed on it; a newspaper clipping with *The Arizona Republic* and a date, six days ago, written in ink across its top above the bold-type heading "ALLEGED EX-GANGSTER SHOT"; and a faded three-by-four-inch photograph of a little kid. It was either a boy or a girl, I couldn't tell for sure, but whatever it was, the kid appeared to be about five or six years old, suffering some kind of anguish or severe pain, and preparing to fall into a swimming pool.

There was also a large pale green check with "Worthington, Kamen, Fisher, Wu, & Hugh" printed in little tiny thin letters, and in big fat letters the name "SHELDON SCOTT" and "$2,000.00." Attached to the check was a small piece of paper at the top of which was scribbled a message signed with a "B" trailing off into a long wavy line that presumably meant "entley." The scribbling was, "Retainer, to pique your interest, or greed. Whichever works. You are now morally obligated to find little—but now presumably bigger—Michelle by no later than, say, Monday (which, as you read this, will be today). So get cracking, old boy!"

Get cracking? Had Hazel, in addition to despoiling my wonderful day, been reading my mail?

I read my mail. The letter, dated Sunday, September 30, or yesterday, began:

> Sheldon: On the afternoon of Monday, September 24 (one week ago as you read this), our client, Mr. Claude Romanelle, was shot (see newspaper clip), not fatally, by two assailants, identity and whereabouts unknown. Today I visited Mr. Romanelle in the Scottsdale Memorial Hospital, where he is recovering from his wounds. I there presented to him a document, prepared at his urgent request, providing for the transfer of substantial assets, until then the sole property of my client, into joint ownership with his daughter, born Michelle Esprit Romanelle (see enclosed snapshot).

I put the letter down for a moment, picked up the old and faded photograph. So the kid was a little girl. Apparently, little boys and girls are identical. She was wearing only a pair of baggy swim trunks, her legs angled in toward each other as if maybe she was knock-kneed, and her lips were pulled away from white teeth while at the same time her entire face was scrunched up sort of in a bunch at its center, as she either squinted into bright sunlight or chewed on some grapefruit sprinkled with alum. Rather an ugly little tot, I thought.

The letter from Bentley went on:

> This evening in my presence Mr. Romanelle signed the document, thereupon immediately transferring joint control of those substantial assets to his daughter. Said documents urgently —*urgently*—require her signature. You, Sheldon, are to ensure that this is accomplished expedi-

tiously and discreetly. That is: Only you and I are to know the identity of our client. The name "Romanelle" is not to be revealed in your investigation, broadcast or bandied about. Neither is the name "Michelle Vetch" (see below).

On a separate enclosure, you will find the given name of my—our—client's daughter (which name, apparently, she no longer uses) together with the date when and place where she was born, the names of her parents, and such helpful information as her weight, length, and sex at birth. Mr. Romanelle states, upon information and belief, that one Michelle Vetch may have been living in Los Angeles at some time during the last several months and this person may—or may not—be the daughter he seeks. That is all we know. Except, of course, what she looked like twenty years ago (see snapshot).

I have, however, assured our generous client that the information supplied, meager though it might appear to some, will be more than ample to enable a man of your peculiar and exceptional abilities to successfully, discreetly, and speedily —*speedily*—conclude this investigation, discover the present whereabouts of Michelle, and deliver her to me in my offices at the Hall-Manchester Building (for her signature on the document aforementioned). *After* this is accomplished, you may then restore to Mr. Romanelle his long-lost daughter, and accept the $10,000 bonus I've wangled for you as a reward for a job well and speedily done.

There was a typed P.S. at the bottom of the page, with something else scribbled beneath it. The typed P.S. said, "I twice, above, used the word 'discreetly.' This is because Mr. Romanelle indicated to me that certain former associates of his might, should they become aware of what you are doing, attempt to dissuade you from doing it. These associates may—*may*—be the people who shot him."

I lifted my head and gazed at the guppy tank, gazed at a little spot on the wall, undoubtedly gazed with a distinctly sour and pained expression on my chops, much like that of the little tot in the faded photo atop my desk. Then I deciphered the scribble: "P.P.S. Call me if you have any questions, Sheldon."

I smiled. It was not a smile that would have gladdened the heart of Bentley X. Worthington, had he been seated across the desk from me. I examined the other material, starting with the six-day-old clip from *The Arizona Republic* headed, "ALLEGED EX-GANGSTER SHOT." Below that, in smaller boldface type, was the subhead, "Gunned Down in Hospital Parking Lot."

I read the story twice. Summed up, it reported that on the previous afternoon Claude Romanelle, who two decades before had allegedly been active in an Illinois criminal organization referred to, at that time, as "the Arabian Group," had been shot three times in the parking lot of the Arizona Medigenic Hospital on McDowell Drive in Scottsdale. The victim had been about to enter his new Mercedes-Benz sedan when two men drove up in another car, described only as "a dark gray sedan," and fired "a fusillade" of shots. The assailants then sped east on McDowell, headed toward the city of Mesa; they had not been apprehended.

The writer stated that Romanelle had been taken by ambulance to the Scottsdale Memorial Hospital where —at the time the story was written—he had been undergoing surgery. But then the writer went on, "Moments before arrival of the ambulance, Mr. Romanelle, who was fully conscious during our entire discussion, expressed the desire that he might once again see and speak to his daughter, his only child. 'I hope it is not too late,' Mr. Romanelle told this reporter. 'It has been twenty years now, but I hope I can still find her, and . . .' He left the statement unfinished."

It occurred to me, on my second reading of the story, that Romanelle might have left the discussion unfinished because about then an ambulance skidded to a shrieking stop, attendants tore him from "this reporter's" grip, and bundled the possibly expiring citizen onto a stretcher. I couldn't help wondering if the inquiring reporter, while Romanelle was presumably sprawled flat on the parking lot's asphalt and perhaps spouting gobs of blood from several holes in him, had also inquired, "Any last words for our readers, Mr. Romanelle? How does it feel to be shot so many times? What are your thoughts about gun control, sir? Do you think any of those bullets pierced your heart or lungs or bladder?"

But I also wondered why, if Claude Romanelle had been gunned down in the parking lot of the Arizona Medigenic Hospital, he had been driven several miles to Scottsdale Memorial.

I jotted that note on a pad, plus bits of information from the rest of the story. Romanelle was fifty-eight years old, a resident of Scottsdale for twelve years. Since the dismissed indictments twenty years ago, he had not been in any trouble with the law. At the present time he was "a legitimate businessman," a vice-president of Cimarron Enterprises. The president of that company was a wealthy local resident named Alda Cimarron, active in real estate development, mining ventures, manufacturing (of restaurant equipment), and apparently well received philanthropy.

The separate typed sheet of bond paper Bentley had included with his letter contained only a few more bits of info. Under the name of Michelle Esprit Romanelle were the date of her birth—she would have been twenty-six years old this past April 23—and the names of her parents: Claude M. Romanelle and his wife, Nicole, who were then thirty-two and twenty-four years old respectively.

Bentley had also included for me Romanelle's room number at Scottsdale Memorial, the address and phone number of his home in Paradise Valley, and a statement that he would probably be released from the hospital on Monday night or Tuesday morning.

I picked up the phone, placed a long-distance call to Bentley X. Worthington's offices in Phoenix, Arizona.

Collect. In less than half a minute, Bentley was on the line.

"Sheldon, old boy," he said in his most winning trial attorney's baritone, "I rather expected you might call."

"I rather expected you might expect me to," I said.

"How is the good life in Southern California?"

"Not so good."

"Ah, Sheldon, this doesn't sound like you."

"It isn't me. This is a conglomerate composed of Sherlock Holmes, Javert, and three clairvoyants. This conglomerate is supposed to find a woman once upon a time named Michelle Esprit Romanelle, who is now maybe or maybe not known as Michelle Vetch, possibly residing in California or perhaps one of the other forty-nine states, and we are to accomplish this expeditiously without using her name or anybody else's name while the people who massacred her father attempt to dissuade us, presumably by employing such persuasive means as guns, knives, baseball bats, and bazookas."

"Precisely," he responded jovially. "I am gratified that you have placed your finger so quickly upon the crux of the problem that faces us. I knew you would speedily penetrate to the heart of—"

"Bentley—*Bentley*—"

"Sheldon, please. Attend to this closely: Considering the limited and peculiar nature of the information I have available, I could not possibly present this case to any normal or *average* investigator, could I?"

I squeezed the phone in my fist, looked around till I found that little spot on the wall, scowled at it. "O.K., O.K.," I said. "You're really serious about this one?"

"Absolutely."

"With regard to this document that urgently—repeat, urgently—requires the daughter's signature. You wrote that it transfers joint *ownership* of certain assets, and in the next paragraph that it transfers joint *control*. Maybe it doesn't make any difference, but which is it?"

"Both. Since you are not an attorney, Sheldon, I feared you might be dismayed should I lay upon you legalese and Latin and ponderous specificities. However, the document is in fact an *inter vivos* trust, the trustor being Claude Romanelle, the trustees—only two in number—being Claude Romanelle and his daughter, or the cotrustee, Michelle—"

"O.K. Sorry I asked."

"—Esprit Romanelle. You might, yourself, prefer to think of it as a 'lifetime trust,' although in legal language it is essential that specificity and clarity of intent be—"

"Wait. Stop. You're right, I am getting dismayed. Even a little depressed. So, quickly, another question that occurred to me—and your answer may be imprecise, even illegal. Concerning this transfer of assets into whatever it is, you used the word substantial. How substantial?"

"There are certain elements of attorney-client confidentiality and privilege—"

"Good-bye."

"Hold it. Ah, several millions. I think I do not overstep my required bounds by telling you that much."

"Millions—of dollars?"

"Yes. A considerable number of them. Multiple millions. We are not talking nickels and dimes here."

"How come if this Romanelle hasn't seen his daughter for twenty years, he suddenly wants to lay a bunch of these millions upon her? And why *hasn't* he seen her for so long?"

Bentley explained that a little more than twenty years ago, shortly after his daughter Michelle's sixth birthday, Romanelle had simply walked out, split, abandoned his daughter and his then wife. "'That cantankerous old horse,' he called her," Bentley went on. "Referring to his ex-wife, I mean."

"No kidding? Horse?"

"Also poison-tongued termagant, viperine Amazon, whinnying virago, and razor-mouthed Xanthippe."

"Has a way with words, does he? If not women. Apparently it wasn't a match made in heaven."

"Not quite. As to your question, why now? Judging by Mr. Romanelle's comments to me, I assume it is because, for at least a few seconds last Monday afternoon, he realized what is most important about living because he thought he was dying. Apparently still does, for that matter."

"Still thinks he's dying?"

"That is my impression."

"I thought he was being discharged from the hospital today or maybe tomorrow."

"That is correct. Two of his wounds were superficial, and the more serious abdominal injury has been expertly repaired. Mr. Romanelle informed me yesterday evening that his physicians told him he is out of danger and suitable for discharge soon."

"Then why—?"

"I have asked myself the same question, Sheldon. I have not answered it."

"Well, I suppose I'll have to call this Romanelle, see if I can get something sensible out of him."

"Ah. Then you're taking the case?"

I was silent, considering the question.

He said, "Sheldon?"

"I'll give it a shot, Bentley. But I can't give it full time for a day or so. I'm still wrapping up some odds and ends on the Amber case, my last job."

"Amber. Was that . . . Miss Nude Something?"

"Naked. Miss Naked California. Among other things. That one is all wrapped up, really, but I have a couple of time-consuming—"

"Sheldon, that won't do. My—our—client is, well, you would probably say antsy. He is consumed by his desire for speedy results. I *must* tell him you will commence your preliminary investigation immediately, and be on it full-time by . . . by tomorrow, no later."

"Thing is, the local police insist that I spend a little time with them explaining . . . Well, I could maybe get that all done today—it's why I'm in the office so bloody early."

I paused, thinking. "O.K. I'll talk to the law, sign a statement, get that done today, this morning if I can. And I'll put some lines out on this Romanelle kid . . . Bentley, lines out for *what*? Usually when I'm looking for some-body, I've at least got a name, or a description, or an alias, *something.* Of course, you haven't forbidden me to use the lady's first name, Michelle. Maybe I could run an ad: Michelle, get in touch with me and I'll give you millions of dollars. Then all I have to do is eliminate the nine hundred thousand phony Michelles—"

"Splendid. Run an ad. Put your lines out. Consult your informers and informants. Get cracking."

"Bentley—"

"That's the spirit of the Sheldon Scott I know. So, then, I shall inform Mr. Romanelle that he can count on you? That his worries are over? That momentous events are—"

"Knock it off. I'll inform Romanelle myself, as soon as you stop arguing your case and hang up."

"Excellent. Since Romanelle is still at the hospital, and you will therefore be placing your call through the switchboard and/or nurses' station there, do not identify yourself as Sheldon Scott."

"Not as—me?"

"No. Identify yourself to hospital personnel as William W. Williams, and Mr. Romanelle will not only know it is you but will accept the call; otherwise he probably would not respond to it. Mr. Romanelle does not want the name Sheldon Scott to be recorded in hospital records, or even in the memory of employees of Scottsdale Memorial —should, that is, anyone of a curious nature ask who has been in contact with Mr. Romanelle. Clearly, he does not desire that anyone learn that he has been in contact with a private investigator, and this is his means of ensuring that result."

"Yeah, I see. But, Bentley, you're beginning to make me a little uneasy. Who might these people of a curious nature—"

"Well, now," he interrupted. "Just as I expected that you would call, I expect that you have a few additional queries of me. What are they?"

"For starters, what's this about our client's being involved way back when with something called the Arabian Group? Or some kind of criminous, maybe felonious, activity?"

"You refer to the 'Alleged Ex-Gangster' appellation on

the clipping I mailed you. I've no idea, Sheldon. I did bring the subject up, gently, with Mr. Romanelle. He merely replied, and I quote him, 'That was long ago and far away, pal. I've forgotten about it. You do likewise, Charlie.' He has, at times, a rather colorful way of expressing himself. Colorful and, oh . . . ominous, perhaps.''

"Ominous-perhaps, huh? Is he a big ugly ominous ape?"

"Oh, no, not at all. About six feet but very slim, quite thin now of course, and pleasant enough but slightly . . . satanic. Mainly he has a certain, well, forcefulness of expression. I had no difficulty in not pursuing the subject further, even though he was flat on his back in a hospital bed.''

"Anything recent on the two Charlies who plugged him?"

"Nothing. The police have come up with . . . empty, I believe is the argot.''

"How did Romanelle happen to contact you? Were you acquainted before?"

"I had not previously heard of him. Obviously, he had heard of me, and been favorably impressed. He phoned the office yesterday morning, early, and insisted upon speaking to me. 'The head honcho,' he told my secretary. He explained his situation, told me the kind of document he wished prepared, and was quite precise about how he wished it drawn. I told him any of my firm's attorneys could handle the matter, but he insisted that I represent him.''

"He explain why? Other than the fact, of course, that you are a widely known, very visible, much-publicized genius attorney?"

"He did not explain. But he was quite persuasive, and . . . generous. Generous, perhaps, hmm, to a fault. In any event, I personally took the document to Scottsdale Memorial and there secured Mr. Romanelle's signature. And check. It was at that time I suggested you as the investigator who might best determine if his daughter was still in the Los Angeles area. You have not yet thanked me for doing you this favor.''

"I hope that's what it is. Thanks anyway. Last question:

If I should happen to locate this Michelle Romanelle, who of course cannot be so identified at any time or place, I'm to bring her to you posthaste? Not to her antsy father first?"

"Correct. Mr. Romanelle placed considerable stress upon this point. Not until her signature has been affixed to the document several times mentioned, which is now here in my vault, is she to attempt to see her father. Nor, for that matter, are you."

"I think I ought to see that document. There seem to be some curious—"

"See it you shall. When you arrive here with Miss Romanelle. Or with Miss, Mrs.—well, who knows?"

"Wonderful. O.K., Bentley, I'm on the case. Part-time today, until I'm through with the cops, and full-time from then on. However . . ."

"Ah . . . Is there something—?"

"If, unfortunately, I happen to severely injure or even severely kill anybody during this simple little missing-person caper, Bentley X. Worthington himself will defend me, and get me off scot-free."

"Of course. Shell-Scott free." He paused to chuckle. Alone.

We hung up. On the sheet of bond paper before me was the phone number of Scottsdale Memorial Hospital, and Romanelle's room number up on the sixth floor. For some reason, I was a little reluctant to dial it. I wondered exactly what Worthington had meant by that ominous-perhaps line. I wondered *who* those Charlies, and other associates, were. I was already committed, of course, by what I'd said to Worthington. But once I spoke to Romanelle and told him I'd do what I could, then I was *really* committed. All the way to the end, then, come hell or high water. Word of honor, Scout's oath, a man's word is his bond, all that jazz.

On the other hand, even though, so far as I could recall, I'd never heard the name Claude Romanelle until this morning, the guy was starting to intrigue me. Also, I had me an interesting puzzle: How do you find somebody when you don't know who it is or where it's at?

But, looking back, I could recall a case or two that had

started by my getting conked on the head; and when you begin a case unconscious, it doesn't go a long way toward building up your confidence or that rugged-private-eye self-image. So this way was a lot better. For a change, all I'd do was read a little, and spend some time on the phone. Maybe I could solve this one with my index finger, just dialing about, calling a lot of people, asking cogent, probing, incisive questions.

Sure.

And I felt a little heavy in my swivel chair, as if all of my 206 pounds were settling down, and down, under the influence of unusual gravity. Me, the vigorous and vital full-of-beans lad who, not half an hour ago, had thought he could float.

I pulled the phone back over in front of me. The damn thing weighed a ton.

Chapter Two

CLAUDE ROMANELLE DIDN'T sound like a man who'd been shot three times only a week ago. The voice was deep, strong, a little hoarse. And loud.

I had identified myself to the bored-sounding lady who put my call through to room 608 in the West Tower of Scottsdale Memorial Hospital as William W. Williams, and a few seconds after that my client's voice was bending my eardrum inward:

"Williams?"

"Right. I'd like—"

"That means you're this hotshot investigator, Sheldon Scott, right?"

"Well . . . right. And I'd—"

"The Williams cuteness is only to keep the people here dummied up, just in case, no point in putting up signs."

"Signs for who—?"

"Our mutual friend, Worthington, laid quite a pile on me about you, said you're the man for this job, you'll get it done one way or another even if it's by accident, I won't be disappointed. I better not be. If that silver-haired counselor was conning me, I'll get two guys from Texas to cut his balls off. Even if you're as good as he says, which nobody is, I don't suppose you've located Michelle yet. Or have you?"

"If you'll turn your mouth off for a minute, I'll try to tell you." I wasn't sure, but I thought I heard a chuckle. I went on, "No, I haven't found Michelle. I haven't even started looking for her."

"Man, *get* started. *Get* looking. I don't have any time to waste—"

"Mr. Romanelle, will you kindly clam up?"

Yeah, it was a chuckle. But he remained silent for a little while, and I continued, "I've just talked to Worthington. Now I need more from you. But let's be sure I know exactly what you want me to do. First, you want me to find your daughter. Second, see that she gets to Worthington and affixes her signature to whatever documents you had him prepare. And third, when that's accomplished, deliver your daughter to you, presumably at your home in Paradise Valley. Right so far?"

"On the button. Except, let there be no when-and-if here, Scott. Cut that down to when. And fourth is, get it done now without dilly-dallying or dawdling—"

"No, sir. Fourth is, I'm supposed to do this in an hour and a half blindfolded and with my hands tied behind my back."

"What does that mean?"

"It means this: I'm not looking for a Michelle Romanelle, because your daughter doesn't use that last name now, but you can't tell me what name she *does* use. Moreover, under no circumstances am I to utter or use the name Romanelle, or even Claude, for reasons not yet made clear to me. You think your daughter *may* be somewhere here in the L.A. area—or maybe not; you aren't sure. So far, then, all I've really got is the name Michelle and a few maybes. And that's not enough. I somehow get the impression you don't want to wait very long."

"I sure don't, can't. That's a fact. If it takes you a week or two, forget it. Got to be quicker than that. But you do have a point. I'll tell you what I can. It may not be much." He paused, and I heard him coughing. Then he cleared his throat and said huskily, "What do you want from me?"

"Start with why you think your daughter might be in or near L.A. And why you think she *might* be using the name Michelle Vetch."

"O.K." He was silent for several seconds. Then he said,

"I send my ex a little money from time to time. Mainly—" He coughed again, sort of a deep honk, and I missed, or thought I missed, his next few words. Sounded like some kind of "spree," and "booze" and filling up the food larder.

I broke in, "What was that again?"

"Money for whatever, pay the rent, buy clothes, replenish the booze larder. That fire-breathing dragon likes her booze, at least she used to. She'd snort it up her cavernous snout and then breathe it out as fire and smoke, all the while belching poisonous hiccups—"

"Mr. Romanelle, please. I care not about your marital difficulties in the past century. What I asked you was—"

"Right. Nicole—that's my ex, the fang-filled mouth of my dumb days, the saw-toothed she-creature . . . Well, let that go for now. My ex, my former unblushing bride, moves around a lot. She knows I can't send her any gelt unless I know where to send it, so—if I haven't called her for a while—about once a year, or every time she relocates, whichever comes first, she rings me up and tells me where to send the money, not forgetting to screech into the phone that I never send her enough, she needs more, *more, MORE*—"

"Let that go, too, for now," I suggested gently.

"Last call was from Los Angeles, about six months ago. Nicole mentioned she was living in Monterey Park, right next to L.A., you know, and recently divorced from a guy named Vetch. But she said I could make out the large check, which she knew I must be eager to send her, to Nicole E. Vetch, the name she was continuing to use temporarily."

"Temporarily? Well, no matter, if you sent her a check, I can start with the address you mailed it to, right?"

"Wrong. I mailed it to General Delivery, Monterey Park, as instructed. I think she was maybe living with some Charlie and didn't want him snooping her mail. Anyway, I sent her a nice cashier's check including an extra nickel to make her happier, which is no more difficult than making Medusa's hairdo look prettier than the shimmering tresses of Rapunzel—"

"Mr. Romanelle—"

"Send the money quick, she howled, because she was about to marry another guy—probably the Charlie Snoop she was shacked with but she didn't tell me this one's name, probably didn't *know* his last name yet—and move to North Dakota. I think it was North. South, North, whichever—hell, even if it was one of the Poles, it wouldn't be far enough . . . Ah, yeah."

"At least I may assume she was, for sure, in Monterey Park six months ago, right?"

"For sure long enough to pick up my bucks at General Delivery, which is the only address I got. For all I know, she was living at the post office. See, she keeps moving around, gets rid of the old husband—I think she kills 'em and buries 'em in the backyard, then—"

"O.K. Enough. That takes care of Nicole for the moment. Nicole, the razor-mouthed Xanthippe—"

"Hold on, there. You can't talk about *my* ex-wife like that, Scott. *I* can, but—"

"Sorry. I thought I was merely quoting you."

"Humh. I think you were, at that. So you were saying?"

"That places Nicole in the L.A. area. What reason is there to think Michelle might have been here?"

"Nicole, my—my ex, mentioned that Spree dropped by to see her every week or two. I deduced that she would not drop by from Cairo, Egypt—"

"Right. A sensible deduction. Can you narrow it down to, say, the lower half of the state of California?"

"No. That's all I've got."

"Incidentally, did you say spree? Didn't you mention something like that before?"

"That's Michelle. Michelle Esprit. When she was a little girl—before I split, of course—we called her Spree. Nicole and I both did, then." He paused. "Spree. She was the sweetest, brightest, loveliest little miniature lady who ever lived . . ." Then he coughed a couple of times and said brusquely, "What else, Scott?"

"You may not want to answer this one, but I think you'd better if you want me to move fast, without—without dilly-dallying and dawdling, as you so sweetly phrased it."

He laughed softly, a rumble deep in his throat. "Just trying to get a line on you, Scott. Not so easy to size a man up on the phone. Be easier if I could look you over."

"Why do you have to size me up?"

"Man, you got to size *everybody* up. There's little old ladies who carry knives in their bustles, guys named Percy who—"

"Let me finish the original question, O.K.? *Why* all this secrecy, all this cloak and dagger, don't use the name Romanelle and so on?"

"Well . . ." He fell silent for a few seconds, then said, "Some of my associates—former associates—*if* they knew a guy named Sheldon Scott was doing a snoop for me, might try to throw some little roadblocks, shall we say, into your path."

"*Why* would they do that, Mr. Romanelle?"

"We'll set that question aside. It truly has nothing to do with you."

"O.K., I'll let that simmer for now. But these little roadblocks you mentioned. Shall we say, like a tank armed with heat-seeking missiles, maybe?"

"If they happened to have one handy, no doubt."

"Great. So name the associates."

"You don't need that. All I'm asking you to do is find my daughter—"

"Mister, I need it. If you think I'm going to throw rocks at a tank or try to de-fang the snakes in Medusa's shimmering tresses without knowing who's driving or what's hissing, think again. And the longer you think about it, the more time you—you, not me—waste."

"You're starting to talk like me, Scott. Maybe you'll do after all. The only name I'm sure of—sure you ought to know, I mean—is a man I worked with in various enterprises until very recently. As recently as this past Monday, about four P.M. His name is Alda Cimarron, and it's ten to one he's the sonofabitch who had me shot."

"O.K. That should help."

"Didn't help me much."

"That's not what I meant."

"I know. Couldn't resist it."

"You say various enterprises. What kind?"

"Just various."

"Can you clarify that a little?"

"I won't."

"How about the two guys who plugged you? You make either of them?"

"No. I've got no idea who they were. Well, an idea—I'll give any odds it was Alda hired and paid 'em. But I didn't even see the fleepers. Just blam-blam, and there I was flopping around on the asphalt like a hooked mackerel. Thought I was a goner."

"Correct me if I'm wrong, but I'd guess their aim was pretty lousy, since you're being released from the hospital fairly soon for a gunshot victim. And, too, I got the impression from the newspaper story that maybe you weren't hit too bad."

"Not too bad, no, not from your point of view, Scott. In fact, didn't bother you at all, did it? The truth is, it was a lot of fun. I can hardly wait to do it again. Certainly added spice to my day—"

"I didn't mean to imply—"

"Those goddamn Charlies drilled me clean, no bone-hit, through the muscle of my right shoulder, which wasn't all that bad except I won't be shaking hands with the doctors here, when I thank them for poisoning me with half the pharmacopoeia, for another week or so. And one slug kind of chewed on my side, hardly enough to bleed. But the last one—last, first, second, who counts?—hit me in the gut. That's the one that knocked me down and spoiled my appetite for dinner at La Champagne."

"What I meant was, I gathered from the story in the *Republic* that you were able to talk with the inquiring reporter for a minute or two, and mentioned hoping to see your daughter again, so at least you weren't killed instantly."

"Nicely put. But yeah, that goddamn reporter. Here I am, halfway into the next world, I can feel myself getting charbroiled, and this kid, looked to be about twelve years old, is hunkered down on his heels eyeing me like I'm a specimen. Would you believe?"

"Yeah. In fact, I'd wondered if—"

"This misbegotten child of a high school black mass hunkered there and asked me at least eleven hundred wonderful questions, of which I answered maybe two or three, and I've been kicking myself for not buttoning my yapper ever since. Stupid of me to tell that jerk I was hoping I could see my little girl again. But, like I said, I thought I was a goner. And I'd been thinking about little Spree, anyway, a lot lately, running things over in my mind, and . . . Well, at least I didn't mention her name."

"Something else puzzles me. You were shot in the parking lot of the Medigenic Hospital, but the ambulance took you to Scottsdale Memorial. Why not into Medigenic, since you were already there?"

"Because I told everybody in the general area if they didn't take me to Memorial I'd make sure they got their arms and heads fractured by personal friends of mine, and I'd sue them for ten million dollars, plus I would personally pry off their kneecaps. No way I was going to let them roll me into Medigenic."

"Why not? Something wrong with the hospital, they only treat vegetarians or—"

"No, it's a nice place. Professional, color TV, at least a couple nurses that don't look like male wrestlers or morgue attendants. I just wasn't about to be stuck in there."

"Don't you think I ought to know why?"

There was silence for a while. Then he said, "You're probably right. The joint is owned by Alda Cimarron. You recall his name, don't you? By him and the president of the Board there, doctor named Bliss, Phillip Bliss. Hell, I've got a little piece of it myself. Does that answer your question?"

"Sure does. O.K., not much more. The info Worthington sent me, he had to get from you. What you could remember, I mean, not from documents, records, birth certificates, that sort of thing."

"That's right."

"O.K., if you remember, I need to know the full maiden name of your wife, place and date of your marriage, name of the man she married after you two split—the first man she married after that, since I gather there's been more than one."

"There's been more than a couple, and still counting. I think she was getting ready to absorb number five—"

"Mainly I need the first one after Claude Romanelle. And where Michelle—Spree—was born." Something wiggled up in my head.

Romanelle told me his wife was Nicole Elaine Montapert when he met her, and maybe he should have left it that way. He remembered the date when they'd been married in Fort Lauderdale, Florida, which was also where Michelle Esprit Romanelle had been born, in the Lauderdale-East Hospital. But he couldn't remember any of Nicole's names that he'd sent cash or cashier's checks to a number of years ago—the surnames, that is, of his ex-wife's subsequent husbands—except the most recently divorced one, Vetch, whom she had met, married, and lived with in Reno, Nevada. And I didn't think that would be much help to me. If Michelle had adopted a different surname after her parents separated, most likely she would have assumed the next husband's name rather than the name of number three or four.

I said, "The info I got was merely that Michelle does not go by the name Romanelle anymore. But is that for sure? Is it just an assumption, or do you *know* she dropped the name she was born with?"

"It's a fact. She hasn't used the name since maybe a year or two after I walked out on them. Nicole made sure of that." He paused, then continued, "I see where you're going, Scott. Maybe I should give you a little background. Never mind why I split, I just got fed up and left. Abandoned wife and child, walked out free as an eagle. Not very noble and long-suffering; but no excuses. I've told you, I send them some cash every six months or so, at least every year. So I've been talking once or twice a year to my ex for twenty years now, and each call ages me about a year or two extra. Say, that would make me about . . . ninety-nine now. You wouldn't know it, would you?"

"You could have fooled me."

"Well, I build myself up with vegetables and raw meat

and push-ups, and about three shots of Jack Daniel's, before each time I call her, or figure she's due to call me from some new place, because I know it'll give that nonstop mouth of my pre-eagle days a chance to tell me, one more time, everything I did wrong since the first time I crapped a diaper. The first couple of years, way back, I asked to say hello to Spree, but you can guess how that went over. So I never again said hello to little Spree, or asked how she was, or got to tell her . . . tell her I was sorry."

He coughed a time or two, then said, "Nicole, dear, sweet Nicole, who in another incarnation gave tips on technique to Lucrezia Borgia, took pains to let me know she'd confessed to *her* daughter, which presumably she gave birth to by dividing in half like an amoeba, exactly what kind of a cruel, heartless, Jack the Ripper rake and libertine the virtual stranger, once known to them by the alias of Claude Romanelle, really was." He paused one more time. "I don't know what Michelle's name might be now. But I know it isn't Romanelle."

I said slowly, "Just a thought, Mr. Romanelle. When I was talking with Bentley Worthington, more out of frustration than anything else, I mentioned something about running an ad for anybody named Michelle who happened to be alive in the universe, just a facetious comment. But there might be something wiggling here. I've never heard the name Spree before. There wouldn't be many more of those, if any. Now, I know you don't want me to use the name Romanelle, but is there any reason why I couldn't use the name Spree? And also Michelle, for that matter."

"You mean in an ad? In a newspaper?"

"Right. Maybe in the Personal Message column. I haven't given it a serious thought until this minute. But the name—strike that, I won't use it as a name, just a word, the only *name* will be Michelle. And the *word* spree wouldn't mean a thing to anybody except your daughter, except to somebody named, or once called, Spree. It's one way to go. And there aren't many other ways."

"Well . . . Maybe." Silence for ten seconds. Then, softly, as if more to himself than to me, "None of those sonsofbitches would know what we called Michelle back then. No hassle." Then, with his normal loudness, "No problem, Scott. Can't think of any."

"O.K. Last question. It's been twenty years, so you probably wouldn't know your daughter if you saw her. And I don't know beans about her. As a kid, did she have any identifying marks that she'd still have today?"

"Marks?"

"Marks, scars, a wart on her nose, anything."

"Just the birthmark. On her chest there."

"On her chest where?"

"Little brownish or tan splotch—it's in the photograph I gave to Worthington for you. You got it, didn't you?"

"Yeah. Just a minute."

I picked up that faded old photo, grimaced one more time at the little kid's tortured expression, then looked over the rest of it. Sure enough, there was something, a little blotch on the skin over the ribs, on the left side. Not large. At first I thought it was from a hole in the negative, or a fly speck, though it was too big a speck for any but a monster fly. I held the picture near my face and squinted, and could make out a small blotch of darker pigment. On little Michelle, it would then have been only about half an inch wide and maybe an inch or so from top to bottom, but irregularly shaped, with what looked almost like a little wheel at the bottom and another arched line on top.

I said to Romanelle, "Right, got it. That's good enough. You understand, it's at least possible another lady, *not* Michelle, might try to claim she *is* Michelle. So it could be important to have something as proof of identity other than the right answer to the question 'What was your mother's maiden name?' and so forth."

"Humh," Romanelle said. Then, "Scott, I've been thinking. As you spoke, my mind was wandering. Back to the days when Michelle's mother-to-be and I met."

I wondered what he was getting at. He was speaking almost dreamily, in a kind of singsong. "I may not have been completely fair in my comments about old Garbage Mouth—I mean, Nicole," he went on. "Actually, the first couple of years weren't all that bad. And a lot of the troubles were my fault. Like, oh, when she caught me bare-assed in the kitchen with the cook. While Cookie was fixing dinner. Ruined the dinner—little things like that."

"While . . . ? How—?"

"But what I want to say is, when we got married, Nicole was a fine-looking woman all around. Very pretty face, good legs, damned bright head on her shoulders. But the thing was, the memorable thing about Nicole was, she had the biggest, most astonishing, most perfect, most gorgeous pair of tits west of Zanzibar."

"She did, huh?"

"She sure did. Why, it was nearly a month after we met before I realized she had a little mole at the corner of her mouth. Now, some men might not understand my fascination with what others—even you, perhaps—might consider mere anatomical protuberances. Right, Mr. Scott?"

"Me? Oh, no, I wouldn't . . . call 'em mere—that."

"I didn't think you would, Mr. Scott."

Something cuckoo was going on here. And twice in a jiffy he'd called me "Mr." Always before it was just Scott.

"How would you know?" I said suspiciously.

"I have had—reports."

"Reports?"

"Reports. It would, therefore, be best for all concerned —assuming you are indeed swiftly successful in finding little Spree—"

"Little Spree? Yeah."

"—if you satisfied yourself about her identity merely by asking such questions as, 'What was your mother's maiden name?' "

"You got that from me. Just a minute ago."

"You see, Mr. Scott—"

"Incidentally, what happened to plain old Scott?"

"—it is, perhaps, a bit late for me to start becoming protective—overly protective, even vengeful and maniacal —about my innocent little girl."

"Vengeful? *Maniacal?* Romanelle, are you out of your cotton-picking tree? Man, she's a grown woman. She's got to be twenty-six years old by now. That's pretty *old.*"

"Precisely. Consider what that means. Perhaps to *some*

she is a grown woman. But, to me, to me she is still my tiny sheltered child."

"Ah, come *on*. If this is what it sounds like—and I think it really sounds like what it sounds like—then you have popped your cork for sure."

"It is my cork. And if I wish to pop it, who is to say nay? I am attempting to convey to you my intent, my concern, that no harm, of *any* nature, be visited upon my little Spree until I see her once more."

"Do you think you could stop calling this old woman your little—"

"Let me make my request clear—let's call it a request, shall we, Mr. Scott?" And he went on from there for a minute or so, all in that gentle singsong, about how, should any discomfort not desired by his—yeah, his little—Spree be visited upon her, specifically by me, what he had promised those people in the parking lot, who suggested taking him into Medigenic, would be merely openers for Sheldon Scott. I gathered that his "personal friends" might leave parts of me in Glendale, and parts of me in Pasadena, and bits and pieces in other places not polite to mention.

When he finished, or ran down, I said, "Who am I talking to here? Is this the ninety-nine-year-old invalid who cuddled Cookie in the kitchen?"

He chuckled. "It isn't easy to scare the hell out of you, is it?"

"Not too easy. And not lately, Romanelle."

"Well, I think you'll do," he said. "So find her quickly, will you?"

"That's another damn thing, Romanelle. What's all this baloney about speed, quick, hurry? What's the difference if it takes an extra day or two?"

"Just a day or two might not matter. But much longer . . ." He stopped. "I did not intend to mention this, but perhaps it will accelerate your efforts somewhat. Perhaps not. I suppose I've been . . . clinging to a curious kind of pride. The doctors did an excellent job on my wounds. But when they went—went inside, as they say, to repair the gut-shot, the surgeon discovered a previously unsuspected gastric carcinoma in there."

"Cancer?"

"That is the layman's term, yes—physicians live in fear that we may understand what they tell us, don't they? Well, they cut out what they could, but were unable to get it all and fear it has metastasized. So the doctors are impatient to cook me with cobalt and then administer sufficient chemotherapy that I will be able to kill cockroaches merely by breathing upon them. Oh, I'm not going to expire in a week or even a month. But such news does lend a certain sense of urgency to one's days."

I didn't say anything.

He added, "Do you have the information you need, Scott?"

Back to Scott now. What had I done right? "I think so."

"Then good luck. Get busy, get to work, get out amongst 'em—"

"If you say 'Get cracking,' I'll quit."

"Find Spree for me."

"I will," I said.

By 10 A.M. I had called two detective agencies, one in Reno, Nevada, and the other in Fort Lauderdale, Florida. The first would try to run down anybody named Vetch who had been married in Reno to a woman named Nicole, and if he was found simply ask him what his stepdaughter's name was and where she and/or his ex-wife was living now. I hoped it would be that easy. Fort Lauderdale would start with the marriage of Claude and Nicole Romanelle, and the birth of their child, Michelle Esprit, and try to trace them forward from that point toward today, hopefully discovering Michelle's full name and whereabouts long before reaching here and now.

I had also—in fact, it was the first thing I did—called in an ad for the Personal Message and Missing Persons columns of the *Los Angeles Times*. I was lucky to get the call in early enough—in addition to pulling the string of an acquaintance who worked for the advertising department of the paper—so that the ad would appear in tomorrow's morning edition.

The ad copy I'd scribbled on my pad was atop the desk, and I read it one more time, to see if I'd broken any of Romanelle's rules. Even though the ad itself might have been more fetching, the rules appeared to be intact. The copy read:

MONEY FOR A SPREE
If your name is Michelle and your 26th birthday was last April 23, you may be eligible for a money spree, a dollar bonanza! If you are the one, a very large fortune is awaiting you.

That's the way it came out, and the only change I'd made was to strike out "sizable" and make it a "very large" fortune. I had also included the instruction that the right woman should "Call Shell Scott," and listed my office phone for daytime hours and my apartment number for after five.

The ad sounded a little as if it was one of those promotional come-ons that promise you prizes like "either a new Rolls-Royce automobile or a toaster" if you'll simply spend a few hours examining the property and let their crew of experienced hypnotists tell you about the wonderful opportunity in their Fairway Estates condominiums near the proposed eight-hole golf course.

No matter; if it came to Michelle/Spree's attention, I would undoubtedly hear from her. I pushed the phone onto the corner of my desk, put all of Worthington's info, and my notes, into the padded envelope again, and shoved back my swivel chair.

From here on, the case would be getting tougher. I was going to have to leave the office.

After saying, "Hello again, you little devils," to my frisky guppies, and "Good-bye," I went out, locked my door, and stopped briefly at the cubicle personed by Hazel at the end of the hall.

"If you need to reach me," I said, "I'll be down at the Police Building. Answering a few final questions about my last job, the Amber case."

She finished pecking at keys, spun around on her stool.

"Oh, *that* one," she said, rolling her eyes prettily.

"Yeah, *that* one. Only reason I have to visit the LAPD is that the police insist upon giving me a medal for cracking the case. For the various misdemeanors and felonies I committed while cracking it they will, during the rest of the afternoon, be beating me with rubber hoses."

She didn't laugh. Or chuckle. Didn't even smile. Instead, Hazel peered up at me and asked sweetly, "Have a nice nap, Shell?"

"O ye of little faith," I said. "Have you forgotten all those vitally important calls you just placed for me? Why, I want you to know that, already this morning, I have taken on a *new* case, accepted a sizable retainer with the promise of *much* more, talked to my client, to his and my attorney, and to a pair of detective agencies far away. Moreover, I have arranged for an ad in the *L. A. Times*, which probably means the case is half solved already."

She glanced at her little glittery watch, and back at me. *Then* she started laughing. Great sense of humor, this kid.

"Oh, Shell," she snorted. "Sometimes you're *so* funny."

That's the way it goes, when it's too early in the morning.

Chapter Three

DUSK WAS FALLING gently over the city when I got back to the Hamilton Building, and my early morning mood of exuberant euphoria had gradually been worn away by the hard bright edges of the day. I'd spent several hours at the LAPD, filling out reports and answering questions—and I guess it was what those questions made me think of that brought me down a little. Hell, I know that's what did it.

This morning I had awakened with an indefinable sadness, gossamer dolor clinging thinly, as though from some sweet sorrow unremembered. And that isn't like me. It really isn't. I awaken slowly, true, *very* slowly. And usually grouchy and grumbling until hot coffee puts some gas in my tank and adds spark to the plugs and ignition. But almost never do I start the day actually down, depressed, with the feeling that somehow all's *not* right with the world.

So, for a while this A.M., unusually early despite having slept very little, I had stood in my bedroom gawking at nothing, wiggling my bare toes on the thick black carpet, and wondering what the hell. Was I sick?

And then I remembered. Aralia. Sure. The last case, the Amber investigation: hoodlums and holograms, con games and fun games, beautiful bodies and stiffening corpses, pulchritude and parties and Miss Naked U.S.A. Ah, yes, Aralia Fields. Warm and wonderful Aralia.

And Aralia was gone. As of Sunday, yesterday.

I'd known she was going a long way. Long and long,

probably too far for me to reach. It had been sweet and memorable and splendid while it lasted, but I knew, no question, it would never again be the same; those moments were done, vanished, gone.

Even so, I had stood there in my bedroom for quite a while, wiggling my toes on the carpet and running through those movies of the mind. But after a bit much of that I said to myself: Hey! To *hell* with this dumbness. Whereupon I let out a growl, like a large dog sniffing a stranger he is preparing to bite hugely, and told myself aloud that I would *not* mope about and ooze moodiness and spoil what otherwise might be, what could be, a wonderful day. Correction: not might be or could be but *was*, if I didn't screw it up on purpose. Don't magicians and gurus tell us we create personal realities by private thoughts, build tomorrows from the harmony or static we self-generate now in our noodles? Sure they do. So wasn't I standing here wiggling forlorn toes and inviting large constipated birds to fly over and dump on me, or even more dire events to transpire? Sure I was.

So I instantly ceased the toe-wiggling, and instead jumped vigorously up and down and about; and then, in the shower, sudsed up hot and rinsed cold while singing "Home on the Range" in my most thunderous ex-marine bellow, finishing with a pair of allegedly obscene limericks, blessed by tag lines of sufficient sizzle to pierce delicate eardrums, while beating on my chest with the soap.

Magic! By the time I was dressed and finishing aromatic black coffee I was feeling dandy again. Only a trace of Aralia remained, so I said, "Bye, kid; wasn't half bad," patted her marvelous bare derriere, then shook my head and flung her into limbo, or at least in that general direction.

I had been quite pleased with myself. Because it *had* turned into a wonderful day, or morning, or at least part of a morning. Certainly I'd been euphorically floating on my way to the office and perky-pretty Hazel this A.M. But, later, all that jazz with the LAPD, the repetitive questions —going over and over and *over* much of it, the way some psychiatrists and analysts deepen and *deepen* grooves and gouges of raw memory in an already-crippled brain—had brought back the malaise, or at least part of it. Well, dammit, I told myself, if you kicked it once you can kick it twice; you kicked it this morning, so do it again.

I strode through the Hamilton's lobby for the second time this day, and up the stairs, taking them only two at a time this trip. Almost everybody else was long gone by now, though. And an empty building has an air of desolation about it, a lifelessness that doesn't exactly quicken the spirit. I trotted into the office. Fed the fish, watched the industrious scavenging of my little *Corydoras paleatus* snuffling along sand at the bottom of my guppy tank. Observed half a dozen male guppies prodding females with their vigorous gonopodiums, in the shameless and terrible way they have.

Then I locked up, hastened downstairs, and into Pete's Bar, conveniently next door to the Hamilton Building. It was that in-between hour, and the place was nearly empty.

Pete nodded silently at me, reached for my usual bourbon.

"Give me something else, Pete. Something I've never had before."

He moved a few feet away behind the bar, cocked his head, started picking up bottles. No comment; we'd known each other a long time.

When he placed before me a murky, suitably dangerous-looking concoction in a tall glass, I heard the front door open, then *shoosh* closed. I took a sip of my drink, glancing around to see who'd come inside.

It was a woman. Tall, dark-haired, young. She'd come in out of the gathering night, and in a strange way it was as if she'd brought part of the night, or dark, inside with her. She sat at the far end of the room, around the curve of the bar, in shadow. It could even have been someone I knew, but the light wasn't bright enough so I could be sure.

Soon she slid from her stool, walked around the curve of the bar and up to me. Tall indeed, and very lovely in an odd, "foreign" way. Probably in her middle or late twenties, full-formed woman's body, simple expensive-looking blue suit, dark, smooth, smart. Long-lashed dark brown eyes, black hair and thin black brows, lovely full lips.

"Do you know me?" she asked. "You were looking at me so . . ."

I needed to shake the last bits of that blue chill that had been sneaking up on me. Besides which, she was overflowing with a kind of sultry-looking gorgeousness. Besides which, what the hell, nothing ventured—

"Sure," I said. "Don't you remember? We met that glorious weekend in Acapulco. I was diving off a rock—"

"Oh, way up high there, at La Perla?"

"No, it was just this . . . rock. Well, how has it been, Madelyn? I mean, of course, how have *you* been?"

"Wonderful."

"I knew it."

"But my name isn't Madelyn."

"Boy, you don't remember *any* of it, do you?"

It was a slow smile. Slow, warm, getting warmer.

"Why don't we move to a booth?" I asked her. "I'll have Pete bring us booze in champagne glasses. Doesn't that sound fun?"

"No. No, it really doesn't. But I think I'd like to, anyway."

"You're starting to remember. Maybe if I described this rock—"

"I have to wait here, and I don't know how long it could be. So I might as well wait with you."

"Thanks a lot, Evelyn—"

"It's Kay. Kay Denver. And I didn't mean that the way it sounded." The warm-warmer smile again. "I meant, I have to wait here for a while, and maybe you can help me. Either you or—" She turned, looking for Pete.

I said quickly, "No, no, he's a—a deaf mute. But you can count on me, Miss Denver. Kay?"

"I came here, to Pete's, because a friend of mine told me there's a detective who gets bombed here some nights. But he's supposed to be quite good, even if he drinks and all."

"What do you mean, 'and all'?"

"My friend said this fellow's name is Shell Scott, but I don't know what he looks like, or anything else about him. I called his office, but he hasn't been in all afternoon. I thought maybe you could help me find him."

"There's no maybe about it. But, ah, it happens I have some small talent in this detecting business myself —though you would never know it to look at me, would you?"

"Goodness, no!"

"You're not supposed to say that." I stood up. "Come with me. I have reserved a booth."

I led her across the small dance floor to a booth in the corner, waved at Pete, ordered a drink for Kay—a Tanqueray martini with two pearl onions, waited until it was before her. Then I propped my chin against my fist, and, comfortable enough to last through even a long story, looked with interest at Kay Denver's interesting face.

"What would you do with a detective," I asked her, "if you had one?"

"Oh, I couldn't possibly tell you," she said, shaking her head slightly from side to side. "I hate to tell *anyone*, and I'm certainly not going to tell the story twice."

"Just tell me once, then."

"No, it's too . . . ghastly. I won't tell anyone except this Mr. Scott, and I might not be able to tell *him*, even. I don't know. I'd have to meet him first, make sure he's . . . sympathetic."

"He is a paragon of sympathy and empathy. And you've met him already. That's me."

"What's you?"

"Shell Scott is. I mean, I'm him. I'm Shell Scott."

"No, you're not."

"Sure I am. Wouldn't I know?"

"I don't believe you. Who are you, anyway?"

I blew some air out my nose, had a slug of my murky drink, put the glass down, and took out my wallet. "Observe," I said, showing her my wallet card, attesting to the fact that I was a private investigator licensed by the California Department of Consumer Affairs' Bureau of Investigative Services, then my driver's license. "See?" I said.

She pressed her full lips together, then pooched them out a little, pulled them back in again. They kept moving for a while, and I watched them, fascinated by the poochiness of those fantastic lips as they moved out a little almost joyously, then back a trifle in what struck me as clear disappointment, then out a little again, and in, as if maybe she was sucking on a mint that was half sweet and half sour, but surely all melted by now, which would have been true even of a cold-rolled-steel ball bearing, it seemed to me, were it to be nuzzled like that by those wild lips.

Then she stopped moving. That is, her nuzzly lips stopped moving in and out in that fetching way they had, and she eyed me curiously. "Why did you lie to me?" she asked.

"Lie? When? About what?"

"About who you are."

"Oh, that. I didn't lie. I just . . . didn't tell you *who* I was. Or am. Right? Think back."

She thought back. At least her lips got very active again and she slanted the dark, heavy-lidded eyes to one side. "Well . . . maybe so. But"—she glanced toward the bar, then back at my face—"he's not a deaf mute, either. I heard him talk to you when you ordered my drink. And you said he *was*. I want an investigator I can *trust*. Especially considering the awful . . . problem I've got."

"Hey, you can trust me. Honest. I just told you that about Pete as a . . . little joke. I wanted you to talk to *me*, not him." I paused. "Just a little joke, see? Play on words. Like, if I told you it was raining cats and dogs, you wouldn't say I lied just because little kittens and puppies weren't actually falling down all over the place. You wouldn't run outside to see if the air was filled with animals, would you?"

"Well . . ."

"Listen, do you think I would have let you hear Pete talking if I really wanted you to think he was a deaf mute? Wouldn't I have ordered in *sign* language? Wouldn't I . . ." I stopped. "What the hell am I doing?"

"You're trying to make me believe I can trust you. So I can tell you about my . . . awful problem."

"I suppose. But I mean, how did you get me on the defensive so all-of-a-sudden? Look, when I came in here tonight, I was in an odd kind of mood. Loose ends, a little blah, maybe. Then I saw you come inside, and you looked —interesting. You're very lovely. You were alone. I was alone. I thought maybe we'd get acquainted, and run away together. To a tropical island. Build a grass shack and drink coconut milk, and—"

"You're weird," she said.

"Well, strike the grass shack and coconut milk. What I'm getting at, Miss Denver . . . May I call you Kay?"

She hesitated, pushing her lower lip slowly up over the upper one and then rolling it down again, up and down several times. Which may not sound extraordinarily exciting, but was. In fact, I was getting more out of just watching this lovely's mouth move around than I'd gotten on some entire dates including drinks and dinner and dancing.

I leaned toward her. "I'll let you call me Shell," I said.

And finally the lips parted, showing the even white teeth, and she smiled, warm-warmer and finally warmest. "Oh, all right," she said. "Shell. But you're still weird."

"Now that we're on a first-name basis," I said, "what's this problem you mentioned?"

She frowned, black brows pulling down over the dark eyes. Then she lifted a leather handbag from the seat beside her, placed it on the tabletop, and opened its clasp. She reached inside and pulled out an envelope, took something from the envelope, and extended it toward me. I barely got a glimpse of what appeared to be several photographs, about four-by-five-inch color shots, then she jerked them away, stuffed them into the envelope and stuck it back in the leather bag, placed the bag in her lap.

Maybe I'd gotten only a glimpse, but the top photo had unquestionably been of a woman, nude, facing the camera and with her arms raised, hands holding a fluffy pink towel atop her head, the cloth covering her hair and falling down along one side of her face.

"I don't know if I can do this," Kay said. "I thought the detective my friend mentioned—you, I mean—I thought you were older. Like middle-aged. Maybe ancient and decrepit, and . . . Well, you're *not*."

"You noticed."

"Maybe I'd better explain a little first."

"O.K."

She took a deep breath, sighed, then said, "It's the craziest thing, Mr.—Shell. There's *no* way it could have happened, but it has. Somebody has taken a lot of pictures of me, photographs, in my apartment. But I live alone—I have a suite in the Dorchester. And if somebody was taking photos of me I would have *seen* him."

"Him?"

She looked at me, rubbing the tip of her tongue slowly back and forth across the upper lip. Sort of a nervous gesture, I supposed, the way someone else might crack his knuckles or drum with fingertips on a tabletop, but much prettier and stupendously more sensual, of course.

"I just assumed it was a man," she said finally. "Why would a woman want photographs of me naked?"

"Why . . . ah, indeed?"

"Anyway, there's just no place he could have been without my *seeing* him. I mean, if you studied the photographs and realized where he would have had to be—well, people aren't invisible."

"Uh-huh. If I studied the photographs . . ."

"And if you saw my apartment, I mean, the way it's set up. There are pictures of me after I got out of the shower, and putting on my—well, getting dressed—and even one of me lying on my bed naked. It was warm, and I was letting the air-conditioning cool me, you know."

"Sure."

"Well, he couldn't have been up there on the *ceiling*, could he?"

"Doesn't seem likely," I said. "Maybe if I studied—just took a quick peek at the snapshots. And if you described your apartment—like, are there a lot of mirrors? There are one-way mirrors people can see through, you know, like they have outside the I rooms in most police departments. And, well, there could be a number of explanations, probably."

"I don't know about technical things like that. What's an eye room?"

"The letter *I*, short for interrogation. Where they ask questions of the prisoners and suspects."

"Oh. Well, you'd know about all those things. Yes, maybe you really can figure out how he did it." She took the envelope from her bag again and held it toward me. Well, sort of. She started to push it toward me, then pulled it back just as I was about to snatch it from her, and held it pressed against her breast.

I was getting a little twitchy. Either this Kay Denver knew a whole lot about how to build up suspense in a man, or she was in a terribly ambivalent state, possibly requiring the services of a psychiatrist more than a detective. But perhaps I was being unfair. Which made us even.

She was saying, "I haven't even asked you yet, Shell. If you *can* help, would you start right away? I don't mean right now, tonight, of course. But tomorrow first thing?"

"Well . . . Actually, no. I've just finished a case, and normally I'd be free. But something came up this morning. I've accepted a job for a new client, and usually I concentrate on only one case at a time. Usually. I've always felt I should concentrate all my energies and attention on the single job at hand, instead of . . . Usually, that is. I suppose there could be a situation—"

"Will it take long? This case you just got?"

"I—it could, but I don't think it will. The more I think about it, the sooner I bet I wrap it up."

"What kind of case? Is it a long, complicated thing, Shell?"

"No. Well, yes, it's a little complicated in a way. But, no, I don't think it'll take long. I just have to find, locate, a—person. I put some lines out today, talked to my client, ran an ad, that sort of thing. Just preliminary getting-started angles. I won't really know until tomorrow whether any of the angles might pay off. Probably late tomorrow, if then. So there's really not much left for me to do tonight. Unless—"

"An ad? You mean advertisement? Is that how detectives solve cases? I don't understand."

"This is just an ad . . ." I stopped. But there was no reason not to tell Kay about that message; all of L.A. could read it tomorrow. So I went on, "An ad in the Personal Message and Missing Persons columns of the *Times*. I'm hoping to locate a girl, a woman, and I'm much more optimistic about the thing working than I was a minute ago—several hours ago, I mean. Very good chance I'll wrap this case up in a . . . jiffy."

"But you won't really know anything for sure until tomorrow, or tomorrow night?" She took her hand away from her breast, casually placed the envelope on the table before her. "Probably late tomorrow, you said?"

"If then, yeah. But I might get lucky. I'm a lucky fellow. Usually. And usually—"

"I was thinking, Shell."

"O.K."

"If you get everything finished tomorrow, or tomorrow night, then you could concentrate on me—working on this for me, couldn't you?"

"Sure. Wrap it up in a jiffy."

She pushed the envelope toward me. Not far. Maybe a couple of inches. "I could let you take these photos with you—"

"Sure. Yeah. I'll study them—"

"—and then, if you get time tomorrow, you could come over and look at my apartment. And maybe figure out how whoever did this is doing it." She shook her head. "I just can't think of *any* way it could have happened."

"There's a way. I'll bet I find it."

"So you take these, Shell. Quick, before I change my mind."

I picked them up quick, and had two fingers inside the envelope when she cried, "Oh, no, don't look at them *now*. Wait until I'm gone."

"Gone?"

"I couldn't sit here with you while you looked at all those photographs of . . . me. Of me . . . you know. Some of them are—well, whoever did it is probably a professional photographer. Maybe that's a clue for you. They're so clear, and sharp, you can even see—I just couldn't, that's all." She paused, then went on, "Maybe you can tell something from the paper they're printed on, or the kind of camera he must have used, things like that."

"Maybe. Probably. Incidentally, how did you get them? Were they mailed to you?"

"No. That's part of how crazy all this is. They were inside the front door of my apartment, on a little table there, when I got up yesterday morning. *Inside* my apartment."

"Yesterday? Not this morning, then."

"No, yesterday. I just . . . stewed for a while, didn't know what to do. And there wasn't any note or anything, just the pictures. In this same envelope they're in now."

"No message 'I'm watching you' or 'How about a date?' or demand for payment of money, nothing?"

"Nothing." She shook her head slowly from side to side. "Only those damned photographs."

They were still in my hand. I put them in my coat pocket. "You don't have any idea who might have taken the shots?"

"No idea." She looked soberly at me. "Shell, this may seem odd to you, and maybe not very important. But it's important to me. And . . . the worst thing is not understanding, and . . ." She stopped, went on softly, "I'm *scared.*"

"Well, there's got to be an explanation, Kay. I mean for *how* it was done. As to the why, and who, I'll dig into that as soon as I can." I paused. "Wouldn't it be funny if some guy invented a camera that could take pictures at a distance? Just set the dials for latitude X and longitude Y, and *click*, you've got a picture of whatever's there. Or whoever."

"Is there something like *that*?"

"No, no, I was just saying what *if* there was? Wouldn't that be great? I mean, great invention . . . not so great for *you*, of course. There'd be all kinds of amateur photographers dialing your latitude and long . . ."

She was giving me a strange look. "You're—"

"Don't say it," I said. "Let's start over. About tonight—"

"Why don't I call you tomorrow, Shell? Find out how you're doing, when you might have time for me."

"Sure. But I was saying, about—"

She scooted sideways in the booth, stood up. "I'll call you around five P.M., all right? Of course, you could call me *before* then if you've solved your case, or whatever it is, and you're free. Couldn't you?"

"Sure. But I've got a better idea, Kay. Even when I'm working, I have to eat. So do you. Everybody does. So why don't we do it together?"

"Do . . . what together?"

"Eat. Go to dinner. I'll call you tomorrow, when there's a break in my feverish activity, which there will probably be plenty of, and take you to some fabulously expensive bistro. For dinner. How about that?"

She was standing by the booth now, so I slid out, stood next to her. She hadn't let out any squeals of pleasure, so I said, "O.K.? How about that? Great idea, huh?"

In heels, she was only an inch or two shorter than I, which would have made her pretty close to five-ten, a tall lady. Tall, with a full-to-the-brim figure, prominent high breasts pushing against a V-necked white blouse and the dark blue cloth of her suit, obviously curving hips. Not a lightweight, but tall enough to carry all of those splendid pounds with ease and grace, she looked good to me.

No question, she did know all the tricks of keeping a guy in suspense. Not a peep from her yet. But her lips were saying something that was probably significant. Yes? No? Maybe? Only if you like my pictures? Only if you don't like my pictures? Only if you don't *look* at my pictures?

But then, after at least three or four seconds, she smiled warmly and said, "Fine. I'd enjoy that very much, Shell. You can tell me how you're doing on your case, and I can tell you if I hear any more from, or see, my Invisible Man."

"Done. I'll call—"

"Why don't I just meet you here again, Shell? Like . . . five o'clock? Or later?"

"Five's fine. But I can pick you up. I'll even get the car washed."

"I'd rather meet you, Shell. I'll be out most of the afternoon anyway. I don't want to just sit around in my apartment, and wait. I'm . . . uncomfortable there now.

Let's meet here, and we can start with a martini. Or two."

"Or three," I said.

"Three . . . at the most."

So Kay knew that sexy martini-toast, too. And this time her smile wasn't just warm, it was *hot*. Lips curving, tip of tongue held between white teeth, those dark brown eyes almost smoldering, one arched black brow raised. There was something more than sultry about that face, something almost savage. At least, at that moment there was.

Then she smiled. "Five o'clock, then. Here. You and me and martinis. Then off to your bistro—fabulously expensive, you said?"

"You better believe it. Just a plain glass of water's a nickel."

"I like a man with class. Well, bye. I feel better, Shell. Really. I think you're going to help me."

And then she stretched upward a bit, moved slightly closer, and kissed me very gently on the lips. Just a touch, a brief pressure, a moment of warmth and smoothness and perfumed softness, before she turned and walked away from me. She moved with a long firm stride and an almost poetically rhythmic sway, hips swinging in sensual undulations as if their joints and sockets were immersed in and lubricated with hot honey.

I sucked in a deep breath, sat down in the booth again, pulled the envelope from my coat pocket, and took out the photographs. I could still feel the gentle pressure of Kay's mouth pressed lightly against mine, see that hot-honey undulation of her hips, as I took my first look at the photos, in living and lascivious color, of lovely and luscious Kay Denver.

Who, it developed, was even lovelier and more luscious than I had guessed.

Chapter Four

HOME IS THE Spartan Apartment Hotel on North Rossmore in Hollywood, near Beverly Boulevard. At 8 P.M., after stopping for a steak dinner on the way, I parked in the garage behind the Spartan, trotted into the lobby, and headed up the stairs, waving a quick hi to Jimmy, the young night man behind the desk.

I let myself into 212, my three rooms and bath on the second floor, and flipped on the overhead lights. There was already soft illumination in the living room from the two fish tanks against the front wall. One of them is a ten-gallon aquarium like the one in my office, also bright with guppies, several of which, after the commotion of my entrance, zigzagged about in all directions through and around the green clumps of anacharis and cabomba, darting up, down, and sideways like the colorful tumbling of a kaleidoscope or a small star shell exploding.

I accepted this as the fishes' way of saying they were glad to see me, and paused for a moment in front of the larger of the two aquariums. It's a twenty-gallon tank in which I keep the two black mollies—*Poecilia sphenops*—four little sharklike *Panchax chaperi*, two red swordtails, a pair of *Rasbora heteromorpha*, a couple of little catfish scavenging on the sandy bottom. Plus an adult pair of *Paracheirodon innesi*, or neon tetras, along with my two all-time prizes, a pair of frisky personally-raised-from-little-bitty-eggs *baby* neons. The colorful dandies are so-called because of the bright bluish-greenish strip extending from eye back to caudal fin, so vivid it's actually like a thin neon sign, glowing, shimmering, iridescent.

But I called those two little ones my prizes not because of their electric brilliance, but because I was essentially, or at least by one remove, their daddy. I had placed a healthy adult male neon, and a particularly fetching gravid female fat and heavy with eggs, in a separate aquarium, carefully pH— and temperature-controlled, and fed them the fish equivalent of steak and lobster and organic vegetables and wheat germ and vitamins. Which is to say, with lots of live food like tubifex worms and brine shrimp and wiggly daphnia, until they presented me with a whole slew of little-bitty eggs from which, eventually, emerged and grew three dazzling offspring. I was almost proud enough to pass out cigars.

Well, maybe you're not all that interested. But, if you wondered why, when I had three baby neons to start with, there are only two in the tank now, that's easy: One of the little fellows died. Just keeled over. No, I didn't dig a hole and stick him in it, with a card saying "Here lies Elmer," etc. I may be a little eccentric, but I'm not that dumb. Besides, the other fish ate Elmer. He was just floating there, belly up at the top of the tank, and *zip*. Gone. Makes a man think.

I dropped a little dried salmon meal on top of the water in both tanks, then turned on the table lamp next to the chocolate-brown divan. The apartment consists of living room, kitchenette, bath, and bedroom. In the living room, a low black-lacquered coffee table rests in front of the divan, and beyond the table are three large leather hassocks, seldom in the same places on the yellow-gold carpet. The carpet itself is thick with a heavy shag nap and beneath it is a double-thick pad that feels almost like a mattress under the feet, especially when they are bare feet. Plus a gas-log fireplace, and on the wall above it my provocative Amelia, the somewhat garish yard-square nude I picked up long ago in a pawnshop.

In the bedroom, black carpet, oversize bed, stereo and TV with VCR, walk-in closet filled with a few suits and dress shirts, plus lots of sport jackets, shirts, slacks, some of them in very bright hues indeed, slippers and shoes including several pairs of polished reddish-brown cordovans.

The kitchenette is small, with a breakfast booth big enough for two friendly people, microwave oven, refrigerator and freezer, cabinets with dishes, bourbon, vodka, gin, and vermouth, and a few ambrosial liqueurs, should a lady desire something like crème de menthe or Frangelico.

I flopped on the divan, propped my feet on the coffee table, and examined those photos of Kay Denver again.

In Pete's, I had been impressed with the dark, sensual beauty of her face, and guessed that the tailored suit and V-necked white blouse covered a full-curved woman's body as lovely and impressive as the face. I hadn't been wrong. The photos—there were three of them—eliminated any need for guessing. In one of them she was seminude, in both others completely bare and beautiful.

The photo I'd gotten a mere glimpse of when Kay first started to hand them to me was of her apparently leaving the shower. Part of its frosted-glass door and a strip of chrome edging were visible behind her. Her arms were raised, both hands holding a fluffy pink towel around her head. Drops of water sparkled on her high full breasts, on the smooth skin of her abdomen, in the dark nest of pubic hair, on her long firm thighs. Her eyes were closed, pink tip of tongue at one corner of her mouth.

The second shot was of Kay, nude, bending slightly forward as she pulled on a pair of lace-trimmed pink panties that were halfway up her thighs. The last shot was of Kay lying on her back, on a large bed covered with a smooth white spread, the ornate design of brass bedstead slightly out of focus beyond her head. None of Kay Denver was out of focus, however. Her head, resting on a pillow underneath the white spread, was rolled slightly to one side. Her lips were parted, eyes half closed. I could see each individual black lash, almost make out the pores in the pink skin of her breasts.

This was the shot of which Kay had said, "He couldn't have been up there on the *ceiling*, could he?" She had exaggerated about that one, because the shot had clearly not been taken from high overhead. As a guess, I would have said the camera was some distance from the foot of the bed but not more than six or eight feet above floor level. Three or four feet above Kay's bare body, yes; but hardly "on the ceiling." That still didn't answer any of the questions about who could have taken those shots, or how.

All three photos had been printed on glossy Kodak color paper. They were so sharp and clear that I assumed they were contact prints rather than enlargements from 35mm film. Which only suggested that the "invisible" photographer's camera exposed a four-by-five-inch negative, not what kind of camera it was. And I couldn't tell much about where the photographer, or at least that camera, might have been from the photos themselves, not without looking over Kay's apartment. Which would have to wait at least until tomorrow, if not longer.

So I put the three photos back in their envelope, left the envelope on the coffee table, got up and walked into my bedroom. I had pushed the vision of Kay's loveliness, of those full flowing curves, out of my mind, I thought. But as I undressed and glanced at my bed, for a moment I could almost see her there, long bare body atop the spread in the same pose as was enticingly displayed in that color print of Kay relaxing nude in her apartment, lips parted, eyes half closed.

So I firmly pushed her out of my thoughts again, took a quick shower, walked back to the bed, asked Kay to please move the hell over, and climbed between the sheets.

I pulled myself up and sat on the side of my bed as the second alarm stopped with a *ting-ting* and final *ting*, and I smacked my lips, opened one eye, and said, "Bluh."

Over black coffee, I checked the *L. A. Times*, found my ad. It was one of half a dozen, but happened to fall at the top of a column in the continuation of those Personal Messages, so the opening boldface "Money for a Spree" line sort of jumped off the page.

I wondered how many other people in and around L.A. were reading the same paragraph; and if Spree would see it, and call me, and let me wrap up this case in a jiffy; and if Kay Denver had found any more gorgeous—but admittedly disturbing, even frightening—photos in her apartment.

After forcing down a piece of toast for breakfast—none of my appetites get up until an hour or so after I do in the morning—along with more black coffee, I called my office number in the Hamilton Building and got Hazel on the PBX. It was just after 9 A.M.

"*Sheldon Scott, Investigations*," she said brightly. "May I help you?"

"Hi."

"Oh, it's you. At least it sounds sluggish and gummy. Is this the late Shell Scott?"

"Don't make me think, Hazel. You know I don't wake up until it's time to go to bed."

"Sex, sex, that's all you men think of—"

"Check the morning *Times*, will you, dear? Personal Message section." I gave her the page number in the classifieds, and a line or two of the message. "There may be a call coming in to the office, in response to that ad." I paused. "In fact, because I was dumb enough to use the phrase 'very large fortune,' you might get two or three calls. The lady I'm looking for, the one who really *is* in line for a large fortune, is not only named Michelle but her mother's maiden name was Nicole Elaine Montapert. Write that down, will you?"

"It's down. Spell the last name."

I did, then added, "If you do get any freako calls, only the right lady will know the mother's correct maiden name. All the dingdongs will claim they can't remember because their mother got amnesia when they were born, or maybe they'll just say oops and forget it. Easy, O.K.?"

"Easy's easy for *you* to say. I suppose you're going back to bed, assuming you're not still in it."

"Hazel, my love, I am going forth into the city. Down those mean streets. Out into the lethal smog, and crack-ups of the Freeway . . . Hello? Hazel?" She'd pulled the plug on me.

So I did what I'd told Hazel I was going to do, went out into the smog, and onto the freeways. I spent three hours in

Monterey Park, two hours at the L.A. City Hall, and another hour in the newspaper morgue at the *L.A. Times* digging into twenty- and twenty-five-year-old files until I found the stories I was looking for, the ones that mentioned Claude Romanelle. Which, actually, was about my only accomplishment—other than developing eyestrain from peering at microfiche records and frustration from talking to bored employees in recorders' and city clerks' offices—because what I came up with on Romanelle's ex-wife Nicole and daughter Michelle was zilch.

One problem: While it's comparatively easy to follow the trail of a Dudley Smitherson from Cincinnati to Taos to Pasadena, whenever and wherever a Mary Jones enters wedlock and becomes a Smitherson, there Mary's trail —and maybe something of Mary—vanishes. So by the middle of the afternoon I was back in my apartment at the Spartan, busy on the phone again.

I checked with the detective agencies in Florida and Nevada. My contact in Reno told me that Vetch, first name Robert, had been married there to Nicole—who by now, in my mind, was Nicole Elaine Montapert-Romanelle-Wallace-?-Vetch-?—and moved, according to a change-of-address form unearthed from the Reno post office after the expenditure of "considerable time and expense," to Redondo Beach, California. But Mr. and Mrs. Vetch had remained at that address for less than six months, and no clue to their subsequent whereabouts had yet been found.

The Fort Lauderdale agency had discovered that, soon after divorcing Claude Romanelle, Nicole married one Edgar Hopkins Wallace—hence the Wallace preceding "Vetch-?" in the name I was building in my head. They had found evidence of their divorce, recorded a couple of years later, but no indication of Nicole's later marriage.

Thus, bits and pieces, a line here and a name there, but nothing at all on Michelle Esprit so far. I did know a bit more about Claude Romanelle. From the morgue at the *Times,* plus calls to contacts in Fort Lauderdale, Detroit, and Chicago, I had learned enough to convince me that my new client was a pretty slick and slippery crook. Or, at least, *had* been, twenty to twenty-five years ago. Claude and a half-dozen other men, all of them young, in their twenties and thirties then, had operated a variety of successful—for them—scams and con games.

The scams and cons of the Arabian Group—as it was dubbed by the Chicago newspapers of that day—were always local, never national in scope, and there was never any evidence of organized crime affiliation. They were just a group of crooks banded together for a time, five or six years, in the pursuit of crookedness and the ill-gotten profits thereof. Profits which were, if the occasional hyperbole of old newspaper reports could be half believed, in the neighborhood of ten million dollars, which is a lot of money now, but was a stupendous quantity then.

The gang got its name from the presumed leader of the criminous group, one Keyser Derabian, who later was indicted, tried, convicted, and jugged, and died in prison of pneumonia. His brother, Sylvan, was also part of the group, but I was unable to discover what happened to him. However, the real brains of the outfit, or so the reports indicated to me, was Claude Romanelle. The word "genius" is used with remarkable imprecision by some crime reporters, as in "evil genius of the underworld," or "Numbers-Racket Genius Indicted in Calculus Scam," but the word had been used often enough in connection with Claude that it was a pretty sure bet he was no dummy.

Interestingly, Claude never did any time, though he was twice indicted. The first charge was initiated by the SEC, and alleged that Romanelle had run a boiler-room operation that sold nine million shares of stock in an oil-pipeline company that had only two yards of pipe. The second indictment charged that he'd cooperated with executives of a Chicago brokerage firm in profiting illegally from inside info, first regarding a forthcoming low-earnings report, then from advance news of a takeover bid, in both the buying and selling of shares in a company called Skyland Enterprises. Skyland was the owner of five amusement parks, complete with bumper-car rides and Ferris wheels, in Illinois, Pennsylvania, and Florida. Both indictments were eventually dismissed.

Busy man, my new client. At least in those days. Interestingly, he had not engaged—at least, there was no available evidence that he had—in such slippery and felonious behavior during the last twenty years. Or since about the time he'd split from the abode then shared with Nicole and "little Spree."

By 4:30 P.M. I had completed all I felt could be accomplished this day, and was out of the shower, admiring my dazzling reflection in the mirror affixed to my walk-in-closet door. I wondered if I had gone too far, laid it on a bit much. I had not forgotten I was to meet Kay Denver at Pete's, around 5 P.M., and I did hope to impress her rather more than I apparently had last night, when zip, she was gone.

Yes, I wanted to impress her, thus I had dressed with some care and a lot of positive thinking. But . . . well . . . I looked like a guppy. I had to admit it. A pink sport shirt with cornflowers and ferns on it, scarlet trousers with white belt, white shoes and socks, and a custom-tailored jacket the color of . . . well, like when they mix a lot of paints together in a can and then dip a piece of canvas in it. No, more like if you could freeze a rainbow and then hit it with a sledgehammer. No, more like . . . well, yeah, like a guppy. That was where I'd gone wrong.

I dashed back into the closet, hung up the colorful jacket, and slipped into a white sport-type coat, one of my favorites. It wasn't cut like a regular suit coat. The guy who made it for me in a little shop—I forget exactly where —said it was the style worn at times by white hunters in Africa, or even maharajahs in their summer palaces. Except for its dashing cut, it was very simple. Just plain white, or various whites, blending in a kind of rippling effect, and a little red and blue piping around the lapels and down the front. It was really keen. The red would blend with my shirt, or pants, and the blue . . . what difference did it make?

I had already phoned Kay a couple of times without any luck. The desk clerk at the Dorchester confirmed that Kay Denver was registered in suite 42, but there was no answer in her rooms. But, then, she'd told me she expected to be away from her apartment virtually all day. So I stopped at the coffee table, picked up the photos of Kay that I'd left there the night before, stuck them into my keen coat pocket, then breezed down to the Spartan's parking garage, and into my sky-blue Cadillac Coupe de Ville convertible.

Just in case Kay was late for our date, I would at least have the company of her pictures.

By the time I'd pulled into my space in the lot behind the Hamilton Building, it was only a couple of minutes before five. I stuck my head in the door of Pete's and spotted him behind the bar.

"Any gorgeous ladies waiting here for me?"

"Nope. Just the usual, Shell. Two process servers, one heavyweight wrestler, and an angry father looking for you and his daughter. Angry, armed, and dangerous."

"Don't say that." For some reason, when he said "angry and armed" I thought of Claude Romanelle and those exaggerated comments about his "little Spree," as if she were still his wee infant. But, yes, "dangerous," a guy with his background might be. Especially if he turned out to be nuts.

"Tell them all to make appointments," I said to Pete. "But there is a long, lissome lovely named Kay Denver —the lady I met here yesterday—who should be along in not less than a minute and a half. Tell her I'll be right back—have to see Hazel for a minute."

"Tell Hazel hi for old Pete," he said, smiling.

He liked Hazel. She'd sat at the bar here with me a couple of times, and Pete was impressed. He thought she was orange blossoms and sugar candy, sweetness and brightness. He had actually said things like that, or things very close to them, in speaking with pointed approval of her. As if maybe I should take *her* out for dinner at a fabulously expensive bistro. She was cute, sure, and bubbly and fun. But she was just a *friend*.

"Right back," I said, trotted out, next door, and up the stairs inside the Hamilton. Hazel was still in her cubicle, putting papers back into their folders. The monitor of the IBM PC was dark.

"Hi, friend," I said cheerily.

She turned slowly on her stool. "Don't friend me," she said darkly.

"What's this? A bilious Hazel? Pete just told me to say hi for him. He'd marry you if he were a hundred years younger—"

"Handle my call or two, he says. My call or *two*."

"Three? What happened? Did you get . . . more than three? Four? Hey, I'll buy you a—a pencil with a real eraser."

"You'll buy me a lobster. No, a mink. And gold and silver and diamonds."

"Sure. Anything you say."

"There were more than a *hundred* calls. All because of your damned *ad*." She picked up some lined yellow sheets of paper held together by a paper clip and threw them at me. "More than a *hundred*."

"You're kidding," I said, shocked.

I *was* shocked. A hundred? What was happening to all the people who used to read the story of the Founding Fathers, of little Georgie Washington, big Ralph Waldo Emerson?

I looked at Hazel's eyes, burning into me like little arc lights. "I guess you're not kidding. Um. That many?"

"A hundred and six plus three who actually came *up* here. Fourteen Michelles, all born on April twenty-third, and ninety-five females who didn't give their names, or couldn't remember who they were. Those are the check marks."

I glanced at the pages. Mostly checks, in blue ink. The checks, I noticed, got bigger and bluer toward the end of the last page. Toward the end of the day.

"Well," I said. "That's—something. Well, uh, 'thanks' seems . . . inadequate. Ah, besides the mink and gold and silver and diamonds, can you think of anything nice I can do for you?"

She snorted fire out her delicate nose. At least she snorted, and there appeared to be little blue flames in it.

"Well," I said, "I'll think of something. But right now, I've got to run. Uh, I don't suppose any of these—these one hundred and nine knew Nicole's maiden name, did they?"

"They didn't even know their own. If one of them had passed the test, I would have told her to get in touch with the—with that—with *you*, you . . ." She stopped, got up from her padded leather stool, and stepped closer to me, leaning on the top of the counter between us. She looked me up and down.

"I heard you say you have to run," she commented pleasantly. "Run where? Are you in a track meet?"

"Track—?" I stopped. I glowered at her. "Well, Hazel," I said stiffly, "there went your damned diamonds."

She smiled. Or almost did. Certainly it was the first expression so far that might be said even to have approached a smile. "You've got a new *date*, don't you? Oh, Shell. You always do *something* ridiculous when you're going out with a new one."

"Something ri*dic*ulous? Why, that's—ridiculous. That's —dumb. That's . . . Hazel, do I really look . . . ?" I stopped again. How was I going to phrase it? "Ah, not dashing? Like an African maharajah in the bush . . . that's not what I meant."

Her expression changed oddly. Sort of softened, I guess. "No, no," she said, and she did have a more smiley smile on her face now. "You look really nice, Shell. Just a little—unusual. But you're an unusual guy, aren't you?"

"Don't ask me. However, I am *not* color-blind. I remember once you accused me of thinking yellow was a shade of purple, so I had them tested. My eyes, I mean. Well, gotta ru—go. Bye. See you tomorrow."

"Tomorrow," she said. Then, "You really *do* look nice, Shell. Bye."

Kay was there when I walked into Pete's again. She'd apparently come in just before me, because Pete was showing her to a booth. The same one, I noted, where we'd sat last night. She was still standing, and turned to look at me as I came inside, the door *shooshing* closed behind me.

She was wearing black. Black suit, smartly fashioned

jacket fastened with a single large white button at her waist, and with odd lapels that rose up into the air and ended in points at either side of her chin. Snugly form-fitting black skirt hugging the flaring hips. White blouse, cut low, exposing the soft roundnesses of those fine firm breasts. She wore the black hair up, piled loosely atop her head, and everything together accented the blackness of her eyes, the sootiness of her long lashes, the slashing arcs of those thin dark brows. She looked fabulous.

I stopped next to her. "Kay," I said, "you look wonderful. Fantastic. Gorgeous." I beamed at her.

"Thank you, Shell."

On an impulse—or maybe because Hazel had shaken my confidence and I wanted an unbiased opinion—I asked, "What comes after thanks? I mean, how do *I* look?"

The black brows pulled closer together, the skin at the bridge of her nose forming a little furrow. "Do you really want to know, Shell?" she asked.

"I'm not—sure now."

"You look——"

"Never mind."

"—like a very large tropical bird."

"Huh. Great." I paused. "Wonderful." I paused. "Well, that's better than a fish, isn't it?"

She didn't know what I meant by that. Neither did I. "Well, we'll have to hurry," I said. "Let's go."

"Go?"

"Yeah. I was just out at a track—the racetrack—I —entertaining the crowd at a circus, O.K.? So we'll spin by my apartment, O.K.? So I can change into something suitable for the exciting evening ahead. Wait'll you see my suitable black suit," I went on. "It'll nauseate you. Keen for funerals, though. I wore it when Mad Dog Gicci was assassinated——"

"What are you talking about, Shell? I've already ordered martinis. Isn't that what you said last night?"

"Who knows what I said last night?"

But she had indeed ordered. For at that moment Pete walked up with a tray on which were two martinis, one with a pair of pearl onions in it, the other with an olive for me.

"You two just going to stand there?" he asked.

"Not you, too, Pete," I said dully.

He placed the martinis on our table. Kay and I sat down on opposite sides of the booth and she lifted a martini with two onions and said, "Cheers. Did you find your client's daughter yet? This Michelle you said you were looking for?" She took a sip of the martini, and started doing sexy things to one of the onions with those disturbingly mobile lips.

I ate my olive. "I didn't think I'd told you the woman's name," I said casually. "Just that I was trying to locate a woman."

"You *didn't* tell me her name, Shell." Down went the lucky onion. "You said you were busy, busy, you'd talked to your client, run an ad—you even told me it was in the Personal and Missing Persons columns of the *Times*. Don't you remember?"

"Yeah, I remember now. The truth is, I was a little distracted. By you. You do derail a man's train of thought at times, Kay." She smiled, white teeth flashing behind the curving red lips, and I went on, "But I still don't remember mentioning the lady's name."

"Shell, I read your ad in the *Times* this morning. After talking to you, and hoping you could help me with—help me." She lowered her eyes, glanced to one side. "Well, naturally I was interested. And the *ad* mentioned a Michelle, whose birthday—whatever it was." She looked at me, her expression quite sober. "Is something wrong?"

I shook my head. "No. Not with you. With me, maybe. Guess it's the business I'm in. Always looking for discrepancies, slipups. Clues, you know. And then there have been so damned many Michelles already, calling to claim their fortune."

"Oh? You've had a response?"

"You can say that again. And again . . . and again. I should have realized you must have seen the name Michelle in the ad. Half of L.A. must have."

Something was bothering me. One of those little uneasinesses below the edge of consciousness, something Hazel had said about the women who'd phoned the office number listed in my ad. Plus three—

But at that moment Kay took a large swallow of her martini, zonking down nearly half of it, and said, "Did you—did you get a chance to look at those photographs I gave you?" She smiled, pink tip of busy tongue sliding slowly across her lips, from left to right and back from right to left, then she bit down gently on it and grimaced. "I guess that's a silly question."

"Not so silly. Just kind of unnecessary. Yes, Kay, I did examine the photos closely, in the interest of investigative thoroughness, of course." I stopped, started over. "Look, I don't want to sound as if I'm making light of your problem. I'm not. It's just that, um—"

"I understand. Probably you couldn't tell much about who did it, anyway. Not just from the prints."

"Partly it's that. It is also the fact that you are a sensational-looking lady. And in the altogether, well, lady, the mind wanders off into the boondocks. I did conclude that the prints were made on glossy Kodak color paper, thus I could narrow down the places where that paper is sold to maybe a thousand stores. No, I'd say the way to go is to check out your apartment, concentrate on the how."

"I've been thinking about that, Shell. It's impossible a man could have *been* there—from where the photos must have been taken, I mean. So there must be just a camera, or mirror . . . or something."

"Something, yeah. You get any more photos since last night?"

She shook her head. "No. Thank God for that."

We chatted a little more, finished the cocktails. Kay moistened her lips, let them play with each other for a few passionate moments, and said, "Two more martinis, all right? I'm buying."

"Two more, yes, indeed. But buying, you are not."

She raised an eyebrow. "I don't believe this. I don't have a keep-the-lady-in-her-place act here, do I? A male supremacist kick?"

"Just male, kid. You want to buy the booze it's O.K. by me. Just invite me to the pool hall. But I invited *you* out for this mad, unforgettable evening, remember?"

"Mad?" she said. "Unforgettable?"

"That's discouraging. We've barely started, and you've forgotten already."

She smiled. "Must have had too much to drink."

"O.K., O.K." I wiggled two fingers at Pete.

He brought the drinks. Halfway through those second martinis I realized that Kay got a lot more out of her onions than I did from my olive. I just popped it in, crunched it severely, and boom, down the hatch into the hooch. But she sort of sneaked up on those pearly little vegetables, nuzzled them, seduced them, probably drove them half crazy, then apparently let them dissolve somewhere near her molars. It was fascinating. I could hardly wait to see what she'd do with a steak or lobster. Probably get us both arrested.

"That reminds me," I said, "after this one, let's head for Hollywood, all right?"

She nodded, and I went on, "I have selected, with the help of a computer data base and several knowledgeable maître d's who don't eat where they work, a flamboyantly seductive and sinfully romantic restaurant on the outskirts of Hollywood. The food ain't too bad, either. On the way we will be passing within a furlong of the Spartan Apartment Hotel, wherein your host resides. There, if we can stop for not more than two minutes, I will change swiftly into my pallbearer suit."

"Do you have to talk like that?"

"Well, it's black. What's wrong with pall—"

"No, that junk about sinfully romantic, and all."

"Junk. Well, I usually drink bourbon, but this perfume must have gone to my jaws. Three of them and I'd probably recite poetry to you. 'Shoot if you must this old gray head, but spare—'"

"To Hollywood. But we stop at your apartment on the way?"

"Right. O.K.? Of course, I could go like this, but I don't think you'd like McDonald's—"

"You wouldn't be thinking about getting me to your apartment and trying to seduce me, would you?"

"Wouldn't I? My dear Miss Denver, you do me a great wrong—"

"Not yet, I haven't," she said, smiling.

"That's not so great. Really, all I intend to do—at least *before* dinner at this sinfully romantic joint—is get out of these duds and into something more depressing. That would please you, wouldn't it?"

"I think it would."

We went. As I passed the end of the bar, Pete leaned forward and said to me, "How's Hazel?"

That was Pete's wonderfully subtle way of telling me he liked Hazel better than Miss Denver. But he liked Hazel better than *any* of the ladies I might happen to be with. So I merely said, "Haven't seen her since she ran off with the plumber, Pete. But I got the license number of his Porsche."

Then, *shoosh*, and we were outside. But Pete's comment reminded me of something I wanted to do. A couple of doors down Broadway from Pete's was a little flower shop called Jeannie's, which wasn't presided over by a Jeannie but by a nice gray-haired old lady named Mrs. Nestle, from whom I had purchased a ton of posies in the past. We exchanged our usual small hugs and I told her I wanted some roses sent to the Hamilton, to be delivered by 8 A.M. tomorrow morning.

"How many, Sheldon?" She was one of the few people who always addressed me formally.

"Nine dozen, all of them long-stemmed red roses. Yeah, red's O.K. Plus one white rose."

"Nine *dozen*? Why nine *dozen*?"

"Plus one. I have sinned, Mrs. Nestle. This is so maybe I won't live in hell for a week. And because nine dozen plus one add up to a hundred and nine. Which—skip it. Tied or glued onto the single white rose, include this note, please."

I scribbled a message on one of the little "Jeannie's" cards, but didn't sign it. Just "Hazel—Wanna go to the fights?"

"The white rose symbolizes purity, doesn't it, Mrs.

Nestle? Goodness and truth and niceness, all that jazz?"

"Well . . . purity. Virginity—"

"That's close enough."

"Red roses usually express love. Devotion."

"Hell, I don't want this gal to get the wrong idea. She's just a—friend. They're for Hazel."

"The *wrong* idea? Nine *dozen*?" She looked at me intently through gold-rimmed eyeglasses. Then she sighed, "Where do you want all these flowers put up there?"

Mrs. Nestle knew where Hazel worked, at the end of the second-floor hallway. So I said, "Just scatter them around. Have the boy put some on the computer, the PBX, on the counter, wherever."

She sighed. "I'll deliver them myself, Sheldon. I don't know why men are so dumb."

"Dumb? Mrs. Nestle, I have had *just* about enough today from the entire female sex—"

"Dumb, dumb, dumb!" she said, smiling.

"Well," I replied stuffily, "we can't *all* be women, can we?"

She said that was smart.

We were rolling up Beverly Boulevard, two or three miles from North Rossmore, when I realized what had been bugging me about Hazel's earlier comments. It was her saying that three of those ladies had descended upon, or rather ascended to, her cubicle on the Hamilton's second floor. Her words, I recalled, had been ". . . plus three who actually came *up* here."

It's funny how the great sprawling vastness of a man's subconscious mind will gather into itself all the information about nine billion different things, and select only one or two of them to bug him about, and often select what appear to be relatively unimportant items at that.

What belated realization told me *now* was something I should have deduced *immediately*, the instant Hazel told me of those three enterprising females who, instead of simply phoning the number the lucky lady was supposed to call, had instead taken the trouble to discover the office address of "Shell Scott." And slyly hastened to that address, in the hope of thus outmaneuvering all the other impostors.

Moreover, with my powers of deduction thus sharpened to a shining point, the next conclusion was almost beautiful in the purity of its logic: If three females were smart enough to discover the location of my office, it was at least conceivable that three other even smarter females had similarly discovered the location of my dwelling, my apartment, my home.

Thus there might, at this very moment, be one or two—even three—females waiting, waiting nervously, waiting impatiently, waiting greedily, to pounce upon me in the lobby of the Spartan Apartment Hotel.

Wrong.

Not three.

Thirteen.

Chapter Five

IT HAD BEEN a pleasant drive.

Kay and I chatted easily, laughed a little, learned some more about each other. Not a whole lot. Just that she was single, a writer of nonfiction, she'd grown up in Wisconsin and never wanted to see snow again; and that I had always wanted to go to Hong Kong and hoped someday a client from thereabouts, say Singapore, would hire me to investigate the true origin of chop suey. Negligible miscellany, light but pleasant chatter.

However, when Kay and I walked up the steps and into the Spartan's lobby, I became immediately aware of a flutter of movement and an unusual but rather pleasant hum of well-modulated sounds, as of little animals cheeping and rustling in a bosky jungle.

Then Jimmy, the night man on the desk, called out to me, "*Shell!* Boy, am I glad to see you! Eddy said some of these ladies have been here for *hours*, and—"

He probably went on, but I would never know what he might have said, because his much-too-loud "*Shell!*" was a trigger transforming those nice little animal sounds that brushed almost delicately against the ear into the howling and shrieking of cannibal headhunters pursuing their fleeing dinners. Simultaneously, the flutter of movement became what was unquestionably some kind of female catastrophe with twenty-six arms and twenty-six legs and *at least* thirteen mouths—all of which were wide open —its dismaying entirety converging upon me from every

63

direction except straight down and obviously impelled by the desire to burst eardrums.

I say obviously because, although somewhere in the shrill cacophony that had suddenly erupted I thought I picked up a couple of *Shells* or maybe *Michelles* and a *me* and a *you* and some *I-I-I*, most of what hurt my ears, and even hurt my whole damned head, was simply NOISE, absolutely impossible to describe but much like the disembodied lungs of the entire Metropolitan and Italian operas all squashed together and being jumped up and down on in the lobby of the Spartan Apartment Hotel.

After a while I'd had *quite* enough. Clearly it was up to me to bring order into this bedlam, time to silence these women and make them *listen* to me. Before we were all deafened. Time to find out what had brought them all here—as if I didn't know—and cleverly get rid of the twelve impostors. Or thirteen. And then take Kay out to dinner. If, of course, any of that was remotely possible.

I pushed *that* negative thought out of my mind right after it discouraged me, and quickly replaced it with: Piece of cake . . . No problem.

To think—finally—was to act. I faced that gang of women squarely, raised both arms, and shouted in a commanding bellow, "All you yammering babes, knock off the yammering and listen to me!"

Nothing.

"Hey! *Listen* to *me*, you hear?"

It was disheartening.

There was still a whole bunch of howling and yammering. Actually, unless my ears deceived me, which was entirely possible after what they'd been through, it was getting louder. I began seriously to wonder: What if this piece of cake couldn't be stopped? What if it was a self-perpetuating cataclysm that would just go on and on, shrieking throughout eternity?

But, no, I wouldn't give up. I was an ex-marine! So I hoisted myself up onto the lobby desk behind me, got to my feet, and looked *down* at the women. "*Now hear this!*" I barked. "*Shut the hell up or I'll knock you on your thirteen asses.*"

They heard me at last. You wouldn't believe how quiet it got. The only sound was from somebody in the back row, saying, "How many?"

"*That's better!*" I yelled. "I mean, that's much better, ladies. Now, pay attention, and I'll straighten everything out in a jiffy."

I leaped lightly from the desk, started descending toward the floor.

It's fascinating how speedily the mind can work when it wants to. When it is, so to speak, given free rein. Though I was swiftly descending, my mind was going even faster. It was zapping along like lightning. I was thinking: That's the secret, I have to stop treating these people like women. I have to stop being *afraid* of them. The key was to act with authority, domination, command, and treat them like *men*.

That's when I knew everything was going to be all right.

And that's when my feet landed lightly on the carpet, and my legs buckled, and I banged one kneecap with *quite* a crunch. I tried not to grunt as I straightened up, grunting. "All right, you miserable dogfaces," I groaned. "Line up there." I pointed. "Elbow to elbow, that's it. There's a fortune at stake here, right? Right! Shape up that line! Suck those guts in! Stick those chests . . . ah."

Well, they did get into a line, if a line is a figure S with a couple of hyphens in it. They hadn't moved with military snap and polish, but at least I'd gotten them away from me, and all thirteen were facing in my direction. Sort of.

So I told them that I was indeed the Shell Scott who'd run the Personal Message in today's *Times*, that the fortune was real and available, and each and every one of them probably deserved it, right?

No question about it. They all nodded and wiggled and even started making a little noise again, but I cut that off quickly, merely with a wave of my fist.

"Now hear this," I said slowly and deliberately, but loud. "There are thirteen of you here to claim the fortune. But only one of you can be the real Michelle. Therefore, twelve of you are out of luck. Hold that thought in your minds. All right, *I want you twelve impostors to leave*"—I swept an arm around dramatically and pointed a rigid finger at the Spartan's exit—"*RIGHT NOW!*"

Believe it or not, three of the gals broke ranks and started ankling across the carpet, heading for the exit from the lobby. The first one kept on going speedily and disappeared into the night. But both of the others stopped after only two or three steps. One of them banged her fists together and shook her head rapidly. The other simply paused, in an attitude of dejection, shoulders slumping. But then both of them went out, not once looking back.

I glanced over at Kay Denver, who was leaning against the lobby desk. She was either smiling aloud or laughing. It ticked me off. But then she moved away from the desk, walked toward me with that hot-honey fluidity of hips and lips and just about everything else, and I became instantly unticked.

She stopped next to me and said, "Not *too* bad, Shell. Three down. How are you going to get rid of the other ten?"

"Beats me," I said. "You got any ideas?"

"It's your problem," she said. Then after a pause, "You were in the army?"

"Army? Ah, you refer to the authority I laid on 'em. The domination, power, command. It should be obvious I was in the marines. The You-nited States Marines—"

"Please. Don't sing the 'Halls of Montezuma' to me. Shell, you must know how to determine the *right* one of these women, if there is a right one. Or at least how to eliminate the wrong ones."

"Well, yeah. Matter of fact, I do. But . . . I can't quiz them all at once, with all ten hearing the questions at the same time." I glanced at the ladies, still standing in an S. "Not this bunch. A couple of them might split and come back later with the answers. I may not know much about women, not today anyhow, but I know my crooks."

"So ask them one at a time. Like . . . in your apartment?"

"I was going to think of that myself, Kay. But there is a small problem. If word should get around that I—well, some narrow-minded people have foisted ridiculous rumors upon the public ear, that is they've made almost entirely baseless charges that . . ." I stopped, started over. "If it became advertised, or even hinted, that I took ten women into my apartment, one at a time and one after another, even if only for the briefest—actually much too brief—"

"I understand," she said.

"You do? That was quick."

"Why don't you let me be your chaperone? I'll be your unimpeachable witness that you were a perfect gentleman with all ten sex-starved ladies."

"Who said *sex*-starved? They're after *money* . . . Ah. Your little joke, hey? I'm glad you're having such a great time, Kay, dear. Yes, I'm glad one of us is. Now, if you'll stop snorting, I'll congratulate you on a peachy idea. Thanks."

"You're welcome," she snorted.

"O.K., let's do it."

A couple of minutes later, after I had explained to the ladies that I would talk to them one at a time in my apartment and we had all trooped upstairs, Kay and I were in my living room with a young and attractive lady named—what else?—Michelle, and the other nine crooks were outside in the hallway.

Kay sat at one end of my chocolate-brown divan, and I sat at the other. Michelle stood before the divan, on the far side of the black-lacquered coffee table.

"All right, Michelle," I said. "What is your birthday?"

She had the year right, and the month and day. I said, "So this past April twenty-third you were twenty-eight years old, right?"

"No, twenty-seven . . . Twenty-*six*." She paused, a pretty picture of confusion. "The ad in the paper said twenty-six, didn't it? That's what I am."

"Sure, you are, you darling." I smiled at her. "What the hell made you think you could get away with it?"

"Screw you," she said.

That left nine.

The next six were almost as easy, but I had to ask five of them to tell me their mother's maiden name. That, of course, was as far as they got. The next one, number eight of the ten, came closest of the bunch. She was a short brunet, about five-two, and heavyset, probably twenty pounds overweight. She claimed to be Miss Michelle Mort, twenty-six years old. But I guessed she had to be at least ten years past twenty-six, if not more, with a sour and rather grimly fixed expression as if she were biting down on a piece of human gristle. She was "dressed young," though, and perhaps even overdid it with a knee-length pink skirt, fuzzy pink sweater, low-heeled white walking shoes, and a little red ribbon in her dark brown hair. Still, of the ten, she gave me the biggest shock of all.

"All right, Miss Mort," I began. "Michelle. Birth date?"

No problem. Also no problem with her age, which for sure was twenty-six. But when I asked casually, "Ever called anything else, Michelle? Nickname?"

"Mickey, sometimes," she said. "And sometimes Spree."

I'd been getting bored, going through the same routine so many times. But that answer shook me, not only because it was "Spree" but because the word came from this grim and sour babe who, to my eye, was only a hop from her forties.

I took my first really close look at her, and noticed her dark eyes burning into mine, undoubtedly now—and during the questioning before now—looking intently for any twitch of eyelid or curve of lip, any sudden or involuntary change of expression.

This was a smart one. Best of the ten, by far. Of course, she was a hell of a lot older; more time to get smart. But she'd reached for, and grabbed, the connection with the "Money for Spree" in my ad. I stood up, looked across the width of the coffee table at her.

"That's odd," I said mildly. "Doesn't sound like short for Michelle. Like the 'Mickey' you first mentioned. Which I'll bet didn't get a twitch out of me."

Those dark eyes didn't waver. But there was no doubt she was well aware of what I meant by that. "No, it isn't," she said evenly. "And only my oldest and closest friends call me Spree."

"No kidding. Oldest and closest. Well, then, some of

them must be pretty . . . close."

Just a little bit of a change at that. Not much. Slight tightening of the thin lips. Maybe the eyes burned more hotly.

"O.K.," I said, "maybe you're the one. Won't take long to find out. If you're really the lady I'm looking for, then you've got a small birthmark right about there." I pointed in the general area of her left breast, careful to keep my finger at least a foot away from her fuzzy pink sweater. "And you can tell me your mother's maiden name." I smiled. "Then maybe you'll be rich."

There wasn't much change in her expression even then. But there was enough so I had not the slightest doubt that she knew for sure the jig was now up.

She ignored my comment about the maiden name. Instead, she raised her right arm, clutched her left breast in her hand. Actually, I figured she could have clutched it in two fingers. However, she cupped it in the whole thing, but gingerly, as if even she didn't like it much, and *then* her expression changed quite a bunch.

Lips twisting in what appeared to be definite distaste, she cried hoarsely, "So, you're one of *those*, are you?"

"One of what those?"

"One of *those*. Birthmark—yah. I know what you're after. Next, I suppose I'll have to take off my brassiere, right?"

"Wrong!"

"So you can check, and peek, and fool around—"

"Heavens, *no*."

"And then—I know your kind—you'll say I've got a mole on my sitter, and I have to take my *pants* off."

"Oh, Lordy. Wonderful. Could you lower that stentorian cackle just a little—?"

"Well, I won't do it, I won't. I won't take off my bra and pants for *any*body."

"I'm certainly not suggesting you ever *did*. Not even once in the last forty—"

"I'll tell the others, too." She was already on her way out, halfway to my front door. "I'll tell—"

"*Wait* a minute."

I scooted after her, but she had the door open and was thudding down the hall. By the time I reached the open doorway she was almost out of sight, clumping down the stairs, bits of foaming dialogue trailing after her. Some of which was, "Don't let him take *your* bra off. Or your *pants*. He tried to do it to me—"

I stuck my head out the door. "Tattletale!" I yelled after the old bat.

There were only two Michelles left in the hallway by then. One of them, a cute little redhead, put a hand over her mouth and laughed merrily.

I was thinking it would be great if the real Michelle had a reasonably healthy sense of humor, and I was going to invite the redhead in next. But then I noticed—and it is a measure of how unnerved the sour babe's screeches had made me that I had not noted the fact instantly—leaning against the wall, where he had apparently been lounging while engaging those last two ladies in conversation, was my next-door neighbor, Dr. Paul Anson.

Paul is a friend of mine. A good friend. Also a fine, very high-priced physician, and a very eligible bachelor. But not even once a year would he allow a chance to dig me, to stick me with a zinger, pass without critical or acerbic comment, some of which uncalled-for remarks were as sharp as the scalpels he used for cutting patients in two, or almost so. Tall, lanky, with a kind of "rangy" look, like a western hero sauntering in off the plains after ending the Indian wars single-handed, he was a good-looking guy. Too good-looking, it sometimes seemed to me. Particularly when he breathed hotly over a date of mine, as if attempting to dry her hair with his mouth while simultaneously assuring her that she was obviously too good for a lout like old Shell.

He straightened up, flashing a crooked grin at me.

"You're Scott, right?" he said happily. "Recognized you from your mug shot. I'm Sergeant Anson. It's warm in Los Angeles. I'm working out of vice—dum-de-dum-dum."

"Paul, dammit. I don't need this. Knock it off."

"I hope you'll come along quietly, Scott. Again. You have the right to several expensive attorneys, free of charge—free to *you* of charge—even if you are innocent, but especially if you are guilty as sin. You have the right to remain clammed—"

"*Paul*—" I stopped, took a deep breath, started over. "Can't you see I'm working?"

A glance at my pal's expression, indicating clearly that he was about to crack up, convinced me I had not chosen the most felicitous response. I flapped my hands up and down against my thighs, looked at the little redhead, and said, "Your turn. If anybody cares."

"I—" She looked from me to Paul, back at me again. "I don't know if I really should, really."

I jerked a thumb at Paul. "Don't worry," I said. "The idiot sergeant there will protect you."

"Oh. Well, all rightie, then."

That's really what she said. And, her fears put to rest, she walked up to where I stood in the open doorway of my apartment and on inside. Followed closely, of course, by Dr. Paul Anson. Paul always walked right on inside, uninvited, if the door wasn't locked, and particularly if I was at the same time walking in with a creature of surpassing or even passing attractions.

Fortunately, the last two interrogations went rapidly. With the little redhead I started right out with, "O.K., tell me your mother's maiden name."

And she said, "Oh, pooh. I never thought of that."

Just about the same with number ten, except that she slapped her forehead with the heel of one hand, saying, "*Stu*pid . . . *stu*pid." Then she, too, was gone.

I let out a sigh, collapsed against the cushions behind me. Paul ambled over, sat on the edge of the coffee table. About six inches from Kay Denver.

"How do you do?" he said, showing Kay all his teeth except the upper molars. "My friend, Shell, my dear bumbling old buddy, is a dazzling detective, is he not?"

Paul, presumably, was hoping the lady might say she hadn't been all that dazzled yet—which would surely have been true enough—but instead she said, "Actually, I'm beginning to think he may be quite good. I wasn't sure at first."

"You weren't? Well, trust those first impressions, my dear. Avoid jumping to hasty conclusions. Consider the man's limited and unimaginative technique. Or, instead, let me try it out on you. What is *your* maiden name?"

"Kay Denver," she said, smiling, and making little wiggly heat waves in the ether with her lips.

She glanced at me as I noticed Paul raising his eyes to the ceiling and blinking rapidly. I'd have trouble getting rid of my pal now, I thought. Then he bent even closer to Kay, saying, "By the way, I am Paul Anson. I live right next door. It would please me very much if you would call me Paul. Or call me next door. In the meantime, my advice to you—"

I broke in, "Kay, this character who is apparently trying to drop his teeth into your lap is *Dr.* Paul Anson, a fact he refrained from mentioning. Refrained for fear that his license would be jerked. Jerked because of the operation he is now attempting without sufficient anesthesia."

"Tut, tut," Paul said, attempting to look handsome, amused, blasé, and aloof all at the same time, and very nearly succeeding. "The blighter is trying to come between us already. Shouldn't we ask him to leave, love?"

Kay had an odd little smile on her face as she looked directly into his eyes and said softly, "Paul, darling, he'll stop that foolishness once he knows you slept with me last night." Pause. "And . . . that it was our wedding night." Another brief pause. "But, dear, after your performance, I filed for divorce this morning. I'll mail you your shorts." The smile widened, didn't reach her eyes. "You can't win 'em all, Paul."

For a moment, Paul looked as if he might never win another one. It was the only time I ever saw him open his mouth to speak and leave it ajar, open it wider, and then shut it firmly. He first lost the amused expression, then the blasé, then the aloof, and finally even some of the handsome.

But after all that, he managed a fairly good crooked grin and said lightly, "Sorry, love, I was worrying all night about my indictment for polygamy." Then he scowled. "Best I could do in a hurry. You win, Kay. You're really very good." Then he got to his feet, looked down from his rangy height, and added slowly, "You know where the balls are, don't you?"

He waved a casual hand at me and went out.

I was still trying to absorb all that myself. "Kay, dear," I said finally, "I'll bet if you really tried, you could get almost mean."

"Mean's easy," she said pleasantly. "I was nice to him because he's a friend of yours."

"That was nice, huh? I'd hate to see rotten."

"I *can* be nice, Shell. I mean, *really* nice."

I looked at her. "I believe it."

"Do you have gin and vermouth?"

The change of pace caught me off guard. "Gin?" I echoed. "Vermouth? Sure. Even onions and olives. And frozen peppers. I like to be prepared for any emergency."

"So why don't you mix us . . . let's see. Earlier we had two at Pete's, right?"

"Right."

"And—how does it go? Three under the table?"

"And four . . ." I let it pass.

The familiar, and somewhat crude, old toast goes, "One martini, mmm . . . two at the most . . . three under the table . . . four under the host." But I assumed Kay meant something else by her comment, or perhaps didn't know the entire toast after all.

But she said, "So make two more for you, Shell." Then a big sigh, tongue moistening those restless lips. "And . . . two for me."

She knew the old toast, all right. Including two verses I'd never heard of.

I was already about half awake, in that nebulous no-where between dreams and the day, when I felt, more than heard, Kay slip out of bed.

Then I did hear some definite noises, clinks and little clatters from the kitchenette. I hoped she wasn't suddenly getting domestic and cooking breakfast. Kay sure hadn't been domestic last night—unless domesticity is wildness and abandon, beauty and softness, and an uninhibited sexual athleticism unique in my personal experience, and possibly in the memory of the planet.

I heard water running briefly, something faintly bubbling, scraping of metal against metal. Yeah, she was cooking some kind of alleged edible. Which was a mistake. No matter what she was cooking, if it wasn't my usual lumpy mush or burned toast, it was wasted effort as far as I was concerned. Probably I should have told her I never eat a hearty breakfast before lunch. But we hadn't gotten around to the subject of nutrition.

Five minutes later, fresh from a hot and cold shower, I dressed in white slacks, white loafers, and a wonderfully colorful sport shirt. The shirt was one of my all-time favorites. Its basic cloth color was a kind of lavender-orange but not much of it was visible because that was the background for about a hundred little peacocks. Little male peacocks with their little tails spread open. I really like peacocks. I think maybe they're my favorite bird. Next to fried chicken—but fried chicken would look really dumb on a shirt.

I admired my reflection in the full-length mirror. When I wiggled back and forth rapidly, it looked like the peacocks were flying. After a little of that, I inhaled some huge breaths and sent them whooshing out like Pete's door closing.

"Was that you, Shell? Did you say something?"

It was some broad out there in the kitchenette, clattering around. Kay. Yeah, had to be Kay. I ignored her. First, before I even attempted intelligible conversation, I had to finish waking up. I sprang about for a few seconds, then decided nothing was going to help much except the passage of considerable time.

So I closed my eyes, finally cranked them open again, walked out of the bedroom, and peered into the kitchenette.

I had been correct. It was Kay in there, clattering. "Hi," I said. "You're Miss Denver, I'll bet."

She turned, smiling. She was wearing the same outfit she'd worn into Pete's last night, but minus the black jacket with up-slanting collar points. Just dark skirt, and white blouse with the deep V exposing smooth curves of soft breasts.

"You win the exploding cigar," she said brightly. "Did you have a nice sleep, Shell?"

She was just full of loathsome zip and zing and energy and smiles and vitality. It ticked me off.

I know it's foolish, and not in the least admirable, possibly inexcusable. But, perhaps because it is a minimum of half an hour after I get out of bed before my blood begins to move, much less warm up, I feel it is unconscionable of other people to arise and act *healthy*, act as if they're having *fun*. At least, so ridiculously early in the *morning*. It shows crude insensitivity, and a lack of consideration for the rest of us. It is cruel. It is heartless. It is really dirty. The more I thought about it, the more ticked off I got.

"Oh, *yeah*?" I said.

"What? Shell . . . didn't you hear what I asked you?"

"Umm. Yeah. But . . . I think I forgot the question."

"I asked you if you had a nice sleep. It was just —conversation."

"Well, I had a nice something. Don't remember if I got any sleep. Until now. Well, good morning. O.K.?"

She pulled her head back, looked down her nose at me. "You're not Dr. Jekyll in the morning, are you?"

"Dr. who?"

"Jekyll. I think I'm seeing your Hyde side."

"No, I told you, I'm Dr. Who. What's going on here? A *medical* conversation? Before I've had my *coffee*? That's proof of the insensitivity—"

"Coffee's ready," she said a bit icily. "Should I pour it into your mouth?"

"Don't get picky," I said. "But, as an emergency measure, it's worth considering." I shook my head rapidly back and forth, rubbed both hands over my chops. "Look, Kay, I apologize. I should have warned you not to speak to me until after my eyes open . . . to just lead me around by the hand and point at things."

She took my hand, hauled me over to the small breakfast nook, and pushed me into the curving seat. Then she

placed coffee before me. And pointed at it. I had a sip.
Then another.

"Breakfast is going to get cold," she said.

"That's all right. Doesn't make any diff—"

"And I went to so much trouble. There wasn't much to
work with, but I fixed—"

"Don't tell me. Dear, really, I'd rather you didn't—"

"—what I could find, some steak, and some eggs—"

"Oh, God."

"—and some green peppers."

"Those were for my special margaritas."

I did manage to finish my coffee, and even got down
most of another invigorating cup, before she slid a plate of
stuff in front of me. I knew I couldn't look at it just yet. I
also knew I should have told her long before now that the
normal "hearty breakfast" impresses me like a plateful of
germs. Toast and coffee, maybe a little mush, in the A.M.,
that's my dish.

I really felt bad. Here Kay had gone to all this trouble
fixing a nice breakfast for me, and I wouldn't even look at
it. So I forced myself to take a peek. The steak didn't look
half bad. But—there they were. Those other things. The
bane of my gustatorial life. Two eggs. Both fried. Both *ugly*.

The thing that's important about eggs, at least in the
early morning, is that only a little while before then you've
been asleep, and maybe dreaming. And in some of those
dreams there are these great gooey creatures that slither
around and gobble you up. Usually they have—at least
mine do—these huge bulging yellow eyes, or maybe red or
purple or bloodshot but usually yellow, and they look you
over with this piercing yellowish gaze before—ack, it was
turning my stomach.

I looked up at Kay, who of course was beaming expec-
tantly upon me. "I knew it," I said.

"What, dear?"

"Don't dear me," I said. "But . . . boy, I've got to hand
it to you, girl. You really went to a lot of trouble."

"I hope the eggs aren't cold."

"Yeah. That'd be a crock, wouldn't it? I probably
couldn't eat 'em if they were cold."

Well, I didn't want to hurt her feelings. I'm not mean. So I picked up a fork. Looked down at the plate. Maybe mean was better.

"Look at those eyes!" I said. I didn't mention it to Kay, but I knew the rest of him had to be down there under the plate. "Golly, it looks like a huge Elmer."

"What's a hugelmer?"

"Just Elmer. I buried him in a little hole. But I tell everybody the other fish ate him."

"I'm going to freshen up," she said.

She hadn't even sat down in my little kitchenette breakfast booth yet. "Aren't you going to eat?" I asked her. "Or did you already?"

"Oh, I'm never hungry in the morning. But I know how much a big *man* can eat."

"Sure, you do."

She walked away, toward the bedroom. When she went out of sight, I was still nodding slowly, and saying, "Uh-huh."

I got the remains down my garbage disposal before Kay came back, makeup expertly applied, carrying her black jacket and large black handbag. She put the bag on the floor, near the end of the coffee table, then sat on a hassock and looked at me.

I was seated on the divan, just getting ready to call the Hamilton Building and check with Hazel. It was only a few minutes after eight, but I knew she'd be there working. Or moving a bunch of roses around—I'd almost forgotten about those posies—before firing up her IBM PC.

I was reaching for the phone when it rang.

Ah, Hazel had found the flowers. She was hugging them to her bosom, sniffing in their sweet fragrance. She was calling to thank me profusely and tell me she wasn't mad at me. Mad? Ha-ha, silly boy—

Smiling, I plucked up the phone and said, "Hello, hello. Is this the rarest flowerpot of them all—ah, flower. *Really* meant flower, dear. Sorry. Not quite awake yet. Well, is . . . *Is* this—"

"What in the world . . . ? Have I got the wrong number?"

"Yes."

"This is—are you Mr. Shell Scott?"

It was a lovely voice. Not Hazel, of course. Someone who spoke in soft sweet tones that had a strange kind of music in them. It was vibrant, pleasant, a little husky. Still, I was sorely tempted to reply No, Mr. Scott had just stepped out and would not return until he finished having his head fixed.

But, instead, I said, "Sorry. I thought you were someone else—my . . . gardener. No, that's not true. Why should I lie? But, yes, I'm Scott. Who's this?"

"I'm . . . not sure . . ."

"You don't know?"

"I don't know if I should *tell* you. Are you *really* Mr. Shell Scott."

"Yeah. Really. Honest. I'll show you my driver's license. Look, would it help if I told you I just woke up recently? And I'm not at my best for a *long* time—"

She had interrupted me with delightful lilting laughter. Then she was saying, "Of *course*! Now I understand why you sounded so absolutely *ding*dong—"

"What do you mean, *ding*—?"

"I thought maybe I was the only one."

"You?"

"Me, too. I'm exactly the same way. I'm just *awful* until I have my coffee in the morning."

"That's . . . that's beautiful."

"I'm grouchy, and stupid, and even *mean*."

"No. Not you. I'll bet you don't have a mean bone in your body . . . do you?"

I'd started getting carried away there for a moment. Almost forgot women were all over the place, trying to trick me. And right then this one confirmed my suspicions by saying, "I'm calling in response to your *Times* ad, the one in the Personal Messages."

"Ah, that little dandy. Sure. Winners are arriving from all points of the compass. We may have to stop them at the borders."

Either my comment didn't impress her or she chose to

ignore it. "I think I'm the woman you're trying to reach, Mr. Scott."

"Sure. You'll be number . . . Let's see, number one hundred and twenty-three, plus the calls last night and maybe this morning."

"I don't understand." I didn't comment, and she continued, "Anyway, everything seems to fit me, the name, the birth date—"

"What *is* your name, Miss?"

"Michelle Wallace."

"You got the Michelle right. And what's your mother's maiden name?"

"Oh . . . golly."

While she, presumably, was cleverly trying to remember a name she'd never before heard in her life, I sighed, and was beginning to wonder, once again, how there could be so much more deception, dishonesty, greed, and plain old crookedness around than even I had suspected, when the lady at the other end of the line said:

"Montapert."

"What?"

"Golly, I feel so *dumb*. I just told the nice lady that name, then I went and forgot it *again*. That *is* pretty dumb, isn't it? But I hadn't heard it in so long I just drew a blank again. But that's it, my mother was Nicole Elaine Montapert. She's Mrs. Steuben now, though."

"Steuben."

That's what I said, but I wasn't paying much attention to what I was saying. This, for the first time, was the correct name, and hearing it jarred me almost as much as had listening to sour Miss Mort here yesterday.

"That's pretty good," I said. "You're right."

"Of course I'm right. I simply couldn't remember for a moment."

"Well, maybe . . . You know, you *could* be the one."

"I'm sure I am, Mr. Scott. I mean, I *think* I'm the Michelle you want—at least, I'm Spree."

Maybe it was because I'd just been thinking of the unpleasant lady who so greatly prized her bra and pants, but the word, and this Michelle's statement, didn't bowl me over the way it should have.

I said, "Spree? From what? I mean, what name?"

"It's from Esprit. My middle name. I'm Michelle Esprit Wallace. Originally, it was Romanelle. That's my father's name. And, Mr. Scott, tell me something, will you?"

"Sure."

"Is it my father—Mr. Romanelle—who wants to give me all that money, or fortune, or whatever it is? If it *is*, I'm not at all sure I want it."

"I'll be damned," I said. After a few moments I went on, "I don't think the rest of this should be on the phone. At least you've convinced me we should meet."

"All right."

"Where are you now?"

"I'm phoning from my car. And I'm almost to Beverly now, Mr. Scott, on my way to Hollywood. I could stop by your apartment, if you'd like. It's number two-twelve, isn't it?"

"That's right. O.K., meeting here makes it simple . . ." Then the comment stuck me a little. "Incidentally, a number of ladies have already discovered I live here at the Spartan. But, if you don't mind, how did you find out?"

"Your secretary told me. When I called your office number."

"Hazel? Well, she's not actually my—you talked to her?"

"Uh-huh. Just before I phoned you. She gave me your apartment number, and suggested I call you at home."

Hazel must have been favorably impressed, I thought. "What did you tell her?"

"Just what I've told you, Mr. Scott. That's why it was so dumb not to remember my mother's maiden name for a minute. I'd just got *through* telling your secretary. Or this Hazel. She was awfully nice."

So far, everything fit like a fat hand in a thin glove. Still, there was something else I'd wanted to ask Miss Wallace. Couldn't pin it down at that moment.

"*Now* I understand what she meant," my caller went on. "This—Hazel, after suggesting I phone, told me if you sounded like Dracula at noon I wasn't to pay any attention. Just to keep telling you the same thing over and over."

"She said that, did she? Hazel's a dear girl."

"I didn't understand what she meant at all. Not then. It was just a big mystery."

"Then? I suppose that means you're crammed with sweet understanding now?"

"Oh, sure. Oh! She asked me to tell you something else. Hazel did."

"Wonderful. I'm on pins and needles."

"It was a message from her to you. I wrote it down." She was silent a few moments, then, "Woops—I'll probably almost get another ticket before I find it."

That puzzled me. So while she was looking for whatever fun thing she'd written down, I asked, "Almost? How do you almost get tickets? Mine are never in doubt."

"Oh, they never give me tickets. They just stop me and talk a little, then smile and laugh and tell me not to do it again."

"They smile and *what*? You're not talking about cops. Traffic cops?"

"Yes. Those nice young men on their big bikes."

I completely failed to comprehend what she was telling me. Cops *love* to give tickets. Give them a choice between winning a cruise to Bermuda and giving you—or at least me—a ticket, and they'll never see Bermuda.

"Here it is," she said. "It's a question. Quote, You couldn't find any diamonds? unquote. Is that another case you're working on, Mr. Scott?"

"Apparently it is. And I think it's going to be a tough one."

"Well, let's see . . . I should be there in ten or fifteen minutes. All right?"

"Fine. See you here in a few minutes, then."

We hung up. I tried to sort out what she'd told me or maybe hadn't told me. But then Kay rose to her feet holding the black bag in one hand, jacket draped over her arm. There was a gold-monogrammed "KD" on the bag's flap; and I could see, inside the jacket's collar, a small label that said "Goldwater's."

Then Kay was saying, "I've got to run, Shell. But I'd love to talk to you later, when you're fully recovered."

I stood up. "I was hoping to take you to lunch. Especially since we missed dinner last night."

She smiled. "I didn't miss it at all. And there'll be other nights. For dinner, I mean."

"I hope so, Kay. But, as for lunch, I may be busy the rest of the day."

She nodded. "I know. I was listening to your conversation. It sounds as if you've found your mysterious missing lady."

"It's possible. Might also be another Miss Mort, though. But I should know before the day's out. Maybe by this time tomorrow, you can hire a full-time detective. Cheap."

She smiled again, her lips parting, and for a moment it appeared that each lip was smiling at the other one. Or maybe gently waving, but not waving good-bye. That might sound not only impossible but almost unattractive. Believe me, they not only did it but it was more exciting than watching two little lady mud wrestlers.

"I was just thinking," Kay said, after she got control of her mouth, "about my invisible photographer. The one you're going to catch and beat up for me."

"Yeah, I'll wrestle him to death. No, I'll break his leg. No—"

"Wouldn't it be funny if you were right, Shell, and he's got this crazy high-tech camera with calibrated dials and longitudes and all? What's the latitude and longitude of your apartment here?"

"This may astound you, but nobody ever asked me that question before. What diff—ahk, *mamma mia*! Why, that bastard! He could be out there dialing and fiddling, and yelling 'Gotcha! Gotcha!' Oh, I'd hate to think I could never again . . ."

I stopped, and scowled at her. "Kay, that was cruel. For a minute, or half a horrible second, you almost had me believing—"

She had stepped close to me, and stopped my words with her lips. Just a quick light kiss, much like that first filled-with-promise pressure she'd bestowed on me two nights ago in Pete's.

Then she turned quickly, walked to the front door, glanced back and spoke a silent paragraph or two, or three, with those encyclopedic lips, and was gone, the door closing gently behind her.

Chapter Six

LESS THAN FIVE minutes later my front-door chimes went *cling-clong* and I took a last look around the living room.

It was presentable. Looked lived in, but there were no olives or peppers on the coffee table or carpet.

Besides tidying up a bit I had done a little thinking in advance of my caller's arrival. The question I'd forgotten to pursue on the phone was if, just possibly, my caller might happen to be acquainted, even well acquainted, with a dumpy lady named Mrs. Mort. Wouldn't necessarily prove anything if she did, of course, but it was a question I intended to ask.

Ask quickly. Because, if my half-formed suspicions were correct, I could still take Kay Denver to lunch, and embark upon her interesting case just as soon as I got this little meeting over with.

So, having nearly convinced myself that I was moments from meeting a Miss Mort clone, I pulled the door open and said, "Come on in, and let's get this o—o—o—"

"Mr. Scott? Hi, I'm Spree."

It was the same sweet-soft voice with strange music in it, but this was no clone, not of anyone I'd ever seen. I didn't say anything. I just stared. Silently stared.

People who know me are well aware that I am almost never at a loss for words. Not a complete loss, anyway. What comes out may not be the right word or phrase, but *something* will come out.

Not this time.

There before me was what appeared to be a rather large blond woman about five and a half feet tall, young, wearing something oddly striped and quite shapeless, almost like a hoodless parka, or the loose and baggy serapes Mexican farmers wear in the rain. It was made of rough nubby cloth, with alternating blue and beige vertical stripes, and came down to about six inches above the lady's knees. Beneath it was a pale blue skirt, open-toed high-heeled blue shoes, and very neat and trim-looking ankles and shapely calves. Which might have surprised me considerably if I'd pursued the thought at that moment, which I didn't, because the rest of the torso seemed to be quite large, even fat.

But all of that was only partially absorbed, and only with a kind of peripheral vision and attention, because what I was staring at was, without question, the most beautiful *face* I had ever seen.

It was ravishing, heart-stopping, angelic. And that smile —gentle, bright, warm, more than warm, both soothing and blood-boiling, a blend of sweetness and sauciness and natural-as-breathing sexiness that was down-to-earth but at the same time something else, something more in sensual harmony with sunbeams and moonglow, space winds and starshine, than with earth and its lovely earthiness that a man sees every day.

The lips were full, softly curving over white, even teeth. Or almost even. A little, very little, crookedness on the right there, the incisor on the left just a trifle too short. Plus arcs of new-moon-shaped dimples at the corners of her mouth, like parentheses enclosing and caressing her smile. Her eyes were green. But "green" doesn't say it at all. They were large, seeming almost huge at the moment, almost glowing as I looked at her, great green eyes *almost* the color of certain fine old Chinese jades, or of molten emeralds, or that one four-leaf clover that makes the genie appear. Maybe that glowing aliveness in her eyes was most like the ephemeral green you can see, moments after the rain stops falling, right in the center of a rainbow.

Hell, I don't *know* why that face was so beautiful. It just was. Sure, there are hundreds, thousands, of truly beautiful faces. Just as there are thousands of magnificent sunsets.

So how do you describe one gorgeous sunset in a way that will set it apart from all the rest? How can I describe that face so you can see it, *feel* the softness and sweetness and rare loveliness of cheek and brow and curve of lip, firm flesh, glowing skin, the magic in curve and plane and arc and line? Can't do it. No way.

You can take apart a fine watch and count and catalog every bit of it except the tick, because by then it won't be ticking. So I guess what finally made that face of Spree's so indescribably beautiful was some kind of Spreeness that made it tick, and kept it ticking. Maybe it was the brightness of an inner spirit that glowed from those great green eyes, maybe the warmth of a true and gentle heart, or a special fire in the blood. Who knows? Who knows what beauty is? Or Beauty?

Just say she was gorgeous. Say she was rare. Say she almost stopped my heart and stole my breath. But that still wouldn't say it. Forget it. All I know is that something different, something new, happened to me, came to me, when I saw that face. And it never went away.

I'm not sure how long I stood there like a dummy. But she waited, silently, however long it was. That smile of hers didn't dim, or diminish, or go away. If anything, it might have gotten a little wider, perhaps a little brighter. So, even then, in some part of me, I knew she'd been here before, observed the effect her beauty had on men, waited for them to get their tongues untangled or their eyes back in focus, or perform artificial respiration on themselves until the emergency was over.

Undoubtedly, then, she knew not only that she was beautiful but just *how* beautiful. That's dangerous knowledge. I hoped it hadn't ruined her. On second thought, I didn't care a whole bunch if it had. I'd save her. I'd talk some sense into her pretty head, read magazines and maybe even whole books to her, help her to understand that there was *more* to a woman than—*boy*, she was gorgeous.

By the time I'd mentally saved her from the dangerous awareness that was ruining her life, and we were having

Nui-Nuis on the beach at Bora-Bora, I was back to normal. Well, almost.

I took a long deep breath, and I guess she recognized the symptoms of my ghost returning to its body, or whatever had happened. Because she spoke then, finally.

"May I come in?"

"You'd better," I said. "I'd kick myself around the block if you didn't."

She came inside. I shut the door, then said to her, "Please, just stand there until I get back. O.K.? Won't be a minute."

"All right."

I zipped into the bathroom, shut the door, ran cold water in the basin and splashed some on my face, rubbed the chops dry with a towel. Then I looked at myself in the mirror, raised and lowered my eyebrows, stuck out my tongue and hauled it back in. Everything worked. So I banged myself on the chest a couple of times, and went back.

I walked over next to the young lady, Michelle Wallace, presumably—and I hoped—born Michelle Esprit Romanelle, stopped, looked down at her upturned face, and said, "*I* wouldn't give you any tickets, either."

She laughed. Abruptly, spontaneously, a brief but very merry outpouring of what impressed me as genuine pleasure, almost like the uninhibited delight you can hear, and see, when a child cracks up in glee and rolls on the grass.

I grinned down at her still-smiling face. "I didn't know it was that good," I said.

She laughed a little again—much less than before—and said, "Pretty good, Mr. Scott, but some of that was relief. I mean, after the way you sounded at first, on the phone."

"Yeah. Well, I wasn't quite awake then—sure am *now*, though. And I assumed it was someone else calling."

"I know. But I was still afraid I might be coming up to see somebody who'd look like, oh, Igor. You remember, in the Frankenstein movie?"

"Sure do. And I hope you aren't telling me you're disappointed." I squatted a little, crooked an arm ending in clawlike fingers, and said hoarsely, "Come wizz me, missy? See master bolt new head on Dummy?" Then I straightened up, scowling. "Sorry. You probably make a lot of guys take deep breaths and suck in their stomachs till their faces get purple. I'll try not to act like an idiot again."

"I'm just glad you turned out to be so nice. And attractive."

"Me? Nice?" I started to smile, but made a strenuous effort to keep it from showing. Might make me seem conceited. "And attractive?"

"Well, more"—she started laughing softly again —"more attractive than Igor."

"Ah . . . swell. Thanks a bunch. Well, will you"—I extended an arm, no spastic fingers this time, toward my chocolate-brown divan—"join the nice man on the nice couch?"

She walked over to it, sat on one end. I went around the coffee table, seated myself at the other end next to the little table with my phone on it.

In two or three minutes we'd gone over all the "evidence" of Michelle Esprit Romanelle's identity that had been mentioned on the phone, plus other items about her childhood days, her father's leaving when she was six years old, mostly odds and ends I was already familiar with. She was easy to talk to, bright and articulate, and there was, so far as I could tell, not the least indication of deception. If she wasn't the real Michelle Romanelle Wallace, she was good enough to convince me.

Then she said, "Shell"—it was Shell and Spree by this time—"it *was* my father who hired you to locate me, wasn't it? Claude Romanelle?"

I nodded. "I talked to him on the phone day before yesterday, Monday. He had an attorney draw up papers transferring quite a valuable hunk of his estate into joint ownership with you. Mr. Romanelle has already signed them. My job was to find his daughter, make certain she wasn't an impostor, then deliver her—you—to that same attorney's office for your signature."

"You mentioned something on the phone about impostors. Or at least that I was . . . number a hundred and something? What was that about?"

"Before you, there were a hundred and twenty-two plus a few more." I told her of all those calls Hazel had received yesterday, the three ladies who'd climbed the stairs in the Hamilton Building, the thirteen who'd appeared at the Spartan last night, and some additional calls I'd received here after that. "They're probably still phoning Hazel," I said. "I think I'm in trouble. And I'm afraid to look in the lobby downstairs, though maybe it's too early—"

She broke in, "Isn't it funny, all those women so anxious to get something they don't have any claim to, while I'm really his daughter and I'm not sure I want it?"

"Yeah, you mentioned that before. Why not?"

She sighed. "Depends a lot on how he *got* that money, or whatever it is. I don't know him at all, you understand, Shell. Last time I saw him, I was six. Haven't seen him since, and I barely remember him. But . . ." She hesitated, then continued, "According to what Mom has told me, back then he was a little crooked. Actually, a *lot* crooked. And, Shell, if he wants to give me anything he's *stolen*, well, forget it."

"I can understand that. Still, it's a refreshing attitude."

"Do you know what the assets are? Or what's specified in those papers I'm supposed to sign?"

"Nope. I guess neither of us will until we get to attorney Worthington's office. I know Worthington pretty well, but all he told me is that the amount involved is in the millions. Several million bucks. Nothing to sneeze at."

She crossed her arms in front of her body, pulled them against that tentlike blue-and-beige-striped jacket, or parka, or whatever it was, leaned forward, and said, "I know it isn't. It's tempting. I mean, no matter *how* Daddy got it. I just . . . don't know." She paused, thinking, faint frown lines forming at the bridge of her nose.

"Well, you've got to decide," I said. "My job is just to find you, take you to Worthington in Phoenix, Arizona, and then present you to your father at his home in Paradise Valley. And I should call him there soon."

She stayed in that same pose, silently, for half a minute, then looked up at me. "Shell, with that much money involved, obviously everyone concerned will have to be *sure* I'm Claude Romanelle's daughter. Not just you, but that attorney, and even Daddy, too. I wouldn't know *him* if I saw him today, so how will he know *I'm* Spree? Fingerprints? I don't think I've ever been fingerprinted in my life. I suppose Mother could make an affidavit, or whatever the legal term is. And there are my school records . . . It's not all that easy, is it?"

"Easy enough. Might take a little time, but you've already answered the most important questions. Like a lot of background, your mother's maiden name, your own name, Spree, from Esprit."

That little frown line was still between her eyes. "Yes, but couldn't one of those other ladies, those other Michelles, have found out those things—if they knew you were hired to find Claude Romanelle's daughter?"

"Well, sure, I guess so, *if* they knew . . ." I paused. "That's a good point. But it was Claude Romanelle himself who told me you were called Spree as a tot, and that few if any other people would know that. Oh, yeah, he also said that after twenty years he undoubtedly wouldn't recognize you today, but his little Spree"—I smiled, a trifle stiffly, remembering other comments he'd made about his wee one—"could be positively identified by a birthmark on her ches—" I stopped. "On her, that is on your . . ."

"Birthmark?"

"Yeah, a little, oh, fly—no, not fly, bee?"

"Flybee? What's a—"

"Bee. *Just* bee. I mean, honeybee. You know, little bugs with wings, that sit on flowers and eat pollen, or—"

"Oh!" She smiled brilliantly. The lights went on. The sun came up. Comets and asteroids collided like angel's sparklers. She sure had a great smile.

"You mean my butterfly?"

"Butterfly?"

"I hardly ever think of it anymore."

"Butterfly—yeah. Why didn't I think of that? I don't remember it *exactly*, but I'd say that's about right for describing the little grabber there on your . . . there on . . . Where is it, anyway?"

"Right here." She pressed her fingertips on the left side of that baggy serape, or sweater, or outside vest, or body armor, or whatever it was. "Here, on my . . . body."

"Yeah. That's where it is. I remember, it's almost exactly right there. Of course, at first I thought it was a bug, or fly sp—well, call it some little-bitty animal—"

"Shell, that's twice now you've said you *remember* it. That's crazy. *You've* never seen it. Hardly *anybody* has ever seen it. So why do you—"

"Hey, that's easy," I interrupted her. "Didn't I tell you? No, I guess I didn't. But I've got a picture of it."

"You *what*?"

"I've got a picture of it—of *you*. Look, it's an old photograph your da—your father gave me, of you when you were an ugly little—when you were a little kid. About six years old. You were sort of wearing swim trunks. And there's this little—thing, mark, on your chest."

Her somewhat startled expression had become more normal as I spoke, and now she was nodding. "I see. At first, I didn't quite understand. But of course. After all this time, Daddy wouldn't know me from Emily Zilch. Even if I ran up to him and said, 'Daddy, I'm little Spree!'"

"Might confuse him. Might even alarm him. It's very curious, Spree, but he still thinks of you as his *wee* little—"

"But only I—I mean, only the real Michelle Esprit Romanelle—would still have the little butterfly birthmark. So that's the one *certain* way to prove I'm Spree."

"Makes sense. In fact, that's why Mr. Romanelle gave me the picture." I paused. "Along with several warnings, and rather ominous—"

"I guess I'll have to show it to you."

"You . . . will?"

"That's the quickest way to prove who I am." She nodded, looking at the corner of the coffee table. "Yes. I'm going to follow this thing through to the end. Daddy really *does* want me to sign those papers, for millions of dollars, doesn't he?"

"Yep. Millions. A whole bunch."

"So . . . Well, I guess I'll have to tell you."

"Tell? What happened to show?"

"You see, Shell, my butterfly, the birthmark, is sort of right here." She moved her fingertips gently up and down over the significant area. "Just a little of it shows under my bra," she went on, "like the edge of its wing."

"That's all, huh? No feet, or eyes, or—"

"The rest of it curves up, on the underside of my . . . of my breast."

Either I imagined it or a flush of pink colored her soft, smooth cheeks. Must have imagined it. Women, young ladies, girls don't blush anymore. No matter what. Maybe sock you on the jaw. But blush, no.

She sighed. "Well, I said I'd have to tell you. And I will. It's just still . . . difficult, even after all these years. Not as difficult as it used to be, not nearly, but I still get nervous. Embarrassed. I know it's silly."

"I think you lost me. What's silly?"

"Oh, damn, this really *is* dumb," she said. And then she went on in a rush, the words tumbling over each other, and—there was no doubt about it now—as she continued she was unquestionably blushing. Her face got very pink. Still astonishingly beautiful, but very, very pink.

"It started when I was about twelve or thirteen, my breasts got so big everybody was always looking at them, at least the boys were, and then I got bigger, I mean older, and *they* got bigger, and by the time I was sixteen I'd gotten *so* self-conscious about them, and all the guys thought it —they—was—were—so great, they'd whistle and whoop and say the most horrible things about what they'd like to do with them, especially when the first rockets and space capsules went up—"

"Rockets and space—?"

"—so I finally just decided to *hide* them, and that's what I *did*, I *hid* them."

"You did? Hid? Where? *How*?"

"I covered them all up. With billowy baggy things like this. Like this cover-up." She plucked at the blue-and-beige-striped contraption I had eyed askance upon first glimpsing her.

"Ah," I said. "Umh-humh."

"When I wear things like this, nobody can tell if I'm

flat-chested or barrel-chested or what, at least nobody can know my breasts are so, well, healthy—I mean, nobody can see that they're so *big*, and stick out so *far*—"

"This will probably sound a little odd, Spree, but would you mind saying that again?"

"And finally, from the time I was sixteen, I could at least stop feeling so embarrassed all the time, and blushing all the time. I thought I was almost over it, and I *hate* to blush—I guess I am now, though."

"You sure are. It's a beauty."

"Well . . ." She let out a big, *big* sigh. Having been forewarned, I could see the nubby cloth of her cover-up rise, and rise, and start to fall, like a sheikh's tent in the desert preparing to sail away in a gale.

"I'd better stop chattering away like this. And putting it off. I know I've got to show you my butterfly sooner or later, Shell, so I might as well do it right now."

With a smooth fluid movement, she lifted the thick garment up and past her face, over her gold-blond hair, dropped the blue-and-beige-striped cloth on one of the hassocks. Above the blue skirt that had been visible below the bottom edge of the blanketlike cover-up, she wore a simple pale blue blouse with four large ivory-colored buttons down its front, the cloth of the blouse concealing, but concealing only in comparison with the cover-up's totality of concealment, and stretched tight over, what had to be the astonishing magnificences Spree had been complaining about.

Spree's left hand was resting in her lap. With her right hand she unbuttoned the first ivory button, then the second. I reminded myself that we were conducting a serious investigation here. We were merely uncovering a vital clue. Even so, I was not entirely disinterested. In fact, my jaws were starting to ache. There went the third button, and then the fourth. Fourth and last. My jaws felt as if they had become permanently locked. Which probably explained why my teeth were starting to ache.

Spree shrugged and slipped the blouse from her left shoulder, shrugged the other way and slipped it from her right shoulder as well, then dropped the pale blue blouse on the hassock and rested both hands in her lap, though some of her kept shrugging for a little while. Quite a bunch of her did.

I was astonished, and in a strange state of shock, not only because Spree's bra-covered breasts were of such magnificent and eye-stretching proportions but because my first only-half-aware assumption that my caller must be "large" or even "fat" had been produced *only* because of the false impression caused by that striped camouflage tent she'd been wearing. Spree's waist was actually slim, the hips full and well rounded but certainly not fat, and even in those first seconds of our meeting I had noted the trim-looking ankles and shapely calves, which—now—I could see were in splendidly appropriate proportion with the rest of her.

Spree sat still for a few seconds, both hands resting in her lap on the pale blue skirt, the now-exposed brassiere —which, though it is not of stupendous importance, was also pale blue and edged with a kind of frothy laciness —rising and falling with near-epic grandeur on her long slow breath.

It was one hell of a time for it, but at that moment I heard clearly—as clearly as if it were the devil himself hissing hotly into my ears—Claude Romanelle going on and *on* about how overly protective, even maniacal, he had become concerning his "innocent little girl," his "tiny sheltered child," and even a few additional imbecilities he obviously made up while hissing.

That was quite enough all by itself, but a second curious factor was that when I looked at Spree, whose great green eyes were now fixed on my face, I was able to look way down into those liquid and glowing depths, and there I saw that dumb innocent little tot in swim trunks, with her face scrunched up and lips pulled away from clenched teeth.

With all that on my mind, Spree took a deep breath and let out another big wonderful sigh, looked closely at me, and said, "Shell? Are you all right?"

"Nnnuh . . . nope."

It's possible she didn't understand my reply, because she

went right on, "Well . . . now that I'm finally *started*, it's not so bad."

"Nope."

"At least I'm not blushing anymore."

"Nope."

"You can understand why I was so embarrassed all the time, when I was little."

"Yep."

"I mean, when I was younger."

"Yep."

"There. That's a little bit of it."

"Wha-at?"

"Just a little piece of a wing. See?"

She had placed her left hand beneath the bra, and lifted the left half of everything up an inch or two, or three, without apparent strain, and was pointing with her right index finger. Then she rolled those big green eyes up to look at me, still down at the far end of the divan but leaning *way* over.

"Shell," she said curiously. "Are you—yawning?"

"Certainly not. I was just stretching my jaws around, trying to get some circulation back into my gums."

"Can you see it all right from over there?"

"Oh, sure, I hope to shout—ah . . . you mean the little . . . No, not very well, actually."

"Maybe you ought to scoot a little closer."

I came very close to overscooting, but bounced to a stop as Spree pointed again, saying, "See? There?"

"Ah, so. Yep."

On her smooth skin, over the rib cage and below the bottom edge of the bra, was a small light brown area, curving down only about a quarter of an inch and then sideways half an inch and up again, up and away to disappear beneath the wild blueness yonder.

"Yeah, boy, I can sure see it *now*," I said enthusiastically. "No doubt about it, there's some of the little, um, insect. That's what it's got to be."

"Insect?" Spree said, still holding her splendid breast aloft.

"Well . . ."

For a moment I couldn't remember what the damned little bugger was supposed to be. "I know it isn't a bird," I said. "And I know it isn't a, well, any kind of hairy animal—"

"Butterfly?"

"Butterfly! That's it! I knew that. It was right on the tip of my . . . erumm." I examined it closely.

"That's only a little bit of it, of course," Spree said.

"Oh, sure. I can see that. Merely a mere piece of a wing, exactly the way you described it. Rest of him must . . . Or her. Hard to tell about—let's say him. Must be, mmmm, hidden in there. Looks like he's trapped, struggling to free his little flapper, and then fl—"

"When you see all of it, then it really *does* look like a butterfly. There's a lot more, of course."

"Of course."

Spree—or at least Michelle, though I already felt quite confident about calling her Spree—had stretched her arms behind her back and was fiddling with one of those Chinese-puzzle doodads women use to hold the back ends of their brassieres together in an iron grip, sometimes forever. She fiddled for a while, and I started wondering if she had two doodads.

"Well, here goes."

That's what she said. But she was still fiddling. Ah, but no. She'd solved the Chinese puzzles some time ago. The bra, and everything, was still in place only because she was hugging her arms to her sides, a slight frown on that lovely face. "Let's see," she was saying, apparently to nobody in particular, certainly not to me, "how . . ." The suspense was excruciating. "How . . . shall I do this?"

"Any old way?" I suggested.

But then Spree cupped one pale-blue-bra-covered breast in her right hand, slipped her left hand under the other side of the bra, and let the cloth there fall to hang dangling, left hand cupping and covering that suddenly unveiled breast, or at least hiding some of it. Not a whole lot, really.

She repeated the process of lifting her now-bare breast an inch or two, or three, up in the air, but it was an entirely different process from the one she had processed only a minute or so before. It was movement in a different dimension entirely, a fragment of erotic fantasy, a—

"What did you say?" I said.

"It does look a lot like a butterfly, doesn't it, Shell? I just asked if you recognized it."

"Ah. So that's it. I got the funny feeling I was about to say 'No, I sure don't' and I couldn't even remember the question. But—sure. Yeah. That's it. Got to be. What else would it be?"

"You told me the truth, didn't you, Shell?" She sounded suspicious. "That you have a picture of it? To compare it with? A picture that Daddy gave you? I'd hate to think . . . Oh, I'd *hate* to think—"

"Don't think. I mean, don't panic. Hold it right there!" I stopped, knowing I was grinding my teeth again. "Funny—that's what private eyes are supposed to say to tough guys when they want them to *freeze*! Hold it right *there*, turkey! But I sure don't want *you* to free, Spreeze. Ah . . . Forget it. It's not important."

"But you *do* have—"

"Yep. Yep. A picture given me by your da—father. Photo of you by a pool, or plunge, taken when you were an ugly little—when you were a wee kid. Let me collect my thoughts here. Yes. In the photo, you can see the little butterfly on your, ahh, umm, chest. A butterfly, I mean, once you know what it *is*, of course. First time, I thought it was just a little fly speck—damn! Did it again, diddle I?"

"Diddle—what?"

I was shaking my head in wobbly frustration. Women simply do not screw me up so entirely. Not ever before, anyhow. I told myself that I would from now on force myself to remain cool, cool and aloof.

"Just—hangover from an old, old joke," I said. "See, this weird-looking old guy goes up to the meat counter and says, 'Gimme a pound of kiddlies.' Butcher says, 'What?' Guy says, 'Gimme a pound of kiddlies.' Butcher says, 'You mean *kidneys*, don't you?' Guy says, 'I *said* kiddlies, diddle I?' " I paused. "Great. How's that for aloof?"

"A *what*?"

"Loof," I grumbled. "Guy tells dumb jokes at a time like this, that's *cool*."

"Well, you can see it's not a tattoo," Spree said.

"A what-too?"

"Tat."

"You're starting to sound like me."

She smiled. Spree was still holding her bazooka, or bazoom, or whatever it was, up in the air, prominent nipple and part of large pink areola visible between index finger and middle finger. Or, I thought—as the sound of her father's voice flashed before my eyes, assuming such a phenomenon is possible—middle and trigger finger. Idly, I wondered if Spree's left hand, and arm and shoulder, maybe her whole left side, was getting tired.

"Well, why don't you take a good look at it," she said, "and compare it, or whatever you have to do to make sure. And then I can get dressed."

"Don't mind if I do."

I did. As best I could, I pushed Claude Romanelle out of my ears, and also little six-year-old Spree out of my mind, and intently scrutinized the biggest clue I'd come across in this case so far. Yes, it was reasonable to call the thing a butterfly, if one assumed it had been played with by a lazy cat and then hit with a large load of pesticide.

I said, "He's come a long way from his wee cocoon, hasn't the little bugger? Grew from just a little fly sp—ahhg . . . a little baby butterfly to this monster—ahhg . . . this lovely wingéd birdie. Next step should be, I guess, to compare him with his baby picture. If I can remember where I . . ."

"Yes," Spree said. "The photo of me that you got from Daddy."

"Could you call him Mr. Romanelle? Or Claude?"

"Why don't you go get that photograph, Shell? That will be the final *proof*, won't it? And . . . well, my arm is getting a little tired."

"Figures. O.K. If I can just remember where . . ."

In my bathroom, in the tiled wall of my combination tub and shower, there is a loose tile behind which I sometimes hide thin things. Thin, so they'll fit behind the tile. Like photographs, papers, and thousand-dollar bills if I had any. That's where I had put the old snap of young Michelle Romanelle. I recalled seeing it there when I'd stuck the photos of Kay Denver behind the tile.

Yeah, Kay. I shook my head. My life was either getting completely disorganized or wonderfully organized in a totally incomprehensible way.

Also, something else was bothering me. I had never looked at that photo of six-year-old Spree through a magnifying glass. So all I'd really observed on her youthful chest was a spot. A kind of blot with curlicues. Could have been a little piece of mud. Certainly not anything fascinating like a tired butterfly crawling up over the Andes. Only when I could magnify and study without prejudice that blot on little baby Spree could I ever be *sure* it was the same baby insect I'd just been getting inordinately attached to the adult of.

That didn't sound exactly right in my head, but I continued thinking furiously. I really wanted to be *sure*. That is, I very much wanted this lovely, this gorgeous, this astonishingly contoured and convoluted woman to *be* Spree. The *real* one, wee Michelle Esprit Romanelle twenty years later. But—and this was the truly crunching thought —what if the blot and the butterfly failed to match? What if the little blot was just a little blot? Why, that would mean Spree was an *impostor*. And I'd have to put her in *jail*. And I wouldn't *do* it.

"Jail?" Spree said. "What's this about jail?"

I looked at her wonderingly. "How did you do that? You read my thoughts, didn't you? Hoo, I hope you didn't read 'em *all*—"

"You were mumbling something. I thought you were talking to me."

"No. No, I wasn't. You mean I was actually mumbling? Mumbling aloud?"

"There's another way?"

"Spree, this is serious."

"Yes, you were. But very softly. It sounded like 'jail' and 'wooden doot.'"

"Hoo. That's what it was, then. Thank goodness. I'm

glad you *can't* read minds, Spree. That could ruin me. That could ruin *any*body."

"Were you going to get that picture, Shell? My arm—"

By then I was gone. I zipped into my bedroom, yanked open a drawer, found my big umpteen-power magnifying glass, then zipped into the bathroom. I stepped into the tub so fast I slipped, but I didn't go down, just clattered around a bit and clunked my head slightly on the shower nozzle.

I pried out the tile before my secret hiding place, grabbed the photo of Spree in its transparent plastic folder. I couldn't wait until I got back into the front room. So I slipped the protective envelope off and dropped it, then held the snapshot under my magnifying glass, focused, got the view sharp. And—

Chapter Seven

EUREKA! NO DOUBT about it! It was the same butterfly!

Well, almost. The upper wing was much larger now, due to the obvious fact that in the ensuing twenty years the part of Spree on which that upper wing rested had grown much more than the other parts of Spree. Other parts of almost anybody. But, taking that into consideration, the two were essentially identical. I really felt good about it. I felt so good I kicked the side of the tub a couple of times. Then I jumped out and zipped into the living room.

"Eureka!" I cried, thumping over the yellow-gold carpet to stop next to lovely, slim-enough but super-shapely, gorgeous, voluptuous, angelic, heart-stopping Michelle Esprit Romanelle, vital-evidence snapshot in my left hand, big thick magnifying glass in my right hand. "Eureka!"

"Eureka?" Spree echoed. "What does that mean?"

"It means I found your picture."

"What was all that clattering and banging?"

"Oh, that was me in the bathtub."

"In . . . the bathtub?" It appeared for a moment as if she might be going to pursue that angle a little further. But then she smiled. "Oh, I see. Isn't that what Archimedes said when he jumped out of the tub?"

"I found your picture?"

"No—Eureka."

"Beats the hell out of me," I said. "No matter. Spree, I've got the proof that you're Spree. Right here."

I lifted the picture and held it toward her.

But then I thought: Gah-*damn*! *Left* hand is the picture. In my natural excitement, I had raised my *right* hand. In it, of course, I was holding my umpteen-power magnifying glass. I was holding it by the round black handle, and the glass part itself—maybe eight inches in diameter—was almost touching Spree, actually about an inch from her—

"*Shell!*" she cried, looking down at it. "I don't believe this!"

"Well, hell, I don't believe it, either."

She started to say something else, those great green eyes getting even greater and wider, but I silenced her by saying, "Wrong hand. *This* is what I meant to show you—*this* is what we'll look at through my magnifying glass."

Her gaze fell on the faded old snapshot which I'd lifted up before her face, and she understood all, immediately. The expression of something approximating curdled alarm faded from her eyes and her face.

And then she sort of squealed happily.

"*That* picture!" she squealed, reaching for it. "Oh, Shell, I haven't seen that photograph in twenty years, but I still remember it. I was at the Riverview public swimming pool and . . ."

Some more came after that. Quite a lot, in fact. But I missed it all. Because Spree, in her delighted preoccupation with that old photo, had taken it into her hands in order to examine it closely. This meant that she forgot not only to hold in place the right half of her pale blue brassiere but also to continue clutching and at least partially concealing her left breast, the one with the butterfly sort of underneath it, since she was using both hands to hang on to that little picture.

She continued chattering happily for a while. Difficult to say just how long. But then, suddenly, Spree became aware of what had happened when she reached so enthusiastically for the snapshot, what had happened to her and therefore to me, and with a quick movement she crossed both arms over those big bare breasts, and looked up at me from eyes that appeared enormous.

"Oh-oh," she said, mouth as round as her eyes. "I guess . . . the damage is already done."

"I guess," I said.

"I just wasn't thinking. I'm sorry."

"I'm not."

We looked at each other in silence then. I took a step closer, sat next to her on the divan. I looked at that extraordinarily beautiful face of Spree's, drank it in with my eyes, letting them linger on arched brow and thick pale lashes, smooth cheek, soft sweet curve of lip. That face grew larger as I leaned toward her. Her green eyes were enormous. Slowly the lids drooped, her eyes half closed, and her lips parted as her head tilted to one side. Then her lips and tongue were melting against mine. Her arms went around my neck and pulled gently, with a slow pulsing pressure. I felt those magnificent bare breasts warm and yielding under my hands, and then against my lips.

The pressure of soft arms around my neck was gone. It took a moment for me to realize that Spree had her hands pressed against my chest and was pushing, pushing me away.

I looked at her and she said "No" silently, only the movement of her lips, without sound. Then, very softly, but audibly, "No, Shell," shaking her head.

I took a deep breath but still had trouble with my voice. "That didn't sound like yes," I said finally.

"It wasn't."

"I got a little carried away," I said. "Maybe more than a little. I hope you're not—"

"I'm not, Shell. At least, I'm not angry. This was more my fault than yours. All my fault, really. But, Shell, if we're going to . . . get that involved, shouldn't we know each other more than an hour?"

I tried to keep it light. "Sure. Why don't you"—I glanced at my watch—"wake me up in twenty minutes?"

She smiled. We both did. But it was over.

Not the memory, though, of her soft mouth on mine, my hands on her warm breasts, her arms around my neck; no, that wasn't over.

At 9:30 A.M. I dialed Claude Romanelle's number at his home in Paradise Valley.

Spree was going to accompany me to Arizona. She still wasn't certain she would sign those papers Worthington' was holding in his office, but she had agreed to go at least that far and find out what was involved. Also, she did want to meet her father again, after these many years.

Spree and I were in the same places on my chocolate-brown divan where we'd been when this thing started, me way to the left near the phone, Spree over on the right. Every time I looked at her she smiled, and every time she smiled I could feel something like hot iron filings spinning in my blood, or the faint gnawing of ancient hungers, or at least something strange and unique and very nice, and Spree smiled a lot.

"Hello?" That voice in my ear again. But it sounded hoarser, rougher.

"Mr. Romanelle?" I said.

"Right. Claude Romanelle."

"Shell Scott here."

"Mr. Scott! I've been waiting to hear—have you found my daughter? Have you found little Spree?"

"I've found *big* Spree, Mr. Romanelle. You'll really have to get accustomed to—"

"Where are you? Where is she? Is she all right?"

"Of course she's all right. At this very moment, your daughter and I are together in my—" I stopped. Mentioning my apartment might not be too wise. "In Hollywood," I continued. "Everything's fine, under control, and we'll be in Arizona some time tonight."

"That's wonderful. Good work, good work, Mr. Scott. Worthington did not exaggerate your abilities. What's your flight, when will you be arriving? I'll have someone meet you—"

"Slow down, will you? I don't even know yet when we'll be leaving. Couple of things to take care of here first. Besides, I don't *want* anybody meeting us. When we land in Phoenix, we'll take care of first things first, as instructed, then I'll bring Spree to your home. O.K.?"

"First things? What first things?"

That response rubbed me the wrong way. In fact, I

started to get a little prickly sensation on the hairs at the back of my neck. I said slowly, "You're supposed to be the guy who laid down the rules, Romanelle. *Is* this Claude Romanelle? You sound different—"

"Of course I'm me, you idiot! You mean Worthington. Yes, see him first, naturally. But hurry. I'm . . . anxious. Even a little nervous. Twenty years—"

He broke off with a kind of whooping cough or snort, followed by fainter sounds of more coughing, and what I guessed was Romanelle blowing his nose with a combination honking and flapping technique.

"Excuse me, Mr. Scott," he said after a few seconds, his voice even more hoarse and husky than before.

"Cold worse?" I asked, those earlier suspicions undiminished.

"No, of course not," he bellowed in a distorted gargle, "it is gone, gone forever. In order to eliminate my cough entirely, the passionate doctors who cured me of it removed fourteen pieces of mestatasized cancer from my gut and transplanted it into my lungs. In medical circles, this is referred to as 'curing the common cold' by injections of carcipneumonia." He honked and hacked for a few moments more, then said, "Therefore, I must be perfectly well by now. Does that answer your question, Mr. Scott?"

"Sure does," I said, grinning. *That* sounded more like the acerbic and overactive mouth of my client. Also typical of Romanelle, he wasn't through yet.

"In their desire to inoculate me against every malady known to medical science," he continued, "my dedicated docs instructed the cleaning lady to sweep up all the bugs from the floors of Intensive Care. Then they drowned the little bastards in sterile distilled water and squirted their corpses up my—"

Basically what he said was that they'd given him an enema with it. I shook my head. This guy was weird. But also bright, clearly a very intelligent man, even though —perhaps—still somewhat crooked. Right then something started to form in my brain, as if scattered thoughts were being pulled together into a critical mass, but the something dissolved, disappeared.

I said, "Glad you're feeling better. We'll see you tonight sometime."

"Excellent. I'll have a bonus waiting for you, Mr. Scott. Five thousand dollars. Sound all right?"

"Sounds fine."

I thanked him, and we hung up.

I looked at Spree, enjoyed her smile, then dialed the Dorchester Arms. I would be out of town for at least a day, maybe longer, and felt a certain obligation to let Kay know that, and tell her I'd be in touch upon my return.

I asked the Dorchester's desk clerk to connect me with Miss Kay Denver's suite, and Spree asked me, "Who are you calling now, Shell?"

"Could be another client. Not yet, but soon—I think. Just want to take care of this before we leave."

Then the desk clerk was saying, "Miss Denver has checked out, sir."

"She—what? Checked out? When?"

"One moment, please. At eight fifty-five A.M. About half an hour ago."

"Could you tell me . . . Never mind. Thanks."

I hung up, wondering what the hell, then said to Spree, "I'm going to call and make reservations for our flight. But before we drive to the airport, do you mind if we make a quick stop? I'd like to check something at the Dorchester."

"I don't mind. Kay Denver?"

I blinked. "Yes. Do you know her?"

She shook her head, yellow-gold hair shimmering like corn silk. "I heard you mention the name just now, that's all." Spree was silent for a few moments, head cocked to one side. Then she said, "This may be woman's intuition gone totally askew. But would she perhaps be a very beautiful young woman? Dark, black hair, good figure. Really quite eye-catching—especially dressed in a lovely black suit just right for evening, but not for early in the morning."

I was completely out of whatever was going on here. "Dressed . . . how? Well, that's pretty close," I said. "But how the hell—"

"I was simply describing a lovely woman who was in the lobby when I got here this morning."

"In the lobby? But that was five or ten minutes after she left . . ." Oh-oh, I thought. Blew it that time. I suppose I could have gone on and said rapidly, "after she *left* having dropped in for a *jiffy* on her way to work at the cookie factory" and so forth. But, no, that wouldn't have been true. Also, it wouldn't have worked. Also, my mind went blank.

Spree continued, just as if the San Andreas Fault had not opened up directly beneath me, "I noticed her only because she was looking at me so intently. That's when I saw how beautiful she was—and the strange way she was dressed for early morning."

"Strange. Morning. Uh-huh."

"I've had jealous women stare at me the way she did. But *that* couldn't have been why. She'd probably never seen me before. Certainly I'd never seen *her*. Isn't that odd, Shell?"

"Odd. Yes. Tell me, where was this strange lady when you came in and saw her? Hanging from a great sticky web on the ceiling?"

"No, of course not." Spree laughed lightly. It was very light. I could hardly hear it. "She was sitting on one of the couches in the lobby."

"Excuse me a minute. Be right back."

Downstairs I spoke to Eddy, the day man. "Earlier this morning, a lovely young blond woman came here to see me. On business. When she arrived, a little before eight-thirty, another young lady was sitting here in the lobby. Right?"

He nodded, pointing toward a corner couch. "She came downstairs," he said, "made a phone call, then sat there. After the pretty blonde came in, I don't know what the other one did. I had to fix Mrs. Murchison's TV right then."

"She made a phone call? You're sure?"

"Sure I'm sure. Used the pay phone there." He indicated one of the two pay phones in the lobby.

"Did you notice if it was a local call or long-distance?"

"I think she put a bunch of quarters in."

"And you don't know when she left?"

"Nope. Only that I took maybe fifteen minutes to fix the TV—Mrs. Murchison won't leave those little knobs alone, no matter how many times I tell the old bat—"

"Was the woman still in the lobby when you got back?"

"Nope. Gone by then."

"What time would she have been making that call?"

"I came on at eight. It was maybe ten, fifteen minutes after that. Call it a quarter after eight."

"O.K. Thanks, Eddy."

Spree had arrived at 8:20 A.M. So if Eddy's estimate was close, Kay had waited here in the lobby for several minutes. Why?

When I went back into my apartment, Spree was standing before the two fish tanks. I joined her as she said delightedly, "They're just beautiful, Shell. What's that one?"

So I told her, and we chatted about tropical fishes for a minute. Then I said, "It was Kay Denver in the lobby, all right. Waiting to get a look at you, I'd guess—but I've no idea why. So I'm going to make another call or two."

Ten minutes later I hung up the phone. Of my two contacts at the phone company, the first one hit the bull's-eye for me. A two-minute long-distance call had been made from the Spartan's lobby phone at 8:16 A.M. The call was to a business number, a company called Exposé, Inc. I got the address, and the phone number, but didn't place a call. Whatever Exposé was, I intended to check it out in person. The address was on North Hayden Road in Scottsdale, Arizona.

I did, however, make one last call to Arizona, to Bentley X. Worthington. I filled him in, told him my companion and I would see him this evening—no time specified—and asked him to wait in his office till we got there.

I had already packed a suitcase, so I went into the bedroom, strapped on my gun harness, pressed my Colt .38 Special into the clamshell holster, then put on an off-white sport coat. When I sat down at the end of my couch again, Spree joined me. I thought it was nice that she sat down only a foot away, instead of at the far end. I looked at her for a moment, still marveling. I always felt like smiling when I saw that face. Maybe because Spree smiled so often herself.

I said, "We'll drive to your apartment, then stop at the Dorchester. After that, to LAX and on to Phoenix. You'll see your father an hour or two after we get there."

"Did he ask about me when you were talking on the phone?"

"Yes, wanted to know how you were, said he was —anxious."

"But he didn't ask to talk to me, did he?"

"No."

"I think that's a little . . . odd."

"So do I."

"And that beautiful woman in the lobby. I wonder what it means."

"I don't know, Spree. Maybe nothing."

I was silent for a few seconds, thinking of all those women who had called Hazel, and had even shown up here at the Spartan, in response to that little ad of mine. After my years in this business, knowing some people would *kill* for an amount of money so small it was almost a debt, I should have expected that. That and a good deal more. Because we were talking about a *lot* of money, several million bucks.

"Maybe nothing, Spree," I repeated. "But . . . maybe it means the fun's over."

Spree drove her sleek Chevy Corvette back to her apartment building in Monterey Park, and I followed her in my Cadillac. She left her car in the underground lot, packed one large suitcase plus a smaller overnighter, then joined me for a late lunch at a nearby café. By 4 P.M. she was seated next to me in the Cad as we rolled up Wilshire Boulevard.

At the Dorchester Arms, I offered the bell captain twenty bucks, bargained shrewdly, settled for fifty. That came to twenty-five singles for each minute I spent inside Kay Denver's still-empty suite. One minute would have been enough. I checked the shower, bedroom, bed, all the rooms. There wasn't a single place in the suite where any of those nude photos of Kay could have been taken.

It cost me nothing to confirm that Miss Denver had checked out at 8:55 this morning, and that she had reserved her suite by telephone on Monday afternoon and registered, or checked *in*, three hours and twenty minutes later, at 7:15 that night. This was Wednesday. Kay had "lived at the Dorchester" for slightly less than thirty-eight hours.

Before we were halfway to L.A. International Airport, I knew the black Pontiac Grand Am was on our tail. I edged over into the Freeway's right-hand lane, slowed to forty-five miles an hour, rolled down the window on my side, then pulled out the Colt .38, held it in my lap.

"Shell," Spree said. "Is that a *gun*?"

"It's a gun. Don't let it bother you."

"How am I supposed to do that? I *hate* guns."

"I'm probably being overly cautious, Spree. But I figure that's better than not being cautious enough."

The Grand Am wouldn't pass me. It pulled over into the right-hand lane also, but stayed well behind my Cad. I said to Spree, "I may be driving a fraction over the speed limit for a mile or two. Depends."

"How . . . much is a fraction?"

"Whatever it takes."

I eased into the next off-ramp and slowed almost to a stop. The only other car within a quarter of a mile, in the far right lane with me, was the black Pontiac sedan. I left the decision up to them, knowing they couldn't actually park the damned thing behind my Cad. The driver elected not to pull in behind me, but instead roared by in the far left lane going about sixty miles an hour and accelerating. Two guys in the car, both in the front seat of the sedan. That was all I could tell from the brief glimpse of them I got.

I swung off the Freeway, then right back up the adjacent on-ramp as Spree asked, "What was that all about?"

"I thought a car might be tagging along behind us. Could be my imagination."

"Why would anybody be following us?"

"I wish I knew. It's probably nothing."

Our flight was a Western Air Lines 737 departing LAX at 6:08 P.M., arriving at Sky Harbor in Phoenix an hour and ten minutes later. But because California was still on daylight saving time and Arizona was not, it would be only 6:18 in Phoenix, or about sunset, when we landed.

By 5:30 I'd found a place in the lot for those parking a full day or longer, locked the Cad, and got our luggage from the trunk. Then I walked with Spree toward the Western Air Lines terminal.

And that's when I saw the black Grand Am again.

We were in the lined crosswalk, moving from the parking area toward the terminal, when I spotted that familiar Pontiac sedan about twenty yards away on the right, coming our way. Two men in it, driver and one guy next to him, both of them gawking around like teenage drama students on their first visit to the Big Apple, which is why I never did get a good look at them. Because the driver spotted us at the same time, or maybe half a second sooner—with my size, white hair and brows, I'm not easy to miss, and neither is Spree—and all I saw was the driver's mouth moving just before his big hand went up and covered most of his face.

We waited while they went past us as speedily as they could move in the traffic, guy on the right looking away from us toward the terminal, driver rubbing his face as though it itched severely.

Spree knew something had happened. She looked up at me, toward the car moving along at a pretty good clip by then, and back at my face. But she didn't say anything.

Spree hurried through the security checkpoint ahead of me—we were running a little late and there were only about ten minutes left before takeoff—and I had actually started to zip heedlessly after her when I stopped suddenly, thumped the palm of one hand against my forehead, backed up, stepped out of line, let a stout lady carrying a small suitcase go through ahead of me. Through the little passageway that guides you past the magnetometer. The magnetometer that detects any stray chunks of metal you may have secreted upon your person. Like, say, a Colt .38 Special with a two-inch barrel and six cartridges in its cylinder. Like that.

I caught Spree's eye, wiggled a hand at her, and when she joined me again, looking puzzled, I said, "I goofed. I'm still carrying my heat."

"Heat? What's your heat—?"

"Shh." I put my mouth close to her ear and whispered, "My thirty-eight, my gun. Since we've already checked our bags, I'll have to leave my little Colt—"

"Oh, good. I told you, I *hate* guns—"

"*Acck—shhh!*" My mouth was still near her ear. Not that the position of *my* mouth was helping me much. "Don't say anything, dear, just listen. No, just wait here —I'll explain later. Be right back."

Then I sprinted for the nearest bank of lockers. Later I could explain to Spree that if I had cleverly packed the Colt in my luggage, in a hard case, with the cartridges in another package separate from the gun, and declared it, and gotten permission from the airline, then I could have shipped the Colt to Arizona. And that I had not done any of those things.

I stuck two quarters in the slot, put my Colt Special in the locker along with a five-dollar bill in case I was gone more than a day or two, slammed the door and took my key, and sprinted back to Spree.

We made it aboard with at least a minute to spare. I fastened my seat belt and tried to relax, thinking that although I was still wearing my gun harness there was no Colt Special in it. But I didn't really feel naked without it. Not at all. I merely felt as if I'd come aboard without my pants.

By the time the "Fasten Seat Belt" and "No Smoking" signs came on during the approach to Sky Harbor, I had spoken to all four of the female flight attendants, and found one who'd worked a Monday afternoon flight from Phoenix to Los Angeles. The flight had left Sky Harbor at 1:35 P.M. and arrived at LAX at 3:45 L.A. time.

The timing struck me as pretty good. I knew Kay Denver had phoned the Dorchester Arms and reserved her suite at about 3:55 Monday afternoon, and I was thinking that she just might have been calling from the airport. But the young and bubbly flight attendant drew a blank when I described Kay.

As we fastened our seat belts, Spree gave me a blinding smile and asked sweetly if I was making dates with all four of the young ladies. So, naturally, I had to tell her what I'd been doing.

Spree said, "Why do you think she could have been on that flight? Just because of the timing?"

"Not entirely. There wasn't any point in burdening you with the info before now, but while she was in the Spartan's lobby—just before you arrived—she made a phone call to Scottsdale, Arizona. And I remembered . . ."

Once again, I had almost put my foot squarely into my mouth. What I had started to say was that learning Kay had called Scottsdale triggered memory of where I'd heard the name "Goldwater's," which was on the tag inside Kay's black suit jacket. It was a large and luxurious department store at the corner of Camelback and Scottsdale roads in the heart of downtown Scottsdale.

Having cleverly not finished that virtual confession to Spree, I could not think of how to get cleverly out of the situation, so my last words sort of hung in the air, faintly echoing, "remembered . . . embered . . . ered . . ."

"Remembered what?" Spree asked.

"I . . . don't remember. Ah—but, anyway, the flight attendant couldn't *remember* seeing her, although I described her—" I stopped. No way out of it. "I described her with the keen eye of a trained investigator. Because, of course, I knew—know—the lady, I have seen her, and therefore know what she looks like . . ."

"Of course. You described her to the stewardess?"

"Yes. But she couldn't remember—"

"How did you describe her?"

"How? Why, with the keen—"

"No, Shell, I mean—describe her for me."

I did, stating that she was about twenty-five or -six years old, possibly twenty-seven, tall and slim, with a good figure, dark hair done like a professional wig, very attractive, with dark eyes and very interesting lips, et cetera.

"Et cetera?"

"Well, I was just—compressing it."

Spree gazed straight ahead, chewing on the corner of her mouth for five or six seconds, then she said to me, "Call her over here for a minute, will you?"

"Call Millie?"

"Whoever the pretty little stewardess is."

"That's Mil—she told me her name was Millie."

Spree nodded, and as Millie happened to be walking by our row of seats at the time, I crooked a finger at her and she stopped.

Spree leaned toward her, smiled beauteously, explained that Mr. Scott—a thumb indicated me—was trying to find out if a Kay Denver had been on her Monday flight.

"Yes," Millie said, nodding. "He already described her, but I couldn't recall—"

"Let *me* describe her for you, all right?"

"Sure. Sometimes men get things a little twisted. Even *wrong.*"

"*Don't* they?"

They were smiling at each other like old chums having an ecstatic reunion. This continued while Spree said, "She's about five-nine, maybe five-ten, nice figure except she's quite hippy, hair is dyed black. She's probably over thirty, maybe thirty-one—"

"No, no—" I started, but only started. *Both* of them glared me into silence. "What'd I do?" I asked. But nobody was listening.

"Quite beautiful, but very hard-looking, you know?" Millie knew. While she nodded, Spree continued, "Almost the look of a high-priced, *very* high-priced call girl." She went on for another few seconds, describing somebody totally different from Kay Denver, or anybody else I had seen lately.

But for some reason Millie said, "Sure, that's her. Now I remember." She pointed to a seat several rows ahead of us. "There's where she was sitting. I talked to her a couple of times. And her name *was* Kay. But not Denver. It was Kay Dark."

"Thanks, dear."

They shared some secret joy for another second or two, then Millie went on down the aisle and Spree said to me, "Dark. Kay Dark. Isn't that interesting?"

"Yeah. Fascinating. How did you do that?"

"Do what?"

I shook my head. "Never mind. I don't want to know."

After we picked up our three pieces of luggage, Spree walked with me to the VOS RentaDrive—VOS being short for Valley of the Sun—with whom I'd arranged for a rental car at the same time I'd made flight reservations. They had only two Cadillacs available, and I'd arranged for the use of one of them.

But at the desk I canceled the request for a Cadillac and chose instead a year-old Chrysler Laser sedan. The young man behind the VOS counter looked about twenty years old, but he was efficient, with sharp eyes.

"Has anybody asked here if I reserved one of your cars?" I said. "The name's Scott. Shell Scott."

He shook his head. "Not me, sir."

"Anyone else? Besides you?"

"Well, maybe Jeannie." He glanced toward a girl ten feet away, stacking several white cards together. "Just a minute."

He spoke to her briefly, came back. "Yes, sir. A man, about forty, tall, mustached. She doesn't remember anything else about him. Just remembers that much because he said he was meeting you, and asked which car was yours."

"I suppose she told him it was the Cadillac?"

"Yes . . . Is anything wrong? I hope—"

"No problem." I smiled. "Just a chap who wants to surprise me. And thank you very much."

I found out where the Cadillac was parked. It was thirty yards from the Chrysler that Spree and I got into. I drove clear around the lot so that I could pass the Cadillac with it on my left, near my open window.

Not far from that Cad I'd originally arranged to rent were two guys who couldn't yet know I'd switched to another car. So they perhaps should not have been able to recognize my face—particularly since both of them were doing most of their eyeballing toward the Caddy. But they made me. Both of them. And there was no doubt about it. In fact, their reaction told me for sure they were the lads hoping to "meet" Shell Scott. And, very likely, meet Spree.

The taller of the two was about six-three or so, lean, wearing whipcord pants, a beige western-style jacket with brown trim, a dark brown shirt, and a bola tie around his neck; he was about forty, with dark hair and bushy dark brows, a bristly black mustache. The other man was smaller, maybe five-nine and thin, approximately my age, wearing dark gray slacks, a pearl-gray open-necked sport shirt, and a lightweight white cloth jacket. He was a good-looking black man with arched brows that probably gave him an almost constant expression of surprise. But what was most remarkable about the men was how stupendously surprised both of them looked when they lamped me, and how wide and staring all four of their eyes instantly became.

Five minutes later, when I was sure there was no tail on us—which I hadn't expected there would be, since those lobs had been afoot when I'd startled them—I said to Spree, "Time to bring you up to date, I think."

"I think so, too."

"I didn't want to alarm you unnecessarily before. But it's no longer unnecessary. There was definitely a tail on us—two guys following us in a car—when we were driving to LAX. And now two guys here, at *this* end, waiting to pick us up. So we know for sure that somebody—somebody with a long reach, a lot of pull, muscle—is very damned interested in you. You, Spree, not me; I'm an incidental character at this point."

"But why? Just because I'm here to see my father again, and sign those papers?"

"That's got to be part of it. Maybe all of it. We just don't know enough of the why yet. We'll know more when we see Worthington." I paused. "If we get there."

Maybe that was an extreme statement of our position. But I didn't want Spree thinking this was a lark, getting complacent, not being aware of what our position *might* be. I honestly, now, thought Spree might be in danger.

Leaving the airport, I had taken the 24th Street exit north to Van Buren and there turned left toward downtown Phoenix, heading for Central Avenue.

"Those two men here . . ." Spree said hesitantly. "They were just—watching, weren't they? Maybe they weren't even looking for us."

"Dammit, no more wishful thinking from now on, O.K.? The tall cowboy asked for me at the VOS desk, remember? But you're right, they were just watching—and that's what bothers me. I think they expected to take us right there at the Cadillac. If they were planning a tail they would already have been in their own car, ready to follow us. Damn, I wish I had my gun. I wish *you* had a gun."

"Don't say that! Shell, I told you, I hate guns and violence, men being brutal, and hitting each other, and . . . It's stupid, just stupid! Violence *never* solves anything—"

I interrupted her. And maybe my tone was sharper than it should have been. But her attitude was typical of the innocent. And it's usually the innocent who get taken. Or killed. I said, "Lady, I'll give you eight to five the next frog you kiss won't turn into a handsome prince with a marshmallow castle no matter how much you'd like to believe it—"

"You don't have to be sarc—"

"If some miserable thug is pointing a gun in my general direction and squeezing the trigger, and I get a chance to blow the creep away, I'll blow him right off the planet. If he misses and I'm lucky, that violence solves *my* problem. And if a meatball tries to cave in my head with a hammer, the first chance I get I'll kick the bastard in his balls and solve *another* problem—"

"Do you have to be vulgar? And sarc—"

"Yes, Spree, I do. Consider: two guys in California, two more—at least—here in Arizona. That spells out planning, organization, specific and probably criminal intent. How did they know we were flying from L.A. to Phoenix? How did they know when we'd arrive here?" I was silent for a moment. "Maybe I'm overreacting. But I don't think so. And I sure don't want anything happening to you."

After a short silence Spree said, "I . . . don't either. But thanks, Shell, for worrying about me. Don't ruin *all* my illusions, though."

"Look, all I'm trying to tell you is nobody *wants* to get hit on the head or ripped off or shot, but sometimes it happens. Even in fairy tales. Something had to turn that prince into a frog in the first place, right?"

I stopped at the intersection of Van Buren and Central, took a right. The fourteen-story Hall-Manchester Building was a mile away on Central Avenue, and that was where we were going. Not as the crow flies, however. Halfway up the block was a Mobil gas station. I spotted an outside payphone booth, pulled the Chrysler alongside it, and got out. It was nearly dark at 6:45 P.M. but there was an almost metallic glow in the desert air, and it was hot. The air temperature was probably ninety degrees Fahrenheit, but after the air-conditioned coolness inside the Laser it felt like centigrade. I dialed Worthington's private number. He answered immediately.

"It's Shell, Bentley. The lady and I just got here. But there was a tail on us in L.A., and a couple jokers waiting for us when we landed at Sky Harbor. We're a few blocks away on Central now, but we aren't about to stroll in through your front door inviting unpleasant attention if we can help it. Any suggestions?"

He said briskly, "Go to Second Street, two blocks east of Central. The Dillingham Building faces Second and backs up near the rear of the Hall-Manchester. The two buildings are separated by a small alley. Go out the back of the Dillingham, and into the rear of the Manchester."

"Sounds good. I know there are four elevators in your lobby, but—"

"Don't use those. When you come in the rear entrance, turn left. Freight elevator there. Only about ten feet, you can't miss it."

"O.K. Anything new come up since I talked to you on the phone this A.M.?"

"Not really. Our mutual client phoned me shortly after you did this morning."

"Romanelle? What did he want?"

"Merely reported that he had spoken with you, and that I should expect to see you and his daughter some time this evening. Asked me to call him when his instructions had been carried out." Bentley paused, then added, "He sounded terrible."

"Yeah, he's got several varieties of flu, apparently. O.K., we should see you in about ten minutes."

After parking in the Dillingham's lot, Spree and I walked through the building, across the alley, and into the Manchester. No problems. We found the freight elevator, stepped inside it, and I pushed the "10" button.

"I thought we were going up to the twelfth floor," Spree said.

"We are. We'll walk the last couple."

"Shell, you keep making me—nervous. Do you *really* think all this . . . cloak and dagger is necessary?"

"Maybe not. But isn't it fun?" She gave me a bleak look, made no comment.

We creaked up to ten, stepped out and found the stairs, walked up to eleven, then on to the closed door leading into the hallway on the twelfth floor; the passenger elevators would be halfway down it on our right. Twenty feet farther, but on the opposite side of the hallway to our left, was the main entrance to Worthington's suite.

I twisted the doorknob, began easing the heavy door open an eighth of an inch at a time, one eye near the slowly widening gap between door's edge and frame. Spree was standing close on my right, and I saw movement as she shook her head. I glanced at her and she silently mouthed the word "fun."

Little did she know. When the door was cracked half an inch, I could look all the way down the hall, see the closed door to Worthington's suite of offices. But I could also see, not quite halfway down the hall, or about ten feet short of the elevators, the forms of two men.

They weren't looking my way, but toward the elevators and Worthington's door beyond them, their backs toward me. I eased my viewing crack wider until I could see clearly enough to be sure. The shorter of the two men was black, and lounged against the wall. He wore gray trousers and a white cloth jacket. The taller man, wearing a beige western-style coat, stood with his legs wide apart, hands thrust into the hip pockets of whipcord pants.

No doubt about it, even though I hadn't seen their faces yet. They were the two men who'd been waiting near the VOS rental Cadillac at the airport.

I eased the door shut, started taking off my shoes.

Chapter Eight

SPREE SAID, "WHAT—" but I flipped my right hand up, pressed a finger over her mouth. Her eyes got wide when she realized I wasn't playing games.

Holding my finger against those soft lips, I whispered, "The two characters who were waiting for us at Sky Harbor are waiting again. Right down there." I took my finger from her lips and pointed.

There were a lot of questions in those big green eyes, but she didn't ask any of them. I said, "When I get this door open again, hold it, O.K.? So it doesn't clunk shut. What I *don't* need for the next minute or so is any noise—unless I make it."

She nodded, her eyes enormous.

I added, "If you happen to hear any gunshots, just get the hell out of here. And, whatever happens, I don't think you'd better watch." I thought about it. "Yeah. I don't want you watching *any* of this, O.K.?"

When I got my big shoes off, she automatically took them from me, held them under her right arm. I eased the door open again. The men were in the same positions as before, looking away from me. When I pulled the door wide enough for me to slip through, the tall cowboy moved and I froze. But he reached into his trousers pocket, took out a pack of cigarettes, got one lighted, left the smoke in his mouth, and stuck his hands into those hip pockets again.

The men were nearly fifty feet from me. It looked longer.

But I took a deep breath, slid through the doorway, made sure Spree was holding it open, then moved fast. I went forward in a gliding half run, thick socks on my feet sliding silently for an inch or two after each long step. The men were thirty feet away, then twenty. I saw the cowboy's right hand come out of his pocket, reach for the cigarette in his mouth. If either of them turned around, or glanced this way—

But they didn't. They were ten feet from me, and then I came to a stop right behind them, a foot and a half from the nearer of the two, the cowboy type, who was about an inch or more taller than I, at least six-three. I balled my right hand into a fist and hauled it back, ready to launch it if I had to. Then I yelled at the top of my lungs, as loud as I could yell, "FREEZE!"

They went straight up into the air. Both of them. The smaller guy, the black, had been leaning against the wall, and he just went right up against it for, I'd swear, at least two feet, before he started down.

"DON'T," I yelled again, with equal loudness, "DON'T turn around or I'll blow your goddamn heads off!"

The big guy had landed and gone into a crouch, right hand high at the left side of his chest, while the black man was still kind of tilted against the wall, with one arm extended straight out in front of him, fingers splayed. Why he'd stuck his arm out there I didn't know. Probably he didn't, either. Their heads were waggling, moving a quick half inch toward me, but then back the other way. They weren't *quite* willing to look at me.

I felt the clenched fingers of my right hand start to relax a little. "Lyle," I called—not so loud this time—"watch these apes while I shake them down. Spina, keep that smokepole on the fleepers. Just be goddamn sure you goddamn miss me if you have to bring 'em down."

After that, it was a ridiculously simple thing to reach around the tall guy, brushing his still-frozen and slightly trembling hand, and haul out his Smith & Wesson .38-caliber revolver from a shoulder clip, then pat the second man and kidnap his Colt .45 automatic from a belt holster.

The adrenaline was still flowing, almost squirting in me, from that fifty-foot glide over the polished floor, and I simply proceeded with what, it seemed to me, was the logical progression of events already begun. I hauled back my right hand again, but this time with the heavy Colt automatic gripped in it.

Without really thinking about it in any depth, I knew I couldn't simply shoot these guys, and I had nothing to tie them up with, and I couldn't at the moment turn them over to the law—something flickered nervously in my mind at that point, but then faded and died without becoming more than a flicker—so I simply swung my gun-weighted hand around in a tight arc, pivoting slightly on my sock-covered left foot to maintain my balance, and clunked the cowboy solidly on the back of his skull. He didn't make a sound. He didn't even grunt. Just went straight down like beef falling from a hook in the meat-market freezer.

And that was the precise moment when that flicker flickered again, more brightly this time, and I thought an almost paralyzing thought that somehow had not occurred to me before this too-late moment:

"*Oh*, boy," I said to myself, "could these guys possibly be *cops*?"

It didn't seem likely. But who the hell knows what is really *likely* at such a moment. I knew, however, that I had crossed my Rubicon, burned my bridges, and whether the cowboy was a crook or a cop, or even the mayor of Phoenix, it did not matter much at this juncture because whoever he was I had really clunked him a terrible one on the back of his head.

And there was one more clunk to go. Right or wrong, I couldn't stop now, not with the job I'd set out to do only half done. So I hauled back the heavy Colt again, starting to size up the black guy's head.

And at that moment two things occurred one after the other, each of which disturbed me plenty, but the louder one disturbed me considerably more than the initial softly gassy one. The first thing was that the cowboy's various muscles, relaxing completely, allowed what apparently was quite a bit of accumulated internal gases to escape from the nearest point of exit, with a kind of bubbling musicality that even at another time and place where it would have been more appropriate might have been considered unduly prodigious and even inconsiderate. What bothered me about the event was my knowledge that this sort of thing, and more, came to pass when a man *died*. But all I'd done was knock the guy unconscious. Hadn't I? It was a confusing moment. Made even more confusing by the really *loud* event.

I was just starting to swing the Colt at the side of the black guy's head, aiming at the tight-curled black hair just above his ear, when some woman—in only an instant I realized it almost had to be Spree, because there weren't any other women up here—let out a horrendous ear-piercing wail that sounded like, "NOooooOOoo—don't DO that!"

Whatever, it was of such curdling intensity that I almost missed the black egg's head entirely. But I got him somewhere in that general neighborhood at the very instant his impossibly-wide-open eyes fell on my chops, and with sufficient neatness that he, too, went away, if not into the hereafter at least into a more peaceful place. Presumably one where guys did not get slammed on the head by blunt gun-instruments.

With both men sprawled on the polished floor at my shoeless feet, I turned and scowled at Spree, who was standing not more than two yards away from me. Me and the two unconscious cops, I thought nervously. Then I groaned. What I'd meant to think nervously was *crooks*. It was ridiculous to assume they might be police officers. It was only because of that mental process whereby, if you get some dumb idea or picture—like a blue-striped giraffe —into your head, even after you shoo it sternly away the damn thing keeps sneaking back in unbidden and bugging you.

So there I was, thinking about cops and a blue-striped giraffe instead of doing whatever came next, which I hadn't figured out completely yet, not with the sound of Spree's stupendous shriek still rattling my eardrums.

She was an odd but nonetheless still pretty sight. Yes, pretty, even with her mouth open and her tongue sticking out of it, and both arms held rigidly at a forty-five-degree angle from her sides, fingers splayed much as had been the black guy's until I hit him.

Scowling at her, I began, "*Dammit*—"

"Don't hit me! Don't hit me!"

"Don't *hit*—will you shut—*I* won't hit you. That's dumb. Of *course* I won't hit you."

"Are you . . . sure?"

"Am I *sure*? What kind of ridicu—dammit, I told you not to look."

"I looked."

"I know. I heard you. I guess those are my shoes, huh?" They were on the floor near her feet. Must have fallen there when she stuck her arms out in that angular way. "Thanks."

I put my shoes on, then checked the two guns I'd taken from the men before they became unconscious. The .38 revolver was fully loaded, but only three bullets were in the automatic, two in the magazine and one in the chamber. When I slapped the clip back into the butt of the .45, I was feeling a trifle better about the men. Not many police officers carry half-loaded .45-caliber automatics. But I checked their wallets to be sure. No police ID, no badges. The tall cowboy was Jay Groder, forty-one years old, with an address in the Arcadia district between Phoenix and Scottsdale. The slim almost handsome black guy was Andrew H. Foster, thirty-two years old, five feet ten inches tall, weight 155, address in Tucson, Arizona.

I stuffed the wallets back into their coat pockets, thought about moving the men, then straightened up and glanced at Spree. She had been watching my every move, fascinated.

"We'd better get you into Worthington's office," I said, "even before I clean this mess up. Some of their pals might be—"

She ignored my comment, peering soberly up at my face. "That was a *terrible* thing you just did to those poor men," she said.

Ah, I thought. Not fascination after all. Revulsion, maybe. Or sudden disillusion. I had clunked two innocent bystanders on their heads.

"I thought of asking them to dance," I said. "But sapping them on their skulls seemed like more fun. I haven't time to explain. There could be others—"

"But, Shell, they hadn't *done* anything to you."

"That's *because* I sapped them on their heads," I said, with what struck me as irrefutable logic.

But then, finally, Spree seemed to hear an echo of what I'd been trying to tell her. "Others?" she said. "Other men? You mean that Lyle and Spina you yelled at?"

"No, no, those are *my* guys. *My* team." I pointed vaguely at the ceiling. "I made them up. I was referring to possible reinforcements for the two lobs here on the floor. So let's get inside."

I took Spree by the elbow, guided her to Worthington's office entrance. On the dark paneling of the door, in small gold block letters, were the names "Worthington, Kamen, Fisher, Wu, & Hugh."

Before going inside, I stuck the Colt automatic under my belt at the small of my back, and tried fitting the S&W .38 into my holster. I was still wearing the gun harness, but that clamshell holster had been specially molded to fit my own .38 Colt Special, and the S&W, though also equipped with a two-inch barrel, didn't slide in as smoothly or nest there as tightly as my own gun would have. If I jumped around a lot, the thing might even fall out. But, no matter: I felt much better than I had before.

I opened the door and Spree started to step inside, but I stopped her, poked my head in, and looked around before letting her come in with me. Before us was a wide, low receptionist's desk with a white leather chair behind it, empty. Soft lights illumed the dark mahogany-paneled walls, two oil paintings in heavy ornate frames, two overstuffed chairs covered in what looked like pink silk. Thick gray carpet was underfoot. On our left, light streamed past very large carved double doors that stood open. As I looked past them into the spacious office, Bentley X. Worthington appeared in the doorway, smiling.

"I see you made it," he said in the rich, caressing baritone voice that had swayed dozens of juries, and now either soothed or stimulated—depending on his intent—a lot of well-heeled clients.

"After only a couple of problems," I said. "Which, in about half a minute, I've got to finish taking care of." But then I stepped forward and gripped Bentley's outstretched hand. As Spree came up near us, I said to her, "This is your father's—and your—attorney, Bentley Worthington. I can't tell you for sure how good he is—it's rumored he's top of the hill—but I guarantee you can trust him. Bentley, this is Spree, or Michelle Esprit Romanelle."

He took her hand in both of his, gazing at that radiantly beautiful face. "My God, you are an exquisite creature," he said.

She said, "Thank you, Mr. Worthington," and smiled. And Bentley, I knew, was lost.

He cleared his throat. "Herrum, I will have to charge you an exorbitant fee, if only to prove I have not lost my wits because of you, Miss Romanelle."

"It's Miss Wallace now. Formerly Romanelle."

He looked at me and started to speak, but I said, "This can't wait, Bentley. We met two guys outside, who, it may be presumed, were not lurking in the hallway to consult you about torts. They are temporarily indisposed. Have you got a closet, small room of some kind, where I can lock them up while we conclude the business here?"

"Yes. Storeroom. Several of them. But first, Sheldon, the young lady states that she is Miss Wallace. Formerly Miss Romanelle. Is there any doubt *whatever* that this is the fact? Before proceeding, I must have your unequivocal assurance—"

"Don't worry about it. You've got it. She's Claude Romanelle's daughter."

He nodded, the soft light rippling gently over deep waves in his thick white hair. "If you are satisfied, Sheldon, I will accept that. Come into my office, please."

I said to Spree, "You go ahead. I'll be with you in a minute."

As Bentley and Spree walked inside his office, I went

back to the entrance and into the hallway. The first thing I noticed was the lighted number above the door of the elevator, the "4" changing to a "3." And the next thing was the complete emptiness of the hallway. A few seconds later, bending over, I could see the parallel waving lines on the polished floor, extending from where I'd left the two unconscious men to the elevator itself. Heel marks, undoubtedly, as one of them pulled the limp form of the other. Had to be the black guy, Andrew Foster, hauling the cowboy. I hadn't got him as solidly as I meant to, not with Spree making that noise like an earthquake in a tin factory.

When I walked into Bentley's office again, Spree was seated in one of two overstuffed chairs placed side by side before Worthington's enormous black-walnut desk, and he was just turning from a brushed-steel filing cabinet, a two-inch-thick red cardboard box in his hand. The box was about ten inches by fourteen inches, large enough to hold a lot of legal-size papers.

He placed the box on his desk, opened it, and took out a long official-looking document that appeared to consist of several sheets of white bond paper with neat lines of typing under the printed heading on the top sheet.

As I sank into the chair next to Spree, I mentioned that the guys I'd left in the hallway were no longer in the hallway, but had split for parts unknown. Bentley nodded silently, then handed the document to Spree, saying, "This is the document I prepared in accordance with Mr. Romanelle's wishes. I would like for you to read it, at least all of the first two pages, after which I will explain my view of the document's significance. You may then wish to read it again, before you sign it. The other pages are simply a listing of Mr. Romanelle's assets, which he desires be transferred into joint ownership with you, his daughter. Those assets, as you will see, are substantial."

Spree read the first two pages and glanced through the others, shaking her head slightly. Then she extended the document toward me, looking at Bentley.

He said, "Yes, I think Sheldon should read the document, since his work is not yet finished."

So I read the thing. It was headed "Claude Romanelle

Inter Vivos Trust" and couched in the usual legal terminology, much of which seems deliberately designed to depress meaning and elevate obfuscation; still, I thought I understood half of most of it. Following a paragraph referring to immediate joint ownership by both signatories of the "list of assets attached as Exhibit A and by reference incorporated herein," and arthritic language that appeared to embrace and include future additions to or subtractions from the totality of those assets due to inflation or deflation or increased or decreased market value or natural catastrophes and/or acts of God, presumably including pestilence and famine and termites, a separate paragraph provided among the whereases and hereinbefores that upon Claude Romanelle's death for whatever reason his daughter would become the sole beneficiary of the trust, whereas should Romanelle be predeceased by "the other signatory"—which I assumed referred to Spree—the trust assets would thereupon be distributed outright to a charitable entity called the Omarac Foundation—which I'd never heard of—after which the trust would terminate.

Despite the legalese and some paragraphs totally impenetrable by any merely human mind, the basic purpose of the document appeared, at least as I interpreted it, to be reasonably transparent: Upon signing the final page, where Claude M. Romanelle's graceful-looking signature was already affixed, Spree would—and at the same time would not—become richer by half the amount of Claude Romanelle's net worth, which according to the summation on the next to last page of the document had amounted, on the day the papers were prepared, to a fraction over twenty-three million dollars.

I mentioned my interpretation to Worthington and he replied, "Quite good, Sheldon. That is almost correct. But it is the 'almosts' that create havoc should imprecise agreements be subjected to the nit-picking analysis of attorneys. You may be sure that this document will survive any such analysis unchanged and unchallenged. It is true that Miss Rom—Miss Wallace both will and also in a sense will not become richer by many millions of dollars upon signing. The entirety of the assets listed therein"—he nodded his white-haired head toward the document, which was now back in Spree's hands—"will become part of the trust, of which Miss Wallace and her father, Mr. Romanelle, will be the joint beneficiaries the instant she affixes her signature at the place provided. However, from that moment forward, neither of the signatories may dispose of any of the listed assets without (a) the approval of the other, which approval must (b) be in the form of a written addendum to the trust agreement, signed by both parties in the presence of the designated attorney for both, Bentley X. Worthington, and none other."

I thought about that. "Unless I went astray somewhere," I said, "Miss Wallace can't dispose of any of the assets —can't really consider any of it her own—unless her father, Claude Romanelle, agrees to her so doing, and not only agrees but signs a statement to that effect in your presence."

"That is correct. However, that stricture inhibits not only Miss Wallace, the daughter, but also the father, Mr. Romanelle. Not even he can dispose of the listed assets without her approval—approval, to repeat, in my presence."

"What I'm getting at," I said, "is that it's almost like giving away a box of candy but keeping the sweets. Or not *really* giving anything at all."

"On the contrary, Sheldon. And Miss Wallace." He looked directly at Spree as he continued. "The moment you sign this document, you will, in effect, be invested with absolute *negative* control of the described assets individually and in their totality. You cannot, without permission and agreement of the other signatory, dispose of or consume any of those assets yourself, but you can absolutely prevent their disposition or consumption by the other signatory, should you so desire, merely by withholding your agreement. The same, of course, is true of Mr. Romanelle—once your signature has been affixed and witnessed by me."

Spree said, "I believe I can understand the reason for all this, Mr. Worthington. After all, my father doesn't really know who—or what—I am. Isn't that right?"

"Precisely," Bentley said, smiling upon her. "You have cut to the heart of the matter. The provisions we are discussing here are not unprecedented, or even unusual. If I may speculate . . . ?"

Spree didn't mind if he speculated. I didn't, either.

"Mr. Romanelle," Worthington went on, "is in less than excellent health. Further, he was recently shot and injured by unknown assailants." He paused and asked Spree, "I assume you have been informed of those facts?"

"Yes. Shell told me all he knows about those things before we left Los Angeles. But it wasn't very much. I'd certainly appreciate it, if you know any more—"

He interrupted gently. "Sheldon, by now, probably knows a good deal more about the situation than I do. But let me continue. Whatever his personal character and personality require that he do, it is my assumption that Mr. Romanelle truly desires that his daughter benefit from the estate he has amassed during his lifetime. She might inherit it—which essentially will be the case should Mr. Romanelle, for whatever reason, become deceased, after the document is signed. Or she might share some of those benefits during the life of the other trustee. However, we have at issue here a considerable estate, many millions of dollars, and the most elementary prudence suggests that it not be given away to, or divided with, one who is, essentially, a stranger. Not, that is, without certain reasonable and essential safeguards."

Spree was nodding. "That's what I was suggesting a minute ago. I really think it would be stupid of my father to sign over, or hand over, even a dime to me when he hasn't seen me in twenty years. He'd be a fool to do anything like that before we've even met, after all these years. And I don't believe he is a fool."

"Precisely," Worthington said again, again beaming upon Spree. "He has, therefore, caused me to include in the document's language those provisions mentioned. After all, what if his daughter should turn out to be some kind of monster, a modern Ma Barker or Typhoid Mary . . ."

"Or Medusa?" I offered.

"Or Med—" Worthington stopped, looked curiously at me. "Medusa?"

"Or Xanthippe."

"Oh." Bentley saw the light. What if the daughter turned out to be, in the father's eyes, worse than the mother?

"Well, obviously you are none of those things," Worthington said. "I don't know what Mr. Romanelle is thinking. He might even have wondered: What if she is gruesomely *ugly*?" He beamed. "Which, I say without fear of contradiction, it is evident that you are not."

Spree gave him a smile. It was only a little smile, but there wasn't a trace of ugly in it.

"So, then," Worthington went on, "Mr. Romanelle has thus wisely, with my considerable assistance, protected himself against the possibility that he might discover his daughter not . . . shall we say worthy? . . . of his generosity. Such an unworthy offspring might seize all the assets available to her and flee with them, laughing all the way to Rodeo Drive." He glanced at me, almost reluctantly removing his eyes from Spree's face. "In Beverly Hills."

"I know where it is, Bentley," I said. "Don't get so carried away—"

"But I have not the least doubt," he finished, again gazing at Spree, "that once you and Mr. Romanelle have met, he will surely, surely, find all of his quite natural fears and misgivings laid to rest. How could it be otherwise? My goodness, Miss Wallace, you *are* an exquisite—"

"Bentley." I squeezed the word in, then continued, "May we assume it is your expectation that, once Romanelle becomes convinced his daughter is not a female Attila the Hun, he will probably limit or lessen some of the strictures presently set in cement in your document?"

"Ah . . . yes. I do assume it. And Miss Wallace will become a wealthy woman on the instant."

"We haven't discussed this," Spree said. "I mentioned it to Shell. But . . . I'm not sure I want the money, his assets. I'm just not . . . sure."

"Eh?"

Bentley X. Worthington's healthily pink and handsome face appeared to become less pink on the instant. Then it assumed the forceful, wise, somewhat rigid expression of the attorney who senses that his case, and wonderfully large fee, may be on the edge of the toilet.

He leaned toward Spree, saying earnestly, "That is a perfectly understandable reaction at this point, my dear. Understandable, and wise. The sensible procedure would be for you to sign the trust document now, and *then* determine, in your own good time, the course you wish to pursue once you have seen, and talked with, your father. Your father, who, though you have not seen him in long and long, may have grown, changed—as we all change in our path through this hard life—become a different person, a new man, a true father to the child he aban—has not seen for two decades."

"I agree with part of that," Spree said. "It's true, isn't it, that—after I sign—I can, if I wish, change my mind? In a sense, erase my signature?"

"Absolutely. If you so wish. Merely by resigning as trustee and signing a statement to that effect in the presence of Mr. Romanelle and me."

"That's what I thought, from reading the document," she said. Spree was silent for almost a minute, chewing the corner of her lip, as I'd seen her do before in my apartment. Then she said, "I'll sign. First, though, sum up the nature of those assets for me, will you? I glanced through those pages rather quickly."

"Certainly. There are two bank accounts; in round numbers, one amounts to $100,000, the other $65,000. Mr. Romanelle's residence in Paradise Valley, owned free and clear, is appraised at $560,000. One free-and-clear two-bedroom condominium in Villa Monterey, Scottsdale, currently rented year-round at $800 a month, valued at $90,000. A Mercedes-Benz automobile valued at $60,000. Furnishings, jewelry, gold coins, three bags of junk silver, valued currently at approximately $250,000. Plus 1,700,000 shares of Golden Phoenix Mines, Incorporated, listed with NASDAQ and quoted today at fourteen bid, fifteen and a half asked. Present value just under $24,000,000."

"If anyone could sell that many shares without knocking

the price down under a dollar," Spree said. And her next question was, "What's the float? Do you know, Mr. Worthington?"

"Umm, one moment." He pawed through papers in the red box, pulled one out. "Fifteen million shares authorized," he said. "Twelve million issued, five million of that closely held by principals."

"Three million in unissued stock, then, and five million that's probably under SEC Rule 144, control securities," Spree said quietly. "So, for practical purposes, only a seven-million float, maybe less. I wonder—do you have the names of the principals, with the amounts of their positions? And if they've held their stock for three years or more?"

"Not at the moment. But I'm sure I can get that information for you if you wish."

"I'd appreciate it if you would, Mr. Worthington. Do you know much about the company? Golden Phoenix Mines?"

"Only the public pronouncements and releases, prospectus, latest annual report. However, I'll look further into that, you may be sure."

"Thank you. It seems advisable. Of the total assets, that stock accounts for . . . let's see. Total twenty-four nine-two-five. And twenty-three eight for the shares max. So the shares account for ninety-five-plus, just under ninety-six percent of the entire estate."

"Yes," Bentley said, looking slightly dazed, but no more dazed than I. "Yes. Fine."

In another five minutes, the last questions had been answered. Spree signed the document, then Bentley wrote in the date and his own signature, spelling the entire name almost legibly this time.

When Spree and I stood up, ready to go, Bentley said to me, "I mentioned speaking with Mr. Romanelle by phone this morning. He asked me to call him when this was done."

He was reaching for the phone when I said, "Don't call him yet, Bentley. O.K.?"

"Why not?"

"I told you some of what's happened in the last few hours. Remember, those two guys I clobbered in the hallway were lethally armed—and they were gone by the time I got back out there. Look, call Romanelle in, say, an hour. That's after the signing, which is when you said you'd phone him."

"Well . . . All right. An hour from now, then."

"Good. Incidentally, when we leave here we're going to see Romanelle for the first time. It might help if you'd describe the man again. In more detail than you did on the phone."

He did so, quickly and concisely, after which I said, "Thanks, Bentley. We're off. I'll let you know how it goes."

He sighed. "Let me know in the morning, Sheldon. I'm taking my wife to the club tonight."

Chapter Nine

RUMBLING DOWN IN the freight elevator, I looked at Spree, trying, for a change, to see past the radiant loveliness of that special face. She was obviously intelligent enough; but maybe there was something more, something else I'd missed, or simply hadn't looked for.

It's a strange blindness, but even when we know better, we men too often assume that if a woman is extraordinarily beautiful, she must not be particularly brainy—when, in reality, the reverse is almost always true. Whatever it is that builds this house the spirit lives in, that forms the bone and blood and nerve and flesh, forms the living brain as well. It would be a poor carpenter who built splendid sturdy rooms and a roof that leaked, a poor mason who built a wall of the most expensive brick with the cheapest mortar. No, we're all of a piece, consistent, homogenized in a way; whatever the integrity and quality of a person is, it doesn't change between an arm and a leg or a thighbone and a nose, it's stamped indelibly on every piece and part from head to toe and on all the goodies in between. Even if, sometimes, we see a woman or man possessed of obvious cerebral splendor combined with what appears to be pronounced homeliness of feature or even *ugliness*. And then we get back to the question of what beauty really is. Or Beauty. Which was much too deep for me.

So as the elevator descended, I merely enjoyed the caress of Spree's soft lips, and brow, and golden hair against my eyes, and said, "Where'd you pick up that stuff about float—and the ninety-six percent of assets bit, you do that in your pretty head?"

"I worked in a small brokerage firm for six months. Didn't like it, but I learned a little about equities, companies going public, how the market capitalizes earnings. The percentages thing, it's just a kind of mental trick—Mom told me Dad could do the same thing. But let's talk about that, if we do, when we're a mile or two from here. You've got me convinced, Shell. Or those two men convinced me. And . . . I'm glad you've been so cloak-and-daggerish, so foolishly careful."

"Anytime," I said. "You should see me when I'm reckless."

She gave me a small smile. "I thought I had." Then that little frown line appeared between her brows. "Do you think those men, or others, may still be around? Looking for us?"

"Sure. But they weren't planted at the rear entrance when we arrived, and probably won't be when we leave. Even if they are, we'll be O.K., Spree." I grinned at her. "I've got *two* ugly guns now."

Another small, very small, smile from her. Then the elevator stopped at the ground floor. I went out, .38 S&W in my hand, its hammer cocked. But there was no trouble. In another minute we'd walked out the Manchester's rear entrance, through the Dillingham, and were back in my rented Chrysler Laser. Ten minutes after that we were on Camelback Road, rolling north toward Scottsdale.

Spree had been telling me about her current job —writing programs for a small computer-software company in L.A. called OmegaWare, and mystifying me hugely in the process—when she abruptly changed the subject. I'd swung over to Lincoln Drive and we were at the edge of Paradise Valley when she said, "Shell, you wouldn't *believe* how nervous I am."

"I might. It's an odd situation."

"I hope I . . . like him. Now, that's odd enough, isn't it? I hope I like my own father? But it's as if I've never met him, not really."

"Well, neither have I, Spree. Just talked to him on the

phone those two times. Incidentally, when I spoke to him this morning he sounded like a guy with multiple pneumonias, so don't be overly disturbed if he's less than a hundred percent."

"I understand." She leaned forward, hands clasped. "How much longer?"

"Nearly there."

Romanelle lived on Desert Fairways Drive, so called because it bordered several fairways of the Paradise Valley Country Club golf course. It was a prestigious area where many of the well-to-do and even very rich rich lived. We were a block from the traffic signal at Tatum Road, and as I pulled into the left-hand lane, the light ahead turned green.

"Just across Tatum we take a left, then slide into the next little street, which is Desert Fairways. So call it another two or three minutes."

"That soon?" she said softly.

I checked my watch as we swung off Lincoln at the entrance to the Camelback Inn, then took the next left into Desert Fairways Drive. It was straight-up 9 P.M. Another block or two and I could see the house on our left. It was a one-story rock and redwood place, low and wide, set back behind what they refer to as "desert landscaping" out here, which to a Californian looks exactly like a lot of dirt and cactus. The street number was in red and white mosaic tiles on the face of one of two stone pillars flanking a black asphalt driveway that curved up and around before the house. A light was on above the entrance door, as though to welcome guests. But it was enclosed in a wrought-iron and red stained-glass box and the glow from the bulb inside spilled splashes of reddish pink across a flagstone deck before the entrance, like shallow pools of anemic blood.

I drove slowly by, checking the place out. Just past it was a vacant lot and I turned around there, letting the Chrysler's headlights illuminate the lot, briefly revealing a stretch of green fairway beyond its farther edge and then sweeping over the side of Romanelle's house. I didn't see anything disturbing, so I swung into the asphalt driveway, parked close to the flagstone deck opposite the entrance doors. I left the engine running, the Chrysler facing toward Lincoln Drive. Then I turned to look at Spree.

"When I get out," I said, "I'll slam this door and both doors will be locked, windows rolled up. You get behind the wheel. I'm going to look around a little. If anything . . . unusual happens, get the hell out of here fast and find some cops."

"Couldn't we get some cops first?" she asked.

"No way. They'd think we were freakos. Nobody's *done* anything to us yet. No menace, no threats even. Hell, the shoe's on the other foot. *I* recently assaulted two upstanding citizens and turned them into downfalling citizens, who may even have reported me for assault and battery by now. I'm not joking. It's happened to me before—and that was in Los Angeles, where most of the cops *like* me."

"I wish there was another way."

"I can't think of any offhand."

"But you'll be so . . . exposed. It scares me."

How about that? I thought. I had assumed Spree was tense and nervous merely because she was about to meet her father. I had underestimated the lady. She'd been up with me all the way, maybe ahead of me.

"You think our lads might be out there among the cacti, too, don't you, Spree?"

"Of course. You had damned well better be careful."

"Count on it."

"One other thing—and don't argue, Shell. If anything unusual does happen, you get back to this car as fast as you can. I promise to open the door for you." She smiled. "No one else."

I started to argue, then said, "Play it by ear," and got out of the car, pressed the lock button down, slammed the door. The air outside was hot, really *hot*. I pulled the Smith & Wesson revolver from its holster, thumbed back the hammer, held the gun down low against my thigh. I could smell the scent of orange blossoms. Odd, I thought, to smell orange blossoms in October. Maybe false bloom or mock orange; but the scent was thin and sweet in the desert air.

I walked halfway down that curving drive, trying to see

into the darkness, feeling most of my muscles trying to form granny knots. But nothing happened. There was a garage down there, its door open, glint of metal and chrome inside. That was all. I turned around, walked in the other direction and past the idling Chrysler, on down nearly to the rock and cement pillar near Desert Fairways Drive. Nothing. Except that the soles of my shoes were getting warm. The asphalt, baked all day by the Arizona sun, was like a heating pad under my feet.

When I got back to the car and crooked a finger at Spree, she turned off the engine, pulled the keys from the ignition, opened the door on her side. I held her close with my left arm around her shoulders, kept the revolver in my right hand as we walked over the flagstone deck to the reddish entrance door.

I poked the button, looked around as a deep velvety *clonngg* boomed somewhere inside the house. When I pulled my head back toward the door, it opened suddenly and a short heavyset man about fifty years old, wearing glasses that reflected the reddish light, poked his big bald head toward us, saying rapidly, "Mr. Scott? Miss Wallace? Is this really little—really Spree? We thought you were going to phone—"

He went on to say something that I think was, "Come in, do come in, Claude is in the Arizona Room," but I wasn't listening closely. This fat pappy would never know how close he'd come to getting shot.

I lowered the revolver, eased its hammer down, slipped the gun into my coat pocket. "Who the hell are you?" I said.

"What?" He looked at me, blinking owlishly through the horn-rimmed glasses. I noticed a faint thin scar low on his left cheek. "Oh, of course, you wouldn't know. I'm Dr. Simpson. Robert Simpson. I'm attending Claude—Mr. Romanelle."

"I didn't know doctors still made house calls."

Yeah, he was a real doctor. That bugged him. Stiffly, with his heavy chin thrust forward half an inch, he said, "Claude is not merely a *patient*. He is a friend."

He turned, and we followed him across a big living room warmed by half a dozen lamps, all glowing. I got an impression of heavy couches and easy chairs, colorful pillows, heavy Oriental-looking table lamps, as we went on through a second room and then through an open archway into what the doctor had referred to as the Arizona Room, which in California we might call a patio room, or even a den. This one, as are most in Arizona, was at the very rear of the house, adjacent to the backyard or patio beyond which would be the Paradise Valley Golf Club's eleventh fairway.

As we stepped into the room several separate impressions brushed my mind. First, Claude Romanelle, not on his feet to greet us, not dancing over the off-white carpet to embrace "little Spree" or even shake my hand, but seated at the near end of a long low couch on our right, facing the rear of the house and what my first glimpse through glass patio doors suggested was a heavily landscaped yard with palms and lush greenery surrounding an oval swimming pool, underwater lights turning the water a softly rippling blue.

Romanelle was wearing an expensive-looking shiny black robe edged with yellow piping, his head was turned toward us, and as the three of us entered he pushed against the divan's arm with his left hand and started rising, apparently with considerable effort, to his feet. This was the first time I'd seen my client in the flesh, but I recognized, from Worthington's description, the high wide forehead and face narrowing down to the pointed chin. Also he was the right age, about fifty-five to sixty. Still, for all I knew, this guy could be middle-aged Joe Schmuck with a high forehead and pointed chin, so I looked him over pretty good. He was quite pale, almost shrunken, and until he managed to stand erect I thought his height was less than Romanelle's even six feet. But once he was standing I could see he was only two or three inches shorter than I.

He glanced at me, nodded, then fixed his eyes intently on Spree and said in a hoarse, soft voice, "Is it really you? My God, are you my Spree?"

It was a very curious moment. The reunion of strangers. Nobody seemed to know quite what to do. Romanelle stood there, one hand pressed against his middle, the other arm raised toward Spree, with the palm up, as if he were offering her a gift. I had moved well into the Arizona Room, just getting out of the way. Dr. Simpson stood inside the open archway where we'd entered. Spree was four or five feet farther into the room, standing immobile, facing Romanelle.

After what seemed a long time, she said quietly, "Yes, Daddy. I'm Michelle. I'm Spree."

Then she stepped toward him. Romanelle raised both hands, clasped her hands in his own, and said something too soft for me to hear. Then, hesitantly, he put one arm around her shoulders.

I glanced out at the green-filled patio and blue-water pool. Reflected in the big sliding-glass Arcadia doors I could see Spree and Romanelle close together, the doctor still in the doorway to the room. And I knew something was out of joint.

I hadn't made up my mind yet just what was digging at me, but I knew something here was very queer indeed. It wasn't the fact that I couldn't be absolutely *sure* the man was Romanelle. Or the presence of the doctor, Simpson —or a man who'd said he was Dr. Simpson. My unease was based on something else. Maybe several something elses.

I still had my right hand in my coat pocket, palm pressed against the revolver's butt. I tightened my fingers around the gun's grip, index finger resting on the smooth curved trigger. Everything slowed down, almost stopped. Except my thoughts. Thoughts, one after another:

In that second conversation with Romanelle, on the phone this morning. He hadn't asked to speak with Spree, his daughter, not seen or spoken to for twenty years. Odd. Nothing to build a felony case on. Just—odd.

But also in that conversation he'd never called me simply "Scott," but always "Mr. Scott." Which was how Romanelle, in our initial conversation, had referred to me *only* when expressing real or feigned umbrage, irritation, threat. Throughout that second call it had been "Mr. Scott" each and every time. Odd.

I thought I smelled the faint perfume of orange blossoms again. Maybe it was my imagination. But that real or imagined scent made me remember the muscle-knotting walk along the asphalt drive out front, down the drive and back. And—nothing. That's what was bugging me. That nothing. Considering what had preceded this moment, somebody *should* have been out there, waiting for us, waiting in the darkness outside. And nobody had been waiting. At least not *outside*. But, maybe . . .

A small slow ripple of movement was reflected in the glass door, something glittering like a snake's eye, there where Romanelle stood. Romanelle and Spree. I was already moving. Not thinking about it, just doing it, turning and lifting the gun, feeling the hammer catch on cloth, ripping it free.

The Smith & Wesson was still pointed at the floor but my head was twisted around far enough for me to see the man and Spree. He held her tightly with his left arm, right arm extended toward me. That snake's-eye glitter at his fingers was light reflected from a heavy gun he held, a gun that blasted enormously. I could see flame spit from the round muzzle, feel the cracking sound of the gunshot slap my eardrums.

Spree was just starting to struggle, trying to break free from that encircling arm. Probably that's why he missed me. I heard the slug snap past my head, heard the long-drawn-out shattering and crisply tinkling sound of glass in a window behind me breaking and starting to fall, separate pieces whirling in the air and colliding with silvery *tinks* and *clings*.

I got my right arm up, parallel to the floor. Butt of right hand cupped in left palm and fingers, right hand pressing forward while the left pulled back. Legs bent, squatted in a low crouch, thigh muscles stretched and trembling. I had the hammer thumbed back on the gun, but couldn't fire. Spree was moving, jerking. Still held close, too close.

He fired again. Nicked the top of my left shoulder. It felt like a blow of a hammer. And I still couldn't fire. I learned a lot about what I felt for Spree then, in that unending second or two. The heavy gun in his hand wavered away, exploding again, harmlessly, as Spree jerked—silently. Not a sound from her. I could see her lunge, twist, see the golden shower of her hair, see her red lips stretched, teeth pressed together. I was holding my breath, could feel the thud and thump of blood inside my head, clear down into my arm, into my hand squeezed around the gun's butt, into that finger light on the trigger.

Spree raised one foot, slammed it down, heel driving at the arch of the man's foot. I heard him yell, saw him jerk, saw the heavy gun swing away then back toward me, dead on me, saw Spree spin, whirl, topple away from him.

Just far enough. I shot the sonofabitch three times.

One, two, three. Low, middle, high. Three bony fingers plucking at that shiny black robe he wore. Low, in the groin. Middle, centered in his chest. And high was in his throat. That last slug tore through his neck, ripped open the carotid artery. Blood spurted from his throat, spurted astonishingly, a red ropelike arc glistening in the overhead light as it curved outward and down, fell splattering onto the white carpet. His gun took an impossibly long time to fall.

The man's legs bent loosely, simply came unhinged, as if all the muscles and nerves and tendons had been instantly cut, and he went down slanting backward in the air, his head striking the arm of the low couch and then thudding against the floor. He lay there, arms still raised, legs slightly lifted and moving. It looked in a queer, shocking way as if he were trying to get up. He wasn't. He was dead, or no more than half a heartbeat from death, but for a stretched-out taffylike segment of time his hands clawed, legs pumped slowly, like a man riding an upside-down bicycle in quicksand. Then his legs straightened, the arms dropped, his fingers stopped moving, still curled into pink-flesh claws.

I walked toward him. I knew he was dead, but I pulled back the S&W's hammer one more time. Spree was screaming. Running. Running somewhere. I stopped over the dead sonofabitch and almost shot him again. Instead, I swore at him. But there weren't any intelligible words, just a husky grunting sound. Grunts, mumbles, and my teeth gritting together.

Slowly, time stopped standing almost still. Slowly, I eased the revolver's hammer back down. Slowly, I felt my lungs fill with breath, smelled the acrid scent of gunpowder, felt my chest rise, became aware of the fire, the burn, jagged teeth biting at the tip of my left shoulder. I could feel a little stream of blood running down the arm, cooling on my biceps.

Those high harsh screams had stopped but I could still hear the chilling sound inside my head. Neither Spree nor the irritable doctor who made house calls was in sight, and I heard no sounds of running—heard no sounds at all, except the soft hum from a pump behind me, out there at the swimming pool.

I called out, yelled "Spree!" Nothing. I ran to the front door, outside. "Spree!"

A car, black sedan, Lincoln, was sliding right at the end of the driveway, lunging into Desert Fairways Drive. My rented Laser sat where Spree and I had left it—how long ago? Twenty minutes? Fifteen? I looked at my watch. Four minutes ago.

I ran down the drive, past the now-empty garage, along both sides of the house, then inside again and through all the rooms. I checked the area around the pool, crashed through vines, thick-leaved green plants, flowers. "Spree! *Spree!*"

I wouldn't let myself think she might have been in that speeding Lincoln, in it with the good doctor, who might soon get his own one-two-three plus one more in the head. She was around here somewhere. Scared, sure. But nearby. She had to be.

I went out front once more, walked over the flagstone deck, opened the Chrysler's door, and slid inside, not really thinking what should be done next, just wanting to sit and think for half a minute. Maybe if I started honking the horn—

"Shell?" It was tiny. Muffled. I barely heard it.

"Spree?"

"Oh, Shell. God, I was so scared." She was behind me, rising up from the floorboards in back. She came tumbling over the seat, sort of crooning, "Scared—and sick, really sick, I thought I was going to throw . . . up . . ."

"Hush."

She was pressed against me, her face buried between my chest and right arm. I pulled her close, held her. She was shaking. Well, so was I.

"Oh, God, it was awful. I saw him, trying to shoot you. And then—him. When he fell. I got sick, really weak. All that blood. I started to shake, I couldn't—"

"I know. Hush. It's O.K. now, Spree. Really. It's O.K."

Then, for a while, I just held her. Pulled her into my arms, my mind, my breath. After a while she stopped trembling, quivering. And finally she moved away. Not much. An inch or two. And looked at my face.

"I'm all right. I suppose we could go somewhere else, don't you think?"

"I sure do."

I started to switch on the ignition, then stopped. I hadn't heard any sirens yet. There'd be plenty soon; but maybe there was time.

I asked Spree, "Will you be all right for half a minute? I mean, right here, alone."

"Yes. But why?"

"I've got to go back inside. Just for a few seconds."

"All right."

I wanted to know who it was I'd just shot. Shot three times with somebody else's gun. If it was Claude Romanelle, that was one thing. I'd merely killed my client, and Spree's father. If it was not Romanelle, then who was it? Who had sent him here? Or had it been his own idea to shoot me, at his earliest opportunity, preferably in the back, and then take Spree—where, for what?

And, finally, if the corpse there in Claude Romanelle's Arizona Room was *not* my client but merely a deservedly dead stranger, then where in hell was the *real* Claude Romanelle?

I swung the car door open, got out.

Out into the humid heat of an Arizona October night.

Smelled yet again the faint sweetness of orange blossoms.

And heard the distant—but not distant enough—sound of approaching sirens.

Chapter Ten

THE DEAD MAN lay on his back, oddly twisted. The blood that had spurted from his ripped throat had landed four or five feet from the body and now formed a thick snakelike stain, clotted like a bloody bas-relief on the white carpet. It was shockingly red, dark scarlet against the tightly woven nap. And on the front of the man's black robe, on the white shirt and dark trousers underneath it. His neck, too, was smeared with thickening blood, brilliantly red like cuts of meat under those special lights in a butcher's display.

I could still smell the sharp odor of burned gunpowder —plenty had been burned, six shots had been fired in this room—but it was almost overpowered by the sour stink of the newly dead. Everything that had happened earlier to the cowboy when he'd flopped unconscious at my feet, and more, had happened to this guy, doubled and redoubled. Maybe that's life's final indignity: the slimy stink in your pants when it ends.

I bent over the man, gingerly patted his pants pockets, pulled out a key ring, dirty handkerchief, black plastic comb with several teeth missing, handful of change, and a brown leather wallet. I put everything back except the wallet, flipped through it. Several C-notes and some smaller bills—I didn't count them—credit cards, a driver's license.

The Arizona license had been issued to Claude M. Romanelle, of this address on Desert Fairways Drive, Scottsdale, AZ. Height 6'0", weight 145, hair brown, eyes brown, age 58. It was signed in the same graceful script I'd seen on the document in Worthington's office. In the lower right-hand corner was a small color photo of—the dead guy. The man I'd just killed.

That would have caused an even more severe commotion in my digestive system if I had not already seen those credit cards issued to somebody named Frederick Keats. I pulled Romanelle's license from its transparent plastic envelope—and there beneath it was another driver's license. Frederick R. Keats, Tempe, AZ, address, 5'11", weight 170, hair brown, eyes blue, age 54. The small color photo was identical to the one on Romanelle's license. With that obvious clue in my hands, I could see that the duplicate on Romanelle's license had been glued onto the plastic. I could feel the ridge made by the substituted photo's edge, rather than the plastic rectangle's normal smoothness.

I stuck Romanelle's license into my pocket. I wasn't certain it was a 100-percent-wonderful idea for me to take that ID, thus removing significant evidence from the scene of a crime, especially not with Paradise Valley police cars already on their way here—and, by now, a lot closer. However, I wanted a leisurely look at that concealed photo of Claude Romanelle. It seemed high time that I found out, for sure, what my missing client looked like.

So I stuffed the dead man's wallet into his pants pocket and ran back outside, piled into the Chrysler. Spree already had the engine idling and was seated on the passenger's side of the car.

There wasn't any conversation until we were back on Lincoln Drive. During that time I felt under my coat and shirt, fingered my left shoulder. That arm was throbbing, the point of fire only a small blaze now, but constant. There was no difficulty in moving the arm, just increased pain, running from shoulder to neck, when I lifted it. So I didn't lift it much. But with my fingers I felt the wetness, traced the pulpy furrow on the outside flesh just below the bone, barely below. I wiped my fingers on a handkerchief and stuck the folded cloth over the moist furrow, drove with only my right hand on the wheel.

Two police cars were coming this way, red and blue lights flashing on their roofs. I pulled to the right of the road as the white Dodge sedans with blue stripes along their sides whipped past us, siren on the lead car wailing like a great cat being pulled apart on a rack.

The first word of conversation after I got the car moving speedily again was "Whew," from Spree.

"Two or three whews," I said. "That was close."

"Close back at that house, too. What—what happened there, Shell? That couldn't have been Dad. I *know* it wasn't."

"You're right, it wasn't. Guy named Keats, and I've never heard of him. But how did you know? Did you see something—?"

"No, I just knew, somehow, I'd never seen that man before. Not when I was a child, not ever. But I wasn't certain what to do, and walked over to him. Then, after that, everything happened so fast . . . ."

"It was supposed to be fast. Over in a hurry before the questions started. But if there were questions, Keats even had a faked ID to con me with. And, Spree . . . well, I owe you. The trouble you gave that guy probably saved my life. Strike 'probably.' I know it did. After that first shot he never had a chance to aim."

"Mostly I was just trying to get away from him." When I glanced at her she added with a soft smile, "Mostly."

"Thanks anyway, Tiger."

"You don't owe me anything. I saw you. I remember those few seconds so clearly I'll never forget them in my life. You just stood there, all squatted down like a huge rock, with your gun pointed right at us. And you didn't shoot at him for . . . it seemed like forever. You could have. I know you didn't shoot him because I was so close. You don't have to tell me, I know. But, Shell, you should have."

"Well . . . maybe I would have, if I'd been carrying my own gun. But I'd never fired that Smith & Wesson even once. Might have shot my own foot off."

"Uh-huh." Spree was silent for a few seconds. "What now?"

"First thing, and one of the many reasons I didn't want to dance around all night with the cops, is to get you somewhere safe. Get you tucked in until I can figure out what's next."

"Tucked in?"

"Figure of speech, dear. Same thing as behind locked doors and barricades."

"Uh-huh."

I could drive way the hell out of town, I thought, up north to someplace like Carefree. But that would be too far away for me to handle all the things I felt I'd have to do in the next several hours. And it would mean, too, when I came back to Scottsdale or Phoenix I'd have to leave Spree alone for too long. Much longer than I cared to.

So I slowed for the light at Lincoln Drive and Scottsdale Road, made the green, and turned left, heading north. Then I said to Spree, "I want your opinion. You're the lady at risk here." I listed some of the options, including twenty-miles-away Carefree, and finished, "We're almost at the Registry Resort. Maybe if we pull in there very speedily, and I register alone but for two, man and wife, Mr. and Mrs. William Williams, say, you'll be tucked away about as safely as anyplace else. Maybe not, but—"

"Safe enough," she interrupted. "*You're* the one who's probably going to get shot."

"Thanks a lot—"

"But also, you ought to get rid of this car pretty soon, shouldn't you?"

"Even sooner. That Simpson guy, the doctor, there's no guarantee he checked the plates. No guarantee he didn't. But he for sure knows we're in a year-old Laser."

The swank Registry Resort, less than a mile north of the Scottsdale Road and Lincoln Drive intersection, was on our right. I eased into the driveway, avoided the entrance, and kept going until I could park far back at the rear of the hotel property in near darkness.

I unlocked the trunk, opened my suitcase, uncrumpled a wide-brimmed hat I'd packed and stuck it atop my white hair, traded my torn and bloody coat for a blue leisure jacket. Then I left Spree locked in the car, and started walking up front to the Registry's main entrance, having a hell of a time carrying Spree's two bags and my big suitcase. But the rest of it was easy.

When I walked into the Registry's spacious and lovely lobby, taking a deep breath of air-conditioned coolness as the melodic tinkle of softly played piano caressed my ears, for a strangely disturbing moment it was an almost physical shock to realize that all of this was going on at the same time and in the same world as the one in which I'd just shot and killed a man named Frederick Keats.

Little more than three miles from here, a photographer from the Paradise Valley police department might by now be taking pictures of the corpse. But blending with that bloody image in my mind were mental snapshots of well-dressed men and women strolling through the Registry's lobby, laughing, heading for bars or restaurants here, or out there on the town.

Instead of the stench of feces and urine, blood and burned gunpowder, in my nostrils were the faint and delicate odors of foods and spices from luxurious La Champagne and chef's *hors d'oeuvres* from the Fountain Bar here in the lobby, mixed with the too-sweet scents of perfumes, after-shaves, paints and powders. Too sweet? Maybe not.

At the desk, I asked for the quietest and most private rooms available, registered as Mr. and Mrs. William Williams, then rode with the bellman transporting our luggage to villa 333—which turned out to be one of the "bilevel suites" separate from the two-story main building, in the rear and not far from where I'd parked the Chrysler.

Inside the suite I glanced around the downstairs sitting room, shower and dressing area, wet bar, then followed the bellman upstairs and into the single bedroom. There were two double beds side by side up here, another bath, closet, outside sun porch. I gazed about at this with an air of languid disinterest, mumbled, "This'll do," as I handed the chap five bucks, still uncouthly wearing my wide-brimmed hat. I figure if you pay three hundred and eighty-five bucks a night for lodging, you can uncouthly wear any damned thing you want to.

The bellman smiled with moderate enthusiasm, or about five bucks' worth, placed my key on a dresser, trotted down the stairs and left.

I'd carried both guns, concealed on me, to the villa. There'd been only three cartridges in the Colt .45 when I took it from the cowboy outside Worthington's office. Coincidentally, the Smith & Wesson revolver also had only three slugs in its cylinder now—because I'd put the other three into Frederick Keats. That gun, therefore, was very hot, and so, if my identity should become known, was I. Still, I left the more familiar snub-nosed .38 in my clam-shell holster and put the Colt automatic on the closet shelf far back against the wall.

Then I got gauze pads and tape from my suitcase and went into the bathroom for some do-it-yourself repairs. Five minutes later I had a reasonably comfortable and secure bandage taped to my left shoulder, and was wearing a clean white sport shirt with the white trousers and blue leisure jacket. Five minutes after that Spree was in the villa with me.

She looked around, quickly inspected the upstairs and downstairs, then came over to where I stood near a dark wood cabinet enclosing the color TV set.

"You travel first-class, don't you?"

"Nothing but the best for my wives, ma'am."

"How nice for us. And I am now Mrs.—who? Mrs. what?"

"Close," I said. "Mrs. Williams."

"Of course. Silly of silly me to forget so soon, Willie. I *suppose* I call you Willie?" Spree batted long thick lashes rapidly at me, either coquettishly or in an attempt to air out the room.

"Absolutely *not*," I said. "I registered as William. So you may call me William. Not may, must. Outside this room, anyhow."

"O.K., Bill."

"No, no—you're much too sophisticated to call a William a Bill. Except . . . well, maybe when we're intimate, like taking showers together, or . . ."

She was giving me a very bleak look. "Mr. Williams,

weren't you going to move our Mercedes? Or Rolls? Or Porsche?"

"Sure. I'll move all three of them. Or—which one did we bring?"

"We flew."

"Ah, yes. Well, I'll go park the plane. As for you, kid, park that sophisticated bod in yon bed. When I return, I will watch over you all night long like your guardian Willie."

She looked up at me for a moment, then leaned closer, lifted her face, and kissed me quickly, gently on the side of my jaw. I put my hands on her shoulders, slid them around her back, and pulled her close. It was another one of those impulses. A nice one. Spree didn't pull away, just sort of snuggled against me as if this were something we'd practiced forever. I hugged her gently for a few fine seconds, then let her go.

And out I went. Into the Valley of the Sun. Into darkness.

It was over an hour before I got back to the Registry. I parked the Laser two blocks from a VOS Car Rentals office on 40th Street in Phoenix, left it there with the keys beneath the floor mat. Then I walked a mile to the nearest Hertz agency, address from the Yellow Pages, and rented a dark blue Mercury Capri. For the second time tonight I had to produce my driver's license and a credit card in my name; and while, so far as I knew, nobody was yet looking for Shell Scott except perhaps a few crooks, at least two of them with severe headaches, leaving this kind of paper trail gave me a definitely uneasy feeling.

When I let myself into suite 333, all the lights were out except for one table lamp upstairs in the bedroom.

Spree was in bed, asleep. Her face was soft, relaxed, very young. She looked at that moment about sixteen years old. At least her face did. But she must have turned, moved, after falling asleep. The blanket and a pale green sheet were pulled down to her waist. She wore a simple nightgown that covered everything normally covered. But it was white, lacy, not completely opaque. And those magnificent breasts swelled beneath the cloth, prominent nipples and large shadowy areolas only half concealed.

I pulled the covers up beneath her chin, and *then* she looked sixteen again. Long, slow breath . . . making a small *p-p-p* sound through her barely parted lips when she exhaled . . . lashes like long thin shadows under her eyes.

I took off my jacket and shoes, pulled a large overstuffed chair next to the bed, put the revolver on a nearby bedside table, then turned off the light and settled down in my chair-bed for the night.

Spree must have heard me. Or almost did. Or dreamed it. Because I heard her say very softly, "Shell," but it sounded like a muffled "Shlull?"

I turned toward her, putting my hand on the bed.

In the darkness, she reached out to me, touched my fingers. Said something completely unintelligible, barely audible, ending in *p-p-p.* I gripped her hand gently, held it like a bird. Not hard enough to squash it, but not so gently it could fly away.

It didn't. Not until dawn.

Chapter Eleven

MORNING.

I awakened slowly, like a beast rising from a murky swamp, to small sounds of movement, another melodic sound almost like a woman humming . . .

I rolled over but kept bumping into something. My left shoulder burned, the arm was heavy. There was a small tight spot at the base of my skull. I peeled my eyes open, saw the arm of the chair I was collapsed into. Memory limped back. The sound I'd heard *was* a woman humming, moving about. Spree. In another minute or two I heard her coming up the stairs. She looked around, then she walked over and beamed down at me.

"Hi, there," she said brightly. "Up and at 'em, it's a beautiful morn—"

"Don't try any of that stuff with me," I said.

"Oh . . . I forgot," she said.

I clambered to my feet, made it into the bathroom for a quick shower, careful of the shoulder bandage, shaved and dressed. Then I joined Spree below in a little alcove, kind of a dining area, and sat down across from her at a small square table.

"Good morning," I said.

"Welcome to the world. I've been up for over an hour now. You hungry?"

"No."

I noticed a cart on wheels, tray atop it, glasses and silverware and dishes on the tray. Spree followed my gaze and said, "I've already eaten. Called room service—didn't want to waken you."

I was no longer asleep, but not yet wide enough awake that I was thinking like lightning. Still, her comment bothered me. I said slowly, "I don't think your calling room service was such a good idea. The idea is for you to hide here, unseen, unapproachable, like Rapunzel in her castle tower—"

"Shell, it's too early for poetry, even though I *have* been awake for an hour. And I had the waiter leave my tray outside the door, then brought it in myself a minute later."

"Good thinking. I don't suppose he was still lurking out there, maybe holding his palm up for a tip?"

"Of course not. At least . . . I didn't notice anybody. And *you'll* add a nice big tip to the check for him, won't you, Mr. Williams?"

"Sure. I'll give him some of my old Krugerrands. Well, room service sounds good about now. How's their coffee here?"

"I'll call and order you a nice breakfast. Eggs, maybe?"

"I knew you'd say that. But no. *Absolutely* not."

"Well, what do you want? Don't you like eggs in the morning?"

"Not before I've eaten. I'll just have coffee."

"Oh, Shell, you've got to *eat*. A big man like you—"

"Here we go again," I said glumly. Not to her. She was a woman. She wouldn't listen. She was going on about proteins and carbohydrates and even vitamins and minerals.

"Just coffee," I interrupted. "And a piece of toast. And you'd better be careful—"

"White, whole wheat, rye—what kind of toast?"

"Burned."

She cocked her head on one side, then the other. "You're not a barrel of laughs in the morning, are you?"

"Sure I am. Not after I wake up, of course. Not *right* after."

She went to the phone. Soon there was coffee and a piece of toast. Burned. The Registry is a class resort. Spree had one cup of coffee with me. I had three, plus the delicious toast. And I began to think the world was a marvelous place to be.

Before finishing my last cup of hot strong brew, I went through the Scottsdale and Phoenix telephone books. There was no Robert Simpson, M.D., listed, so I called both the Maricopa County Medical Society and the Arizona State Medical Association, but neither group carried such a doctor on their rolls. So all I had was memory of the man's fat pink face, bald head, heavy chin—and the fact that he owned, or at least drove, a black Lincoln sedan.

No Kay Dark or Kay Denver was listed, either, but Exposé, Inc. was—at the Hayden Road address I had already jotted in my pocket notebook.

While at the phone, I made a call to a financial reporter on the *Phoenix Gazette*, whom I'd met on my first trip here, when on a case involving a group of *mafiosi* at a senior citizens housing development called Sunrise Villas.

According to him, *Exposé* was a monthly publication devoted to gathering and publishing "inside" and/or "exclusive" information about business and investment frauds, scams, rip-offs, and cons, but also about legitimate enterprises deserving, in the opinion of the editors, of plugs or applause for being notable examples of "the best of free-enterprise entrepreneurship in action." So they touched upon the best from time to time, but concentrated on the worst most of the time.

Exposé, now in its third year of publication, was headquartered in Scottsdale, and during its first year had concentrated primarily upon action in Arizona. Since then, the thrust had become national in scope. It was expensive, three hundred bucks a year, and available by subscription only, not for sale on newsstands. To the best of the *Gazette* reporter's knowledge, *Exposé* was itself legitimate, very professional, and performed a valuable service.

He added, "I know and admire Steve Whistler, the publisher-editor. He's a go-go dynamo and a man with a lot of balls. Necessarily so, guy like that makes some heavy enemies."

"I'd guess he would," I said. "Their info's pretty good,

then? Not just a rehash?"

"Damned good. The *Gazette*'s Arizona's financial news-paper, you know, and we've got excellent sources. But a couple times a year those guys break a story we've barely started sniffing after. They've got good people here in the Valley, correspondents in several other states. I'd say, judging by some of the stuff they've come up with, they might have a line into organized crime as well. Maybe even an undercover man or two."

"That's . . . very interesting," I said slowly. "You got any documentation on that? Or names?"

"No, this is just the opinion of one financial reporter reading between *Exposé*'s lines. They've come up with stuff that wasn't available even to us, and we're not amateurs. Could be a lot of other explanations."

I said, "If the publication knocks a company and its stock takes a dive, anybody knowing about the story in advance could make a bundle by selling the stock short. Other side of the same coin, they give a good guy a boost, any insiders—which primarily here means *Exposé* people —could maybe take a ride up with the shares. Any evidence that kind of thing happens?"

"Not so far. Or if there is, I don't know about it."

"They ever get sued?"

"All the time, Shell. You intimate a crook's a crook, or come right out and say so, you're gonna get slapped with papers—at *least* papers. But they haven't lost any yet. If I was them, I wouldn't worry about lawsuits so much as I would about getting blown away."

When I hung up the phone, I got Claude Romanelle's driver's license from my coat pocket, sat down at the small table again. My reporter acquaintance hadn't been able to give me any startling info about Romanelle or Frederick Keats, although he'd "heard about" Romanelle's being shot last week. Obviously he hadn't—yet—heard about Keats being shot by somebody last night. So I carefully pulled the photo of the late Frederick Keats from Roman-elle's license. Something like rubber cement had been used, and its residue came easily off the plastic when I rubbed it with my thumb.

And there he was. His face, anyway. He appeared to be more youthful than a man fifty-eight going on ninety-nine. High wide forehead, wedge-shaped, almost pointed chin, straight brows over large dark eyes—large, like Spree's.

There was indeed a slightly satanic cast to his features, but he wasn't a bad-looking man at all. He really didn't look a bit like Keats when the two pictures were placed side by side.

I passed the plastic rectangle over the table to Spree, saying, "Claude Romanelle's driver's license. I got it from the dead guy's wallet when I went back into the house last night. So that's what your dad looks like."

She studied the small photo for a long time. "I like him a lot better than the man who *said* he was my father," she said finally. Then, softly, "I wonder if he's still . . . alive."

"I think he probably is. Don't ask me why. I haven't put much of this together yet. But I'll do my best today to find out, try to locate him."

"Have you any idea where to look, where to start?"

"I've got a couple of ways to go. And I'll find some more. Well, I'll phone you when I can—you stay here in the suite, Spree."

"I will. And *you* be careful, Shell."

"Never fear. I'll be invulnerable now that I've had my coffee."

I guess I was fully awake at last, because I looked again at Spree and, finally, really saw her.

She was wearing low-heeled sandals, a bright banana-yellow skirt, and a wonderfully voluptuous white blouse, no "cover-up" this morning, and she was fresh, impossibly beautiful, warm, glowing. Makeup had been expertly applied. Her lips were red as strawberry wine, her eyes that middle-of-the-rainbow green, her golden hair combed with sunshine. She looked like the spirit of spring or the dreams of summer, and she took my breath away.

I smiled at her. "Where were you when I woke up?"

This one was bright on the inside as well as the outside. Besides, she'd been up for *two* hours. "I was out feedin' the chickens, Paw," she said, "so they'd lay lots of yaller aigs. I suppose you'll be leavin' me, now all the chores is done."

"Now all the chores *are* did," I corrected her. "But I'm afraid you're right, child. Wish I could stay. Wish I could stay with you."

"So do I. Maybe tomorrow."

"There's always tomorrow," I said, and left.

The offices of *Exposé* occupied one wing of a small business complex on Hayden Road between Osborn and Thomas. When I parked in their lot, it was 8:35 A.M.

I walked in through double glass doors under two-inch-high white letters on a black base spelling out "Exposé, Inc." A long counter was before me, a hinged wooden gate at its left providing entry to a large room visible beyond the counter. At the rear of the room, along the entire width of the wall opposite me, were three separate offices, paneled in wood for the first four feet up from the floor and with glass extending from that point to the ceiling. From here, anyone sitting down in those offices was out of sight, but the head and shoulders of people standing could be seen. Only three individuals were standing back there, a very tall man in a white dress shirt open at the collar, talking to a shorter man in the central office, and a middle-aged lady in the office on the left.

Between those offices and me were at least a dozen desks at which employees wrote in ledgers, studied computer screens, tapped away on keyboards, even used old-fashioned clattering typewriters. The entire wall on my far left was lined with six-foot-high green metal filing cabinets. It looked and sounded like a busy place.

Behind the counter, at a small desk, sat a dark-haired woman about thirty, with bright blue eyes and a button nose. As I leaned on the counter she got up from her desk and walked over near me.

"May I help you?" she asked.

"Yes, I'm here to see Mr. Whistler," I said briskly, all business.

"Do you have an appointment?"

I took a chance. There were only two men visible in those three offices at the building's rear, both in the central or presumably "main" office. "Say, that's Steve back there now, isn't it?" I said, nodding past her. "Tall man in the white shirt?"

She looked around, back at me. "Yes. If you'll give me your name—stop! You can't do that!"

But I had already done it. I was through the little hinged wooden gate and on my way into the big room. The blue-eyed receptionist scurried to her desk and pushed a button on a desktop intercom about six inches from her already-open mouth.

Just before I reached that middle office I saw the tall guy lean over his desk, depress a switch, and listen, undoubtedly to that open mouth beneath the button nose. He glanced into the room and his eyes fell on me. He turned back to his intercom, then his head snapped toward me again in a classic double take.

I'd left my wide-brimmed hat in the Mercury, so my white hair and brows were just as obtrusive and visible as they usually were. That, plus my size, was more than enough to ensure that anybody who'd seen me or my picture could identify me with a quick glance, much quicker than the long stare the tall man—Steve Whistler, apparently—was giving me as I opened the door to his office, stepped inside, and came to a stop looking at him from six feet away.

He spoke into his intercom, "It's all right, Helen. No problem." Then he looked at the short heavyset man who'd been talking to him and said, "That's all for now, Bren."

The short man hesitated, looked at me, back at Whistler. "You sure? If you want me to stick around—"

"No problem. We'll finish it later, Bren. Out. On the double."

The guy did what he was told. With everything else taken care of to his satisfaction, Whistler turned his attention, finally, to me. With one long arm he indicated an uncomfortable-looking wooden chair before his desk and said, "Please sit down . . ." He hesitated briefly, pulling at his lower lip with two fingers, apparently came to a decision. "Please sit down, Mr. Scott." With that, he sat down himself.

I perched on the edge of the wooden chair, leaned forward with both my elbows on his desk, smiled without an overabundance of joy, and said, "O.K., you know who I am. And I know you're Steve Whistler. Why don't you tell me—just for openers—who Kay Dark is?"

He raised an eyebrow, nodded slowly. "That's pretty good," he said. "My information indicated that, as an investigator, you aren't too shabby, Mr. Scott. But I'll admit I'm surprised you asked me about Kay Dark instead of Kay Denver."

"Why don't you tell me about both the darlings?"

He smiled. "I think I will. But . . ." He paused, rolled his eyes up and to the right for three or four seconds, looking as if he was gazing at a far horizon, then came back to me. "I think, though, that we should first come to an agreement about a trade."

"What does that mean?"

"A trade of information. I can answer many of your questions. But *I* have a lot of questions, too. That's my business: questions—and answers that most people can't get. The way to get the right answers is to ask the right questions of the right people. You're the right man to tell me several things I very much want to know."

"Like what?"

"Glad you asked." He grinned. It was a wide, pleasant, happy kind of grin. "By way of foundation. I expected to see you here—eventually. But not this soon. That impresses me. As I mentioned, my information is that you're a good investigator, unorthodox, creative, tough when necessary, you've closed some pretty big ones including two or three here in Arizona. But most important to me, you're afflicted with an old-fashioned integrity, you're honest. You might lie to protect a client, but never to protect yourself at the expense *of* the client—or of anyone else, for that matter. Obviously, you are seriously retarded. You appear to think there's still some virtue in virtue, that a man should pay his own way, whatever the coin. How am I doing?"

"I'm not so sure about retarded."

He laughed.

"Go on," I said. "I'm fascinated."

"Well, as I told you, I expected you to get here, maybe in a week or two. Not so damned soon. You must have arrived yesterday afternoon, right?"

That was his first direct—or, rather, indirect—question. I thought about it. Maybe he already knew, for sure, precisely when I'd arrived. Maybe not. But a number of people did know. The bad guys knew, whoever they were. If Whistler was one of them, my answering his question wouldn't tell him anything he wasn't already aware of. On the other hand . . .

I nodded. "That's right," I said. "So?"

He reached for a gold lighter on his desk, next to a pack of Tareyton Long Lights, picked them up, and looked at me. "You mind?"

"Not at all. Use them myself."

He lit one of the cigarettes, slid the pack across the desk to me. "Go ahead, if you'd like," he said.

I took one of the smokes, ignoring the Surgeon General's horrendous warning on the pack—which I figured, in fairness, the Surgeon General should also arrange to have printed on hormone-fattened meat, pesticide-sprayed vegetables, polluted drinking water, nuclear power plants, the earth and the seas and the smoggy skies—and in the midst of my mental meanderings Whistler leaned forward, flicked on his gold lighter, and lit the Tareyton for me. In a strange, slightly uncomfortable way, it seemed that we'd almost come to some kind of agreement in that moment.

He took a drag, blew out smoke, and said, "To answer your question, which I believe was, 'So?'—so you can tell me if you are, as I strongly suspect, the man who shot and killed Keats last night."

A lot of things spun through my head in the next second or two. If he was *not* somehow allied with Keats and Andrew Foster and the cowboy, Jay Groder—the only names I was sure of so far—then this guy's sources of information were stupendously good ones. But if he was so allied, that was a question he obviously wouldn't need to ask.

I tried to keep my expression only mildly interested. But

I don't think I succeeded. For one thing, my hand holding the cigarette stopped halfway to my mouth for a long second before I got it moving again.

I took a closer look at Steve Whistler. I knew, from the fact that he'd been a little higher in the air than I when we were both standing here in his office, that he was about six-four, and I guessed he'd push the scales to about one-eighty, maybe a little more. He wasn't lean, but neither was he wide except in the heavy shoulders. I guessed his age at maybe thirty-five, give or take a year. The face was smooth except for deep lines curving from his straight nose down to the corners of his mouth, ending at pads of facial muscle that bunched up when he smiled. It wasn't a handsome face, but it was pleasant. And strong. He had a lot of slightly wavy dark red hair and oddly light brows over eyes an almost pastel blue.

He was relaxed in his chair, right elbow on the desk, hand bent easily at the wrist and holding his cigarette, no evidence of strain. I got the impression of a lot of controlled energy under the surface of the man, power in reserve, like banked fires or steam under pressure in a boiler.

Finally I said, "Interesting question. I can think of a lot of possible answers. Like, 'Keats? Keats who?' Or maybe, 'Not me, I'm the guy who pulled Shelley's heart from that bonfire on the beach—'"

He winced. "I wish you hadn't said that. I'll just assume we're both fond of Trelawney. O.K., how about this? I'll tell you what I'm sure you want to know. And then—if I convince you we're on the same side of the table, that we can help each other by sharing information and working together—you answer *my* questions. Fair?"

"Fair enough. Meaning, if we get to that point, I'll then answer questions that don't compromise my old-fashioned integrity. And if my answers—assuming there turn out to be any—go no farther than you, *no*body else."

"I'll buy it," he said, leaning back and propping one shoe on a corner of his desk. "Here at *Exposé*, we make it a full-time job to go after crooks, rip-off artists, primarily in the business and investment communities."

"I know a little about what you do," I said. "Not much, but I'm more interested—"

"I'll get there," he said pleasantly. "What I want you to understand is that we're good. I think we're the best private organization doing this kind of work—there aren't many. But we're also better than a lot of public crime fighters. You like the sound of that, crime fighters?"

"Knocks my socks off."

"We're computerized, hooked into data-base networks that give us access to nearly five thousand periodicals —newspapers, magazines, newsletters—which means access to one *hell* of a lot of good research we don't have to do. And we do plenty ourselves. In five minutes I can give you a printout on almost any sizable U.S. corporation you can name, most of the little ones, and a rundown on nearly everyone from their CEOs to the building efficiency superintendents, or janitors. Or a dossier on a private investigator named Sheldon Scott."

I opened my mouth, but he went racing on. "Four former FBI agents work here, two are in the building now. Plus five former police officers, two of them with a combined total of twenty-six years in police intelligence. I pay good money to six of the best writers and reporters available at any price, including my latest find, Kay Dark, brilliant small-town reporter who rose to become the until-recently-anonymous crime reporter/author of 'After Dark' for the *Chicago Free Times*. You've heard of 'After Dark'?"

I hadn't, but I said, "I've heard of Kay Denver."

"Then I have your attention?"

"I'd say so."

"Recently a man named Claude Romanelle was shot and wounded here in the Valley. We know that Mr. Romanelle owns a sizable number of shares in a company called Golden Phoenix Mines, a curiously vigorous mining company which is right here in Arizona, in Maricopa County. I have visited the site, and it *is* a mine, a mine actually producing gold, not merely a staked claim or a puffed-up paper description. However, the price of Golden Phoenix shares, traded over the counter, has risen from twenty cents three years ago to four and one-eighth asked at the beginning of this year, to about fourteen dollars now. It *may* go to forty. Most of that spurt has taken place in the last month fed by rumors and possibly solid inside information, plus in particular the release of a truly sensational assay report almost two weeks ago, of which assay I shall make further mention if you happen to be interested."

"I'm interested."

"I thought you would be." Whistler pulled his shoe from the desktop, sat up straight, and leaned forward. "Now we get to you."

"Good."

"Well, almost. Soon. *Exposé*—which is to say, me, but also nearly everyone else here in the shop—is very interested in Golden Phoenix, for which the front, or president, is a slick-smooth, possibly dangerous man named Alda Cimarron, in whom we are also much interested. *We're* also aiming at a man named Sylvan Derabian, called Mr. Arabia by his fellow felons—"

"Felons? He's done hard time?"

"Two years only, and that more than twenty years ago."

"More than twenty . . . Arabia?" I stopped, chose my words with some care as I went on, "I recall something about an old Illinois case involving one Keyser Derabian. I think he had a brother named Sylvan, but I don't know what happened to him. That was all . . . a long time ago."

"I sense the dawning of a small light. Mr. Derabian —I'm referring to Sylvan now—was indeed the younger brother of Keyser, who expired in the slam. We may safely say, then, that both Keyser and young Sylvan were, those many years ago, associated with our mutual acquaintance, Mr. Claude Romanelle."

"Who says he's a mutual acquaintance?"

"A great deal of evidence, which you will be privileged to examine, should you wish. Also, Kay says."

I took a last drag on the Tareyton, snubbed it out in a tray Whistler pushed toward me. Then I said, "If we should assume I know someone named Romanelle, I doubt that I would have mentioned the name even to so marvelous a researcher as Kay Denver-Dark."

"You didn't. You wouldn't have to. She is very, very good. In only the two short months she's been with me, Kay has impressed me as much as anyone else in the shop. She's the closest thing to my right-hand man that I've ever had at *Exposé*." He chuckled. "Make that right-hand person. Wouldn't want to call Kay a male anything, would we, Mr. Scott?"

If it was a question, he didn't wait for an answer. For a slightly sticky moment I wondered if Whistler might already have received the definitive answer to that one from his "right-hand man."

But he was going on, "No, you did not mention the name Romanelle. You did mention a Spree—in fact, you ran a widely seen ad about that money spree. Indeed, Mr. Scott, that is how we became interested in you."

"Whoa. Back up just a little, O.K., Mr. Whistler?"

"O.K. And make it Steve, please. You don't know it yet, but we're soon going to be . . . perhaps friends, certainly associates, pooling our efforts in righteous endeavor."

"Righteous endeavor. You make it sound like we're going to sell tickets to the Christian Olympics. But about that ad. Sure, I'm responsible for it. But that Personal Message didn't appear until Tuesday. And Kay happened upon me in a bar . . . well before then . . ." I stopped, finished lamely, "On Monday."

I was gritting my teeth and nodding as Whistler, now Steve, said, "No reason to kick yourself, Shell. No way you could have guessed we'd know about the ad two hours after you phoned it in, or that very soon afterward I'd have Kay on the next L.A. flight."

"Let me catch up here. I can buy your having a contact at the *L.A. Times*, one who'd tip you about that Personal Message *if* it waved red flags at him."

He nodded, smiling slightly, and said, "That's right."

I kept going, "But what red flags were waving? Maybe it wasn't the most clever prose ever written, but I didn't name anybody called Romanelle, and I sure doubt it could have been the spree in money—"

"Shell Scott."

"What?"

"That was the red flag. Shell Scott—your name."

"Come again?"

"A minute ago you asked me to back up a little, Shell. Let me do that now. Keep in mind the megabytes of packed computer memory we've got right here, data-base access, cross-checked files—and a lot of friends, sources, tipsters, sympathizers. O.K., Romanelle was shot, assailants unknown, on Monday, September twenty-fourth. Taken to Scottsdale Memorial, and on the following Sunday was visited in his hospital room by a local attorney, Bentley X. Worthington. Considering our already-active interest in Romanelle—primarily because of his connection with Golden Phoenix—and the super-prestigious nature of Worthington's law firm, that got our attention. The first question we asked was: Why? Why would a hot-shot—"

I interrupted. "One quick question before that, all right?"

He nodded impatiently.

"How in hell did you happen to know Worthington visited Romanelle?"

"Shell, that's really not important," he said, almost with irritation. "But I'll tell you, to spare myself a dozen more questions like it. These things don't just happen, we make them happen. It's our business. O.K., Worthington's well known, top law firm, often interviewed on TV, very visible. In this case, one of Romanelle's nurses at Scottsdale Memorial—two-year subscriber to *Exposé*, by the way—saw Worthington leaving Romanelle's room, the room incidentally of a gunshot victim, and passed that information to us."

He paused, reached for the Tareyton pack, lit up his second smoke, and said, "To save you the trouble, your next question is: Why did she think we'd be interested in info about Romanelle? In this case, simple. Claude Romanelle—along with several other individuals—was mentioned briefly in our last issue. We did a short prelim article on Golden Phoenix Mines, promised an in-depth follow-up to lead off our November issue. That issue will be out in a couple weeks, working on it now."

He pulled open a drawer of his desk, saying, "Here, let me give you a copy of that October issue." He took out what looked like the standard 8½" by 11" newsletter, opened it to the next-to-the-last page, and handed it to me. The "Journal" was eight pages of fairly small type, and while I glanced at page seven Whistler went on, "We publish on the third Friday of each month, put those eight pages into the mail before locking up that day, a separate Express Mail package to each major city so most subscribers get their copies on the following Monday. Most local subscribers, of course, get theirs on Saturday." He pointed. "There's the Golden Phoenix article, and the come-on for November in the box."

Enclosed within a black square at the upper right-hand corner of the page, boldface type proclaimed that *Exposé*'s investigative reporters were continuing their research into the past and present, and the future prospects, of Golden Phoenix Mines, Inc., and that results of those labors plus several of "the no-holds-barred interviews you have come to expect from *Exposé*" would appear in next month's issue.

Top left on the same page, a two-column article was headed "Golden Phoenix—Fool's Gold or .999 Fine?" I skimmed the few paragraphs and noted at the article's end a list of several large shareholders with the number of shares owned by each opposite his name. Seven individuals were listed as owning one million shares each, among them Alda Cimarron, Sylvan Derabian, Phillip Bliss, M.D., and Claude Romanelle. There were three other names, but none of them meant anything to me yet.

Whistler continued, "In checking our file on Worthington, we found that he routinely employs local private investigators to develop information for him. Considering the fact that Romanelle had just been shot by a pair of still-unidentified men, it seemed not unlikely that Worthington might employ such investigators again. However, we also learned that the only *out*-of-state detective he had used was Sheldon Scott, normally active in the Los Angeles –Hollywood area of California. So your name went onto a list—we pulled a total of fourteen names, by the way, not just yours—which was communicated to a number of our associates and friends. With a request that *any* information appearing in newspapers, magazines, on television, hearsay, rumor, about you—and, of course those other thirteen names—be immediately transmitted to *Exposé.*"

He paused, head lowered, looking up at me from the sharp pastel-blue eyes. "Are you beginning to understand how I managed to get one of my investigative reporters next to you, hoping to uncover what you were doing for Worthington and determine whether or not it involved Romanelle, well *before* your money-for-spree ad appeared?"

"Yeah, I am. I'm also beginning to suspect you must spend a fortune keeping those megabytes of memory and a ton of other files up to date."

"We do. Four hundred thousand this year. So far. But we'll spend whatever we have to. Which could be twice our present expenditure if necessary. Our subscriber base is just over eighty thousand and rising, so we're well into the black."

Multiplying eighty thousand subscribers by $300 per subscription told me that Exposé, Inc., had to be grossing around twenty-four million a year, maybe more. Coincidentally, that was almost exactly the total Worthington had said Romanelle's estate amounted to. Which wasn't important, except that it made me think again of Claude Romanelle, and wonder where he was, how he was, and even *if* he was.

Whistler was saying, "I've explained where I'm coming from at some length so you can be sure I'm not just groping in the dark when I say—for example—that I suspect you're the man who shot Fred Keats last night. But *if* you did . . ." He scowled at his desktop, shaking his head slightly, went on, "then there's something *very* damned puzzling about whatever happened there. Something very strange about the gun that was used to kill him."

That jarred me. "How would anybody know what gun was used on this Keats?"

"That's part of the puzzle I'm hoping you can help me clear up. Look, we—that is, I and a very few others here in the shop—know, or can logically assume, that Romanelle hired Worthington, who almost immediately thereafter called you in Los Angeles. You arrived here yesterday, late—but well before Keats was killed. Killed at Romanelle's home, remember. To which home it is almost certain you intended to go, in the company of Claude Romanelle's daughter, or at least a woman you believed to be his daughter. There's a good deal more, but I think here is where we find out if we can work together and make that trade I mentioned. So, one more time: Did you kill Keats?"

"I sure did," I said. "Shot him three times."

It was right then, just before my answer, with the thought of *Exposé*'s very substantial resources, computers, files, tipsters, and "friends" still in my mind, that I decided to level with Steve Whistler, at least as much as I sensibly could. I needed whatever information he might be able to provide more than he needed answers from me. Moreover, my client's interests, and even—in view of what had happened on Desert Fairways Drive last night—his life, if he still had one, might depend on my getting whatever helpful information I could as quickly as I could.

"That's a start, Shell," Whistler said matter-of-factly. "O.K., my turn. I don't have any idea how the hell it happened, but the gun you used on Keats is the same one that put a bullet into Claude Romanelle on Monday, ten days ago."

"I'll be goddamned." I paused, thinking about it, then went the rest of the way. "I took that piece from a long lanky cowboy type shortly after I happened to produce some unconsciousness in him and a friend of his. Name was Jay Groder. He and his black friend both split before I got back to them."

"A black? Young good-looking guy about thirty?" I nodded and Whistler said, "Andy Foster, probably."

"Not probably, for sure. Andrew H. Foster according to his ID. What's the evidence that Romanelle was shot with the gun I took from Groder?"

"Romanelle was shot three times, but only one bullet stayed in him, the one serious hit he took in his middle.

Police got that bullet from the surgeon, of course. When Keats was shot—in Romanelle's home—they naturally compared that bullet on file with the three in Keats. Presto. Same gun."

"Uh-huh. Next thing. I don't know where the hell Romanelle is, and I very much want to find the man. If you know where he might be, or can give me any help locating him, I'll owe you."

Whistler shook his head. "No idea. Wish I did. So do the police, by the way."

"Cops? Why do they . . . ?" I stopped, swore softly. "Don't tell me they think he might have killed Keats?"

"They sure do. And they are attempting, with considerable industry, to find him."

"But why would the cops think *he* could have shot Keats with the gun somebody used to plug *him*?"

"That's part of their puzzle. We've got puzzles within puzzles here. They think Romanelle can tell them how it happened, once they arrest him. After all, it happened in his house. The body was there. Romanelle was not. And that's enough for them right now."

I was doing a great job for my client. Now I had all of Maricopa County's law looking for him. Actually, of course, they were really looking for me, even if they didn't know it yet. Which wasn't a very comforting thought, either.

I said, "So far I'm tuned in to Groder, Foster, and Keats. Who the hell are these guys? The Arizona Mafia?"

"Not quite. They're all associated, one way or another, with Alda Cimarron. Or with Cimarron Enterprises. I'll let you take a look at our paper files on them." He pressed his intercom switch and said, "Send Weinstein in here, please," then started writing the names I'd mentioned on a white pad.

"Add this Cimarron, will you? And a doctor named Robert Simpson, if you've got one. Romanelle, too, if it's no problem."

"No sweat," he said cheerfully.

A short, very young-looking man with a whole lot of hair and a very faint wispy mustache came in rapidly, took the paper Whistler handed him, spun around like a military cadet, and marched out.

"He one of your privates?" I asked Steve.

"Embryo general. That kid's got his eye on tomorrow. IQ about one-eighty, by the way." While waiting for General Weinstein to come back, Whistler said, "You worked for Worthington twice before, didn't you?"

"Right. I also got involved in another case, here in Arizona, when I thought I was vacationing at Mountain Shadows."

"We know all about that—the Sunrise Villas thing, wasn't it?"

"Yeah. Your information's pretty good."

"Very good. We've got quite a file on you now."

"Swell. Where do I send the blackmail payments?"

Perhaps it was fate. Or cosmic coincidence. Or merely interesting timing. Whatever the reason, it was at that precise moment, when we were discussing *Exposé*'s "file" on me and my various activities, that there was the sound of rapid footsteps outside Whistler's office, then the door was pushed open and she—who? You guessed? Yes, she —came inside.

I cranked my head around to see the tall dark-haired lovely taking two energetic strides forward, accompanied by a number of deliciously feminine wigglings and jigglings, especially when she came to a sudden stop. Yes, it was Kay Denver-Dark, the lady who had succumbed so enthusiastically to my charms, helpless in the grip of my hypnotic power.

She looked straight at me, her eyes wide, mouth forming an "*O*"—as in "*Oh*-oh!"—while slowly all that jiggling and wiggling ceased, as though all the separate acts in a little aphrodisiacal circus were simultaneously expiring.

But only for about half a second. Then, again, the whistles blew and calliopes played and the clowns swung from their trapezes as she took two more quick steps straight toward me, those wild lips curving in a smile of—what? Welcome? Greeting? Reunion? Baloney?

"Shell!" she cried. "What a wonderful surprise!"

Chapter Twelve

I SAID, "No kidding, ma'am?" and "*I* know you, you're Kay something," and "You're looking as healthy as wheat germ, kid," while she chattered several phrases of absolutely no consequence either, and then Steve Whistler was standing behind his desk saying, "Kay, dear, when did you get back? I'll bet it was just now, what? Well, Kay, Shell, I won't introduce you two—"

"No," I said.

And Kay finished it, "We've met."

During the next minute, General Weinstein zipped in, placed a foot-high stack of thick file folders on Whistler's desk, spun around and zipped out before I could salute him. Steve barked into his intercom for "Hot coffee, hot, hot," Kay shuffled idly through those files the general had delivered, and I stopped putting words together audibly but in no particular order and just sat there scratching my chest.

Then the coffee arrived, and Steve, with one long cigarette smoldering in his ashtray, lit another and said to Kay, "I've been trying to convince Shell we should all work together. We could make the *Exposé* resources available to him, and he can fill us in with whatever he comes up with. I think we'd make a good team on this thing."

"Oh, I'd like that," Kay said sincerely. "That is, if . . ."

She was looking at what appeared to be a spot in the air exactly halfway between Steve and me, and she rolled her eyes left at Steve, then right toward me, and finished,

". . . if Shell can ever forgive me."

By then she was looking straight at me, and sending me some kind of significant message with her lips. Morse code, maybe. At least, it looked like three dots and a dash. Whatever that was. Maybe those familiar chords from Beethoven's Fifth, the way they would look if you couldn't hear them.

"Oh . . ." I said. "Forgive? Well, I'll think about it. Yeah, I'll think about it a *lot*."

I had a sip of my coffee, which must have been condensed from pure steam instants before they brought it in here. Burned my tongue severely. Which reminded me. "Hell, you're forgiven," I said lightly, waving my tongue in the air to cool it off.

"Oh, good," Kay trilled. "I knew you weren't the kind of man to hold a grudge against me, Shell."

"To what?"

"I'm glad that's settled," Steve said, apparently referring to some other conversation.

"After all, Shell," Kay continued, "when Steve sent me to Los Angeles to find you, talk to you—"

"When you volunteered, dear," Steve said.

"Yes, when I *volunteered* to do it—because I thought I might be able to pull off another coup—"

"To what?" I said again.

"—and prove I can compete with the *men* reporters . . . well, Shell, I didn't *know* you then. Once I actually *met* you, and found out what a sweet, fun person you were —are—then it was . . . too late. I mean, I couldn't *unvo*-lunteer then, could I?"

"Absolutely not," I said. "I guess. Would you run that by me again?"

She turned to look at Whistler. "He knows the whole thing, doesn't he?"

"Just about."

"Did you show him my report?"

"Not yet."

"Oh, good."

"But I think that's a fine suggestion."

"Oh, no. No, it's *not* a suggestion."

"Yes, a capital idea."

"Steve, I'd rather you didn't. After all, it's so . . . cold."

"Nonsense, Kay, you did an absolutely terrific job. It's the best way I can think of to demonstrate quickly to Shell our thoroughness, the lengths we'll go to in order to get the job done, how we pull widely separated pieces together from a number of different sources until, presto, a significant picture or pattern begins to appear. Yes, that's capital. Particularly if we're going to be working together."

He stood up, started to turn.

"Steve," Kay said, her voice a little shrill, "it's a bad idea. Don't. I—I insist."

He glanced back toward her. "You what?"

Then he turned and walked to one of several green-painted metal filing cabinets against the rear wall, opened one of the drawers, and took out a two-inch-thick folder.

I heard Kay sort of muttering, "You damned pseudo-macho men, you bloody blisters" or something like that. Hard to tell. After all, she was muttering it.

Steve extracted some white sheets and put the folder back, then sat down at his desk again and handed the papers to me. There were three pages of white bond paper, neatly typed, and in capitals at the top of the first page was the heading: "Subject: Shell Scott."

I read it all. Not with undistilled delight, no; but with growing admiration for some of Kay Dark's talents that I had remained blissfully unaware of even while they were being energetically exercised upon me, due to Kay's cleverness in keeping them in the background while focusing my attention upon other talents being energetically exercised upon me in the foreground—which, if I understood it, had to be one of her most impressive talents.

Yes, in retrospect, which we never seem to get around to until later, I had told Kay Dark—and *Exposé, Inc.*—quite a lot, even while thinking I was revealing nothing at all.

Subject was approached by Reporter in Pete's, a bar near subject's office in Hamilton Building, at approximately 5:30 P.M. on Monday, October 1. Reporter invented simple cover story designed to interest subject and explain alleged need for employing him.

During subsequent conversation, subject revealed the following information: (1) He had just accepted a case for a new client, something that "came up this morning." (2) His assignment was to locate a person later specified as a woman. (3) He had talked to his new client that day. NOTES: If subject's new client is Claude Romanelle, the mentioned conversation could only have been by telephone; long-distance records should reveal call (probably A.M.) to S. Memorial placed from —or possibly to—subject's office or apartment phone.

Kay had helpfully included both my phone numbers at that point.

Tuesday, October 2, P.M. Subject interviewed and disposed of thirteen fraudulent claimants to fortune mentioned in above mentioned Personal Message. Key question was maiden name of claimant's mother. (See other information in ad copy.) With one claimant, subject's interest was apparently aroused when she mentioned her alleged nickname, "Spree." Subject stated that if she was the lady he was looking for (the "real Michelle") she would have a little birthmark on chest (indicating left-breast area).

Wednesday, October 3. About 8:00 A.M. subject received phone call in apt., presumed to be from the "real Michelle." During conversation, he repeated the name Stooben (phonetic, verified by you as Steuben); later in conversation said, "Spree—from what name?" Agreed to meet her in his apt. Reporter observed this woman upon her arrival at hotel. She is approximately 25 or 26 years old, 5'6" tall, weight (overweight) perhaps 150 lbs, hair blond. Beautiful—*very.* Too risky to attempt pix, but Reporter can identify positively if required.

CONCLUSIONS: Connection between subject and Worthington/Romanelle confirmed. Subject unquestionably employed to locate Romanelle's daughter; accomplished this on morning of October 3. She is identified (as confirmed by you in referenced telephone call, logged 8:16 A.M. Wed. AZ time) as Michelle Esprit Romanelle, daughter of Claude Romanelle and Nicole Elaine Montapert (maiden name), now Mrs. Lawrence Steuben. Rom.'s purpose in wishing daughter found at this time is not known. Whether subject contacted by atty. Worthington or by Rom. not known. Basic assignment completed. END.

I was impressed. Probably Whistler had been, too. But, then, he'd told me that she was very good. I wondered if he knew just how good, and in how many ways. Curiously, I had a hunch—based in part on his reaction to her sudden arrival—that he probably did.

Both Steve and Kay waited silently while I speedily read the report, and when I placed the three pages back upon the desk, each of them was clearly waiting for my response. Presumably for different reasons.

"Wow," I said to Steve, "I see what you meant."

And to Kay, "Brilliant job. I mean it. But you left out at least one thing."

She gazed straight at me, unmoving, even her lips motionless, and appeared to be quite—well, apprehensive. I said, "When we met that second time, Tuesday night, you asked me if I'd found *my client's daughter* yet, if I'd found this Michelle I was looking for. I missed it at the time. Didn't really tag that slip until Wednesday morning sometime. Maybe you missed it, too, Kay?"

"Dammit to hell, I sure did," she said. But she was smiling. Quite obviously relieved.

"I remember saying I hadn't told you the lady's name was Michelle, and you explained you'd picked that up from my ad—the real impossibility, the client's daughter bit, went right by me, though."

"Me, too," she said. "I almost blew it, didn't I, Shell?" And then, apparently apropos of nothing, she softly added, "Thanks."

A few minutes later we had covered quite a bit of ground I was interested in. I had skimmed through the files on Groder, Foster, and Keats, making a few notes, but I spent more time on Alda Cimarron. In addition, because of my special interest in Romanelle, Whistler agreed to make a copy of his file for me, and turned the original over to young Weinstein for duplication.

It was nearly 10 A.M. when I leaned back in my chair and said, "Steve, when I asked you if the people I ran into were Mafia, maybe I wasn't too far off target. At least, these guys"—I waved a hand at the stack of bound files—"will do until the real Cosa Nostra stands up. But right now the main thing is for me to locate Romanelle. And I think I ought to know more about this Golden Phoenix situation Romanelle's into so heavily. The involvement of this guy, Cimarron, along with those Arizona *mafiosi*, doesn't smell good. Is it a scam?"

"Maybe," Steve said. "Maybe not. We don't know —that's why we're interested, digging into it. It's a real mine, a producing gold mine. It was shut down for several years, but the picture started getting interesting about four years ago. That's when Cimarron, and the people back of him, took over and started spending money."

"People back of him? Like who?"

"The money people. We'll get to that. As I was saying, the picture—and profit, rate of earnings increase—that's steadily improved for three years, and now suddenly the stock has doubled since the release of that incredible assay report I mentioned."

He got to his feet. "Fill Shell in on all that, will you, Kay? You know as much about it as I do. I'm going to get a copy of Toker's report."

As he went out, Kay got up and leaned forward to put her empty coffee cup on the desk. Somehow, when she sat down again, her skirt got hiked up far enough that it exposed a lot of bare thigh. A whole lot. To be honest, it exposed that smooth, firm, warm thigh nearly up to where the thigh ends and the next thing begins. It was, I confess, somewhat distracting, mainly because it was so pretty.

But I realized that this stupendously seductive exposure had to be an accident. No *way* any gal could accomplish so much just by sitting down. Even if it wasn't accidental, I'd have bet she couldn't do it twice in a row.

"Shell?" she said.

"Hmm?" My mind had been wandering.

"Thanks again."

"You're welcome. But . . . what are you welcome for?"

"For not telling Steve—what you could have."

"Forget it, Kay. It goes with the territory—I'm in the business, remember? Once I went to a PCP-pusher's house, got in by telling him I was the plumber, then hit him with a pipe wrench."

"Oh, that was a *lot* worse than what I did, wasn't it?"

"Well, yes, now that I think about it. Incidentally, as you've probably guessed, I checked out your rooms at the Dorchester. So where *were* those dazzling photographs of you taken?"

She looked not at me but directly at where Whistler would have been sitting if he'd still been in the room, which he wasn't. "In Chicago," she said, "two years ago, I was still married then. My ex—well, he wasn't my ex-husband then, not quite—took them." She moistened her lips, gazed intently at a filing cabinet. "Well, Steve said for me to tell you about GPX, so I'd better do what the man said."

"What's GPX?"

"That's our shorthand for Golden Phoenix Mines, part of the GPXM ticker symbol a broker punches into his keyboard when he wants a quote on the stock. Let's see, Steve mentioned that the earnings, and prospects, for GPX started getting better four years ago, that's when Liberty Enterprises installed Alda Cimarron as president of Golden Phoenix Mines—it was called Maricopa Minerals, Inc., before that time—and he started spending money, a lot of money."

"Hey, remember this is all new to me, Kay. What's Liberty Enterprises? Also, what do you mean the company *was* called Maricopa something?"

"Maricopa Minerals. It was a producing mine in the nineteen-thirties. Just a marginal producer, mining and milling under a thousand tons of ore a day, with a gold-purity ratio of around two tenths of an ounce of gold per ton. No big deal, but the stock was listed over-the-counter, and traded—if I remember, I haven't got the figures in front of me—from about twenty cents to just over a dollar then. It closed down during World War Two, and was never put back into production after the war."

She stood up, saying, "I think I'll have some more coffee. You want a cup, Shell?"

"No, I'll just watch."

She filled her cup from the tall silver pot and sat down again. That's all, just sat. I knew she couldn't do it twice.

"Liberty Enterprises," Kay continued, "is primarily a real estate development company. They own raw land and developed properties in a dozen states, including Arizona. For several years they've owned about a hundred thousand acres of bare land in Arizona—here in Maricopa County, in fact—but it's just desert, sand and cactus and rocks, *maybe* to be developed down the road sometime. But included as part of that land was the old, closed-down Maricopa Minerals property, including the nine-hundred-foot main shaft, everything that was in place when the mine was in production before. None of it in very good condition, of course."

Steve Whistler came back in carrying a manila folder in one hand, and sat behind his desk as Kay said, "I guess a number of people knew there had to be gold at the site, maybe a little, maybe a lot, but after the war nobody did anything about it. Besides, since the seventies that property has all been owned by Liberty Enterprises. Well, finally they took a good look at the property, and brought Cimarron in to oversee additional exploration and possible further development. He hired engineers, geologists, all the people needed, and in the first year they did a lot of diamond drilling and delineated a fairly significant ore body."

I said, "I don't understand much of this, but I guess the main thing is that there really is gold in the Golden Phoenix. Right? So what's the problem?"

Steve entered the conversation. "Maybe there isn't any. But a lot of things about GPX—including Cimarron and some of the other principals—smell to me. There's gold, sure. But, remember, it isn't down there under the ground in nuggets and bricks. Maybe there's a tenth of an ounce, or if you're lucky a quarter or half ounce, of gold in a ton of dirt. You can't even properly call mineralized rock 'ore' unless you can mine it, mill it, and sell it at a profit—the SEC won't allow it. Just as you can't call your reserves 'proven'—as opposed to the other two, lesser categories, 'probable' and 'inferred'—unless you can mine those reserves at a profit."

"Look." I lifted a hand. "I don't want to operate a mine. I don't even want to buy any stock in one. I just want to know if these guys are crooks or not."

Steve grinned. "It ain't that easy to tell, pardner. No question there's gold mineralization. I guess Kay told you GPX used to be Maricopa Minerals."

"She did."

"Well, when they were in production, before the war, Maricopa produced over seven million tons of ore grading around a fifth of an ounce gold per ton. They didn't shut down because they ran out of ore, but because of World War Two. So there's gold, but the question is how much and what's the gold-purity ration of the remaining ore. If this is corroborated, proven valid"—he waved the manila folder alongside his head—"then Golden Phoenix is a bonanza. Incredible. Especially with the price of gold where it is today."

"If what's corroborated?"

He slid the folder over the desk to me. "That is the latest assay report on new exploration of previously unexplored Golden Phoenix property beginning about three hundred yards from the main shaft. This report became available from Arizona Geological Laboratories only two weeks ago. To be precise, on Friday, September twenty-first —coincidentally, the same day we printed the October *Exposé*, so we weren't able to include it in the brief write-up on GPX that I showed you. Actual work of the assay was done by Thomas Toker, the company's chief geochemist. He has a good reputation, all the credentials. Take a look at the report."

I did. I looked at it for a full minute, and wound up understanding somewhat less than when Whistler had been waving it alongside his head. "Steve," I said, passing the folder back to him, "just explain the high points to me, will you? And keep it *simple*."

"I'll try." He looked at Kay and said, "You should probably get back into the Bennett subdivision hassle, don't you think?"

"Of course. I've got at least three hours' work on that." She got up and walked to the door, but then turned and said, "Now that you're here, Shell, don't be a stranger."

"I'll be in touch."

"Maybe we can . . . have lunch, or dinner or something, before you go back to California."

"Maybe."

She gave me a long look, and appeared to be sending a message to me with her lips. They definitely weren't waving good-bye, but seemed to be saying something more like *au revoir*, which is French for "four at the most."

Steve missed all that, peering at the report, then at me. "The first thing to understand," he said, "is that when somebody wants to find out if there's mineralization —little bits of gold, in this case—on a piece of property, he'll drill a bunch of holes in the ground. From these diamond-drill holes he'll pull up samples of the ore—or, more likely, just a core of plain old dirt—and ship it to an assay laboratory. There the geochemists and various technical people can, from the ground-up sample—which looks about like concrete mix, by the way—determine if there's any gold present. If there is—and often, along with gold, there'll be small amounts of silver, maybe copper, zinc, lead—the technicians can compute the number of ounces present per ton. Then an estimate of the tonnage of ore available, and total number of ounces of gold in that ore, plus the approximate cost per ounce to mine the stuff, can be made."

He lit up another Tareyton. "Basically that's what happened four years ago. Liberty made the decision to return the mine to production, installed Cimarron as president of the renamed Golden Phoenix, brought in geologists, engineers, equipment. They incorporated under the new name, issued stock, and were in business. The original stock issue sold for only twenty cents a share, but within a little more than a year they'd poured their first gold bar, and naturally the stock went up dramatically—it had actually started up months before, as the market anticipated that future production. Well, production has steadily increased, with the result that this year earnings will be well above last year's forty cents a share even without any extraordinary new discoveries or other developments. And the extraordinary has occurred."

I said, "I suppose that's this assay report you've mentioned two or three times."

"Yes, the Toker report. Briefly, GPX has been mining about four hundred tons of ore a day, with a gold-purity ratio of approximately a quarter of an ounce of gold per ton—we'll ignore the silver, the other metals, to simplify this for you."

"Please do. It's already over my head."

"You don't have to understand every detail, Shell. Just keep in mind what I said, which means production of about a hundred ounces of gold per day. Even after costs of production, that's been enough to produce earnings of twenty-five to thirty cents a share. A couple of months ago, Alda Cimarron announced plans to double production —from four hundred tons a day to eight hundred or more—over the next year to eighteen months. And then, last week, the Toker report was released showing phenomenal assay results on a new ore body adjacent to the one being milled at the site now."

"I guess those are the numbers I was looking blankly at in the report you handed me."

"Right. Here's what those numbers mean. If the figures are valid, and can be corroborated, it means Golden Phoenix has discovered drill-indicated reserves of at least a million additional tons of ore grading from fifteen hundredths to six tenths of an ounce gold per ton, with only ten percent of the known mineralized structure drilled so far. Those are exciting assay results. Or, in your language, this could mean not merely a doubling of earnings but perhaps ten times current earnings in the next year or two."

"So that's why the stock jumped up this past week?"

"You bet it is. And that move could be only the beginning."

"You said, if the figures could be corroborated. Corroborated how?"

"There'll have to be more drill holes pulled, and those samples assayed. Maybe by a different lab. If those results repeat, then I'll be buying the damned stock myself. So will everybody else I know. But until that's done, I'm withholding judgment."

"Do you know this Thomas Toker?"

"I know him by reputation—it's good. And I met him this past Friday. Interviewed him, told him I'd be quoting him in the lead article of this month's *Exposé*. He's young, bright, seemed forthcoming and candid. Told me the results excited him as much as they did anybody." Whistler paused. "These guys in assay labs, they might go weeks, even months, without finding any mineralization at all. Then here come samples from Alda Cimarron's chief geologist on the Golden Phoenix site and everybody in the lab gets turned on."

"Alda Cimarron," I said slowly. "I haven't got any proof yet, but there's a pretty good chance he was behind the shooting of Claude Romanelle. Now, I looked through your files on all these guys. Didn't have time to do more than skim them, but I noticed that Foster did time for wire fraud, and Groder fell for ADW and later a manslaughter rap. You mentioned Sylvan Derabian's two-year jolt. What I'm getting at, my impression is that the only one of these cats who *hasn't* been in the joint is Cimarron. Did I miss something?"

"No. He's never been in prison. Not quite. He was indicted for fraud back in Illinois about ten years ago, but was acquitted."

"What was the fraud?"

"Basic Ponzi scheme. He and some other promoters were selling guaranteed-get-rich courses at five thousand bucks a crack. The information wasn't bad, mostly copied from Napoleon Hill, Claude Bristol, Venice Bloodworth, a dozen or so of the classics. Without credit, needless to say, and changed enough so it wasn't clear-cut plagiarism. They guaranteed to pay their 'Investors in Abundance,' as they called the customers, twice their five-thousand investment if they hadn't made at least twenty thousand in the first eighteen months. The eighteen months gave them time to pay off some of the original investors with money coming in from new marks, but it was the guarantee and a couple other cute angles that got them into trouble with the Attorney General. Total of maybe five million bucks involved, and the end result was seven indictments, five convictions. Cimarron, as I said, was acquitted."

I took a look at the man's file again. Each of those *Exposé* "packages" was very complete, including from one to several photographs of the subject, plus dossiers, newspaper clippings, copies of police reports when available. In the Cimarron file were two photos of the man, one a copy of a two-year-old newspaper photograph, head and shoulders only, the professional lighting and background tagging it as a studio portrait. The other might have been the enlargement of a Polaroid snapshot. It was in color, and showed a large man wearing a dark suit about to open the door of a black Mercedes-Benz 560SL convertible. He was looking to his left, toward the camera, the dour expression on his heavy features indicating an almost total lack of pleasure at being photographed.

I estimated his size and weight, comparing it with the Mercedes coupe, which looked oddly smaller than it should have. "Am I wrong," I asked Steve, "or did this guy keep on growing when the rest of us stopped?"

"He's big, all right," Steve said. "He's my height—six-four—but I'd guess he's got close to a hundred pounds on me."

"That's pretty big."

"When I was out at the Golden Phoenix property, Cimarron was tramping around in snakeskin boots and white Bermuda shorts. Each of his calves looked like a full-grown midget, and his arms are almost as big. In those shorts, and a T-shirt, the man looked unreal, like those warped reflections in a fun-house mirror."

"So I won't ask him to arm-wrestle when I call on him. He doesn't sound like a real fun-house-type guy."

"He's not. You planning to see Cimarron, Shell?"

"My next stop, right after I leave here. I've got a couple of questions for the man that he probably won't want to answer."

"If he doesn't want to, he won't." Steve looked steadily at me from the pale blue eyes and said, "I guess you know what you're doing. But watch out for this one, Shell. He's mean."

"I guessed that from his picture."

"Wait till you see the original." He paused, looked at me silently for a few seconds, then said, "You'll agree you know a good deal more than when you came in here half an hour ago, right?"

"Right. You've been very helpful."

"That was the agreement, Shell. You've told me you shot Fred Keats, but little else. Anything you can add to that?"

"Yeah, there is. The agreement also is that none of this is for publication, none of it goes farther than your ears unless I turn you loose."

"Absolutely."

So I told him my story from the beginning, just hitting the high points, the facts as I knew them, but without details of no value to Whistler or *Exposé*. For example, when I finished, he knew I had come here with Romanelle's daughter but not where she was now, only that she was still "in Arizona." And I left out any explanation of the cover story Kay Dark had invented to justify her contacting a private investigator.

Steve leaned back, hooked one long leg over the arm of his chair, and said, "Keats had Romanelle's driver's license in his wallet, with his own picture on it?"

"Right. And his own license beneath it—that's how I knew his name."

"Which probably means Keats, or whoever he was acting for, grabbed Claude Romanelle."

"Grabbed him or killed him. The main reason I came here was on the chance I'd learn something to help me locate Romanelle—if he's alive."

He nodded. "I understand that. This other guy who was with Keats last night. He said he was Dr. Simpson?"

"Robert Simpson. No such physician listed in the phone book, or known to the state or Maricopa County medical groups. I checked that before I came here."

"Describe him again, will you?"

I repeated my earlier description of the short fat guy, adding, "Dark horn-rimmed glasses, thick enough to indicate a pretty good correction, dark eyes, bald, fleshy under the chin."

"Sounds like Bliss. Dr. Phillip Bliss. Little scar right here?" Steve rubbed a thumbnail along the left side of his jaw.

"Yeah, maybe. I think so. But I didn't spend a lot of time with him."

"And you were pretty busy." He pulled his leg from the chair arm, leaned toward his intercom, told Helen to have Weinstein bring in the Phillip Bliss file chop-chop. In thirty seconds General Weinstein materialized with one more thick file, placed it on Steve's desk, and vanished.

Steve opened the file, pulled out a five-by-seven glossy black-and-white photograph, and handed it to me.

"That's the guy," I said. "And he is also associated with Alda Cimarron, isn't he?"

"He is. In the Medigenic Hospital primarily. President of their Board of Directors. But he's also involved with Cimarron as co-investor in a few other enterprises, none of them illegal so far as I know. We haven't anything negative on him in the file."

"Well, you do now. And I've another reason to pay Cimarron a visit."

"Watch yourself. The man is more than just mean, I think he's a little warped. And goddamned dangerous."

"I'll watch it." I shook Steve's hand, and was on my way.

Chapter Thirteen

A COUPLE OF phone calls to Cimarron Enterprises and the Medigenic Hospital drew blanks. Alda Cimarron was not available at either location; nor, for that matter, was Dr. Phillip Bliss—Bliss was out of state, I was told. So I drove toward Paradise Valley, and Cimarron's home, without phoning ahead. If I was lucky, the big man might be there, and if so, I didn't intend to announce my visit.

The town of Paradise Valley is sixteen square miles of mostly desert, and a majority of the people who live there want to keep it that way. Each residence must be built on a minimum of one acre, and some of the big expensive houses sit on many times that amount of land —Cimarron's, for one. I had seen, in his *Exposé* file, a picture of the home along with a diagram of the area, so I knew the house was on a three-acre lot that looked like ten because the site was bordered by undeveloped land that wasn't owned by Cimarron, but still gave him more privacy, more "space," than any other homeowner near him in that exclusive area.

The address was on Desert Park Place, and with help from a street atlas I found myself on Lincoln Drive again, going west and retracing, in reverse, the route Spree and I had driven last night. This morning it was an unusual and quite pleasant drive between Mummy Mountain on the right and the greater mass of aptly named Camelback Mountain on my left, past the Mountain Shadows Resort —where I'd once stayed, during an earlier case—then El

Chorro, and finally the entrance to the Camelback Inn.

I rolled on by, aware of a gentle tightening of my stomach muscles when I realized I was no more than a quarter mile from Romanelle's house, where, not Fred Keats at this daylight hour—the police had probably completed their physical investigation at the crime scene, and by now both they and the corpse would be gone—but a thick smear of Keats's blood would still be slowly drying on that off-white carpet in the empty Arizona Room.

At Tatum Boulevard I turned right, then after half a mile or so swung left into Foothill Drive. In a few seconds I'd found Desert Park Place, slanting upward as it rose toward the low hills on my right. Soon after I headed up the narrow road, I recognized Cimarron's big beige and brown house ahead. Part of the acreage behind it constituted the base of one of the little mountains or large hills dotting the landscape out here. The house itself was situated on a gentle rise sloping up toward the craggy hill behind it, and thus was higher than any of the other nearby homes. With what I guessed would be ten rooms, on three expensive elevated acres affording a spectacular view of Paradise Valley and Scottsdale, the property was probably worth well over a million bucks.

A gray cement driveway rose alongside the house and curved around behind it. On the far side of the house, beyond what I guessed was the property's edge, a dirt road, or at least a rutted path about wide enough for a single car or truck, slanted up the hillside. Probably access to some of those still-vacant lots for a developer or property owner; or maybe just evidence that adventurous high school kids had come up here at night to enjoy the view, and other pleasures.

I drove up the driveway, parked, followed a pebbled path that led around to the front of the house and ten-foot-high double doors there, poked the inch-wide beige button that I assumed was the doorbell. Inside, a softly metallic booming sound accompanied my pressure on the button. But nothing else happened, nobody appeared. I walked around the side of the house to its rear, where there was an oval-shaped swimming pool, more desert landscaping, a couple of chaise longues covered with brightly patterned cushions. But no people.

A narrow pathway, made of three-foot lengths of oil-stained railroad ties set in the earth, extended from beyond the far side of the pool toward the rock-covered hill behind the property. And twenty yards or so up that path was what appeared to be a separate small patio, or at least a cement deck upon which sat a low white table and three white chairs, a large black metal charcoal broiler, and a massive wooden bar with a couple of bottles in view upon it. The whole thing was covered by a canvas roof shielding it from the burning sun.

The fourth white chair had been pulled away from the table, and in it sat a large man with broad burly shoulders. He was facing away from me, unaware of my approach as I skirted the pool and walked over the railroad ties toward him. From the size of that back, and the meatiness of those shoulders, I assumed the man was Alda Cimarron. His right arm was extended but hidden by his body, so I couldn't at first see what he was holding. Then he swung that arm right, body turning slowly, and I saw the gun. It looked like a long-barreled .22 target pistol, with something odd about the barrel, but most of the weapon was concealed from my view by the man's big hand.

He kept turning, as if tracking a moving target, aiming far to his—and my—right. I glanced in that direction and saw, thirty or forty yards away on the down-slanting hillside, a puff of dirt, got a quick glimpse of something running. Out here, it was probably a jackrabbit or rock squirrel, maybe even a Gambel's quail or roadrunner making very speedy tracks.

The man was apparently shooting his odd-looking gun, occupying himself with a little target practice. But I hadn't heard any sound. None at all. No crack of gunshot or even the muted *spat* of a silenced pistol. It gave me a queer feeling; it was odd.

He turned back to his left again, put the gun down in his lap, doing something with it. By then I was only a few feet from the man, and as my foot scraped on the cement deck he turned his head toward me, saw me, appraised me. He didn't jump to his feet, jerk around, say anything. Just swung that big head toward me, slowly, almost ponderously, and poked me with his eyes. It was Alda Cimarron, all right, and, man, those eyes were cold. Cold as a prison camp in Siberia, friendly as measles.

I stopped a couple feet from his chair and looked down at him. "Mr. Cimarron?" I asked.

He took his time about replying. The long-barreled target pistol was in his right hand, and he'd already lifted the loading lever, dropping the base of the bolt down and exposing the rear of the just-fired cartridge case. Deliberately, with thumb and index finger, he took the case out and dropped it onto the cement deck, then uncurled the last three fingers of his left hand, exposing three .22 long-rifle bullets against his fat palm. With his thumb he separated one of them from the others and, again with thumb and finger, gripped the bullet and inserted it into the gun's chamber. Then he pressed the loading lever back down but didn't push down the smaller trigger-cock lever. So the gun was loaded but wouldn't fire, not until the trigger was set—at least, it wouldn't fire *if* the gun was what I thought it was.

After all that, he said, "I'm Cimarron. Who are you and what do you want?"

The voice was low, rumbling, almost metallic like that sound inside the house when I'd poked the bell. The man was big, even bigger than I'd envisioned him. A more appropriate word would have been "massive." He was wearing the same kind of outfit Steve Whistler had mentioned seeing him in at the mine, a white T-shirt and white Bermuda shorts, and Steve had been right about those calves. They looked like flesh barrels. But they fit with the rest of him, including the barrel chest stretching his T-shirt, the almost grossly swollen thighs filling the truncated legs of his shorts, and the thick muscular neck holding up the large and apparently unhappy head.

This guy had to weigh three hundred pounds, maybe even more, and seated in the too-small chair he looked like a weight-lifting Buddha suffering from aggravated constipation. He wasn't larded with muscle as the phrase goes, but muscled with muscle, like a pro football guard or maybe a guard and tackle squeezed together in a large squasher. That big oversize head was almost flat on top, and bald in the middle, with a crown of feathery brown hair high on his forehead and wispy around the sides over his elephantine ears.

"I'm Shell Scott," I said. "I'm a private investigator from Los Angeles, and I flew up here to ask you a couple of questions. Among other things."

"Sure you did," he said, in that bottom-of-the-barrel rumble. His eyes were unmoving on my face.

They were strangely mottled blue eyes, not much warmer than chips from an Arctic iceberg, with visible red veins snaking through the dull white around the irises. Below the staring eyes was a large fleshy nose with flaring nostrils, each crammed with a small jungle of tangled hairs, overflowing and drooping downward like a comically misplaced mustache. Big square teeth that showed when he said "Sure," slightly crooked. Flushed face, ruddy complexion. Thick beige-brown brows tangled like the mustache in his nose, growing together in the middle. His left hand was relaxed in his lap, fingers curled and cupping the long-rifle slugs. His right hand, holding the long-barreled pistol, rested against his hairy right thigh a couple of inches above the knee. The gun's barrel was slanted in my direction, but not directly at me. Not quite.

And now I could see what it was that had struck me as odd about that barrel. It was three or four times as fat as it should have been, close to an inch in diameter, which probably meant that the entire barrel had been enclosed within a larger metal tube. The way Cimarron was holding the pistol, I could see the dark neoprene rubber seal at the muzzle end. And I remembered the last similarly "suppressed" gun I'd seen, a Ruger .22 long-rifle automatic pistol that had been expertly modified by a gun wizard in Florida. So, though I couldn't see them, I could guess that inside the fat barrel was a series of metal washers, each with a hole in its center to allow passage of the original —but now perforated—barrel, and in the rest of the washer a pattern of holes and baffles to swirl expanding

gases around and dissipate them. A silencer. The entire
eight inches in front of the gun's frame was a combination
of the original barrel plus an eight-inch silencer.

"Like what?"

It seemed such a long time since his last words that I had
to think back to my original comment.

"Questions about one of your associates," I said.
"Claude Romanelle. And a few other things."

One corner of Cimarron's wide mouth lifted an eighth of
an inch. In almost anyone else, I might have thought it was
the start of a smile. But that heavy sullen face looked as if a
genuine smile would crack it down the middle and leave
the pieces dangling from those eyebrows and the hairs in
his nose.

"You flew up here just to ask me P.I. questions about
Claude? Bullshit."

I could feel the familiar slow flush start creeping up my
neck. But I said quietly, "I mentioned that I had some
other reasons for coming to Arizona. But I'm beginning to
think that's the main one. Especially since the longer I'm
here the more questions I've got."

"Bullshit," he said again. Then he repeated stolidly,
"Like what?"

The flush was feeling a little prickly now, reaching my
ears. "Like, could you tell me where Mr. Romanelle might
be now, Mr. Cimarron? Like is Mr. Romanelle still alive,
Mr. Cimarron? Like, have any of your friends shot him
again lately? Like, where can I find your associates, Jay
Groder, or Andy Foster, or Dr. Phillip Bliss, or Godzilla?
Like that, Mr. Cimarron."

It all just rolled off him. The little bunches of muscle
rose microscopically at both sides of his mouth this time,
and I even caught a glint of light on the lower edges of his
two front teeth. It was, perhaps, the most unenthusiastic
smile I had ever seen.

"Beats the hell out of me," he said. "It just beats the hell
out of me, Mr.—was it Scott?"

"That's right."

It was curious. Strange. The moment we'd looked at
each other, a couple of minutes ago, even if I had never

heard of Alda Cimarron, I would have been certain he knew not only who I was but more than a little about me. And wasn't overjoyed by any of it. There had been, too—and still was—between us a kind of instant and tangible antagonism, something not imagined but actually felt, a perceptible *push*, almost like the repulsion you become aware of when you move the like poles of two magnets toward each other.

Clearly, there was no way this overly muscled, sullen, and obnoxious beefball and I were ever going to get along; and right then I knew, with the same conviction a man falling off a seaside cliff has about landing unattractively on the rocks below, that Cimarron and I were going to collide, crash together somehow, and one of us was going to crunch onto the rocks. It would for sure happen eventually; sooner or later; maybe now.

But it didn't *have* to be now. Sweet reason demanded that I be nice for a while longer. So I said mildly, "Thanks for answering my questions in such helpful detail, Mr. Cimarron. Incidentally, that's a good-looking piece." I indicated the pistol in his hand, still not pointing at me, not quite. "Getting in a little target practice? Knocking off the neighbors' kids, maybe?"

He scowled. Even before that, his visage had not been such as to encourage the timid. But, scowling, brows pulled lower, corners of the wide mouth depressed, he looked a lot like one of those squat statues explorers find down there in the South American jungles. And not much more fun.

I went on, heedless of sweet reason, "Yeah, I'd say that's a custom job—must be, unless it came equipped with a supercharger, or whatever that thing is on the front end there. I'd say single-shot target piece, probably a modified Hammerli free pistol going for around . . . what? Fifteen hundred clams maybe?"

The squat statue did not move. At least, not the whole statue. Only its nostrils stirred, flaring slightly and then subsiding as breath was sucked in and snorted out, in and out again, disturbing the little jungles of hair in those nasal orifices. For a queer moment I imagined little twittering creatures in there, clinging to the microscopic equivalent of vines and roots and tree trunks, waiting for the storm to subside so they could get on with their lunches. I also thought for a moment that Cimarron might get even more violent, but he merely turned his head and gazed briefly at the far horizon.

When he looked back up at me, the scowl was gone and he said, almost pleasantly, "You got a pretty good eye, pal. This started out as a Hammerli Model one-fifty, but the guy who owned it had it silenced so he could use it as a takeout gun. It's very good—they tell me—for killing people when you don't want to make noise doing it. You want it *real* quiet, then you use subsonic ammo, muzzle velocity of maybe seven hundred feet per second." He opened his left hand, glanced at the two remaining long-rifle slugs in his palm. "Like these, from Fiocchi." Then he looked up at me again and said, "I, of course, only use the gun for target practice, plinking at rocks and twigs."

"Of course," I said. "You hit any? Rocks and twigs, I mean?"

"Well," he said, "I've never missed the mountain."

That one surprised me. It sounded almost like levity. Cimarron shifted in his chair, pressed down the Hammerli's trigger-cock lever, which sprang back up by itself. So the gun was now ready to fire. Meaning, I presumed, that Cimarron intended to fire it. Hopefully, not into me.

All around us were scraggly mesquite trees and creosote bushes that grow all over the desert, here covering the earth and sloping hillside along with some feathery cassia and manzanita trees. About forty feet before us was one creosote bush larger than most, with a narrow crooked spire sticking almost straight up into the air at its top.

Cimarron, still seated, raised his right arm, intricately carved and convoluted wooden grip of the gun snugly nestled into and around his big paw, sighted briefly, and fired. The sound was a sort of *ffft*, no louder than a girl blowing somebody a kiss. But the tip of that upright spire disintegrated.

"That's good shooting," I said. "Damned good."

"Not bad. But you can probably do better, right? Wanna give it a try?"

Actually, I didn't. It was his gun, his party. But I couldn't very well refuse, not when he so obviously wanted me to make a fool of myself. "Sure," I said, with only a small sinking feeling, "why not? But one more little thing, if you don't mind."

He waited, seeming quite pleased with himself. Either because of his making that very good—perhaps even somewhat lucky—shot, or because he'd maneuvered me into attempting to match his already-accomplished bull's-eye, his disposition appeared to have improved slightly. And with him, slightly seemed like a lot. Whatever the reason, when I asked my next question, he not only answered at some length but appeared to enjoy responding.

What I said was, "One other little thing, Mr. Cimarron. I know you're president of Golden Phoenix Mines, and that the shares are trading at about fourteen now—largely, I gather, because of a recent assay report. I talked to a couple of people who say the stock might go to twenty. But some others think it might wind up at a buck and a half. Any comment?"

He startled me. He laughed. He got his mouth clear open and let out a bull-like roaring sound and slapped his thigh with the fist holding the .22 cartridges.

"A buck and a half?" he said, still snorting a little. "I can guess who told you that. The same guy who went long in the market on Black Friday. Or maybe the guy who sold all his International Tabulator just before they changed the name to IBM. Somebody with his head so full of bullshit he craps out his ears, that's who. Yeah, Phoenix isn't twenty yet—by the by, this morning's quote is sixteen and a half bid, pal, you must have got your numbers a day or two back."

"O.K., so it's sixteen and a half. But that's today, and the people I talked to are worried about tomorrow—"

"Screw 'em. Those goddamn losers are *always* worried about tomorrow. I tell you Phoenix is sixteen and a half today, in a week it'll be twenty, and in a month or two it could be forty."

"You giving me a tip?"

"If you've got enough sense to take it, yeah. Too good to be true, right? Worry about tomorrow, right? Scott, how much do you know about GPXM—Golden Phoenix, in case you're a market idiot?"

"Not much. I know it's a former producing mine that was called Maricopa something. And three or four years back, Liberty Enterprises—whoever that is—asked you to check it out, get it running again, named you president, and the stock's done pretty well since then."

"Yeah, pretty well. First year earnings a dime, next year twenty cents, last year forty cents, and we might hit eighty this year, still got a chance—there's nearly three months left. Do you understand what I'm telling you, or are you too goddamned dumb to know I've just described a rate of earnings increase of *one hundred percent*? Earnings smack-doubled each year since day one, and it's gonna happen again."

The change in Cimarron's attitude, his earnestness, and even his expression—which, while not now exactly cute, was at least not horrifying—amounted to a metamorphosis. Either he was a great actor—and most con men are actors deserving of solid-gold Oscars—or he really enjoyed talking about his Golden Phoenix, about mining and shares and rates of earnings increases, maybe even believed what he was saying.

And what he was saying, not having stopped yet, was, "Another thing you're dead wrong about, Scott. Liberty didn't ask *me* to turn Maricopa into Golden Phoenix and make it one hell of a mine—I asked *them*."

"You lost me there."

"I got a hunch that's easy to do. But in this case it's understandable. I'm going to assume you don't know your ass, don't know mining, don't know gold, don't know shit."

"Pretty quick, you're going to bug me—"

"I live in Arizona, right here in Maricopa County. Love it. This place is the nuts. And I keep my eye out for the big cracker, all the time. Now, the Maricopa Minerals property—Golden Phoenix today—isn't far from the Roddy Resources Bighorn property here. A while back,

Roddy brought in an independent engineer to work some of their land and I got a copy of his report. In it he said, about Bighorn, that it had—and I can quote it exact for you, verbatim—'an excellent possibility for the delineation of several million tons of gold-bearing material in the .05 to .10 ounce per ton range which might be mined by low-cost, bulk mining methods.' Now, that's low mineralization, nothing to get me steamed, see? But Roddy drilled thirty-five rotary holes with twenty-eight of them confirming gold mineralization over very impressive widths ranging up to—and here it gets a little more interesting—up to .410 ounces per ton. O.K.? You with me so far, Scott?"

"Well—"

He went right on, "The old Maricopa is just about on strike with that Roddy ore body, and I got a hold of all the old Maricopa Minerals records—skip the how, it's not important—and studied the development work the former operators did back then, in the thirties and forties, memorized the whole megillah like it was the new *Penthouse* special-beaver issue. Those records told me the gold mineralization continued down to a vertical depth of nearly two thousand feet. They never did explore those lower levels, they never went below nine hundred feet—well, hell, gold was thirty-five back then, no wonder. More important than that—we're getting up to the latest assay you mentioned. You were talking about last week's AGL assay report, right?"

I assumed AGL was Arizona Geological Laboratories, and said, "If you mean the Thomas Toker report, I've seen it."

He blinked, pulled the beige-brown brows down over the red-veined eyes. "You've *seen* it, huh? Well, then you know what gangbusters those numbers are."

"Not exactly. I didn't understand much of it."

"Well, it's goddamned good numbers. But what I was getting at a second ago, in those old records there was *also* a report of mineralization due east of the main shaft. They never mapped it, never did a thing about it. Just took the first look and then died on it. Skip the rest. I went to Liberty, told them what I had, and talked them into putting me in charge. Which they did, along with putting up the bucks. Big bucks. Of course, the old shafts were flooded, we had to clean the mine out, buy machinery —*big* bucks."

"I'm kind of interested in that AGL report. Didn't those diamond hole cores, or whatever the hell, just come out of nowhere? Sort of out of the blue, say, as in blue sky?"

Cimarron ignored the implied reference to con games and said irritably, "Diamond *drill* holes, it's a goddamned diamond *drill . . ."* He shook the big head, pulling his lips back far enough to show the square teeth again, not in a smile but a grimace. "Shit," he said. Then, "You asked, I'll tell you. And you'll probably know less then than you do now, which'll be under zero. I always had a gut feeling about that mineralization east of the shaft, and earlier this year I took my chief engineer out there and told him how and where I wanted the holes drilled. He thought I was nuts. I told him, drill 'em. I spit on the ground, and that's where the first hole went. We pulled seven holes, all in a line due north, each one about four hundred feet farther out on the line. My man just about crapped his shorts, but I told him, *do* it." He stopped, looked up at me, rubbing his big chin. "Maybe it hadn't occurred to you yet, Scott. But when I tell somebody *do* it, I don't remember the last time anybody didn't."

"When I figure out what the hell you said, maybe it'll impress me. But probably it won't. Weren't you telling me about drilling for diamonds, or—"

"Shit," he said, not for the first time, grimacing yet again. "So we pulled those seven. That's some of the ore samples AGL assayed for us. First two, forget it. But every one of the next five, we hit ore-grade intersections. It was that once-in-a-lifetime crapshoot, all naturals. Listen to those five assay results. The first hole intersected fourteen feet averaging .151 ounces of gold per ton. The second assayed .198 ounces of gold per ton over eighteen feet. The third, .214 ounces over twenty-one feet. The fourth, .437 over twenty-three feet, and the last .611 over twenty-two feet. You get the picture? That grab you? The farther north we went, the better the mineralization got. We're drilling more holes, and the next assay results should make the stock go crazy."

"Is AGL—this guy Toker—doing those assays, too?"

"Yeah, but there's going to be so much holler we'll probably duplicate the results with a different lab, just to pacify the goddamn losers. This is the big one, I can feel it in my balls. Before we're through we'll prove two million tons of ore minimum with a gold-purity ratio of up to .6 and maybe better than that. Shit, man, Campbell Red Lake mines a grade of only .62 purity. There's a billion down there, a billion bucks, a goddamn billion smackeroos, maybe twice that, I can feel it in my *balls*. Does that grab your ass, Scott?"

"Well . . . Maybe if you could show me some Kruger-rands, or those gold coins with pretty pictures of pandas—"

"*Sheee-it*," he bellowed. "Get the goddamned hell *out* of here, Scott."

"Temper," I said pleasantly. "I guess I don't get to try out that little popgun of yours."

I thought he might throw the popgun at me, but instead he slowly smiled. Which meant I could see a little bit of his two front teeth. "Oh, yeah," he said. "I wouldn't want to miss that, would I? Being a P.I., you must be a real hotshot, right?" He didn't expect an answer to that, and didn't get one.

Cimarron reloaded the gun and sealed the chamber, handed the gun to me uncocked. I didn't really care a whole lot about firing the pistol, particularly at anything I was supposed to hit, but I did want to get a closer look at it. The handsomely crafted piece was a beauty, no doubt about it. Its large wooden wraparound grip, probably mahogany, covered most of my hand as I held the gun. The right side and rear of the grip were crosshatched to provide friction against the shooter's palm and thumb pad, while the left side and front were scalloped with grooves that would fit Cimarron's big fingers. Cimarron's, not mine.

I looked along the barrel, not aiming over the front sight but just getting a feel for the weapon's weight and balance. "That big silencer makes it a little difficult to aim," I said.

"I managed to aim it, hotshot. Besides, we wouldn't want to annoy the neighbor kids' ears, would we?"

I smiled at him. "Certainly not, Mr. Cimarron."

I hefted the gun, feeling at a distinct disadvantage in what Cimarron was clearly viewing as some kind of contest between us. Guys like Cimarron love games they can't lose. What bugged me was that I couldn't easily avoid playing at this point, couldn't avoid letting him win. And I sure didn't like letting this guy feel he was one up on me this early in the game. Well, if I couldn't outshoot him with his own fancy pistol, maybe I could keep him from knowing how badly I missed; maybe I could change the rules a little.

So I said, "I'm not much good at plinking. No incentive. So why don't I pretend a guy out there"—I waved the gun over half an acre—"just took a shot at me, and missed. And I've got to drill him." I tapped the end of my nose. "Right here."

"Sure. Why don't you?" I could see three or four of his big teeth now. This was fun. This was aces wired in five-card stud. "Where is this guy, Scott? Sitting at the bar here?"

"No."

A mockingbird had flown past our canvas-covered patio and I watched it swoop, turn, flutter down to land on the projecting limb of a paloverde tree out in front of us. In front, and at least a hundred feet away. The bird had landed near the end of a thin smooth branch snaking out a couple of feet farther than any of the other branches. It, and the bird on it, were about six feet above the ground.

"That mockingbird just lit on the poor guy's head," I said with forced cheerfulness.

"Tame bird, huh?" Cimarron said, almost chuckling.

"No," I said quietly. "The guy's Fred Keats. And the bird is clairvoyant. He knows Fred's gone."

No chuckles now. Those unhealthy-looking eyes of Cimarron's opened wider, locked on mine. I could see those red veins clearly in the dull whites around the mottled blue irises. Quite a long time passed, or so it seemed, before Cimarron's glare softened a little, wavered, and he looked back toward the paloverde tree.

"For Christ's sake, quit stalling and take your shot," he rumbled.

"I'm not stalling, Mr. Cimarron. I'm waiting. You wouldn't want me to miss Fred and hit an innocent bird, would you?"

Yeah, he would. The look he gave me was one of monumental contempt. Contempt mixed with growing anger. I was standing only about a foot from the seated man, holding the gun down by my right thigh, and he clamped the fingers of his left hand around my wrist, reaching with his other hand for the pistol.

This guy was astonishingly strong. His fingers dug into my wrist like gear teeth grinding. I do not have small and delicate bones, like a bird's, say; but for a second I thought he might break something. Cimarron pulled the .22 pistol from my fingers, his left hand still clamped around my wrist. I squeezed my own left hand into a fist, shifted my feet—as the pressure went away.

I was hot. I was suddenly boiling. I do not like being touched even in friendly camaraderie by those guys who like to slap you on the back and dislocate your cervical vertebrae, or squeeze your shoulder in hearty good fellowship. And when the touch or slap or squeeze is *not* friendly, then something extreme and undoubtedly quite poisonous happens to my blood and various glands.

I had hauled back my left arm and was about to cream this guy, but he wasn't even looking at me. Instead, he had cocked the gun and was aiming toward the paloverde tree, toward that mockingbird on poor Fred's head.

' I jabbed my right hand out, fingers extended, and hit the gun's barrel, knocked it six inches to the side.

It's possible that pleased Cimarron less than his grabbing my wrist had pleased me. His already ruddy face got pink and then quite red. I could see the pulsing of a wide vein over his left temple. My right wrist still ached and I rubbed it, kneaded it, flexed and wiggled the fingers for a few seconds.

Then I said, "Cimarron," for the first time not prefacing his name with "Mr.," "let me give you fair warning. If you ever latch on to me like that again, I'll deck you."

He rose easily to his feet, and for the first time I was looking *up* at those cold red-veined eyes. This guy was huge. He blotted out the little mountain behind him, a flesh mountain himself. "You really think you could do that, Scott?" His voice was soft.

"Probably," I said. "But I'll never know for sure until I try, will I?"

We stood there, angrily eyeballing each other like two idiot kids in the schoolyard. Finally I held my right hand out, palm up, and looked at the gun. He hesitated, then placed the pistol in my palm.

I hadn't seen the mockingbird fly away, but it was gone. I could barely see the little branch it had been sitting on. I took one step to my left and turned my back on Cimarron, stood at right angles to the almost invisible branch I was supposed to shoot at.

Then I took a long slow breath, let half of it out, and spun right, bringing the gun up in both hands at the ends of my extended arms as my right leg swung around in a quarter circle. When my shoe slapped against the cement deck, I went down into a half crouch, legs wide apart, finger starting to press gently on the pistol's trigger. I wasn't sure I could see the selected branch, but I saw the tree and then *ffft*.

I wasn't even sure if I'd hit the mountain. No matter; I'd accomplished my purpose. I'd selected a target so far away it was an almost impossible shot to begin with, and I'd been moving enough that Cimarron would very likely have been watching me, not my target, and thus wouldn't have any idea how widely I might have missed it.

Wrong. Sometimes what you hear compensates for what you can't see. Burglars in a store know the cops are coming because they hear the sound of sirens. A pro golfer in the lead of a tournament knows if the challenger, a hole ahead, made or missed his putt by the noise of the crowd. And I knew I must—somehow, by a crazy fluke—have hit that target I hadn't even really aimed at, knew it by the sound from Cimarron.

It was no more than the same old thing, but very softly

breathed, his softest word of the day. Just that same old "Shit."

I squinted through the heat waves rising from the desert floor, tried to focus a hundred feet away, still not quite ready to believe. But Cimarron was right; he'd called it with an almost beautiful economy of language. I'd hit that shiny branch about a foot from its end; the tip, still attached to the rest of the smooth limb, dangled straight down toward the ground, swaying slightly.

I handed Cimarron the gun.

"You're pretty good yourself," he said grudgingly.

"Pretty lucky," I said. "Well, see you around." I turned and started back toward the house.

I'd taken half a dozen steps, out from under the canvas shade into bright sunlight, when Cimarron, twenty feet behind me, called, "Scott."

I glanced back at him.

He put on another version of that unenthusiastic smile. "See *you* around," he said.

Passing the corner of his house, on the way to my rented Capri, I looked back. Cimarron was halfway to the house himself. No more target practice today. It gave me a little satisfaction to have screwed up his game. But only a little.

The inside of the car was already hot. I put the air-conditioning on high, cracked the front windows an inch, as I drove out the drive and swung left.

I started to pass that narrow dirt road I'd seen earlier, but then stopped, backed into it, kept backing up the rutted dirt for thirty yards. When I stopped, I figured this was just about where Cimarron had been aiming his special pistol when I'd first spotted him. Somewhere around here I'd seen a slug kick up a puff of dirt, had glimpsed a rabbit or some small animal running rapidly through the cactus and paloverde.

I didn't really expect to find anything, but I did. It only took half a minute. It was about a foot from the tangled base of a creosote bush. It was small, fluffy. Gray and white, still limber, loose and warm. A hole had been torn through its neck, half an inch behind the little pink collar.

It was a dead cat.

Chapter Fourteen

THOMAS TOKER LIVED on 20th Street south of Glendale Avenue.

I drove down Lincoln Drive until it became Glendale, took a left at 20th. In Phoenix, houses with even numbers are on the north and west sides of the streets, so I knew Toker's odd-numbered home would be on the east to my left. It was one of those either/or moments we usually aren't aware of, because if I had been looking the other way I would probably never have seen Andy Foster.

But because I was checking houses on my left, I saw the red Subaru XT coupe pull out from the curb in a hurry, half a block ahead. And because it accelerated so fast, rear wheels spinning and squealing as it started to pick up speed, I took a good look at the car, and the man alone inside, when it raced by me toward the Glendale Avenue intersection I'd just left.

He eyeballed me, too. And kept on eyeballing, those already surprised-looking glimmers assuming an expression of much greater surprise, so great indeed that they appeared almost entirely white in the consternation of his chocolate-brown face as his brows shot upward and his jaw sagged open. It occurred to me briefly, though I did not dwell on the thought, that I could now recall three separate occasions when slim, good-looking—usually—Andrew H. Foster had lamped me; and on each occasion it was as though Foster had at the same instant become aware that a laxative he didn't even know he'd taken was suddenly working irresistibly. I'm surprised he didn't run clear off the street and into somebody's cacti, because he was still looking at me—head out the window and looking *back* at me—when I turned to examine house numbers again.

As I had assumed, the number I wanted was right where Andy's Subaru had been parked. I'd phoned AGL, where Toker worked, and knew he hadn't reported in today; he had instead called in sick, and therefore was presumably at home. I made a U-turn, pulled to the curb at the spot Foster had just vacated.

Toker's house sat back from the street behind a lawn rather than desert landscaping of rock and cactus. Perhaps in the winter it had been green and well tended, but it looked neglected now. There are a lot of ryegrass lawns and backyards in the Phoenix-Scottsdale area, but the furnace-like heat of Arizona summers kills most rye so it's often oversown with Bermuda, which, if given a lot of water, sometimes survives the blistering of June and July.

Toker's lawn, bisected by a cement walk leading to the front door of the house, hadn't been mowed for two or three weeks. There were patches of shaggy green, but most of the grass had died down, turned yellow, and now in early October the yard looked diseased, scabrous and sickly.

I got out of the car, walked over cement squares toward the house. It was two stories, frame construction, painted white with yellow trim. A couple of shiny-leaved citrus trees were planted at the lot's left edge, a large silk oak on the right. At the front door I located the bell—whoever last painted the house had painted right over the bell itself —poked the button. After half a minute I rang again, then knocked vigorously. The door, ajar, swung inward a foot. I pressed my knuckles against the wood and pushed the door open wide.

Judging by Andy Foster's hasty departure, it was reasonable to assume he'd been inside, left the door open on leaving. I felt a gentle prickle of coolness along my spine, in the hairs at the back of my neck. I stepped inside, swung the door closed behind me.

"Mr. Toker? Thomas Toker?"

On my way here I had stopped at a sporting goods store and purchased a box of .38 S&W cartridges, so the revolver in my clamshell holster was now fully loaded. I touched its checked grip with my fingers as my voice boomed in the house, died into whispers. On my right was a large living room, and beyond it part of what looked like a dining area, end of polished dark table and three or four chairs visible from here. I walked straight ahead, past a stairway on my left leading up to the second floor, through a large kitchen adjacent to the dining room, on into what looked like a den or office.

I could feel my nostrils flare as I breathed in the same distinctive, acrid odor I'd smelled last night in Romanelle's Arizona Room. Burned gunpowder. A shot, or shots, had been fired in here. And not very long before. Strips of bright sunlight slanted into the room through partly closed plastic miniblinds, fell on nubby variegated gray and blue carpet. The ceiling was finished with squares of charcoal-colored cork, and there were half a dozen framed sepia hunting prints on the walnut-paneled walls.

On my right was a large curved couch, low blond wood table before it, two overstuffed chairs near the table. On my left, a wide low desk of the same blond wood as the coffee table, highly polished. Behind the desk, a large padded leather chair with brass buttons outlining its wide arms and high curved back. I could see Toker sprawled on the nubby carpet—a man, at least, and whoever it was there was no question that the man was dead.

He was facedown on the carpet, his head—what was left of it—and shoulders visible from where I stood just inside the room, his hips and legs hidden behind the desk. I placed my feet carefully, stepped closer to the body. He was wearing dark brown trousers and brown shoes, a beige sport shirt. There were two bullet holes in his back and one in the right side of his head, behind the temple and well above the ear.

My heart was pounding. Without being aware of it, I had stopped breathing when I saw the body. I let out my breath, sucked in some lungfuls of air, then carefully stepped over the corpse, squatted near it. There was almost no blood around those two holes in the beige sport shirt. No wonder. The bullet that had gone in over the man's right ear, after ripping through the brain, had lifted off a hand-sized chunk of curved skull and forehead on its way out.

There wasn't much blood anywhere—nothing like that spout of scarlet from Fred Keats's throat last night—but there was a lot of brain in a lot of places. Hunkered down by the body, I could see the slanting sunlight shining on clots of jellylike pinkish-gray brain tissue at dozens of spots on the nubby carpet. Three feet beyond the shattered head, a larger wrinkled clot glistened, still attached to a curving white fragment of skull.

The man's right cheek was pressed against the carpet, one eye half open and staring at forever, flap of forehead skin hanging down over the other eye and bridge of nose. The face was distorted, but not so misshapen that I couldn't recognize it as the face in pictures of Thomas Toker I'd so recently seen in Steve Whistler's office.

I straightened up, stepped with care over behind the desk. On its highly polished top were a phone, an ashtray half filled with cigarette butts, a calendar, a five-by-seven white notepad with about half of its pages still unused, two pencils, a ballpoint pen with its tip exposed, a pocket dictionary. By leaning to my right I could see that the shiny desk surface was dulled, smeared over much of its left half, by what might have been tiny droplets or a spray of blood, but with a clear and shiny area, like a large *L* or right-angled triangle, at the right edge of that smear, near me at the center of the desk.

Using a handkerchief over my fingers, I opened the desk drawers and went through them quickly, finding nothing of interest. I picked up the notepad, holding it by the edges, toward the light and aslant before my eyes, looking for marks, indentations, impressions from anything that might have been written on the page or pages above. Nothing. The page was virgin, clean, without a dent or ripple.

I made a quick tour of the house—very quick; I was anxious to get out of here. However, back in the den, using my handkerchief again, I picked up the desk phone. I intended to call Steve Whistler, tell him what I'd found here and ask for information I needed from him now. But seeing Toker's shattered skull, an ugly reminder of sudden death at Romanelle's home last night, made me think of Spree again. Since about 8:20 A.M. when I'd left the Registry Resort, I hadn't spoken to her. And thinking of her now squeezed a knot of anxiety in my stomach that had been there ever since I'd left her alone this morning. I couldn't think of any reason why she shouldn't be safe in our room; still, that grawing anxiety wouldn't go away, stayed with me, a persistent and annoying ache in my middle.

So before calling Whistler, I dialed the Registry, was put through to villa 333.

"Hello?"

When I heard her voice, the soft sweetness with that strangely musical huskiness in it, I was astonished by the sudden weakness in my knees, the flood of relief that washed over me. I told myself I wasn't being rational, there was no logical reason to feel Spree was in any danger at the moment—unless there was something I'd forgotten, or overlooked, something part of me was aware of but not at the conscious level. More likely it was being in this room with its sights and smells of death, being forcibly reminded of what it really is that's most important about living.

"Hi," I said, "this is good old Bill again. You're O.K., aren't you?"

"Yes—Bill. Are *you* all right?"

"Tip-top. Nothing to report, yet. A lot of things are happening, but . . ."

"But you still don't know if . . ."

"No, not yet. I will. And I'd better get back onto the trail. I was just worrying—thinking—wanted to be sure you were O.K. Look, I've got to run."

"Run back here when you can—Bill."

"I will."

"I miss you."

"Miss you, too."

We hung up. I looked sappily at a framed hunting print

for a few seconds, then again became aware, from the corner of my eye, of the corpse on the floor near me. I dialed *Exposé*, asked for Mr. Whistler.

He was on the line in five seconds, and I said, "Steve, Shell. I'm at Thomas Toker's home. He's dead, shot."

"Jesus. Who—"

"Beats me. But I saw Andrew Foster leaving here as I drove up, just before I let myself inside."

"Foster. That's . . . the young black guy, right?"

"Yeah. One reason I called you, Steve, when I was going through those files you showed me I made a note that Foster is listed as an employee of the Medigenic Hospital, but I didn't see any home address for him except in Tucson. You got one here in the Valley?"

"Just a minute, Shell." I heard him speaking into his intercom, "Helen, send Weinstein in here on the double."

And then I heard a siren. Still distant. Maybe cops chasing a speeder, or an ambulance heading for an accident scene. But maybe . . .

It took Steve—with the help of speedy Weinstein—not more than a minute to come up with the address I wanted. It was only a few miles away, on 32nd Street. But as I scribbled the number in my book, the siren sound was louder. No doubt about it. Closer than before.

"Steve," I said, "are you recording this conversation?"

"Certainly not."

"Can you? I mean, now, no delay?"

"Sure, just push one little switch and—"

"Push it. I've got to get out of here fast. So I'm going to say this once and split. I want all this on the record in case . . . well, just in case, not only for you but also for the police. And I *don't* mean for the police *now*, but when turning it over to them won't screw me up, along with some other people I'm not going to mention yet. You recording?"

"Ever since you said 'push it.'"

I talked about as fast as it's possible for me to speak, for not quite a minute—because the siren kept getting louder, and now I had no doubt it was at least coming this way, if not straight at me. I hit the high points, mentioning

Romanelle and Worthington—but not Spree, not by name
—and explaining not only that I was the man who'd shot
Fred Keats last night but also why. I covered seeing
Andrew Foster leaving this address and my then finding
Toker's body—and that was it.

"No time for more, Steve. Keep this under your hat for
now."

"You've got it. Where—"

But by then I'd hung up the phone and was gone,
running. Running through the house, out the front door,
leaving it wide open, then to the Capri.

Across the street two middle-aged ladies stood in a yard,
one holding a bunch of cut flowers in her hand, both ladies
scrutinizing me with the fixity of interest usually given to
TV game shows. Thus I assumed they would enjoy describing my appearance, and speedy sprint to my car and
tire-burning flight from the murder scene, to the officers
who would soon be interrogating them.

I made it to Glendale and pulled far right at the stop sign
there before the first car, siren wailing and rooftop light
flashing red and blue, skidded into 20th Street and raced
past me, a second patrol car right behind it.

I gunned the engine, headed east on Glendale Avenue. I
didn't look back; no need; I knew where those officers were
going. This was the second time police cars had passed me
only moments after I'd left behind me a house with a dead
man in it. I'd made the first guy dead, true; but not Toker. I
had a hunch, though, that it might be a little difficult to
convince the law I was an innocent victim of accelerating
circumstance.

And I kept wondering—all the way up into Lincoln
Drive, past a carefree foursome of golfers teeing off on the
par-three fifteenth hole of the Arizona Biltmore Country
Club course, even after I turned onto 32nd Street—if
maybe, just maybe, I was getting in over my head.

By 11:30 A.M. I had been waiting inside Andy Foster's
empty apartment for half an hour.

I had driven straight here, left my rented car—already
hot, but soon to be incandescent—parked obtrusively in

front of the four-unit condominium complex near the corner of 32nd Street and Osborn Road. Foster's unit was ground-floor left, and I'd walked right up to the door and rung the bell like your standard magazine salesman. No answer. No car in his covered parking slot. I had been almost relieved.

So I'd moved the Mercury four blocks away, walked back and around to the rear of the complex, and a minute later let myself inside. After half an hour I was ready to climb the walls, so it's probably a good thing I only had to wait another five minutes.

For one thing, during that long half hour my left shoulder began throbbing again, building an ache that filled the entire arm. It had probably been just as sore, throbbing just as much, earlier in the day; but with my mind fully occupied by externally directed thoughts and with movement-going-doing, I hadn't been aware of pain. I suppose, though, despite my itchy impatience, there were some small benefits. I was able to go over again all the things about the Toker death scene that were wrong, get a little more ready for Foster if he showed.

I thought, too, about my client, reaffirming my awareness that, while I had talked to Claude Romanelle in the hospital on Monday morning, during my later call to his home yesterday A.M. it had undoubtedly been someone else—probably the late Fred Keats himself—with whom I'd had that brief preflight dialogue. The evidence for that conclusion was just a series of little things, small anomalies. Like the increased hoarseness from a more severe cold—or an attempt to disguise the imperfectly imitated voice. And the language, of course. Aside from the fact that the real Romanelle called me "Mr. Scott" only when somewhat bugged with me, while the second man had referred to me *only* as "Mr. Scott," the phony hadn't been as sharp, as recklessly correct in his use of language, as the real one. Like his mention of the *passionate* doctors who removed fourteen pieces of *mestatasized* cancers and transplanted *it* into his lungs—instead of impassioned, metastasized, them. Worthington had spoken to me of the $10,000 bonus he'd wangled for me upon my delivery of

Spree to her father; the second "Romanelle" mentioned a bonus of half that amount, or $5,000. Small things, small words; but words I felt sure the real Romanelle would not have used.

I thought about Kay Denver/Dark, too. And Whistler, Cimarron, others. And Spree; I thought a lot about Spree. But—aside from Romanelle himself—Andy Foster was, for a number of reasons, the person I most wanted to talk to at the moment, the reason I was prepared to sit here for hours if I had to. The cowboy, Groder, had been with Foster at the airport last night, and later at Worthington's; but only Foster had been at the Toker death scene. And there were a number of things about that scene only Foster could tell me.

Actually, he was about the only lead, the only good chance, I had left. It wasn't likely I could get anything out of Cimarron unless I stretched him on a rack. A large rack, big enough to handle a full-grown moose. And Dr. Bliss, if not in fact "out of state," wasn't available, his whereabouts at least for now unknown to me. The name Sylvan Derabian was just that, so far only a name.

So I waited. Even though I wasn't yet sure how I was going to handle Andrew Foster when and if I got him. I supposed I would, as usual, just play it by ear, try to take advantage of whatever came down the pike, go with the flow.

But at least I knew Foster was my man. And thirty-five minutes after I let myself in the back door of his condominium apartment, my man came home.

Chapter Fifteen

I was sitting in the living room, at a spot where I could
see his parking space through a curtained window. At
11:35 A.M. the red Subaru slid into that space and Foster
got out, walked toward the condo with a ring of keys
in his hand. He was bareheaded, wearing peach-colored slacks and an orange sweater over a white sport
shirt.

I stepped to the front wall, stood where the door would
conceal me when it opened, pulled out the Smith &
Wesson revolver, breathed slowly and silently through my
open mouth while I waited for him.

I heard a key in the lock. The door opened and Foster
came inside. Without looking around, he pushed the door
closed behind him, then took a couple of steps forward and
stopped. I knew he hadn't seen me, and I didn't think he
could have heard me making any noise. If he'd heard my
shallow breathing, he had incredible ears. But he just stood
there, looking down toward the floor ahead of him, starting
to shrug out of his orange sweater.

I took two long gliding steps right up behind him, started
to jab him with the Smith & Wesson, but changed my
mind. "Freeze" had worked surprisingly well last night;
why change a winning game? So I leaned forward to get my
mouth as close as possible to his right ear and yelled—not
quite as loud as I had last night, but pretty loud
—"FREEZE!"

Four times now. Same thing.

He hadn't known anyone was behind him, of course. That explained a lot. Still, his reaction was quite remarkable.

He snapped his head toward me almost faster than a speeding bullet, and his eyes grew *very* wide when he lamped me yet again, and his eyebrows went up like jet-propelled caterpillars launching themselves spaceward from his head, and his mouth opened so wide I might have been able to put a regulation softball in it, if I'd had one, with room left over for a couple of hard-boiled eggs.

"You're *dead*, turkey," I snarled.

Yes, I really snarled it. And even as I did it, I knew I was overdoing it. Maybe my uninterrupted series of successes in shocking the hell out of this guy had gone to my head. Maybe I'd begun thinking that merely the power of my *word* was enough, I wouldn't need guns anymore. Maybe part of the addle I kept putting into his noodle was bouncing back on my aura and going to *my* noodle.

Maybe not, but something sure happened to Andrew H. Foster. It was not, of course, possible for him to get really pale. But his smooth brown chops did seem to kind of curdle, like when you pour soured milk into hot chocolate, and then his transfixed head—eyes wide, mouth open, brows sailing away—was sinking down, quickly down, almost out of my sight.

He hadn't passed out. I think his knees just buckled, stopped doing their job, so naturally without anything holding him up he went in the other direction. But his great staring eyes—they, I realized, were what had made me think of hard-boiled eggs—never left my face even when the seat of his peach-colored pants hit the floor.

After a few seconds he got his mouth closed, or partly so. Actually, his jaws were working, the way a fish goes when you keep him out of water for too long, or as though he was trying to say something but had no air coming out. Ah, two or three more tries and he got some air in there, and the word came out at last:

"YOU!"

"Yeah," I snarled. "*Me.* And I've come to *get* you."

Well, not at any other time in our whole conversation,

neither before that moment nor after it, could he possibly have come closer to passing out colder than a frozen penguin than he did right then. I thought, if I took a picture of his chops at that moment, nobody would recognize it as a head.

Only then did I become aware that his lower lip was split and puffed, the left side of his face swollen. But the time to ask him about that was not now.

He sat there on the floor for a while, looking intently at my face, white eyebrows, short-cropped white-blond hair, and finally he said, "Are you this dude Shell Scott, or . . . somethin' else?"

"That's me, all right," I said. "And you're Andrew H. Foster, aren't you, Foster?"

"I guess so. Let me think."

"And you're going to tell me every single thing I want to know, aren't you, Foster?"

"Tell you what? About what?"

"Everything, Foster."

He'd put a hand up to the swollen left side of his face and was slowly moving his jaw back and forth. Now was the time. So I said, "What happened to your face, Foster? Somebody slugged you in the last hour or so, right?"

"Naw. Why would anybody slug me? It's just . . . a boil. On a tooth, on my—um, gums. It's a gumboil. I'm swole because it's already starting to fester."

"Listen, turkey, you start leveling with me right now or I'll slug you myself. In the same goddamn place, see? And then you'll fester faster, Foster."

He gave me an odd look. "You hear what you just said?" he asked me.

"Never mind that. Well . . . I guess you might as well get up off the floor, Foster."

"You mind calling me Andy? It sounds—friendlier."

I didn't answer him until he got up off the floor and we were seated at a table—as it turned out, a table in the small kitchen, where friends so often gather—and he was ready to confess everything he knew. I hoped.

"All right, Andy," I said, putting the S&W back into my holster. "You know I saw you splitting from Toker's house.

What you may not realize is that I went in there myself, so I know he's dead, and that you—"

"I didn't kill him," he said rapidly. "I only . . ."

"I *know* you didn't kill him. What I want you to tell me is what you did with the note. And the gun."

"What note? What gun?"

"The suicide note. And the gun Toker used to blow his brains out."

He didn't say anything. His brown eyes shifted from side to side, then focused on the table before him.

"O.K., Andy," I said. "Or maybe we go back to Foster. Maybe we aren't going to be friendly anymore. I'm going to describe for you your two alternatives, the two roads you can travel from here. One road, easy, no problems, no pain, you tell me everything I want to know and you're home free, I'll let you walk. The other road, you clam, or try to con me or lie to me, and—well, Foster, I'll have to hurt you. I mean, in horrible, excruciating ways. So you should understand before making your choice that I am quite capable of violence."

He couldn't know that the last part was baloney, that there was no way I could make myself pound on the guy, or break his legs, or otherwise torture him just to make him talk. At least, I hoped he couldn't know it. I was counting on the possibility that, having by now produced moderate to severe damage throughout his entire nervous system on no fewer than four separate occasions, I might have him conditioned like a Pavlovian pup: could be all I'd have to do was say "Boo!" and he'd babble. But you never know in advance how these things will go. All I could do was give it a try and see what happened.

Foster was nodding his head slowly. "You didn't have to tell me," he said soberly. "If you hadn't practic'ly missed my whole head last night, I'd of been goin' around with one of them Frankenstein plugs in my neck, assumin' I was still goin'. Instead of haulin' Jay down in the elevator, I'd of been took out in a hearse and a hat box—you know Jay didn't wake up till this morning? Yeah, man, you didn't have to tell me you're capable of dismemberizing me, or whatever you got in your intentions."

"You're convinced, then?"

"Boy, am I."

"O.K., Andy. Start with Toker."

"Now it's Andy again, huh? I guess I'm supposed to be encouraged. Well . . ." He paused, rubbed his jaw, then said, "Straight goods? I spill whatever, and you'll let me walk outa here? I can get in my heap and just drive off?"

"Not exactly. I'll be needing your car myself. I'll let you split, but you'll be on foot. When I say walk, Andy, I mean walk."

"Huh. Gonna steal my car—"

"I'm not going to *steal* it, I'm just going to *borrow* it."

"Yeah, sure. That's what we all say."

"*Goddammit, Foster*—"

"O.K., O.K., *hold* it. Yeah, you got it figured. I took the note, I took the gun. But . . ." He paused. "Don't get mad, now. I'm *gonna* tell you. But—how in hell did you figure Toker blew his own conk off? And there was a note? Man, you're spooky."

"No, it was obvious," I said. "Except for the absence of both the gun and note, it *looked* as if Toker had shot himself in the head and fallen to his left out of his chair, maybe was knocked out of it by the force of the slug that blew off a bunch of his skull. He was shot at least once by somebody—himself, actually—while at the desk. There was blood spray on the desktop's left half, except for an L-shaped area where his writing pad would have been if he wrote the note there. As for the pad itself, it was clean, no marks. Maybe half the pages had been used, but there wasn't the faintest indentation from a pencil or pen. So somebody—not likely it was Toker himself—had ripped off the note and, sensibly, several of the blank pages beneath. There's more, but let's get on with—"

"Hey, that's the way it was, it *is* how. That damned note was on the first three pages. But, man, there was two holes in his back. I know, I put 'em there. And he'd shot hisself in the thinkpot clear back here, not up front or even in his temple." Andy was pointing a rigid index finger at a point above and slightly behind his right ear. "How come you suspicioned a suicide shot hisself in the back of his head and twice in the back of his back?"

"Andy . . . Well, there was practically no blood on his shirt, just two neat holes and a little color. His heart had stopped, his nerves were kaput, he was totally dead when those two pills went in alongside his spine. I told you, somebody shot him *at* the desk. But not in the back, not if he was sitting in that brass-studded high-backed chair of his. As for your other point, a hell of a lot of people who shoot themselves in the head either don't aim at the temple or else miss it by a foot."

"Miss it? How can they *miss* it when it's so close?"

"Andy, if you're just trying to delay spilling your guts, I will find another way to spill them—"

"Hey, don't—O.K. I'm just, well, I'd like to *know*. I want to improve myself. I thought I'd confused everything perfect. Hell, Alda told me what to do, but I did it perfect. I thought."

"Alda Cimarron?"

"Yeah. You know any more Aldas? But, listen, how could you figure he shot hisself clear back there on his conk? How . . . ?" He stopped. "You do voodoo, man? Is that how?" He nodded his head a couple of times. "Yeah, you *do* look like a dude who'd do voodoo."

"A what? Andy, I do *not* appreciate your—never mind. O.K., I'll end your confusion. I'll answer your questions . . . which isn't the way it's supposed to go. But then, Andy, maybe you'll help me out a little?"

"You bet. Glad to help. Anybody does *voo*doo—"

"Stick your finger up there on your head again. On your temple."

"This?" He held up his right hand, rigid index finger extended and thumb sticking up like a gun's hammer. "Like this?" He stuck the finger against his temple.

"Perfect. Now, in just a minute, when I say 'bang,' you're going to blow your brains out—"

He yanked his hand away, held it up before his wide eyes while he waggled his thumb a couple of times. "With —this?"

"Well, just playacting. This is to be a demonstration of the . . . the physical effects produced by vivid visualization, the awesome power of the human mind—"

"Yeah, man, and they call it *voo*—"

"Dammit, Andy, don't start that again—"

"You're not gonna really make me do it, make me blow out my whole—"

"Of course not. Don't be ridiculous. *Dammit, do you want to do this or not?*"

"Sure. Whatever you say."

"All right, put the gun back up there."

He looked at his hand, gave one last little wiggle of his thumb, then stuck that stiff index finger against his right temple, a queer blend of resignation, curiosity, and sheer horror on his features.

"Now, then," I said, dropping my voice to a deeper and more spookily hypnotic level, "you are moments away from ending it all. Good-bye, cruel world. Your cock is gunned and loaded . . . strike that. Your *gun* is cocked and loaded, you feel its cold cruel muzzle against your head. You are about to pull the thumb—the goddamn trigger —when suddenly, hark! It comes into your mind—which you will soon not have any more of—that killing yourself is going to *hurt*. It's going to hurt something *awful*. Maybe only for a little while, but that little may seem like forever while you're dying, while your brains and skull are blowing apart, and apart, and apart . . . You *want* to do it. You're *going* to do it. Any minute now! Any second now! Ah, but how *much*, and for how *long*, is it going to *hurt*—*BANG!*"

Boy, this guy had speedy reflexes. Simultaneously, he flipped his right hand away from him, as if flinging a gun at the wall, while both his feet came up and kicked the bottom of the kitchen table, which bounced into the air maybe six inches.

"Andy, you went and spoiled it," I said, disgruntled.

"Spoiled? Spoiled?"

He had both hands on his head now, and was squeezing it, probing it, fondling it. Looked like he was trying to stick a couple of fingers clear inside it.

"Yeah," I grumbled. "I wanted you to see yourself—"

"How—"

"I mean, become aware of where the gun was, and where

your head was, when you fired."

"I never did fire. You yelled *BANG!* And, man, you got a lethal pair of lungs. Like, last night—"

"The closer you got to pulling the trigger, the more you turned your head away from the gun. You just kept leaning more and more. At the end there, your head was three or four inches away from the gun, which was pointed almost at the back of your noodle. It looked like you were trying to get your head out the door."

"Let's not do any more of this. Why don't I just spill my guts?"

"Now you're talking."

And he was. After he'd spilled the first item or two, the rest of it got easier as he went along. That's usually the way it is.

You just have to go with the flow.

One of the first questions I asked Andy was, "Where's the suicide note now? And Toker's gun, for that matter?"

"I took 'em to Alda."

"Why to him?"

"He's the one sent me to find out what Toke was hung on. See, Toke was supposed to meet with Alda early this A.M. at Alda's house. Eight A.M. I think it was set up for. Anyways, he didn't show. Alda couldn't get him on the phone. Finally he calls me and says to find Toke and bring him back with me. I checked Toke's place first. And found him."

"Why was Toker supposed to meet with Cimarron?"

"Beats me. They don't tell me more'n they have to."

"O.K., what did the suicide note say?"

"Well, I read over it pretty fast, you understand. Even skipped some—with him layin' there. I'm not too crazy about dead guys."

"Uh-huh. So just tell me what you remember."

"It was like—like a confession. He explains about doin' the fake assay on the Golden Phoenix ore samples, sayin' he done it for money he needed bad plus some Golden Phoenix stock, but lookin' back it was the worst thing he'd ever did."

I almost interrupted Andy when he mentioned "the fake assay," but he hadn't been rolling long enough for me to risk slowing him down.

So I held my tongue as he continued, "Then there was some technical-lookin' stuff—I think it was maybe how he done the phoneying, and what the results really were, that he didn't mention since the entire idea was to make it sound plenty better than it was—but I skipped most of it there. Then he mentions he was sure gonna get caught, sooner or later, and some more on how dumb he was and there wasn't no way out. That when Claude was shot up, there at Medigenic, he started thinkin' it was his turn to be next, that if it wasn't the police got him he'd get killed by the same people shot up Claude. And somethin' about this *Exposé* bunch being on him, doing an interview, and it was all going to come out for sure now they were digging.

"Then the last part was to his ex-wife—I mean wife, they wasn't divorced yet. I heard she left him six, seven months ago, went back to Minnesota with their kid. Anyways, he says to her in the note he really did it for the money and the shares of stock, but when this come out they'd go into the toilet. He didn't say it like that, just when it come out, meaning I suppose his killin' hisself and the note and all, the Golden Phoenix shares would go back down to where they belonged, somethin' like that. Anyways, he writes to his wife he hoped with that money plus what he expected from sellin' the shares at the top, he hoped he could get her back, he still loved her more than all the world, that kind of crap. Then just . . . I remember how it ended, he didn't sign it or nothin', just wrote 'And this is how it ends.' Nothin' dramatic like that 'Good-bye, cruel world' you were given' me when I was suppose to blow out—"

He'd interrupted the monologue himself, finally, so I tried a question. "It all makes sense, Andy, but maybe you can fill in a couple of little points. The assay report he faked, I suppose he was paid off for that by Alda Cimarron, right?"

"Well . . ." He hesitated.

"Dammit, Andy," I said vehemently, "I told you going

in, I already *know* the answers to most of the questions I'll ask you, and all it takes is one goddamn wrong answer—"

"Hey, it ain't that. Don't pop your cork. It's just, it wasn't Alda made the arrangements and slipped him the cash and all that, he don't get out front much, stays in the background, you know? The guy made all the arrangements was Claude."

"Claude? Claude Romanelle?"

He glowered at me from the brown eyes, raising and lowering the arched black brows. "Huh. You *didn't* know, did you? You bullshitted me—"

"I thought it was somebody else, Andy. Ah . . . I see. Because Toker's contacts had all been with Romanelle, when Claude got shot Toker had pretty good reason to think he might be the next target."

"I dunno about that, except what Toke wrote in the note. *I* never heard nothin' about anybody plannin' to poop Toke. He could've just imagined that and got his head frazzled, which it must of been or he wouldn't've been killin' hisself."

"O.K., all the contact was with Romanelle. But wouldn't Alda Cimarron have had to approve or give the go-ahead on anything like that? Particularly something as important as a faked assay?"

"Oh, sure, hell yes. *Nothin'* about Golden Phoenix gets done unless Alda says do it. He's the president, but he's also a guy you don't want to screw with."

He rubbed the side of his face again, and wiggled his jaw a bit.

I said, "So, then, it's certain Cimarron would have had to O.K. Romanelle's approaching Toker. Just as certain as that, later, he had Romanelle shot. Right, Andy?"

"Well . . ."

He was looking past my left shoulder—which, it occurred to me, didn't seem to be aching anymore—and I could clearly see a little wobble of his eyes, just a fractional movement, left-right-left-right, and I had a very strong hunch he was getting ready to lie to me about something.

"Foster," I said sharply, "I've already warned you a couple of times—"

"Yeah, yeah, sure, it was Alda says do it. Who else? He's the big cheese, I told you. Don't get so hot over nothin'."

"Just want you to keep your part of the bargain, Andy. Because if you do, I'll keep mine."

"Yeah. *And* my heap. You know I'll have to *steal* a car, don't you?"

"Andy, you don't *have* to—"

"You take my wheels, you're the same as forcing me into a life of crime. You're suppose to be a *legit* guy, ha-ha, now I got to go *steal*—"

"Andy, let's keep it on track here. I'll tell you what's happening from where I sit, and you tell me if I'm on the mark, O.K.?"

"O.K. by me."

"The Golden Phoenix is a complete scam. A con game, a rip-off. The idea is to take some worthless shares and run them up with slick promotion, maybe a boiler-room operation, then a faked assay report or two, dump the shares and split with multimillions, leaving behind a lot of shareholders in a barrel filled with worthless paper. How close is that?"

"Well . . ." His eyes didn't do their little dance this time, so I assumed he was merely considering what I'd said. "Pretty close. Actually, you say it some worse than it is. The idea is to goose the stock up, sure, and get out. But it won't go down to nothin'. Maybe two, three fish, but the idea is to dump everything they can on the way to and just under thirty, which they—Alda, mainly—figure is where they can goose it to. Or *did* figure. This today, this Toke screwup, changes a lot of things."

He paused, but without prompting from me went on, "You're right about the boiler room. Alda had twenty guys on the phones awhile, eased off for a few months, then brought em' all in again this week. This week and the next couple, after another assay report even better, is suppose to be the time to grab it all and get out healthy. Dunno what'll come off now. Of course, nobody outside knows yet about Toke knockin' hisself off. Except . . . you do. You know."

That didn't make my position sound too wonderful if Cimarron or some of his pals got their hands on me, or even got close enough to blow me away.

With that depressing thought in my mind, I said, "It looks like Cimarron put the hit on Romanelle right after the Toker report was released. Was that the trigger? Doesn't seem to make a lot of sense if it was Romanelle who arranged for that fake report in the first place. Did I miss something?"

"You sure did. But there's no way you could help but miss it, bein' on the outside. See, startin' way back, two, three years back, Alda and some of us guys moved a lot of stock whenever there was good news to hype—I worked the boiler-room spiel myself sometimes. Claude and Alda together, somehow, I don't know all the ins and outs, come up with the idea of these mailing lists, especially of rich guys what had bought stocks and other things through the mails or after bein' called on the phone. The ones that done it before is the best marks for doin' it again, O.K.? Well, they made up all these lists for their own, got it onto computers, everything slicker'n spit on a tit, a beautiful setup so they have three or four hundred names to hit again. When they wanted to bail out, you know?"

I nodded. "Sucker list, but it sounds like a fairly sophisticated one."

"Yeah, man, names, phone numbers, net worth, change of address if there was one, all kinds of crap they figured was important when it come to the blowoff. Which, as I kind of mentioned, was suppose to be about now and the next two or three weeks. Well, after Toke's first assay, natural the stock steams up pretty good, and we start callin' the marks. Some was interested—I mean, like crazy, wanted all they could get. But the idea is, keep 'em on the string for a little, till the price is up some more. But then the goddamn catasterphobe."

"The what?"

"Disasterville, ruin-damn-nation. It comes out, a bunch of the marks who'd bought Golden Phoenix, them that had gone for at least ten thousand shares when it was way down—so they now got a bee-yootifil profit, right? On paper, but these marks always got it spent in their heads, so they're ripe, fifty or sixty special marks practic'ly askin' to be took. These are the main ones Alda was countin' on for the big buys when he unloads, see?"

"Like after the next marvelous, exciting assay report that's sure to send the stock to eighty or ninety."

"You got it, they had it figured so they could unload all they had to move without runnin' the price down to a nickel, see? Nickel, that's a joke, but you get the idea."

"Sure. So where's disasterville?"

"Oh, yeah. It comes out, and pretty quick they got this *horrible* picture from the computer, maybe *thirty* of these dudes, maybe half of the whole package, has already sold their shares to . . . somebody. They wasn't supposed to *sell* any, they was supposed to *buy* more, a lot more, when Alda and his inside guys was ready to lower the bim-bam-boom. But when they was *out* of it, havin' no more interest in the goddamn stock, they sure weren't gonna be in the market for *more* of it. No, they was useless for the purpose intended. See?"

I liked the way he'd put that one. Useless for the purpose intended. No longer available for the final screwing. "So who bought all those shares from the marks? And how many shares were involved, by the way?"

"They figure it come to somethin' like seven or eight hundred thousand shares."

I blinked. That—almost—told me the rest before he said it.

"Not that the seven, eight hundred thou by itself is puke city, but that the five, six million they got to unload fast ain't got noplace to go now. At least, not so many places. Which, talkin' about maybe six million shares, is a real cramp in the ass. And when Alda gets a cramp there, that's a goddamn lot of cramp."

"So who'd been buying all those shares? Several guys? One guy?"

"One guy." His eyes did that little dance, very briefly, but he went right on and told me. "Claude."

"I think I'm getting a better idea why Romanelle was shot. Let's see . . . shot on Monday, September twenty-fourth. Toker's report was made public the Friday before then, on the twenty-first. Which was also the day the October *Exposé* was mailed."

"You're not so dumb, once I explain everything to you. But you got it. Claude had been buyin' up all the stock he could get—payin' reasonable since he knows it's goin' to near thirty or maybe over—for a year, year and a half. Used a lot of different names, that sort of thing, nominations, or . . . ?"

"Nominees?"

"Like that. Well, it all come out in the computer paper, and Alda like to disemboweled hisself runnin' to the crapper. Them cramps I mentioned. He was so steamed he damn near pressed his pants from inside hisself. He knew, in the first instant, them that sold their stock was no good to anybody once they was unsuckered. So . . ."—his brown eyes wobbled slightly, briefly—"that was the exact instance when Alda put out the word, and sent a couple of us—them." His brows shot way up, and his eyeballs literally quivered. "That's when he sent a couple of them, them other guys, to blow Claude away."

Sure. Maybe now I had a clue as to why Andy's eyes had been dancing. It had been a couple of them other guys. Andy hadn't been one of them. He hadn't been anywhere around.

I said, "I'd guess Cimarron was a mite disappointed when Romanelle didn't get wasted after all."

"You'd guess? A mite? Disappointed? Man, you don't know that lousy . . . that irritable chap at all, do you? Why, he only went ca-*razy*, I thought he was going to *kill* uh . . . them two guys. Them guys what did it. Or, ak-chully, didn't."

"Incidentally, I saw Cimarron myself this morning, at his home. Is that where he was when you took him the note and gun?"

"That's where he was at—still waiting in case Toke showed up—when I called him about finding Toke. Who, obvious, wasn't going to show up anyplace. So Alda says he has to get back to the Medigenic, and for me to meet him there, and that's where I give him the stuff, there at the hospital." Again, perhaps unconsciously, he rubbed his swollen jaw.

"And he gave you that?" I said.

"Yeah. Just slapped me. Didn't hit me with a fist, which would prob'ly have made my head look like Toke's does now. He got pissed off because I pumped those extra two in Toke's back." Andy shook his head wearily. "See, when I call him from Toke's, and tell him what's what, he does a lot of colorful swearing and then says for me to meet him at Medigenic, bringing the note and gun to make it look like a hit instead of a suicide. He *said* make it look like a hit. So that's what I done. Then that lousy . . . then he says, *after* I done it, he meant *just* take the gun and note, because that all by *itself* fixed it to look like a hit. I made a mistake then. Or my mouth did. I says, funnylike, 'Ha-ha, *now* you tell me'—and pow. I ducked, so he only got me with maybe two, three fingers, and knocked my ass over my belt buckle. I went around like a pinwheel and was out cold a whole minute. They tell me."

"What was Cimarron doing at the hospital?"

"Helpin' Doc Bliss keep an eye on Claude."

"Romanelle—he's *there,* at the Medigenic?"

Andy nodded, a strange look on his brown face.

"O.K. Just one last thing to tell me and you can split. What's the best way for me to get Romanelle out of there? Without getting both of us killed?"

"Uh . . . Well . . . Maybe there ain't much point in gettin' him out."

"There's plenty of point. All you have to tell me is how to get to him and I'll do the rest. You *can* tell me where he is, and the best way for me to get in and out, can't you?"

"Yeah, sure. But that ain't what I was implicating. I mean, Alda and Bliss figured they had to make Claude tell them everything and then some, but he is a tough old cookie. So they sent some kind of electricities through his brains to make him unclam his chops. That is, the doc did—"

"Electricity? What do you mean—*electro*shock?"

"Whatever. Some electricities, with a machine they got there and some kind of paddles, that's what they called 'em. Crazy things, don't look much like paddles. Anyways, I guess they kind of overfried his brains some."

"Overfried? What the hell did they *do* to the man?"

"I don't know the technicals of what they done, but I seen old Claude up there and he ain't a very lively cat. More like a dead one."

Chapter Sixteen

I STARED AT Foster's handsome brown face, his last words blending unpleasantly with the image of that dead cat I'd seen on Cimarron's property.

Finally I said, "Romanelle *is* still alive, right?"

"Barely. You can tell he ain't diseased yet because he drools. And moves a little once in a while. But otherwise he looks like he been embalmed."

I swore.

"Yeah," Foster said. "It's a shame, all right. He was such a brainy guy, really smart. Twice as smart as Alda, and Alda ain't nobody's dummy." He sighed, rubbing his jaw. "Pretty bad, especially when you see him. Hell of it is, I liked Claude, he was always good to me, treated me good."

"Look, if he's not dead yet, then maybe . . ."

"Maybe. Sure. They—Alda and Doc Bliss, and a couple of the guys, they're goin' cuckoo, and Alda's about to have a colonary. They're tryin' everything they can think of to bring him around. But I think they fried his brains, like those onion rings you get at Jack-in-the-Box."

"They're trying to bring him around? Help him? Why —because they didn't find out everything they were after?"

"Why, prob'ly because they're humanitarians," he said dryly, "don't you s'pose?"

I stood up, anxious to get moving now that I knew —finally—where my client was. Or, until very recently, had been.

Foster explained, in response to my questions and with

233

as much detail as he could recall, exactly where Romanelle was on the Medigenic's fourth floor and how I might get to him. He added that at various times Dr. Bliss, Alda Cimarron, and Cowboy Jay Groder were with him; they might all three be there, but at least one of them was invariably present. Romanelle was never left alone.

I already had the keys to Andy's Subaru XT coupe in my pocket. So I said, "I really don't like taking your wheels, Andy, but it's necessary," and told him the name of a parking lot where I'd leave the Subaru in a day or two.

"I'll prob'ly be in Abyssinia in a day or two."

"Might be a wise move. You got any money?"

"Sure, I got enough dough. Unless you was fixing to pay me for my car."

"Andy, consider my use of it payment for your loitering about with Cowboy when I and . . . my companion arrived here at Sky Harbor. And loitering again on the twelfth floor of the Hall-Manchester Building. Or, rather, for what you intended, but fortunately were unable to consummate, doing to us."

"We wasn't . . . Well, we wasn't going to . . ." His eyes were dancing.

"You weren't planning to kill us both instantly? Maybe going to turn us over to Dr. Bliss first? Don't bull me—"

"Hey, I leveled with you. Straight goods so far. So don't put me down."

"Alda Cimarron sent you out for us, didn't he?"

"Yeah. Sure, it was Alda. But he says, bring—bring them, that is the two of you, to him personal."

His eyes were telling me there was at least a little something he was leaving out, something not absolutely on the level. So I said, "Or be sure the lady got safely to him, right? And if I happened to be a little too much trouble, maybe if I didn't make it to Alda's, he'd forgive you?"

"Um . . . ah, somethin' like that, pretty close. I didn't have no idea how *much* trouble you was gonna be."

"O.K., Andy. You can stay here or split, whatever you want to do. We're quits. But remember, if you screw up—more specifically, try to screw *me* up—I'll absolutely dismember you, I'll make it a personal crusade. But besides that, if you talk to the law I can tell them a lot of things about you, including your attempt to kill Romanelle. And if you cozy up to Cimarron all I have to do is tell him you puked to me, reciting chapter and verse, and I won't have to do zilch about you, he'll pluck off your arms and legs one at a time himself."

"He'd prob'ly pluck 'em off all at once, that bugger. But the law won't do too good with me on the Claude hit."

"Why not? You were there, you and Cowboy, right? Even if you haven't come straight out and said so."

"Yeah . . . I think I'll tell you. I really walk, right? You're really gonna let me split, like you said?"

"Like I said."

"Be damned. O.K., well . . . yeah, it was me and Jay Groder on that hit. But I missed. Deliberate. Think back on all them shots, and Claude got hit only three times—all three times by Jay. I hit a couple of parked cars with my .45, which is what I was aiming at. I told you, I liked old Claude, he never screwed me or nothing, treated me like I was a friend of his. Which, damn, I think I was, you know?"

"You mean you blew it, made sure you *didn't* hit Romanelle?"

"That's exact. Hey, I figured Jay'd blow him away easy, I just didn't want it on my conscious. Look, man, I do the grift, some con, I steal from a time to a time. But I never killed *no*body, and I got no plans to take it up even for a sideline." He waggled his head, but his eyes stayed steady on my face. "I don't know why the hell Alda sent me on that, except maybe to get more things to hold on me. And I guess he figured, like I did, Jay was enough by hisself. He's killed a lotta guys already, eight, ten, I don't know —maybe he don't. Him and Keats, they were the only shooters in this setup. And you know what happened to Keats lately. I guess you know."

"I guess I do."

I turned toward the door, then stopped. I was impatient to get to the Medigenic Hospital as soon as possible, but something about Foster's just-completed confessions was bothering me. It wasn't any single thing he'd told me, but rather that he'd been able to tell me so much. For a man who wasn't one of the principals, not a mover-and-shaker of the scam, he seemed to know one hell of a lot about the operation.

What I was planning to attempt at the Medigenic wasn't likely to be easy, even if every single thing Foster had told me was true. But if he'd been inventing part of it, conning me for his own reasons . . . Well, a guy could get killed.

So I looked at him again and said casually, "Andy, I'm a little puzzled. You're not exactly Alda Cimarron's right-hand man, but you seem to know a hell of a lot about what he and his pals are up to, about what's going on here. You sure you're not making some of this up just to cool me down?"

He shook his head. "Must be twice as much I *don't* know zip about. What I do got, prob'ly it just *seem* like a lot to you, Scott, because you're gettin' it all at once instead of pickin' it up over two, three years or more like I did. Outside of the main guys in this—which is Alda and Sylvan and Doc and Claude—there's only a couple of weight-lifters and trash-haulers, plus Groder and Keats —well, not even Keats now. And me. Well, it may flabber-gastonish you to hear me say it right out aloud, but compared to those fleepers I am a ring-tailed gold-plated flamingly illuminated hot-damn genius." He paused brief-ly, looked straight at me, and said gently, "Even though the observed demeanor and spacy visage combined with mer-ciless slaughter of the sweet tongue might lead even a perceptive whitey to conclude that this cat's mental devel-opment ceased entirely at the age of eleven if not sooner."

"What? What did you say?"

While I was still blinking, Andy went on easily, "Well, boss, besides from all that, them main guys is pretty closed of mouths, but they all—everybody does—lets something slip out sideways from a time to a time. That's accidental. But, plus I get told a lot on purpose when I'm suppose to do somethin', so's there's less chance I'll screw up doin' it."

"Like what?"

"Like, well, I mentioned workin' the boiler-room operation myself for a while. What I happened not to mention is I'm the one set it up to begin with. See, I been with Alda more'n ten years, one way or another—longer than any of them other employee types out here. So when he wants to get them phones ringin' he tells me to put the package together, and in order so's I get the right guys and don't mess up this important part of the whole craperoo, he explains to me some of the reasons behind why it's got to be set up just so. Plus I manage to ask a couple of dumb questions, which it's easy for me to do."

"Uh-huh. I think maybe I'm starting to understand just how easy."

He smiled, continued, "And . . . like when Alda found out Claude been buyin' up shares from the marks, Jay and I was both right there, listenin' to him yellin' and swearin'. Hell, we could of been nine miles away and still heard him. Plus, like when he told Jay and me to help Claude into that better world we all dream of where the streets are a-glitterin' with rhinestones and the pretty girls dance with no pants on, he give us a general idea why dear old Claude had to go there."

"Plus you managed to ask a couple of dumb questions, right?"

"One or two." He grinned. "Also one or two when he sent me to find Toke and bring him. Plus, I just got through readin' those three educational pages of Toke's last will and testaments about why and how he done what was his end and who told him to. Plus . . ."

He stopped, scowled slightly, squinting at me. "Scott, I could go on quite some while like this, if you still need the convincers. You say so, O.K. But you really want me to keep doin' this scene, or were you goin' somewheres in my Subaru you just stole?"

I jingled the keys in my hand. "That's good enough," I said. "I'll buy it. But Lord help you if I get killed. I'll come back and spook you. However, I might add that this is one whitey who doesn't conclude your mental evolution and synaptical pyrotechnics—or whatever it was you actually said a while ago—ceased at the age of eleven. At least, not entirely."

He laughed. "I'll be goddamn go to hell. Shucks."

"Shucks, *boss,*" I said.

He laughed again.

"Well," I said, "I'm not sure why I'm saying this, but good luck to you, Andy. Hope you make out."

He grinned hellishly, white teeth flashing. "I'll make out. Maybe I'll even pick up my car—gotta believe you're really gonna leave it in the lot."

He stepped closer to me, stuck out his hand. I shook it. Strange moment, I thought. God knows what Andrew Foster did with his life, besides not shooting people, but he was a very likable guy.

"Can I drop you anywhere?" I asked him.

"Not if you goin' toward Scottsdale, which I suspect is where you're goin'. Me, I may drift the other way, like Southwest Phoenix. Places down there I can plain disappear in the darkieness." He grinned again. "No honkies need apply."

I went to the door. When I left, he was sitting at the table, rubbing his jaw and smiling. I hoped I wasn't making a mistake. Or rather—in case I might have made one or two already—making another.

I turned left off Hayden into McDowell Road, drove east toward Mesa. After two or three miles I saw the twin buildings, joined by covered walkways at the second and fourth floors, of the Medigenic Hospital on my right.

I drove on by, sizing up the place, checking out the location of parking lots and spaces. There was a row of windows on the fourth or top floor of the west wing: twelve rooms up there, six on the side facing McDowell and six at the building's rear. Nine of those rooms were for patients; the other three were a doctors' lounge, a small corner office for the chief of surgery, and a spacious 1,500-square-foot office, with wall dividers converting it into a three-room suite for the hospital's president of the Board, Dr. Phillip Bliss. And that's where Andy had seen Romanelle, in a small bedroom of Dr. Bliss's suite. All I had to do was get up there. And get back out. With Romanelle. Or whatever was left of him.

I turned around, drove back past the hospital and into the parking lot on its west side, took a left, and rolled slowly by the entrance. Both of the large steel and glass doors, each about six feet wide and ten feet high, were closed to keep today's near-hundred-degree heat out of the lobby's air-conditioned interior. Arching above the doors, against the building's rust-colored cement face, shiny black letters a foot high spelled out "Arizona Medigenic Hospital."

Somewhere behind me in that west parking lot was the spot where, thirteen days ago, Romanelle had been shot by Cowboy Jay Groder and shot at by Andy Foster. I drove to the far end of the building, passing another parking section on my left about half filled with cars, turned right, and drove toward the rear of the hospital.

So far, so good. According to Andy, here at the east end of the Medigenic's east wing was the Emergency Room entrance, and just past it at the building's rear was, in his words, "where they temporary dump the stiffs after the emergency's over, till they haul 'em away and hide 'em permanent," or what I presumed was a small hospital morgue. Usually the little room was occupied only by the stiffs, and thus should provide a comparatively risk-free entrance into the hospital for me. And exit as well, with my cargo, if I got that far.

I took a right at the rear of the building and parked opposite a pair of plain unmarked wooden doors, wide doors behind which should be the terminal patients who had terminated. I parked as far to my left as I could get, next to a six-foot-high cement-block wall, left-front fender almost scraping one of the white-painted no-parking signs.

That left a space about eight feet wide between my red coupe—or, rather, Andy's, which I hoped nobody here would recognize—and the morgue entrance. Room for another car to squeak by, but perhaps not enough for a speeding ambulance. I refused to worry about those little things: There were enough big worries to occupy my attention.

I picked up my wide-brimmed hat from the seat beside me, put it on. Then I got out, leaving the car unlocked, stepped quickly to the wooden doors. A couple of feet above my head a row of glass blocks dotted the entire rear wall of the building, like a line of transparent hyphens. Picking the simple lock occupied less than a minute; the doors opened inward. I felt refrigerated air pouring out over me, then I stepped into chill dimness, pushing the doors shut behind me.

I was in a small square room. There were no lights burning here, but faint illumination filtered in through the glass blocks above my head and behind me. In the left wall, dimly visible, was a single row of yard-square metal doors, all closed, all flush with the wall. Probably refrigerated cubicles for corpses. The only furnishings were four body-sized rectangular metal tables, three unused and one bearing a body covered by a bedsheet-sized green cloth. The ankles and bare feet of the body projected beyond the table's end, cardboard identification tag tied to one big toe. I wondered if the tag had a name on it, or merely a number. Or possibly a cryptic phrase exemplifying the new identity assumed by the person upon becoming a patient: Gall Bladder 1991 . . . Kidney366 . . . Lung Transplant 2.

I stepped toward a wooden door in the far wall, arm brushing one of those metal tables. I noticed that its top was grooved like an autopsy table and slanted slightly downward toward one end, little dikes and channels for the gravity flow of sluggish but still-liquid blood.

I walked on past the table with the covered body upon it, then turned back, pulled off the heavy green cloth and bunched it into a lumpy ball, clamped it against my chest with one arm. The corpse was—or, if death is neuter, had been—male. An old man, shrunken, shriveled, waxy skin mottled. His face, for reasons unknown to me, was oddly discolored, almost a faintly purplish hue, like a bleached eggplant with blank frozen features.

I shivered, told myself it was because of the cold heavy air all around me. But from that dismaying moment on, at least until the next dismaying moment, my journey was essentially a breeze, a walk in the park. The wooden door was open. I went through into a fluorescent-lighted hallway and turned right, then left at the intersecting corridor, walked briskly past the closed door of the Emergency Room from behind which a voice—again neither male nor female, just a sound without sex or identity—grunted "*Oh*-ah-ah . . . *oh*-ah-ah." Then, just past the Emergency Room, against the outer wall on my right, the elevator I was looking for. Probably the one in which the old man with the purplish face had been brought down here not long before.

Two nurses in white uniforms walked toward me as I poked the elevator button, their rubber-soled shoes squeaking on the polished floor. Up in the elevator, watching the numbers, 2, 3, 4, watching the door slide open with a hiss, then two steps forward, doors staying open briefly behind me. Ahead of me was a long corridor that extended the entire width of the hospital, from east end of the east wing to west end of the west wing. My destination was clear down there at the corridor's west end, nine and a half miles away.

Well, as the Chinese philosophers say, the journey of nine and a half miles begins with a single step. So I took that step, then another—and stopped so quickly my heel skidded on the polished plastic flooring. I caught my balance, pulled the loose bundle of cloth higher on my chest until it partially covered my face.

From an open door ahead of me, out of the third room from the end on my right, stepped a short, plump, bald-headed man wearing horn-rimmed glasses, stethoscope around his neck, dangling end resting on his chest between the lapels of a dark brown business suit. This was only the second time I'd seen the man; the first time, he'd told me he was Dr. Robert Simpson, in the middle of a house call to cheer and make better his fine friend, Claude Romanelle. Or: Dr. Phillip Bliss, whose photo I'd recently seen in Whistler's office at *Exposé*.

If the sight of Bliss started adrenaline oozing in me, the next sight made it squirt. Because next was the huge, wide, muscle-knotted form of Alda Cimarron coming out the same door and into the corridor, turning toward me. I squatted down on my haunches, letting the bunched green cloth cover everything except my eyes peering out from beneath the brim of my hat, let my right arm drop as if I was reaching for something on the hallway floor. But I pulled the arm back up and wrapped my fingers around the butt of the .38 under my coat.

Neither man paid more than casual attention to me. Disinterested, unseeing glances, then into the next hospital room to check and cheer another patient. I took advantage of those moments when they were entering the room and both backs were toward me to straighten up and move with considerable speed straight ahead, toward the Bliss suite at the end of the hall. The door to the suite was closed, but the knob turned easily and the door moved inward half an inch before I held it steady, glanced back down the hall.

Nobody in sight yet. Cimarron and Bliss were still inside that second room from the end. I pulled the .38 S&W from under my belt, wishing it was Alda Cimarron's silenced .22 pistol, not something that would make a noise half the hospital would hear if I had to fire it.

But then I took a deep breath, opened the door, and walked inside. I was in a large room, desk ahead of me with two windows behind it. Two more windows were in the right wall. So this was the corner room of the suite, the office where Bliss did his work, conducted interviews, held court, goofed off. Expensively furnished: thick royal-blue carpet, lighter blue couches and several overstuffed chairs, three filing cabinets against the wall to the right of the desk. To my left, one door was open revealing part of what was obviously a bedroom. Farther left, away from the rear wall and adjacent to the corridor outside, another door was slightly ajar. And next to that door, relaxed in one of the light blue overstuffed chairs, was long and lanky thick-mustached Jay Groder, the Cowboy.

His head rested against the chair's cushioned back; his eyes were closed. No way to tell if he'd dozed off, was asleep or merely resting. I pointed the .38 at him, walked forward, feet almost silent on the carpet. He didn't move. When I stopped in front of him, a foot away, I could see the bristly black mustache wiggle slightly, his lips fluttering as he exhaled. Cowboy was asleep. I took one long step past him, left arm extended, pressed my fingers against the partly open door, and pushed it inward. Saw a couple of chairs, a wheelchair with wide leather straps dangling from it—end of a cot or single bed, a man's feet, his lower legs half covered by the bottom edge of a green robe. At the foot of the cot was some kind of instrument or machine atop a red four-wheeled cart, a rectangular metal box about a foot and a half square and eight or ten inches high with calibrated dial on its face, electrical connections, two strange-looking paddles of some kind with twin disks at one end and dual handles at the other.

I leaned forward until I could see the rest of the bed and the man lying there. He was on his back, arms at his sides, head rolled to his right, face resting against a white pillow. His eyes were open and staring, lips parted and slack. It was, unquestionably, Claude Romanelle; but I couldn't tell if he was alive or dead. He *looked* dead.

If he was alive, he certainly wasn't excited about my appearance in the doorway. And I had a small problem. If he was dead, my goal was simply to get the hell out of here any way I could. But if there was still some life in that unmoving form, my job was to get it out of here with me.

So I wanted to move on into the small room and check Romanelle's pulse, primarily to determine if there was any. If there wasn't, I'd split; but if there was, I would then—*if* I'd simply left Cowboy here sleeping—have to come back and attend to him before getting on with what I'd come here to do.

It probably shouldn't have been a problem at all. Logically, the way to go would be to crunch Cowboy on his skull right now, no hesitation, and thus eliminate any possibility of later interference from him. Still, I hesitated. It just seemed so . . . dirty. That was it. Clunking him while he was sleeping so peacefully, with his lips and mustache fluttering delicately, would be a *dirty* thing to do. So what? I asked myself. Probably I would have to get rid of more of my scruples if I wanted to succeed in this business. I looked around, spotted a pair of heavy-looking carved-stone bookends holding half a dozen medical tomes together on a small table, grabbed one, hefted it, and eyed Cowboy's skull, right at the hairline.

These hesitations and scruples simply couldn't be tolerated. They had to go. Hesitating, I glanced back at Romanelle's corpse, or whatever it was—and he himself solved my problem for me. He moved his eyes. It was only his eyes that moved, rolling toward me and then stopping as if he could actually see me. But whether he saw anything or not, that was enough for me. Vastly relieved, I swung the bookend in a nice tight arc and slammed it against Cowboy's skull, right at the hairline.

It seemed to make a really horrible thunking sound, like dropping a large watermelon on the kitchen floor, but nothing visibly broke. Cowboy slumped, leaned a little farther over in the chair, that was all. He kept breathing, bristly mustache wiggling and lips moving slightly as air bubbled through them.

I moved swiftly to the small bed, knelt by Romanelle. His eyes followed me, but they were still staring, empty, like orbs of glass. "Romanelle," I said, "Claude. Can you talk to me?"

His lips moved. I grabbed the front of the green robe he was wearing, put one hand at his back, pulled him to a sitting position. He was trying to say something, but only distorted mewling sounds came out. Saliva slid over his lower lip, coursed in a shiny line of bubbly wetness down his chin, drooled onto his robe.

"I'm Shell Scott," I said. "Do you remember hiring me, talking to me on the phone?"

He was apparently trying to speak, but only garbled sounds came from his wet mouth, no words, nothing recognizable. So I quit trying to communicate with him, lifted him bodily, and planted him in the wheelchair. The wide leather straps were securely fastened, one at the seat and the other to the chair's back. In a few seconds I had the lower strap cinched around Romanelle's thighs and the upper one tight against his chest.

Then I draped the sheet-sized green cloth that I'd carried all the way to here over his head. It covered his entire body and most of the wheelchair as well. I didn't expect to fool anyone who might see me into thinking I was pushing a laundry hamper or the day's trash, but at least it would temporarily disguise the truth about exactly what, or who, I was trundling down the hospital hallway.

I wheeled Romanelle out of the room, past Cowboy, who still appeared to be sleeping, and to the door leading to the corridor outside; pulled the door wide, peered around its edge. The corridor was empty.

I didn't have any clear idea how long it had been since I'd sped past Bliss and Cimarron in that second room from the end. Five minutes? More? Less? They could have finished here, gone someplace else. Or they could be in that last room. No matter; I couldn't stop now.

So I guided the wheelchair out and started down the polished hallway, picking up speed until I was trotting, straining at the handles behind Romanelle's bobbing cloth-covered head to keep the unwieldy machine from veering into a wall or toppling over. Wheelchairs are not designed for efficient transport at much over a mile an hour, and guiding it occupied so much of my attention that I first saw Dr. Bliss only from the corner of my eye as he stepped from that last room on my left at the corridor's end.

By the time I saw him he was no more than ten feet away, and I sailed right past him toward the elevator, glancing into the room behind him as I went by. Alda Cimarron was just getting up from a chair, where he had apparently been resting his ton or so of muscle and bone while waiting for Bliss to finish whatever he'd been doing in there. Cimarron wasn't looking my way, and I flashed past so speedily he didn't see me. But I knew that was a temporary condition.

Because when I saw Bliss he also saw me, and after a brief moment of shocked silence which he may have required to convince himself he was truly seeing what he thought he might be seeing, he let out a high-pitched but extraordinarily piercing yell that probably carried faintly clear down to the morgue, and unquestionably informed Cimarron instantly that something undesirable was afoot.

What he yelled so piercingly was: "Jesuschristgodalmighty it's Scott—*it's Shell Scott—Alda, it's— Goodgodalmighty it's Shell Scott right here in the goddamn hall and he's—*"

I didn't hear the rest of it. Rather, I heard but didn't

understand it, because I was occupied with trying to stop short of the elevator. I had speeded up almost to a sprint and was slipping and sliding on the polished floor, pulled forward by the mass of the wheelchair plus Romanelle's weight. Be hell, I thought, with a sort of detached part of my mind, if I rescued my injured client still alive, then killed him by slamming his wheelchair into a door.

But I managed to stop without crashing, merely bumping the closed doors gently. Well, almost gently. Romanelle's head bobbed forward under the sheet, then rebounded, and for the first time I heard the noises he was making, and realized he'd been making them all along. Not words yet, just noises; but they didn't sound like pleased or happy noises. Well, you could hardly blame the guy. I tie him up and throw a sheet over him, then start racing along like a Mexico City taxi driver.

But I didn't have time to listen to what Romanelle was noising. I poked the "Down" button to get the elevator up here, then spun around, jumped back toward the open but still-empty door of that last room, going right past Dr. Bliss again, ignoring him. I wasn't worried about Bliss; not even if he'd been a surgeon with two scalpels would he have concerned me. No, the big problem I was worried about was the guy who had heard Bliss yelling about "Shell Scott" and all that other stuff, the guy who would soon be coming through that open door like a cement mixer, like an avalanche, like the solid part of an earthquake, like . . .

No, not soon. *Now.* There he was. It was really a horrible sight. He was already reaching forward as though to grab and crush something into jelly, arms thrust out and fingers clutching, as he leaped into the hallway. His lips were pulled back from those big square teeth, and the teeth were moving, grinding, as if he were gnashing them. You could tell he was really pissed off, really bugged, about something. And I had no doubt what it was that was bugging him.

But everything at that noisy, tumultuous, shocking moment seemed to have been timed almost perfectly for me. Because as I brushed past still-yelling Bliss and got nearer the door, I hauled back my right arm, bunched my fist into a near-lethal weapon; and just as huge Alda Cimarron leaped through the doorway I was starting to launch that fist; and as Cimarron sailed through the air toward me my fist sailed toward him. It was like when brilliant scientists send up a space probe going along pocketa-pocketa toward a mathematically selected point in space where several years later a planet will arrive and have pictures taken of it by the space probe, one arc tracking through space and intersecting another arc with exquisite exactitude. Like that, only this was instantaneous. Well, practically instantaneous.

I'll say this about Alda Cimarron, he had lightning-like reflexes. As he came growling and grunting and gnashing through the open doorway, he saw me right away. Of course, he was looking for me, and I was right there just about to smack him, so that was no great trick. But he also saw my already-launched lethal fist whirring through space at him and, while it would have been impossible for him to get entirely out of the way, he did manage to move his big head like lightning, jerking it to one side far enough that my fist did not destroy his entire mouth including lips and teeth and maybe gums as well. Instead, my bunched knuckles landed squarely against the side of his massive jaw, the flashing arc of my swinging arm and hand intersecting the leaping and jerking arc of his jaw with a precision as beautiful as space probe meeting planet and with such exactitude that I could not have improved upon it if I'd planned it like a scientist, using computers and drawing paper.

The sound of my terrible fist meeting his awesome jaw was almost painful to the ears, louder and bonier even than the sound Cowboy's head had made when I'd clunked him upon it with a bookend. And I knew it didn't matter how big Cimarron was, how tough, how resilient, that mighty blow had finished him.

It didn't do me a whole lot of good either. It felt as though an explosion of flying bone chips traveled from my knuckles through my wrist and elbow clear into my shoulder; as if somebody had doused my arm with gasoline, and sprained it, and then lit it. Cimarron's speedy exit from the room, combined with his solid mass, kept him going in somewhat the same direction he had originally been moving, which is to say slanting into and across the hallway, but slanting even more now and turning, spinning, his arms flailing.

I didn't even watch him hit the wall over there, but turned toward those double doors at the corridor's end. They were still closed, but I knew the elevator had to be on its way, nearly here, because I'd pressed its button. Hadn't I? Sure . . . Rapid slapping sounds were somebody's feet making tracks down the intersecting corridor. The person was out of my sight, but it had to be Dr. Bliss leaving the scene precipitously. That was O.K. with me; one down, the other one going: I'd make it out of here yet.

I took one powerful speedy leap toward the elevator—I had pushed that damned button, hadn't I?—and made it about a foot through the air. I would have made it a lot farther, except something caught on the back of my coat and shirt, tangled the cloth around my neck, and forced a gassy *"Ghaah!"* out of me. That was strange. I hadn't seen anything that could have done that. It was *really* strange.

I knew the corridor had been empty except for Bliss and Cimarron and me. Bliss was gone; Cimarron had to be lying over there crumpled near the wall, maybe groaning feebly. That left me. And I knew *I* hadn't done it. It was almost scary. No, there wasn't any almost about it. The situation was perplexing, impossible, and *very* scary. Even stranger, whatever it was that caught me had instantly started to yank at me. I'll tell you, when something happens that is *impossible*, a guy can start wondering where he's at. Thoughts of extraterrestrial forces, and bogeymen, flash into the mind. It was what you might feel—like, horrified—if a giant Killer Egg should start eating *you* for a change. And the Thing was still yanking, turning me, turning me enough so I could see . . .

No. Ah, come *on,* I thought.

If I had thundered that mighty blow against Alda Cimarron's jaw, and absolutely ruined him, knocked him senseless against the wall, then who was this huge guy? This guy with his thick lips pulled back from big square teeth that he was moving and grinding and gnashing? This guy with one hand tangled in my clothes, and the other fashioned into a giant lumpy metal hammer like the appendages of those villains in lousy movies?

It didn't really matter much who, or what, it was. The thing was clearly preparing to kill me. Well, at moments of great peril, like death, the mind shifts into a speedier dimension. Thus billions of thoughts were ricocheting around in my head like sizzling bolts of electricity. Calmly, I selected from those billions of bolts a single nut or two that fit them. This thing, whatever it was and wherever it had come from, had to be a *male* thing. Not even on Arcturus could females look as horrible as this. Therefore, it would have at least one, and probably two balls. Even though in its home country they might call them fleepobs or zerkles, no matter. And balls, by whatever name, are exquisitely sensitive instruments, as any fellow who has even slightly injured one or two can swear on a stack of Bibles.

O.K., this guy—I had concluded it was definitely a guy—had his right appendage tangled in my clothing up around my neck, and was swinging the left one at about the middle of my face. If nothing interfered with this process, that lumpy hammer was going to crack me smack between my horrified eyeballs. But the guy was also standing in a slight squat, legs far apart and bent at the knees, making him look a little like a great thick inverted wishbone with the whole turkey stuck on its top and flapping its bony wings. I knew what I had to do. More, I had not a single hesitation or scruple about doing the dirty thing. All I prayed was that I'd get a chance to do it.

Somehow I ducked, got my head down far enough that only part of that speeding missile scraped over its top, straightened up so energetically that the grip near my neck loosened, and I then moved my left foot half a step forward, swinging my right leg and foot out and up in the same kind of scientifically calculated arc designed by scientists or professional field-goal kickers, and I got him with wondrous accuracy precisely at the center of his wishbone.

That did it. That took the fight out of him. It might even have taken more than fight out. He let escape from his widely stretched mouth a totally revolting noise I will not even attempt to describe. His wide face began to resemble the one I had seen on the dead old guy downstairs. He sort of hunched forward, arms crossing in front of him, somewhat like that painting of a nude girl bending forward and shyly trying to hide her priceless.

He was slowly going down as I heard the elevator doors open behind me. I *knew* I'd pressed that button. I spun around, jumped to the wheelchair, scooted it and Romanelle into the elevator, banged the button to take us down. As the doors closed, I could see the guy on his knees, hands pushing against the polished floor, arms straightening.

Nobody else was in sight. There wasn't anybody named Alda Cimarron lying in a crumpled heap at the junction of floor and wall. So I had to face it: the guy straining his preposterously outsize arms to get up off the floor had to be Alda . . .

No. *Pushing?* Getting up? Ah, come *on,* I thought.

Not even Alda Cimarron could have both a cast-iron jaw and solid-steel fleepobs. It had to be some kind of monster. Something inhuman and fiendish. About to leap up gaily to dance after me and grab me and squash me. Cimarron? Alda? I worried about it all the way down to the first floor. Longer than that.

But, yeah, Cimarron. He didn't fight fair, that was sure. Also, if there were other ways to get down here where I was, he would know about them. He wouldn't have to wait for the elevator. Of course, he could probably just give a little hop into the air, and come crashing down through the various floors, or ceilings, 4-3-2-1 *gotcha.* I was beginning to question my invincibility. Almost.

The elevator doors opened and I sped out, pushing the wheelchair before me. I noted again that Claude Romanelle, or whatever was under the morgue sheet, was bobbing his head about and making those unintelligible, and unhappy, noises again. But even if I could have understood them I wouldn't have had time to answer. We careened around the last turn and I skidded a yard, slowing to stop at the open wooden door of the morgue—which wasn't open. I had *left* it open, but it was closed *now*. Why would anybody close it? I wondered. Who was going to leave? If the same dummy had locked it, I was in some kind of trouble.

But the door opened easily, and I got Romanelle lined up so I could scoot him through, listening to the splat-splat of rapidly moving feet, like the speedy feet of Dr. Bliss that I'd heard upstairs. No . . . That had been more of a pitter-patter; this was kind of *thunk-thunk* or *chugga-chugga,* not really like feet at all. More like a lot of trees falling.

Yeah. I turned my head right a little, and there he was. Way down at the far, or west, end of the corridor here in this, the east wing. Or wherever. I wasn't exactly sure. East, west—it could have been north and south, but wherever all this was happening, that was Alda Cimarron down there, speeding this way, bent forward somewhat and maybe limping a little, going *chugga*-thunk, *chugga*-thunk but steadily getting closer, coming right at me like a ferocious locomotive gnashing its cowcatchers.

If I hadn't been a grown man, I might have cried. It's *terribly* disheartening to give a thing your best shot using blanks. Or to try, and try, and try again and *never* succeed. Nobody ever said, "If at fourth you don't succeed . . ." A man's got to have some little successes along the way—or where's the incentive to do good?

Of course, I wasn't actually concentrating on all these flights of nausea. I was scooting Romanelle into the morgue so fast our passage probably warmed the whole room two degrees, then yanking those double doors open, zipping outside. And even before I got to that red Subaru coupe—which at least was still where I'd left it—I realized I'd done something dumb. Just one thing, fortunately; but often one dumbness is enough to do you in.

Actually, it had been a fairly sensible decision to leave the car parked as close to the cement-block wall on its left as possible, to ensure passage for any vehicles that might have to get by. But that meant I could not get in on the car's left side; I'd have to go in the same door as Romanelle

—*after* I managed to get him in there.

So I stopped next to the car, pulled its door open, yanked the green cloth from Romanelle and the wheelchair. Ack, the damned straps. Had to get the straps off him. *Chugga-thunk*. Very close; too close. With the straps undone, I picked Romanelle up and—*CHUGGA-THUNK*—said, "Sorry, old chap," and just aimed him at the door and tossed him in. No sooner was my client on his way than I was spinning around, palm slapping the S&W .38's butt at my left armpit. Right after the *blam*.

Yeah, right *after;* I hadn't spun around soon enough. Cimarron was standing in that open doorway at the far side of the morgue. I got a quick glimpse of him there, clearly visible under the fluorescent lights. The sound of the gunshot was not that of his .22, but more like a .357 Magnum. The slug passed from that open doorway where he stood, through the dimness of the morgue, out the wide double doors I'd just come through, and slammed into or bounced off the flesh of my right side, just above the hip bone, then smashed into the car behind me with the sound of a metallic explosion.

I was sure the slug had barely nicked me, hadn't done real damage, but somehow I was pushed back against the car, my back banging the doorframe with an impact that seemed much greater than the slug's almost gentle slap. I flipped the .38 up, leveled it, fired twice at Cimarron. His bulk loomed for a moment longer in the doorway then disappeared as he jumped sideways and out of my sight.

I literally dived into the coupe, going right over Romanelle and banging his legs somewhat on the way. No help for it. Digging the keys out of my pocket, I said, just in case he had some vague idea of what was going on, "Sorry, old chap. I'll apologize properly later. If there is a later. Just doing the best I can, old chap."

I jabbed the key into the ignition but, before even turning the engine over, leaned far to my right—inevitably squashing Romanelle slightly in the process—fired two more shots at that far door, then started the engine and took off so fast, tires screeching on the asphalt, that the still-open right door of the Subaru slammed shut with no help from me.

I put the pedal to the metal as the race guys say, risked several collisions barreling through the west parking lot and skidding into McDowell Road. My fingers found ragged holes in my coat and shirt, a rip in the flesh of my right side. The gouge wasn't deep, wasn't dangerous, but it was finally starting to hurt. There was hot wetness on my side and hip, like burning blood. Besides that, I had a tight drawing sensation at the base of my skull, a prickling coolness along my spine. Because I recalled Alda Cimarron, clubbed as though by a sledgehammer but still not going down; then going down but getting back up with unbelievable speed; then *chugga*-thunking toward me down that corridor. I knew, I was absolutely certain, that he could not possibly be racing along behind us, reaching out to grab my bumper and throw us away. But, still . . .

So I just kept on going lickety-split, heeding the advice of that wise old Negro philosopher—he was a Negro then, before the National Association for the Advancement of Colored People helped change it to black—Satchel Paige, who said, "Don't look back. Somethin' may be gainin' on you."

Chapter Seventeen

AFTER FIVE MINUTES of trying futilely to communicate with Claude Romanelle, I accepted the fact that he was more vegetable than human, at least for the time being if not for all time, and sat by the phone, dialed Hollywood, California, long-distance direct. The Spartan Apartment Hotel. Room 214, Dr. Paul Anson's apartment next door to my own. Paul worked only a half day on Thursdays; maybe he'd be home.

We, my client and I, were in a really cheesy motel on the edge of Tempe, a few miles south of Scottsdale. I'd finally looked back. No Alda Cimarron, no police cars, no signs of pursuit. And, after making sure nobody could possibly be tailing the Subaru coupe, I had pulled into the first motel I saw with a vacancy sign. The car was parked behind the motel; I was reasonably certain nobody had seen me carrying Romanelle into the room. I had patched the superficial wound in my side, temporarily, with a towel under my belt, and except for a little burning pain it didn't bother me, didn't inhibit my movement. The blue jacket, white shirt, and trousers were of course ruined: torn and stained with blood. I figured Romanelle and I were both safe enough for the moment, but—what next?

At least, I was lucky with the phone call. Paul was at his apartment, not having stopped at his club, or a bar, or lady's boudoir on the way home from his office. Unusual for 1:30 P.M. Arizona time, which would be the same as California's daylight saving time.

When Paul answered, I told him who was calling and went right on with my tale, overriding his "Hi" and "What the hell are you doing in the desert?"

When I'd finished, he said, "Your informant said these heavies sent some 'electricities' through his head?"

"That's what he claimed."

"Describe the equipment with the dials and funny paddles again."

I did, telling Paul everything I could remember, which wasn't a great deal because I'd been more concerned about Romanelle and getting him—and me—out of the hospital. But Paul said, "Sure. The thing on the red table—which is called a crash cart, by the way—sounds like a defibrillator. Those paddles could hardly be part of anything else."

"Is that the thing they use in hospitals when a guy's heart stops?"

"Right. They put those paddles on the chest at opposite sides of the heart, press a button on the handle's end, and send a current from one paddle to the other—through the heart—to shock it back into activity if it's failing. When it works, that is. From what you say, they must have put those paddles on both sides of your man's *head*. That's unbelievable. It would be incredibly dangerous . . ." He paused. "Few hospitals are equipped to perform ECT —electroconvulsive therapy, sometimes electroshock as you called it. But just about any hospital would have defibrillators for use in emergency situations, in the O.R., for critical heart patients. But, my God, to use a defibrillator like *that* . . . ? The current is only in milliamps, but in untrained hands it could ruin a man, even kill him, rip through those delicate neurons and synapses and fragile pathways in the brain like a bowling ball through glass. If that's *really* what they did—but, you know, it does sound like it, Shell. You say the man is not unconscious, but he can't talk. Makes sounds, not words. Apparently attempting to communicate, but unable to make it work. Right?"

"Right. Something's in there. He looks at me. Moves his mouth, nods his head. But that's it."

"Can he walk?"

"I'm not sure. I got him on his feet here in the room, and

he was able to stand. But that was as far as we got. Is there any kind of doctor who might do . . . well, something? Anything? I'm sure Romanelle can't even eat or drink, the way he is."

"Yeah, there's one man, Shell, and he's in Scottsdale. I was going through my book while we talked. No guarantee he can help, but if anybody can, Barry Midland is your man. Barry is something special. He's a fine, superbly qualified orthomolecular physician, but also a homeopath, into a number of unorthodox therapies. Something of a maverick and brutally outspoken at times, thus considered somewhat beyond the pale by his more conservative peers —but he is very, very good. Equally important, he owes me a large favor. And this one sounds maybe gigantic." He paused. "If I get this to work for you, pal, it means he and I are even and *you* owe me."

"You've got it."

"Here's his number. Write it down." He read it off to me. "Wait ten minutes after we hang up, then call him. I'll phone him first and pave the way. No guarantees, but I think Barry will do what he can."

"I hope so. And thanks, Paul. Incidentally, speaking of favors, you might be interested in knowing that Kay, the lovely lady who put you down so unpleasantly in my apartment, did it merely as part of a devious plan."

"How's that?"

"The only reason she was hanging around was to find out about the job I was on, pick up what she could about my working for a client—assignment from an outfit she works for here called Exposé, Inc.—and she got considerably more than I thought I was giving her."

He had started to laugh. "You mean she was investigating the investigator, playing your game?"

"I . . . guess you could say that. Turned the tables on me. And I didn't much like it, now you mention it."

"So, then, this lovely Kay Denver really did lust and hunger for me, as I suspected, and sent me on my way in order to deceive the deceiver. Thus she is probably now pining away, regretting—"

"Yeah, sure," I said. "I thought I would do you a small

favor and tell you this, Paul, to help you overcome your crushing feelings of inferiority. Her name isn't Denver, by the way. It's Kay Dark."

"How about that? Well, pal, I appreciate your telling me. I really do. O.K., I'll call Barry and try to pave your way."

We hung up. I waited ten minutes, phoned the number Paul had given me. The receptionist put me through to Dr. Midland immediately. He was fast-talking, efficient, brisk. He said his good friend, Dr. Anson, had explained the situation to him and he had agreed to help, if he could. He asked three questions about Romanelle's condition and appearance, then asked where the patient and I were. I gave him the motel's address. He said he had to see one more patient in his office, but would be at the motel in thirty to forty minutes. He made it in thirty-five.

When the light knock came at the door, I cracked it, saw a man in a brown business suit, carrying a black medical bag and something that looked like pieces of pipe or thin metal tubing. I opened the door, stepped back as he came in.

He glanced at the revolver in my hand, then ignored it, looking around for the patient. "I'm Dr. Midland," he said. "You're Mr. Scott?"

"Right."

The man was young, I thought, for a doctor of whom Paul spoke so highly. In his middle thirties, I guessed, slim, about five-ten and 150 pounds, a lot of dark brown hair, professionally styled, rimless glasses over sharp brown eyes.

Looking at me, he said, "What happened to you? Those are bloodstains, aren't they?"

He was indicating my right side. I'd taken off my jacket, so the red stains were obvious on my shirt and pants.

"Yeah," I said, "it's blood, but I've got practically a full tank left. I'm O.K., the bleeding's stopped." I jerked a thumb. "He's the patient."

Dr. Midland cocked his head on one side, apparently noting the holes in my shirt. "Would that have occurred in connection with . . . what happened to the patient?"

I said, "It sure did. The patient's name, as Dr. Anson

may have mentioned, is Claude Romanelle. He hired me to do a job for him, which I haven't finished yet. But when I located Mr. Romanelle, I had a little difficulty getting him away from the people who did this to him."

"Hmm. I'll look at your side later."

He turned, stepped to the large overstuffed chair in which Romanelle was seated, placed his bag on the floor and opened it. For the next couple of minutes the doctor concentrated on his patient, speaking to me from time to time but without looking around. He took Romanelle's temperature, then affixed a blood-pressure cuff to Romanelle's arm, started pumping air into it with the small hand-operated bulb. After that he listened to heart and lung sounds through a stethoscope.

I finally stuck the .38 S&W back into my holster, and said, "I appreciate your coming here, Doctor. And I'll certainly pay you whatever—"

"You'll pay me nothing. I wouldn't do this for money."

While speaking, he'd put the blood-pressure apparatus and stethoscope back into his bag and picked up the pieces of what I'd thought was metal tubing. In a few seconds he'd erected a six-foot-high tripod with a projecting hook at its top. When he hung on the hook a plastic bag containing about a quart of amber-colored liquid, I recognized the setup as the kind I'd seen often in hospitals, with fluids running from such a bag through a plastic tube down to a needle in the patient's arm.

Dr. Midland cleaned a spot on Romanelle's left arm using a moist cotton pad, took a hypodermic needle from a glass vial, saying, "Mr. Romanelle's temperature and blood pressure are subnormal, but not seriously so. He's been treated abominably."

I said, "I guess they damn near killed him. I thought he was on his last legs when I—"

For the first time since he'd approached his patient, Dr. Midland looked at me. And it wasn't just a look, it was a glare. He snapped his head around and fixed his eyes on my face, glowering, saying rapidly, "Mr. Romanelle is going to be *fine*, Mr. Scott. There is *no* serious damage. He has suffered physical and neurological insult, but fortunately the symptoms of disability are transient. In a very short time he will be his normal self."

He almost barked the words at me, those brown eyes seeming to become darker. And that was when I decided Barry Midland was not only a doctor for sure, but a damned good one, everything Paul Anson had said he was.

I should have known better than to blurt out the comment I'd just made about Romanelle's condition. It was Paul himself, here in Arizona at the Mountain Shadows Resort during an earlier case, who had told me some very important things that I'd temporarily forgotten. Everyone, even the healthy, is affected by the suggestions—maybe even the thoughts—of those around him. But the already ill patient, particularly one in an impersonal hospital setting, isolated and weakened and with his energies and defenses further diminished by surgery or other treatment, is hypersuggestible. Make him believe he'll get better and the chances are he will; but convince him there's little hope, or even worse that he has a fatuously named "incurable" disease—meaning only that the particular fathead treating him doesn't know how to improve the patient's condition—and there's a wonderful chance he'll obligingly kick the bucket on schedule, thus brilliantly confirming the criminal diagnosis.

But what had struck me most about Paul's comments to me on that earlier occasion—when, as it happened, *I* was the patient—was that even when anesthetized or unconscious or asleep or deep in coma, the patient hears *everything,* all the moaning and negative predictions and "Yuck, will you look at that crap next to the liver?" and "A friend of mine had exactly the same thing and died three days later, poor dear," or "I thought he was on his last legs." Maybe he doesn't consciously hear the words but an always alert inner part of the self hears it, records it with a completeness and fidelity far more perfect than the electronic engrams of a computer's memory, and sometimes lets it seep into consciousness with devastating effect. Or with splendidly positive effects, if the suggestions were like those of Barry Midland.

I watched, with increased interest, as Dr. Midland deftly

thrust the needle into a vein in Romanelle's arm, removed a clamp from the plastic tubing above it, watched the fluid dripping, adjusted the flow to speed up the drip.

I said, "Any objections, Doctor, to telling me what you're giving him?"

"Not at all." He glanced up at me again, and almost smiled. "I'm not one of those physicians who feel the patient is better off when kept in ignorance of the doctor's magical unpronounceabilities." At that, he actually did smile. "I had my nurse prepare this IV bag before I left the office. The base is the usual lactated Ringer's injection, essentially water and electrolytes—little else of value, unfortunately. I think if you're introducing fluids into a patient's bloodstream, that's the best possible opportunity to nourish him, provide nutritional support to restore his energies, support the glands and nerves and cells that will help him recover."

"You keep making more and more sense to me, Doc —Doctor."

"Doc's O.K., Mr. Scott." He touched the IV bag with one finger. "Primarily, and most important, I've added to the Ringer's several grams of sulfite-free sodium ascorbate, vitamin C suitable for venous infusion. In *every* case of infection, toxemia, shock, injury, or trauma—as, for example, the trauma of surgery—ascorbate should be given the patient by the physician, at least in large oral doses, and preferably by intravenous infusion if the situation is acute or the prognosis doubtful."

"Ascorbate. That's a fancy word for plain old vitamin C?" I said, squinting at Midland.

"Plain old *miraculous* vitamin C. Its administration should be routine, especially in hospitals and surgical wards. Sadly, most physicians simply will not employ this extraordinarily safe and effective modality, even though their refusal to do so may, and often does, result in the delayed recovery or even death of the patient."

"*Death* of the patient? Isn't that a little strong, Doc? A little exaggerated, maybe?"

"Not at all." He scowled, looking much as he had when glaring at me a minute before. "Any physician, but particularly any surgeon or oncologist, who withholds needed ascorbate from his hypoascorbemic patient should be considered guilty—and in truth *is* guilty—of criminal negligence and medical malpractice."

"Paul told me you were unusual," I said. "But I'm beginning to think maybe he didn't tell me the half of it." I grinned, and the doctor actually smiled again. "What else is in the soup?" I asked him. "Liquefied prime ribs and potatoes?"

"Not quite. Additional calcium and potassium, plus a seasoning of zinc and magnesium—mostly in the form of orotates and aspartates. Emulsified vitamin A, laetrile, a small amount of dimethyl sulfoxide, or DMSO. We're going to feed those nerve complexes, support the immune system, restore the electrolytic balance disrupted by what must have been quite brutal, and excessive, electrical insult."

While talking, Midland had prepared another hypodermic syringe, filling its barrel with solutions from two separate vials, then affixing a new sterile needle. He didn't stick that one anywhere into Romanelle, but instead introduced it into a port in the plastic line between the IV bag and needle already in Romanelle's left arm. Slowly he depressed the plunger, sending the syringe's contents into the tube, thence almost immediately into the needle and the bloodstream.

"Pentothal," Dr. Midland said, without being asked.

"Sodium pentothal? Like the—truth serum?"

"Same thing. This will relax Mr. Romanelle completely, throughout his body—particularly with the other ingredient of the recipe, which is anectine, a curare derivative. These drugs will also block normal brain-cell transmission. But, later, I'll give the patient sublingual drops of homeopathic acetylcholine, which will reestablish normal transmission."

"Just what I was going to say," I said.

He smiled. Not a bad sort at all, this guy.

Dr. Midland told me it would take perhaps another hour for the IV fluid to drip into Romanelle's vein, even though he was infusing it so rapidly that it could later become painful to the patient. But since he would remain here until the job was done, he might as well take a look at me. Fifteen minutes later he had disinfected and bandaged the gash on my right side, and also replaced the amateurish gauze and tape lumpiness I'd affixed to my left shoulder last night. Had that been only last night? It seemed like a week ago to me.

As he finished, Midland said, "I can see you're not a doctor."

I grinned. "I can see you are."

He pressed a final strip of tape against the shoulder bandage, saying, "Same fellows who gave you the most recent bloodiness?"

"Same kind."

"I'll give you an injection, if you'd like. About five grams of that miraculous sodium ascorbate, plus a few trinkets."

"Fine. Give me a little of everything you've got. Although . . . could I swallow it?"

He smiled, fumbled in his bag, took out an absolutely enormous plastic syringe, and proceeded to fill it from one large and several little-bitty bottles.

"Couldn't I just swallow it?" I asked again.

As he affixed a horribly pointed, and sharp, and ugly needle at the syringe's end, I said, "Doctor, maybe I don't need . . . Uh, getting shot by bullets, that's one thing. But one of those needles, perhaps I should confess—"

"Don't tell me you're afraid of a little needle, Mr. Scott."

"That is *not* a little needle. I have seen samurai warriors beheaded with smaller . . ."

He swabbed my skin, bringing the pointed instrument closer and closer to a bulging vein in my arm.

"Oh-hh," I said. "Hey, I've changed my mind—"

"Just pretend this is a gun," he said.

"Don't I wish . . . *Hoo!* Boy, that *hurts.*"

He smiled some more, the way doctors do, and with his thumb began slowly depressing the plunger.

"That hurts, too," I said.

"Ummh-hmm," he said.

It took about two depressing minutes, but by the time he

slipped the needle out and pressed a small bandage over the puncture wound, I was feeling better. At least, I no longer felt embarrassingly faint.

"That should prevent infection, and also help you get around more easily," Midland said. "Assuming your plans include some moving around."

"They sure do. Right about now, in fact—if you've no objections."

He shook his head.

I said, "I need to get out of here for half an hour or so. And about the only chance for me to leave is while you're here with Mr. Romanelle. At least, until he's less . . . until he's better."

"Mr. Romanelle will be fine, very shortly."

"Are you—" I stopped, started over very softly, mouthing the words, "Are you sure?"

"I'm certain of it," he said in a normal tone, quite loud enough for Romanelle to hear, if he was hearing. I wished I knew if that answer was meant for me, or primarily for the patient.

But I said, "Splendid. Never doubted it for a minute," then walked toward the door.

Dr. Midland stopped me. "You're leaving now? Going out—there?"

"Yeah, out there, into the sizzling desert sands, the cold mean streets . . . What's that for?"

He had taken off the coat of his brown suit and extended it toward me. "You'd better take my jacket," he said. "Without it, you'll look like an axe murderer. Or the victim."

I started to protest, but didn't; he was absolutely right. The bloodstains on my trousers, and especially on the sport shirt, could not fail to be noticed by anyone who might see me. In fact, one of the reasons I had to leave was to return to the Registry for clothing that looked less like part of a massacre. Besides, I wanted to see Spree again. I very *much* wanted to see lovely Spree.

"Thanks, Doctor," I said. "That would help."

It would, but not because I'd be wearing it. The coat was too small; I couldn't get it on without splitting some seams.

"Guess I can carry it, and hide the yuck," I said.

"If you get shot any more, throw it away before you bleed much, will you? I'm fond of this suit."

"Sure," I said. "And if I find time to write a will, I'll leave you my entire wardrobe."

He smiled without much enthusiasm. I went out.

First thing, I had to ditch Andy Foster's car. Alda Cimarron and maybe a dozen of his pals undoubtedly knew that red Subaru on sight. I couldn't park it at the lot where I'd told Andy I would leave it in a day or two, not while wearing these bloodstained clothes; that would have to wait for a while. So I drove half a mile, parked the coupe, and stole a Ford, a new blue Taurus.

Nobody yelled "Stop, thief!" as I drove away, but the thought gave me a twinge, a bit of a chill. I was starting to feel like a criminal. Well, maybe in a way I was; I guess it's largely in your point of view. I intended to make amends, if I could, to the guy whose name was on the registration slip in the Taurus's glove compartment; but I had a hunch he might not easily comprehend *my* point of view—that, perhaps, sometimes the end does justify the means. Which, of course, despite much comment to the contrary, is true.

I parked behind the Registry Resort, walked a few feet to villa 333, and knocked gently, knocked again, and right after that, from just inside the door, "Hello? Is that—you? Is it you, Sh—Bill?"

I must have been more worried about her than I knew, preoccupied below the mind's surface with anxiety and concern, even desire and suppressed longing for Spree, lovely soft-voiced sweet-fleshed Spree, because I was amazed at the tangible wave of relief joined with sudden warm pleasure that swept over me when I heard her speak, the intensity of not easily identifiable emotions that leaped up in me. I was letting this one get to me, slip into normally inviolate cracks and crevices in my armor. And that wouldn't do. At least, I guessed it wouldn't.

"That's me, same old Sh-Bill who hugged you good-bye this morning. Just came back for some hello." I paused. "You going to leave me out here?"

Then there was the sound of clicking and clacking and the door swinging open, and there she was, smiling, both arms held out toward me, unmoving but getting closer —because I wasn't just standing out there, I was moving toward her quite enthusiastically. It was all very simple, automatic, natural. I put my arms around her shoulders, felt her arms slide around my waist, her hands pressing against my back as that incredible, magical, heart-blinding face lifted toward mine. I bent toward her and our lips met gently, tentatively, like strangers saying hello, quested, searched, accepted.

And then for a while, I'm not sure how long—who knows? A few seconds, a minute, a day and a half?—her lips and tongue and mouth, her magnificent breasts and firm thighs, the heat of her loins, and whatever the bright flame was that burned inside her, all were like an extension of me, a part of me, familiar, remembered, right.

With her hands clasped behind my back she squeezed that curving, yielding body even closer against mine, tugging with surprising strength—with one arm somehow right over the bandage Dr. Midland had so recently put there, right over the still-raw wound.

Involuntarily I drew back, letting out a grunt, something like, "Gack!"

Spree, her face flushed, looked up at me then moved her left hand, felt the bandage, dropped her gaze to my side. Her eyes widened. "Oh, Good *Lord*," she said. "What in the world . . . what happened to you?"

"Nothing," I said. "Nothing much. Oh-oh, where's my coat? I mean, the doc's coat? He'll kill me, he'll never trust me again if—ah, there it is."

It was crumpled on the floor near a chair. I had apparently given it quite a toss.

Spree had stepped back, one hand at her throat, still gazing at my stained shirt and trousers—well, the way a woman looks at something *ugly*.

I said, "O.K., a guy shot at me. Barely plinked me. That's all, nothing to worry about."

"But there's so much *blood*."

"Only because I *have* so much, dear. Or had. Now it's

just about right. Actually I feel lots better. All that extra blood slopping around in there was driving me crazy."

She fixed those great almost-glowing green eyes on mine, shaking her head slightly, and finally smiled. It was only a small smile. Small for her, not the full treatment. Still, for a moment I felt as though I might have lost more vital fluids than I'd suspected, as if a bunch had leaked out of me when I wasn't looking. The way Spree's smile always affected me, I thought, must have something to do with witchcraft, or magic; or maybe faint memory of Andromeda, and Orion, and forever.

"Aren't you the lucky one?" she said. "Why, he might have missed you entirely."

"Yeah, that would've been a crock," I said. "Well, hi there."

"Hi yourself. So tell me everything."

"I've found your dad."

Silence for two or three long seconds. Then, "Where—"

"He's . . ." I debated briefly, decided to level with her. I told Spree how I'd found her father, most of what had happened since then except the name of the motel where I'd left him, and finished with, "So he's safe for now. But because of what those guys did to him, I haven't been able to talk with your father at all yet."

"My God, what a terrible . . ."

She stopped, walked to the couch and sat on it. "He hasn't said anything? Not a word?"

"Not a word."

"You say a doctor's with him now, Shell?"

"Right. And he impresses me as a very good man. I'm optimistic. And I'd better get back there. Just came here to change clothes. Of course, I thought I might say hello to you while I was at it."

She smiled. "That was some hello."

It was almost an invitation to say it again, but I knew I had to get out of here without undue delay, so I went upstairs to the bedroom. Five minutes later, after a very careful cleanup in the shower, I put on pale green slacks and a matching sport shirt, added a pair of heavy cordovan shoes plus a creamy-beige jacket, and went downstairs.

Spree was still sitting on the couch.

She said, "I watched all the TV news I could, at eleven-thirty and noon. They mentioned Dad, and . . . what happened last night. There wasn't anything about me, or you, either, Shell. But it isn't likely they'd know anything about us . . . about our being here, would they?"

"Maybe not by noon. But that may change before long. A lot depends on how Alda Cimarron handles his end. Of course, he wouldn't want it known that he was holding Romanelle prisoner. So we may stay lucky. When's the next newscast?"

"Five P.M. I'll watch it."

"I've been trying to decide whether to call the cops myself, get some police protection for your dad. And you, for that matter. But I was hoping I could talk to him first, find out—well, find out a lot more than I know now, and that doesn't look too promising at the moment."

"Would you have to tell the police about last night? Shooting that man?"

"Honey, I'd have to tell them a lot of things. Unless something's changed, the police suspect your *dad* of shooting Keats. I'd have to explain that, and undoubtedly answer several yards of other questions. All of which would keep me tied up for hours. Maybe days. And I can't risk that yet."

I was ready to go. I left the Colt automatic on the closet shelf, but under my jacket was my familiar clamshell holster, in it the unfamiliar Smith & Wesson .38-caliber revolver, fully loaded again. Dr. Midland's brown jacket was draped over my arm.

"Well . . ." I said.

"I guess you have to go."

"Yeah. I'll call you when I can."

"Do, Shell. It—it helps."

"Maybe all the problems will work out pretty soon, and we can just relax a little. Maybe your dad will be his old self by the time I get back to him. Maybe the worst is over, Spree."

"Sure," she said.

I could tell she didn't believe it.

Neither did I.

I parked behind the motel again, walked around and knocked gently on the door of the room I'd left forty minutes earlier. In a few seconds Dr. Midland peered out, then pulled the door wide. I went in, handing him his brown coat and saying, "Thanks for the partial disguise. How's Romanelle doing?" At least that's what I started to say. But I only got as far as "How's Rom—"

Because somebody else in the room spoke then, in a strong vibrant voice. And what the man said was, "Well, either you rented that crazy head in a costume shop or you must be Shell Scott."

Chapter Eighteen

I JERKED MY head around, saw Claude Romanelle still sitting in the chair where he'd been when I left, only now upright, leaning forward, one arm resting on his knee, looking up at me with a half smile on his face.

My reaction was delayed. Only for a few seconds, perhaps because the voice and critical nature of the comment were not unfamiliar, or maybe because shock and disbelief momentarily tilted my brain. But I scowled across the room at him and said, "Listen, Romanelle, if you were about to make some crack about 'rented for Halloween' or . . ." I stopped.

And *then* it hit me.

When it did, the shock was like an unexpected blow. It stiffened my muscles, plucked at my nerves. Unquestionably, that was Claude Romanelle looking at me, *talking* to me. Where was the drooling idiot I'd left here less than three quarters of an hour ago?

It took two or three minutes for Dr. Midland to bring me up to date, in part because Romanelle kept interrupting. One thing Dr. Midland said was that he thought the electroshock had temporarily paralyzed, or stunned, that part of the brain controlling speech, so that though Romanelle might have known what he wanted to say, and have been thinking—at least part of the time—with reasonable clarity, he just couldn't get the mind to instruct his tongue and vocal cords to correctly form the words and make them audible.

"It wasn't merely that area, of course," Dr. Midland continued. "The entire brain was affected. Fortunately, not irreversibly. It could have been much worse."

"Just couldn't talk worth a damn, and half the time I couldn't *think* worth a damn." That was Romanelle again. "But I was aware of part of it and remember part—like you hauling me around in some kind of goddamn tent, Scott, and throwing me into a car, half squashing me, banging me around. Hell, I thought you must be the enemy, maybe working for Cimarron. Or the Nazis—"

"Will you knock it off?" I asked him. "I realize, from your carefully reasoned point of view, I should have taken more time getting you out of the Medigenic, and handled your invalid bod with much greater care, in order that Cimarron could shoot *both* of us several times, instead of just me. I also realize—"

He interrupted. "Shot? You got shot?"

"Only once today. I know this must disappoint you—"

Then Dr. Midland got into the dialogue somehow, saying, "Mr. Scott received a superficial flesh wound, which I've bandaged. But it certainly was a gunshot wound."

Romanelle seemed slightly taken aback. But all he said was, "Indeed. That was . . . nice of you, Scott."

"Will you listen to him?" I said to Midland. "He must not be feeling well."

But then I took another look at Claude Romanelle, still marveling at the change in him. I knew he was fifty-eight years old, but—even after all the man had been through lately—he might have passed for five, or even ten, years younger. He had sharp features, long nose, wide brow slanting down to a narrow chin, a full head of straight dark hair streaked with gray. He did look slightly satanic, as I'd thought when I first saw that photograph of him, but he was not a bad-looking man at all. In fact, some might have thought Romanelle handsome.

I turned to the doctor, who was gathering his things together and preparing to leave. "When did he come out of . . . well, what I left here?"

"About ten minutes before you returned," Midland said.

"And quite suddenly, as I expected would be the case."

"He put some little drops in my mouth, and *zing,* it was like lights started going on inside my head—"

Midland interrupted his patient this time, probably having practiced it during the ten minutes before I got back here. "I mentioned to you, Mr. Scott, that at the proper time I would administer homeopathic acetylcholine, which should reestablish normal transmission of electrical impulses among the brain's cells. When I put the drops under Mr. Romanelle's tongue, his response was almost immediate, and extremely gratifying."

"I wish I'd seen it," I said. "But would I have believed it?"

He smiled. "Probably not. Results from administration of properly selected homeopathic remedies are sometimes —only sometimes, of course, and dependent upon the acuteness as opposed to chronicity of the symptoms—so swift and profound as to appear miraculous to the layman." His smile widened. "Even to most physicians."

"The doc's going to cure my cancer," Romanelle said brightly.

Midland winced visibly, scowled at Romanelle. "I told you not to *say* that," he barked.

"I forgot. Must be because I had all those volts shot through my head—"

"Please don't forget again." Midland looked at me, still scowling. "I have assured Mr. Romanelle that, if he wishes, I will examine him and *attempt* to strengthen his immune system, balance his body chemistry, restore those vital energies essential for optimum health. Sometimes when this is done—usually, in fact—the body will itself eliminate aberrant cells, among other deficiencies, and restore the patient to what should be his natural condition."

"But, hell, Doc, what I've *got* is a gastric carcinoma that's metast—"

Midland ignored Romanelle, looked at me again. "You might, if it is possible, Mr. Scott, remind Mr. Romanelle after I leave that I will not even attempt to cure his cancer, which is a phrase that has here been employed only by him, not by me. Nobody 'cures cancer.' Some physicians, a few, do improve the health and vigor of patients with conditions diagnosed as one or another form of malignancy. But the only authorized methods for treating *cancer,* at least in this country, are cutting by surgery, burning by radiation, and poisoning by chemotherapy—which, unfortunately, don't work. They attack only the symptoms, not the cause, thus they never have worked. Also unfortunately, while those approved methods seldom kill the cancer they often do kill the patient. Gentler methods—*any* other methods —are outlawed in the United States, even if they produce results vastly superior to orthodox treatment."

He mumbled something almost inaudible at the end there. I thought it sounded like, "Especially if they do," but I couldn't be sure.

Dr. Midland, looking intently at Romanelle but with what might have been a half smile on his face, said briskly, "I hope you were listening. If so, I trust you will never again suggest that I might treat your condition by any procedure other than surgery, irradiation, chemotherapy, or burying you alive in an African anthill—unless you *want* me to lose my medical license and conceivably be arrested and imprisoned, like a number of my rebellious colleagues."

He paused, sighed, went on. "There is no reason you shouldn't be all right now, Mr. Romanelle, even without further immediate treatment from me. Just take it easy, get as much rest as you can. On that other matter, your . . . indigestion, make an appointment with my receptionist if you wish to pursue it."

Then he glanced at me. "Good afternoon, Mr. Scott. Tell Paul hello for me when you see him."

"I'll tell him more than that, Dr. Midland. Are you sure I can't pay you for—"

"No." He shook his head. "Just . . . please don't ever ask me to do anything like this again." He paused, then added, "Entirely aside from the treatment I gave Mr. Romanelle, some of which was not entirely orthodox, I also treated a gunshot wound. Yours, Mr. Scott. I will have to report that, you understand. But I can delay the report until tomorrow, if it will help."

"It will. Thanks again."

"I'll delay it then." He shrugged. "Since I have already broken nearly every other medical dictate today, except my Hippocratic Oath."

He went out. I locked the door behind him, then pulled a chair over next to where Romanelle sat and said to him, "Now that you *can* talk, do it. And don't leave anything out."

He looked steadily at me. "First things first, Scott. I hired you to find my daughter, and deliver her to me. Have you found her?"

I shook my head. I still couldn't come to grips with the almost miraculous change in this guy. In less than an hour he'd gone from a near vegetable to this tough sharp-as-before old codger. It was nonetheless true that he probably wouldn't know what had happened in the last couple of days—except what had been happening to him.

"Yes, I have," I said. "She's here in Arizona, and safe. Once I get the two of you together my job's done. But there are a couple of problems that have to be taken care of first. And some answers I need from you."

"You've found her? She's really here? How is she —what's she like, Scott?"

"I told you, she's safe. She's fine. And, well, she's a bright, beautiful young woman. Your little Spree is a big girl now, Mr. Romanelle, and she's . . . splendid."

"When can I see her?"

"When you won't get us all killed doing it." I leaned toward him. "A little while ago, when you said 'first things first,' I thought maybe you couldn't wait to tell me how pleased and relieved and happy you are that I got you away from Cimarron and Bliss and the Cowboy. Before they put your brain in a bottle and stuck it on a shelf with the other pathological specimens. Where did I go wrong?"

He grinned. He really seemed amused, almost pleased. "Goddammit, Scott, I like your style. You must be as cantankerous as I am. Well . . . for some reason, I always had trouble thanking anybody, for anything. Little speck on my beautiful character. But, well, ah . . . thanks. Yes. Thanks for springing me from Alda and Bliss and Groder, even if you goddamn near killed me doing it." He paused. "You know who all three of 'em are, huh?"

"I know a good deal more than their names, Romanelle. And I expect to know a lot more than I do now when you finish filling in the cracks. So start anyplace you want, whatever's comfortable. Just get started."

He nodded. "Fair enough. Well, when I talked to you on the phone Monday, I was in the hospital. Got released the next day, went home that night, and they were waiting there for me, already in the house." He cocked his head on one side. "That was Tuesday night. What day is it now?"

"Thursday. Who was there?"

"Jay Groder and Fred Keats. Fred laid a sap over my head. No need for it, I'd set everything up the way I wanted it, and I wasn't going to run. No need for the damned sap. Somebody ought to kill that crazy sonofabitch."

"I already did," I said.

"What? You what?"

When I had talked to Andy Foster, by pretending I knew more than I did I'd gotten info from him that he might not have spilled otherwise. This Claude Romanelle was a different breed of cat, but it was probably even more important that he be informed, right here at the start, that I knew much more than he might suspect. Sure, he was my client; but I had a hunch he might leave a few facts out of his tale if he believed I wouldn't catch the omissions. And I didn't want anything left out, so I decided to hit him with a lot all at once.

So I said, "I shot and killed Fred Keats last night in your home. He was there—with Dr. Bliss, by the way —pretending to be you, had your driver's license in his wallet. Which I checked after I killed him."

Romanelle's interest was complete. His large dark eyes, large like Spree's but brown, were fixed unmoving on my face as I continued, "You might also want to know that it was the Cowboy—Jay Groder—who shot you last week. Andy Foster was with him but Andy didn't hit you, he didn't even try to. You might want to thank him one of these days."

"How the hell—"

"Toker's dead, incidentally. I don't know—"

"He's dead? Jesus H.—"

"—if that fake assay on Golden Phoenix is public knowledge, haven't seen it on the news, but that part of the con's sure to pop pretty soon. I haven't checked the price of the stock today, so I don't know if it's in the toilet yet. Today, tomorrow, next week, gotta be soon. Want me to call Paine Webber for a quote on GPXM?"

Romanelle took a deep breath, let it out. "You're something else," he said. "Where'd you *get* all this?"

"It's my business."

"And it's all true? Keats, Groder, and . . . Toker?"

"It's all true."

He was silent for at least fifteen or twenty seconds, eyes rolled left toward a corner of the room. Then he looked back at me. "A ton of shit," he said slowly, "is going to hit the fan."

"So why don't you get busy filling me in, Romanelle? Fill in the parts I may *not* know, and maybe we can avoid some of the spray."

He nodded. "I guess you must already understand the basic scam was to run Phoenix way up from two bits or so and bail out around thirty. Only using a real mine, with some real gold ore in it, instead of just a paper play, and building it all up for three, four years, a heavy but careful operation. It was going to be over in another month or so. After one more sensational assay report from Toker —which isn't likely to happen now, is it?"

"Not unless it comes through in a séance."

"I have little faith that it will. Well, Alda and the doc each had a million shares going in, there's three million back East with the money guys, some very hard guys indeed. And I pulled a million for my part in the play. I've got a little more leeway with my piece than they do, because I'm not legally an officer of the company, just a . . . consultant."

He shifted in the chair, crossed one leg over the other, still wearing that green hospital robe he'd had on when I

found him. I'd have to dig up some suitable clothing fo
him; but that small problem didn't concern me much a
the moment.

Romanelle went on, "About my part, maybe it doesn'
look sweeter than sarsaparilla, but I came into this thing
kicking and scratching. None of it was my idea."

"Sure."

"It's the truth, Scott. You don't need to believe it. But
well, it goes back a long way. Back to Chicago, the old days
when I was hooked up with Derabian and his bunch. Alda
Cimarron was just a kid then, tough, smart, nearly as big a
he is now. He was muscle then. Me, I worked a little con
did a scam or two, nothing fancy, and no violence. Bu
then . . . well, I killed a guy. Self-defense, the mark didn'
cool out, blew his top, jumped me. I never carried a gun
but I ducked, picked up one of those big vases with sand i
it, the kind you put out cigarettes in, and hit him on the
back of his head with it. Broke his neck."

Romanelle took another deep breath, let it out with
soft sighing sound. "Cimarron, young Derabian, couple o
other boys, they all saw it. And this mark was a politica
guy, close to the mayor at that time. Nobody got prose
cuted, still an open case, you could check it. And Alda
Sylvan, they could still testify about it—no statute o
limitations on hitting a guy with an ashtray. Even . .
umm." He paused, brows knitted, went on, "My poison-
fanged ex-sweetness was there, too, saw it happen."

"Nicole? She was there when you killed this guy?"

"Is that her name? I've called her so many other things
sometimes I forget. But, yeah, Nicole—hell, we were
already having enough trouble to fill a psycho ward, so I
just split. Came out to the West Coast, later wound up
here, in Arizona. So . . . When Cimarron started up out
here, along with Derabian and Bliss and some peasants
they asked me in. Or told me I *was* in. Take your pick, the
whole thing was one of those unspoken agreements that
can deafen you. I'd play along, they wouldn't dig up that
old corpse in Chicago, and I'd make a few mill along the
way. They wanted my smarts, they said, my brain—which
they just got through damn near ruining—and there

wasn't much I could do about it. The alternative was too depressing. I know those guys."

"O.K., for now let's say you couldn't help yourself. But let's also get back to here, Romanelle. Back to Arizona and the Golden Phoenix, and Toker. And where I came in. You mentioned this whole operation would have been wrapped up in another month?"

"Or less. After one more report from Toker to bump the price over the last hurdle. Maybe you better tell me about Toker. Who killed him?"

"We'll get to that. I already know that you personally arranged with Toker for the fake reports, so you don't have to hold back anything on that account."

He blinked. "How in hell did you—never mind. He wasn't a problem. He was eager. Part of it was that Alda had me set it up with three hundred thousand shares in a fake-name account that was really Toker's. Only he could dispose of those shares, and if Phoenix did get to thirty it adds up to nine million. The man was not reluctant."

"*Only* Toker could dispose of that stock?"

"Well . . . yeah. Just him. Or me if something happened to him. Which, I guess, it has."

"How'd it get set up in such a sweet way for you? How come no mention of Cimarron, or Derabian, or whoever?"

He looked straight into my eyes. "Because I set it up that way, Scott, that's how. You think I'm an idiot?"

"Basically, then, you and Cimarron were going to pay Toker several million bucks, depending on the price he could get for those shares, just for doing a couple of phony reports. Is that the large economy size of it?"

"You're a suspicious sonofabitch, Scott. Glad you're working for me." He paused. "You still are, aren't you?"

"I still am."

"You better be, or my ass remains stuck in the fan. O.K., Alda—not me, it was Alda's program, I just helped him with some ins and outs—was planning, after it all crashed, to let those three hundred thousand shares surface, along with a trail showing they were Toker's, so it could look like he'd maybe faked the assays on his own, his idea, by his lonesome. Profit on three hundred thousand GPXM at *any*

price could make most people believe it. We might no
even have to skip the state."

I nodded slowly. "And Toker wasn't going to deny it
right? Or wouldn't be able to maybe?"

"I knew you'd ask something like that. Alda never sai
it, but the impression managed to grow in me that Toke
wouldn't be around to deny anything. Does that satisf
you, Scott? You sure as hell don't talk like a man workin
for yours truly."

"I am, though, Romanelle. I just don't want to ge
assassinated doing it. Speaking of which, I need to know
more about why you set up that deal with Worthington
apparently making your daughter a rich young lad
overnight—please note the stress on 'apparently.' Spre
and I have both read that document, and on the surface i
looks . . . generous. Kindly old daddyo turning over—"

"Daddyo? Please—"

"—a new leaf. But, Romanelle, if it turns out you wer
using her, using Spree and even putting her in danger jus
so you could work some kind of self-serving con, client o
no client, I will break your neck slowly, so you can hear th
crunching—"

"No way, Scott. Relax. I wanted—still do—Spree to ge
half of whatever I've managed to pull together in fifty-eigh
years, and maybe all of it. Once she signed the papers I ha
Worthington fix for me, that did it. No way I'm going t
take anything *from* little Spree, not from my own daughter
You damn fool, maybe I haven't really been any kind o
father to her, but she's part of me, blood of my blood
Nobody else on the planet I can say that about."

"Sounds good. You almost convince me. But, as yo
know, she did sign that document Wednesday night, an
therefore . . ." I stopped. "Wait a minute. Keats and th
Cowboy grabbed you Tuesday P.M., the day before Spre
and I got here. So how would you know? Unless somebod
told you."

"Nobody told me. But I know she must have signed it. I
she hadn't, I'd be dead."

"Try that again."

"If Spree hadn't signed the document—which is also t

say if you hadn't somehow got her to Worthington's office to do it, so thanks for that, my flowery thank-yous to you, all right?—then I would be stiff as a petrified log in Siberia, planted under a cactus and breaking down into fertilizer to make the desert bloom again."

"Will you try to say it simply, Romanelle?"

"I think I'd better start with when I got the idea, and lead you along by the hand from there."

"Splendid. So when did you get the idea?"

"I think it hit me about the same time those three slugs from Groder and Foster did, maybe a little after that. Or when Groder plugged me—you say Andy didn't do any shooting?"

"He did some, just not at you."

"That's nice. I always have liked that slick young black bastard. Nice lad . . . Well, the thing is, I'd bought up some extra GPXM here and there till it came to about seven hundred thousand shares. I told you, I was roped into this deal. Maybe you didn't buy that, but it's true. And when I get screwed, I look for ways to get unscrewed. Seemed to me like there was a chance here for me to get fat and at the same time take a little bite—which they weren't supposed to notice, at least not this soon—out of Alda and his unindicted coconspirators, not including me, of course. So now I've got me two mill GPXM shares . . ."

He let it sag there, briefly. I guessed he'd goofed slightly, by adding Toker's three hundred thousand shares—already, even while the man was still warm if undeniably cooling—to his million-seven mentioned in the Worthington-Romanelle document. Idly, I thought that the numbers were getting up into the financial stratosphere; but I didn't say anything, and after only a half second of hesitation Romanelle continued.

"After I was shot, and after flashing my life before my eyes when I got out of surgery in Scottsdale Memorial, I found myself contemplating the almost unavoidable conclusion that Cimarron had sent the lads to blow me away so he could get my shares back into his own hip pocket." He paused. "Since that was how the deal on those shares was set up in the beginning. Or, actually, about a month

after they were initially transferred to me, more than thre
years ago."

"Come again? Set up how?"

He sighed. "For various reasons, but primarily so m
original million-share chunk of stock wouldn't go to rela
tives or friends of mine in case something happened t
me—and get dumped before the time was right fo
dumping—Alda drew up a little agreement for me to sig
specifying that I would execute a will leaving those share
to him—but the language used was 'all my interest in a
my shares owned at the time of my death.' He wrote it ou
and I signed it."

"You didn't assume Cimarron might chop off your hea
a week or two after the ink was dry on that dandy?"

"I considered anything like that a remote possibility
Scott. Very remote, particularly at that time. The share
were worth peanuts, for one thing. And Alda and I had
good relationship back then. Which relationship, o
course, has since deteriorated."

"I'd say so."

"The fact is, signing that—that dandy was the only wa
I'd get the million shares and my crack at what they'd b
worth down the road. There was some risk, yes, but
considered it minimal. Hell, Scott, everything in life's
risk. The important thing's the payoff."

"Cimarron drew up the paper, decided on the lar
guage?"

"Yeah, he didn't want an attorney involved in somethin
like that. Which, although he wasn't aware of it at th
time—neither was I—turned out to be a mistake. Becaus
he didn't pay me to sign the thing. Not even a fiat dollar.

"So?" I said. "I mean, so what?"

Romanelle didn't answer, gazing past me as if lost i
thought, or looking at something distant in space, or tim
"I know now," he said slowly, "that Alda learned about m
picking up an extra chunk of Golden Phoenix from time t
time, because he asked me about it when they were ruinin
my head there in the Medigenic. But I still don't know fo
sure *how* he tumbled to it."

"I can tell you that," I said. "He found out when th

boiler-room boys started trying to unload more to the marks who, thanks to you, were no longer ripe for the send."

"Be damned. So that's it. Scott, would you be interested in helping me sell some guaranteed plastic igloos to Eskimos?"

"No, thanks."

"Too bad. You might have a future. Well, the main thing is, Alda *did* find out what I'd been doing. I needed a little more time to cover my tail, but things moved faster than I expected them to. Naturally, none of us were supposed to load up on the stock, but there's no legally unavoidable prohibition against it—except the one about they kill you if you screw up—and, given time, I'd have gotten my end unscrewed. Which, however, I obviously didn't. So . . ."

He uncrossed his legs, crossed them the other way, looked up toward the ceiling. "It was obvious as the tits on Paul Bunyan's cow that I was deader than whoever's buried in Grant's tomb. Alda's errand boys missed, but somebody'd get me for him the next time, or the time after. It depressed the hell out of me to think that sadistic sonofabitch would have the pleasure of wasting me and at the same time get his hands on my GPXM. Consider the numbers, Scott. Just the million-seven, and even if he only moved it at fifteen, that's a before-cap-gain net of twenty-five million. At a lucky twenty-seven or twenty-eight bid he'd stash away forty-six or -seven million of my gain. A little better than egg money, right? Considering that Alda would kill two guys for twenty bucks each if he needed forty for a tip, I was a goner. Unless . . ."

"I think I'm beginning to follow your tortured—and, may I say, criminal?—reasoning."

"Sure. And sure you are. What else was there to do? Alda might still kill me just to keep his hand in, but no *way* I was going to let that musclehead get his hooks on my GPXM even if I was dead at the time."

"So that's when you got in touch with Worthington."

"That's when. I did a lot of thinking about it first —plenty of time when you're flat on your back. I wanted to set things up to protect me—I mean, keep me from getting killed in the springtime of my life—but also to protect Spree, while at the same time making sure she'd benefit no matter what happened to me. And also, for *damn* sure, so there was no way Alda could benefit no matter what the hell happened. Quite a bunch of angles I had up in the air there, and I didn't know if they'd all fly. Well, the first thing that smart silver-haired counselor of ours told me was a surprise, but good news—good, at least, if I could manage to convey that same surprise to Alda without getting shot again or totally dismembered. Worthington said Alda's little agreement, the one I signed so he'd get that million GPXM upon my demise, wasn't worth a bird's turds. Not his expression, by the way."

"I had a hunch. I've also got a hunch you're about to answer the question I asked a while ago, which you apparently didn't hear me asking."

"I heard you. But you're right, I am. According to Worthington, the fact that a person signs a piece of paper doesn't make what he's agreed to enforceable—it's only enforceable if there was *consideration.* Like some kind of payment, something of value—that fiat buck I mentioned, for example. Keep in mind, I didn't know that until Worthington told me, last Sunday. And Alda, naturally, didn't know it either when he sent his shooters out to accelerate my obituary. You get it? That muscle-bound meatball might have wanted me dead anyway, but he wouldn't have expected my GPXM as a reward. Considerably diminished motive for wasting me, right?"

"Maybe. But suppose, in his ignorance, he'd managed to get you killed anyhow—if, say, Andy Foster had hit you a time or two with his .45—who'd be around to contest Cimarron's unenforceable claim?"

Romanelle blinked, then nodded, smiling. "Very interesting. Good point, Scott. I like that. Well, it's academic now. As soon as Worthington finished doing his thing for me, and both Spree and I signed the trust document, it was nailed down: If Alda killed me *after* that, all my Golden Phoenix stock—and everything else—would go to her, and there was no way Alda could grab it. Of course, I still had the same problem I just mentioned, conveying this vital intelligence to Alda without getting killed before I convinced him. If I managed that, if everything worked out and I remained among the living, I meant to see that Spree got half, and I'd keep the other half—wouldn't want to wind up alive and kicking but penniless and on welfare, would I?"

"Somehow I don't think that would happen. I can follow your reasoning that Cimarron isn't likely to kill you *if* that would mean losing his chance at thirty or forty million bucks, or even ten million. But what's to prevent him —once he knows for sure the stock *is* lost to him for good, it's gone, kaput—from killing you for the hell of it?"

"Because Alda isn't about to let that kind of money get away from him if there's even a slim chance to grab it. And he knows *as long as I'm alive* he's got a chance for it. That's why I set it up the way I did, so he couldn't afford to waste me. I know that big slob. Besides, it's worked already."

"Worked how?"

"When Groder and Keats grabbed me, they took me to the Medigenic. Alda and Bliss were already there. But before they tried ruining my brains . . ."

He stopped, as though involuntarily, turning his head to one side, his features sort of flattening as he stretched his lips wider. Obviously, he was thinking back to those "electricities" shooting through his head, and just as obviously even the memory of it still affected him painfully.

He moistened his lips, shook his head rapidly. "Sorry. That . . . treatment, Bliss turning the little goddamn dial, it was hellish, it was godawful, I don't like to even—where was I? Yeah . . . Lucky for me, Alda had his boys snatch me this time instead of blowing me away because by then he'd cooled off some and there were a lot of questions he needed answers to. Somehow he'd found out—don't ask me how—I'd been visited twice at the hospital by Worthington, so he wanted to know what the hell that meant. And he wanted to know for sure who I'd bought all those extra GPXM shares from, and when, and exactly how many hundred thou, in what names, if ownership had legally been conveyed through the company's transfer agent, a whole mountain of crap he wanted from me. And I was the only one who could tell him."

"I suppose you told him."

"Absolutely. No question. I couldn't wait. Hell, even before they started trying to force me to talk I was already singing like the entire feathered population of Birdland —because I *wanted* Alda to understand, number one, that the little agreement of his I'd signed way back was pure ape diarrhea, not enforceable if he killed me, no more weight to it than a flea's fart—"

"Romanelle, in the interest of expediting this, could you perhaps—"

"—and, second, that I'd *already* signed papers guaranteeing that every share of GPXM in my name, in cover names, everything I owned, would go to my kid if I was suddenly croaked or even died slowly of protracted middle age."

"Apparently you convinced him."

"Eventually. It wasn't easy—even with the copy of the trust agreement I finally got him to read all the way through. I think Alda just didn't *want* to believe it, he thought I was pulling some kind of con on him—"

"Wait a minute. Are you saying you had with you your copy of the agreement Worthington drew up, with your signature on it, the works?"

"Of course. Worthington left a copy with me in Scottsdale Memorial Sunday night, and this was the first time I'd been out of the hospital. So I had the document in my pocket when I got home. Keats took it from me, after conking my head, I guess. At least he had it, my wallet, everything I'd had on me. And, yeah, it was the works —except for Spree's signature, since this all happened Tuesday night."

"That wasn't enough for Cimarron?"

"Not at first. Like I said, he thought I was pulling some kind of con, which in truth I had been known to do in the past, in relatively innocent ways. So they turned on that goddamn machine and . . ." He winced, closed his eyes and shrank back slightly, went on, "used it on my head for a time. After a . . . time, Alda was finally convinced I'd given him straight goods. He knew, by then, I wasn't lying. But, well, there was all the rest he wanted to know about—besides which, that psycho *enjoyed* doing it to me, watching it—so they used that contraption on my head a while longer." He grimaced, but at last opened his eyes again. "I don't really know how long."

"I gather you gave Cimarron most of what he wanted."

"All. Not most, all. Everything I could think of or remember—while I *could* remember."

"Including hiring me, talking to me on the phone."

"You bet. Everything. And then . . . well, it all got crazy after a while. I might have told them things that never happened. My head felt . . ."

He put both hands alongside his skull, rubbed the temples with his fingers. "Can't explain it, Scott. At first, it was like hurting, but in a different way, different kind of hurt. When it got worse, well, it plain scared the crap out of me. Paralyzed me, couldn't move, thought I was—dead. That's what I thought, they'd killed me, and if that was what being dead was like I wanted to die one more time and get out of there."

He lowered his arms to his lap again. "No way I can describe how it really was. In the beginning, before I blacked out for good, I would come back and know some of what was going on. Alda would ask me a question and I'd tell him the truth, but he'd say I was lying and they'd have to give me another shot. Then he'd nod at Doc Bliss and Doc would turn that little black dial higher, and put those round metal things against my temples . . . I remember yelling, screaming, swearing I'd told them everything straight, and then—"

He stopped, staring at me but not seeing me, his eyes vacant and haunted. His expression, combined with what he'd said and all that must have been left unsaid, made me shiver. I actually was slightly nauseated for a moment, felt a soft clenching around my solar plexus.

But then Romanelle seemed to pull himself together again. "I must have conked out for good Tuesday night or Wednesday morning. I remember a little about you showing up at Medigenic earlier today—only I didn't know then where I was. And you pushing me in that roller coaster at midnight, throwing me at a car, gunshots, a couple of them in my ear. All very hazy, like part of what had gone before, part of what Alda and Doc did to me. Then the first really clear impression, sharp and real, was sort of coming to right here with a guy I never saw sticking needles in me and putting drops of something into my mouth. It was—queer. Very queer."

"I didn't really understand all you'd been through, Romanelle," I said. "And that, after just getting out of the hospital. You're a pretty tough old buzzard."

"Yeah. Sure. But if you'd seen me up there with those goddamn paddles against my head, you'd have thought I was a little girl, grabbed by the bogeyman. You seize, you know."

"What? Seize?"

"Yeah, when a good shot hits your brains you have a seizure, a fit. Convulsions. God, it was . . . It's funny." His eyes took on a trace of that vacant, haunted look again. "Everything we've ever done, thought, read, whatever we are, all our loves and hates and dreams and . . . it's all up there in our heads. In our brains. Or somewhere in there, in us. And when you can *feel* it going . . . feel everything slipping away . . . it's as if you're dissolving, melting, and there'll be nothing left of you. Just a puddle. Nothing . . ."

I got up, wanting to stretch my legs, move, shake off a kind of uneasiness Romanelle's words had built in me. I paced back and forth for half a minute, then said to him, "Let's get back to here and now. There are still several things that have to be taken care of."

"Right," he said. "O.K. But first, well, I told you, for some reason I've always had trouble thanking people. Seems like that's all I've been doing with you. And I guess I want you to know I'm . . . indebted to you, I mean for finding the doc, Midland, and having him work on me here. I don't know where you got him, or how, but . . . thanks for that, you big white-haired bastard. O.K.?"

"O.K.," I said, smiling. "I called a friend in L.A. and he gave me Midland's name. I guess we're both lucky it was him instead of somebody else. But back to here and now,

Romanelle. I've seen the document Worthington drew up for you. And you just told me Cimarron read a copy of it—probably Tuesday night, right?"

"Not long after they grabbed me at home. Sometime Tuesday night, I'd say. But I'm not real sure of the times on anything past the first hour or two after they grabbed me."

"Close enough. The way I see it, with your signature *already* on the document, Cimarron knew if he killed you right then, all your assets—including the Golden Phoenix stock—would go to your daughter, and he'd be out of luck. Unless—and this is what's starting to stick me—unless he killed her *first*."

"I already asked you once if you think I'm an idiot, Scott. Apparently you remain unconvinced I'm not. If you read the trust document, you saw the little kicker saying if my daughter predeceased me the entirety of the trust's assets would go to a named charity."

"Sorry, Romanelle. I do remember that now. At the time I was looking for other things."

"So was Alda Cimarron. But I made sure he noticed that kicker and knew nothing had better happen to Spree. I mean, I made sure while I was still able to make sure of anything. Before all the lights in my head went *pfft* I realized that Alda, once convinced he couldn't afford to kill Spree, would sure as hell try to keep her from signing the document, because when that was accomplished he'd be out in the icebergs. And I told you, my kind of survival logic says she must have signed. If she hadn't—if *I* was the only party Alda had to deal with, since he already had me in a highly cooperative state of mind—I'd be a dead Claude. By now, one way or another I'd have transferred everything to Alda—with consideration this time—and you wouldn't have found me at Medigenic. But here we are. What happened? I can't believe Alda missed that angle."

"He didn't. But I guess he had to spread his people a little thin." I told him most of what had happened Wednesday night, Foster and Cowboy at the airport, the rest of it.

He was silent for a few moments, then said, "So it really was just Keats and Doc Bliss in my house when you and

Spree got there. Well, Bliss is chickenshit, no balls at all. He would have been there in case somebody got shot —somebody besides you, of course."

"Of course. I was *supposed* to be shot."

"I admire your powers of deduction. I'd guess you also figured out why only Keats and Bliss were there, instead of half a dozen guys."

"Besides the troops being spread a little thin, I'd say they didn't expect me to get as far as your home."

"Absolutely brilliant," Romanelle said. "You must also be absolutely damned lucky. Keats never got taken out before, and I know of at least five guys he killed. Got to be plenty others I never heard about."

"Lucky, sure," I said. "But your daughter's the reason I wasn't blown right out into your patio. Spree kept Keats busy, distracted, just long enough. She's got the same kind of—fire, maybe, that I'd guess you've got in you."

He looked at me, nodding slightly, not saying anything but looking pleased.

I paced to the door and back, just moving aimlessly, thinking, for half a minute. Then I stopped before Romanelle and said, "There's still one way Cimarron can make out, get what he wants and screw up all your plans. I suppose you're aware of that."

He smiled oddly. "One way. I thought maybe you'd missed it, Scott."

"It's not a question of missing the way out for him. Obviously Cimarron will have thought of it by now. His problem would be execution, making it work."

"On the mark. But I told you, I know that musclehead —not that he's dim-brained, he's maybe too goddamned smart. If there's one chance in a thousand, he'll try to make it work. And the odds aren't all that long. If he could get his hands on me again, *and* on Spree, both of us at the same time, and bring in Worthington to do the legal officiating, he could make it work. He could for damn certain force both Spree and me as cotrustees to transfer all shares of the stock owned by the trust—and that's two mill now—over to Cimarron himself, or to Al Capone's heirs, or back to the company as treasury stock . . . and you bet it could work." He was silent for a few seconds, then added slowly, "Of course, he'd kill us both then. After that, he'd have to."

"Well, fortunately, he doesn't have either of you now."

"And, Scott," Romanelle said deliberately, "it's your job to see it stays that way."

"No argument there. But I think it's time to bring in the law. So, understand, when I call the cops they're going to put me away. I mean, I'll be out of circulation until several . . . questions are answered by me."

"I don't think I want you out of circulation, Scott. Besides which, Alda's got a lot of people beholden to him, maybe even on his payroll. I can name, for example, two police officers. If I can name two, there are probably more."

"I've had that possibility in mind for a while myself. But we're at the point where that doesn't matter as much as getting police protection for you and Spree. Even if it means I'll be in jail for a while."

"You mean for shooting Keats?" Romanelle asked.

"That, and half a dozen other things. I've stepped over the line on this one, Romanelle." I walked to the table the phone was on, pulled a chair over, and sat down. "I'm going to make a couple of calls, then we'll decide together. You're still the client."

"You calling Spree?" he asked me.

"No. Worthington first, then another guy. Just testing the waters before I jump in."

"Worthington, yes. Good thinking. I'd like for him to be current on all developments."

I dialed Worthington's office, got his personal secretary, and identified myself.

When I asked for Bentley, she said, "He's in court, Mr. Scott. But there's a message from him for you."

I heard a rustling sound, as if she was flipping a notebook's pages, then she said, "I'll read it to you as it was dictated to me."

"Please do."

"The note is for you, that is for Mr. Shell Scott, and the text is: If the police have not yet arrested you, be advised they are making strenuous efforts to do so. It is alleged that they have in their possession a tape recording made by you in which you confess to commission of the Frederick Keats homicide and several other serious crimes. I will be in court until about five P.M. I advise that you take no independent action until we have discussed this matter."

While listening to the soft voice reading Bentley's note, I went through a complex array of emotions and physical reactions. I started getting hot, my skin actually flushing, then I got cold, a chill rippling over my flesh like a sudden wind. At the end I was getting hot again, both physically and mentally.

I tried to keep the anger out of my voice as I asked, "When did Bentley leave this message for me?"

"He phoned from the courthouse, Mr. Scott, and dictated the message about half an hour ago. At, let's see . . . 3:03 P.M. Twenty-five minutes ago."

I checked my watch. Right on: 3:28.

"All right," I said. "And thank you very much. It's important—very important—that I talk to Bentley soon. Would you give me your name? When I call back, I'll ask for you."

"Of course. Lucille. Lucille Weathers, Mr. Scott."

We hung up. Within five seconds I was dialing *Exposé, Inc.*, and in ten seconds more Steve Whistler was on the line saying, "Shell? Where the devil are you? I wanted to get in touch but didn't know where to call you."

"Never mind that now. How come—" I stopped, started over. "I'm just curious to know if there's anything new concerning our . . . mutual interests."

"There's hell to pay. Shell, that information you had me record . . ." He paused. *"Damn,* I hate to tell you this. The police have it. Correction. They've got a copy of it. Identical. But *not* the tape I made."

"How would the police get the thing, Steve? And what do you mean, it's not the tape you made?"

"I don't know how. But, look, I heard everything you said while it was being taped, remember. And that was damaging stuff—even though I can understand why you might have wanted it on the record. So the minute you rang off, I took that tape out of the recorder, replaced it with a blank reel, and locked your tape in my office safe. I'm on *your* side, in case that's slipped your mind."

"Yeah, I know," I said. "Locked it in your safe—it's still there?"

"Of course it's still there. I checked, naturally."

"How did you find out about this, Steve, and when —how long ago?"

"I got a call here from a police officer who is, let's say, sympathetic, to our work. He told me about the tape recording, plus the fact that there's a local call going out on you—going out then, so it's on the air by now—and an all-points bulletin. Just about the same as if you were the new Dillinger. And that was just after three. Five minutes after three, or almost half an hour ago."

"Wonderful. Do those bulletins suggest that the suspect is armed and dangerous and should be shot on sight?"

"I don't know what they said. I just know . . . hell, it's a mess. Shell, I'm sorry, but I swear that tape hasn't been out of my office safe."

"Who else knows the combination?"

"Besides me, only Bren—Bren Finnegan, the man I was with when you barged into my office this morning—and Kay."

"Finnegan and Kay Dark, huh? After the job Kay did on me, I suppose it's natural that I might wonder—"

"Don't wonder, Shell. Maybe she wasn't on the level with you but she's loyal to *Exposé* and me. More important, I haven't left the building, I've been here since we talked. Nobody could have gotten to that tape."

"O.K., Steve, you've been in the building. But not necessarily in your office every minute, right?"

"True. Doesn't make any difference. The leak wasn't from here, believe me. But the question is, what are you going to do now? You need anything? Want me to come pick you up? Name it, Shell, I'll do it."

I believed him. I really did. Still, I said, "Let me call you back, Steve," and hung up.

I needed time to think, sort out the jangle of thoughts and questions whirling around in my head. It had even occurred to me, briefly, that if a cop or two happened to be standing around in Whistler's office while I was talking to him there might have been a trace on the line. The long arm of the law could be reaching out right now, trying to locate the phone I'd been using, the address from which I'd called. If they hadn't pinned down the location already.

But I didn't really believe that. Maybe there wasn't much reason to trust Steve Whistler more than anybody else I'd met lately; but, for some reason, I did trust him. Most of the time I go along with those gut feelings; and I was going to go along with them this time.

Romanelle had tried to interrupt me while I was on the phone, calling out, "What's the matter?" and "What the hell's going on, Scott?" But I'd ignored him. By this time he'd gotten up out of his chair and was now standing only about a foot away, saying, "What the hell? It sounds like trouble—tell me what's going on, dammit, I'm your client."

"I will, I will. Just a minute."

I got to my feet, waved a hand at Romanelle to try keeping him quiet for a few seconds, started pacing again.

Something was on the edge of my brain, one thought trying to squeeze its way out from among all the others, something about that tape recording I had so recently made, me speaking simultaneously into the phone and onto those slowly turning reels on the machine in Whistler's office.

Assume Steve was on the level; also that neither Finnegan nor Kay Dark had a chance to open his safe and remove the tape, make a quick copy, and replace the original. Assume that much. *If* that was true, then how . . ."

It didn't make sense at first. Then it started to. I felt a chillness crinkle my spine, as if the skin was puckering and cracking like a sheet of ice. Felt hairs lifting on the back of my neck. Still pacing, I turned near the door, took a step toward Claude Romanelle. He was staring intently at me, mouth moving as he asked a question I didn't hear.

Behind me there was a shocking, splintering crash, what seemed like an enormous amount of noise, the splintering followed by a thudding sound and a shout. As I spun around, I started to grab for the .38 under my coat, but hesitated, kept my hand off the butt of the gun. Because I was still thinking of the law, police, cops kicking the door down and bursting in to arrest the guy who'd confessed on tape to half a dozen felonies.

If the police saw me yanking out a handgun, it was possible that would be the last sudden movement I'd ever make. So I left the gun clamped in the clamshell holster but kept on spinning around until I could see the crowd of men bursting into the room.

Only it wasn't the police.

I had time for one quick, crazy thought, a single warped, very negative, and I hoped uncharacteristic thought, and it was:

If these guys aren't *cops, I'm dead.*

Chapter Nineteen

IT WAS NOT a crowd of cops; it wasn't even a crowd. Three men, that was all, one well inside the room and two others close behind, all of them coming at me. It just looked like a lot more because the first man in, the one who had undoubtedly taken the splintered door off its hinges and slammed it into the room, was so big he looked like a crowd all by himself. Sure. Alda Cimarron.

I barely had time to recognize him and Cowboy behind him, plus a third man I hadn't seen before, when my palm slapped the .38's butt and Cowboy shoved his right hand toward me like the short jab of a fist, a fist with a gun in it, and from a foot away, moving on around behind me, Alda Cimarron saying softly in that rumbling bottom-of-the-barrel voice of his, "Don't be a chump, Scott. You're on the hind tit this time."

There was a good deal of truth in what the slob said. Both men before me held guns in their hands, and presumably so did Cimarron, because he slammed me on the back of the skull with something very hard and heavy, even harder and heavier than I guessed his fist must be.

Then I stopped guessing about anything for a while. I wasn't out, but I was down on one knee. I kept getting up but somehow not moving any higher, and I could see everything slightly out of focus, hear the words those three men spoke, hear them clearly but with an odd reverberation like a fractionally delayed echo.

Something moved me, and a hand jerked the S&W .38

from its holster. Then, "I'll be goddamned, goddamned to hell."

That was Cimarron. In a moment I realized he had to be looking at and then talking to Romanelle, because he went on, "No more droolin', hey, Claude, old pal? I thought it might be a week, maybe forever, before you'd get your head screwed on straight. What pulled you out of it, Claude?"

There wasn't any answer.

But then Cimarron said gently, "Do what I tell you to, Claude, or we'll paddle your head some more, me and Doc—"

"*No!* Please, Alda—I'll tell you whatever you want. I *will.* All I know is, when I came to there was a doctor here, working on me. And . . . then I was better. O.K. Almost . . . almost O.K. I still can't remember much—it's true, Alda. It's all . . . fuzzy, except since I came to, woke up here. But I'm pretty much . . . normal . . . except for not remembering anything lately."

I could tell from the sound of his thin shaking voice that Romanelle was very afraid, even terrified, at the thought of further "treatment" by Doc Bliss and Cimarron. But I had to hand it to the guy. He was claiming something I knew to be untrue, that much and maybe most of his recent memory was gone.

"Sure, Claude. Sure. So where is she? Your daughter, this Michelle Wallace, where's this Spree of yours?"

"I don't know. Wait—I swear to God, I don't know. He—nobody told me yet."

I got balanced on both feet finally, tried to straighten up. I saw Cimarron's thick legs move, then one of them and the big shoe at its end dug into my gut. The air shot out of my lungs and I went down flat on my face. I could feel the dirty carpet against my mouth; it smelled like moldy rags. I lay still, breathing slowly, breathing as deeply as I could and trying to ignore the pain in my middle and along my side. He'd broken a rib, I guessed.

I heard one of the men hit Romanelle. It had to be Romanelle, because following the sound of somebody banging into a chair and thumping onto the carpet, I was able to move my head and see Romanelle scrabbling on the floor, slowly getting to his knees, then standing.

I heard him saying, his voice not belligerent but also without that earlier frightened and almost panicky note in it, "I've told you the truth, Alda. I don't remember shit since . . . whenever it was . . . Tuesday night, I guess. Until a little while ago, with that doctor here. I don't even know who he was. And I sure don't know where Michelle is. If I did, I'd tell you."

"You'll tell me if you know, Claude, that's for sure. So will this sonofabitch, Scott."

He turned to look down at me. But not all the way down, because I was starting to get up again. For some reason, he didn't stop me this time. I was recovering a little from the blow on the back of my head. At least I wasn't hearing echoes and seeing double. I straightened up, and Cimarron took a step toward me.

Standing a foot away, both hamlike fists bunched on his hips, right hand enfolding what looked like a long-barreled .357 Magnum revolver, he said, "Maybe Claude doesn't know where his kid is—we'll find out easy enough. But it's a damn sure thing *you* know, Scott. And if you're not a complete idiot you'll tell me where Michelle Wallace is, and you'll tell me now. Believe me, you'll be glad you did."

"Cimarron." I looked at that broad face, the bunched muscle at the corners of his mouth, found his mottled blue eyes a couple of inches above my own, tried to hold them as I said, "If we're talking about now, you'd better kill me now. Right here, while you've got a chance."

He grinned, a real normally wide grin, showing the big square teeth, tangled hairs wiggling in his nostrils. "Isn't that cute, boys?" he said without taking his eyes from mine. "Just like he heard it in a movie."

I kept looking at him and said softly, "You hear *this,* Cimarron. Just suck it in your ears and keep it in that fat head of yours from now on. You try to think of something else and this is going to come right back into your head. Every time. Over and over again. So hear it loud and clear, pal: Either you kill me now—right now in this room, no games, no hesitation, just *do* it—or you're all caught up. I'll take you out."

He started to chuckle, the rumbling rising from the big belly and broad deep chest. I truly did hope I'd grabbed his attention and gotten him to concentrate on what I was saying—in accord with the principle that, usually, if somebody tells you *not* to think of a blue-striped giraffe, you are for sure *going* to think of a blue-striped giraffe. So I kept pushing it a little longer. "But I wouldn't want you to keep worrying about it, Cimarron. Just put it out of your mind. Forget I mentioned it."

"Or you'll take me out—*me*," he said, still chuckling, looking probably as amused as it was possible for him to get. "How do you expect to manage that, Scott?"

"Beats the hell out of me, pal. I haven't the faintest idea at the moment. I won't know for sure till I do it, will I?"

"Have I got a surprise for you—pal." He smiled, showing me the square white teeth again. "And this time I'm *really* going to enjoy it."

My head felt as if it had been split open. I knew it wasn't actually cracked, because while my hands were still free I'd felt the sizable lump on the back of my skull—or maybe two lumps, one next to the other. Cimarron had slugged me only once more, but hard enough the second time to put me completely out long enough for somebody to bind my arms. Then there was movement in a car, parking, being half carried into a building. I saw cars, walls; no signs, but I knew the building was one I'd been to before: the Arizona Medigenic Hospital on McDowell Road.

And now, except for the constant throbbing pain in my head, my thoughts were clear enough. I knew where I was—and what was undoubtedly going to happen.

We were all—Alda Cimarron, Cowboy Jay Groder, the other man who looked like the picture I'd seen of a younger Sylvan Derabian, Dr. Phillip Bliss, and Claude Romanelle still in his green robe—in Dr. Bliss's three-room suite on the Medigenic's fourth floor. Not only in the suite but crammed into the same small room where I'd found

Romanelle earlier today. How much earlier I had no idea; time was taffy, a bunch of rubber bands ticking. I didn't know if it was still afternoon or late at night.

I was flat on my back on a high table. Leather straps, secured to the underside of the table, stretched across my body and were buckled tightly around my ankles and wrists. From the waist up, my body was bare. On my right, only two or three feet away, was that foot-and-a-half-square gray metal box I'd earlier seen here at the foot of Romanelle's bed. It was still atop that same bright red four-wheeled cart—the crash cart. The white face of the box—the defibrillator—was turned toward me. I could see a rectangular glass-covered dial placed right of center with black numbers across its top. At the dial's far left, O . . . then 10 . . . on up to 400 at the far right. Below it the words, or letters, "Watt Sec." At the upper left was the word "Energy," and below it a little black dial with numbers around it, also ending in 400.

Pain like hot redness pulsed inside my skull, seeming to swell and then shrink, swell and shrink. I tried to force my mind away from the pain, looked at the defibrillator's face again. At its lower left was the word "Power," below it a small switch with "Off" at its left and "On" at its right near the words "Armed" and "Charge" one above the other. Beneath the switch was a small tubular bit of green glass, a tiny bulb. But it was dark, not glowing. Not yet.

Behind the crash cart, on the floor, a single electrical cord wiggled over the carpet like a thin black snake, probably to a wall socket, though I couldn't see its end. Resting on top of the gray box were the two "paddles" that didn't look like paddles or anything else I'd ever seen except maybe science-fiction ray guns or unworkable can openers. Each had two thin metal disks at one end, the disks about an inch apart and not more than a couple of inches in diameter. From each paddle extended a pair of round black handles, one of them with a buttonlike projection at its end and another snakelike black electrical cord dangling from it. The things were curious, almost comical in appearance, and actually looked quite harmless. But I knew they weren't harmless. They scared me. They scared me more than a gun or knife would have.

Alda Cimarron had been standing close to Dr. Bliss and the man I'd decided was Sylvan Derabian. He, Derabian, nodded, looked at Romanelle, nodded some more while glancing at me—as if I was a specimen pinned to a board for scientific examination—then gazed at Romanelle again. He raised both hands before his chest, arms bent sharply at the elbows, and shrugged. Sort of a "Why not?" or noncommittal "Aach" movement.

Maybe I was imagining it, but I got the impression that Cimarron and Bliss were explaining to Derabian the treatment they'd given Claude Romanelle, and how splendidly efficient that treatment had proved to be—and perhaps would soon again prove to be—in unclamming the clammed mouth, freeing the recalcitrant tongue, facilitating the spill of guts. I didn't like the pictures those vagrant, almost unchosen words painted before my mental eye.

I'd had time to decide upon my way to go. There were only two alternatives anyhow. Either tell them everything they wanted to know except for the one or two most important exceptions, and maybe only the one—Spree, where she was, where they could find her—or else clam, freeze the chops, say nothing at all.

But I knew that once a man—any man—started to spill, to let just a little leak out while withholding the rest, it was too easy for that leak to turn into a stream, a gushing, a flood. Once started, it could be difficult and maybe impossible to stop. So I'd decided, made my choice: Once it began, admit nothing, say nothing. If I could manage it. I wasn't entirely sure I could. But that was the way I meant to go.

Cimarron left the other men and walked to the padded table on which I lay, to which I was strapped. He looked down at me, looming enormous against the ceiling above him, the too-bright overhead light for the moment blocked out by his head. The light silvered his feathery brown hair, formed an oddly incongruous halo around his skull and face. I could smell him. He was sweating, and the odor was heavy, rank.

"Scott," he rumbled, "there's a lot of things I might ask you to talk about, and you'd answer all the questions. In time. Believe it, pal. You can save yourself, and us, a lot of trouble by answering one question. Just one. Then we'll skip the rest, along with all the misery you'll get otherwise. Just spill where the girl is, Michelle. Romanelle's kid. We know you stashed her someplace. Just tell me where."

"When I shot Keats, she ran out of the house screaming and that's the last I saw of her," I lied easily. "Easily so far, I thought. "If she's still running, she ought to be passing Tucson about now."

"Scott," he said, almost wearily, "don't lay that smartass bullshit on me. One more time. Michelle Esprit Romanelle. Claude's kid. Where is she?"

"Why don't you show your good faith, Cimarron? Tell me how in hell you found Romanelle and me in that dumpy motel."

"Shee—" He started to swear, then cut it off. Slowly he nodded the big head. "Why not? Sure, give a little, get a little, hey? Well, it was easy as scratching your ass. I've got twenty guys do a little phone work for me from time to time. Even got all the telephones wired and in place a couple days ago. So I just had the boys start calling every goddamn motel, even hotel, in the Valley. Only thing they had to ask was *if* anybody checked in between one-fifteen P.M.—you snatched Claude sometime after one—and two o'clock or thereabouts. And it had to be a big guy looked like you, either alone or else with an invalid. Took a lot of calls—we covered Scottsdale and Phoenix before getting to Mesa and Tempe—but once there was a hit all we had to do was go there and pick you up."

He waited, lips closed but spread in what might have been a self-satisfied smirk. Finally he said, "How's that for good faith? O.K., Scott, where is she?"

Silence. Smirk going, gone.

The big face close to mine, small jungle of hair in his nose wiggling as the nostrils flared, mottled blue eyes looking a little glassy, almost manic. Slowly, "One *last* time, you shitty sonofabitch. Michelle Esprit Romanelle. Where's she at?''

I ignored him, took a long deep breath, getting ready for whatever ordeal would fill the next minutes. Or hours. Although it wasn't the sort of thing you can really get ready for, not the kind of exercise anyone practices.

Cimarron didn't make it easier. Still leaning close above me, that broad greasy-looking face shining with a thin film of sweat, he said, "Let me tell you how it goes, Scott. We'll play with you a little, try a couple dandies we haven't worked on much yet. But then, pal, if we have to sizzle your brains like we did Claude's, you'll spill, you'll have fits, maybe bust your spine jerking around. You'll talk, you'll run off at the mouth, you'll beg, but it'll be too late. You saw what it did to Claude. I *know* you saw what it did to him, pal, you grabbed him out of here while he was still a zombie."

Knock it off, I yelled inside my head. *I* was supposed to be the striped-giraffe psychologist here. I tried to shut out his words by testing the straps on my ankles and wrists —again. I wondered if the strap on my right wrist was really looser than the other, or if that wrist was merely more numb.

"We're still figuring out the niceties, Scott," Cimarron was saying, "the artistry. Haven't had the power up all the way, not as high as it goes. That's four hundred watt-seconds, Doc tells me. I suppose if we did, it might cook your brains into . . . what? Like whatever you'd get if you squashed a fly? Just some jelly and juicy fruit and squashed flyshit, maybe. With a couple fly eyes and half a leg in it."

He laughed, gurgling merriment rumbling up from his gargantuan gut and out the gaping mouth a foot from my face.

This strong silent treatment of mine wasn't working too great, so I spoke finally. I told Cimarron to go perform a complicated obscenity upon himself. Actually, that's misleading. What I suggested he attempt is not normally an obscenity. It is obscene only if one does it to oneself during a public parade on Main Street. Which it is physically impossible for even a deranged acrobat to do. Thus, obscenity is a myth, and cannot exist except in acrobatically deranged imaginations. Or so spun the feverish thoughts in my head.

I wondered if my mind was already trying to get away, get out of here, before these bastards even started playing their games with me. I knew I had been consciously trying to relax, willing relaxation, only to find suddenly that muscles were rigid again, cords in neck taut, arms starting to tremble a little from tension too long held.

Let's face it, I was scared, frightened, hugely apprehensive. Not because of anything they'd done—they hadn't really done a damned thing yet—but because of *imagined* future pain and panic and wreckage of the self. And that was ridiculous. Nothing is ever as bad as our exaggerated anticipation of its reality, they tell us; the imagination creates more monstrous terrors than those that are real, they tell us. I was trying to remember what else they tell us—and figure out who "they" were, and if they'd ever been strapped to a table about to be plugged into the lightning—when I saw Alda Cimarron's arm moving in the air above me.

He was waving at one of the other men. Dr. Bliss, it was. "Try the chest thing," Cimarron told him.

Dr. Bliss said, "I'm . . . not sure that's wise—"

"Goddammit, just *do* it. That's what the thing's made for, isn't it? To start hearts if they've conked out?"

"Yes, of course. But—"

"So if it stops his ticker, you do your thing and start him up again, O.K.?"

"I'll do my best. But it's an extremely dangerous procedure—"

"Bliss, quit farting around and do it. This guy pisses me off. He's a smartass and a smart-mouth, and he pisses me *off*. He's supposed to be a tough sonofabitch. We're gonna find out how tough the sonofabitch is."

I didn't believe any of this. Or, I believed it, knew those humanoid monsters were talking about me—and, clearly, about *my* heart . . . my *heart,* about turning it on and off like a plug-in toy—but this unbelievable crap they were arguing about attempting, attempting with me, simply wasn't acceptable. It wasn't real. The mind refused to swallow the concept and digest it, burped it up instead. The mind, I thought . . . what if the mind, the brain and its electron streams and synapses and myriad virtues, was so excessively stressed that—

Cimarron was no longer near on my right. Dr. Bliss was there, one of those queer-looking little paddles in each of his hands. He was speaking, saying something to the effect that he'd already set the current at so-many watt-seconds himself, and the others must be sure not to touch the patient, which could be dangerous to the individual so touching.

The patient? I was going to kill every one of these human goddamn maggots if I ever got the chance . . . which didn't seem likely, even to me. Bliss had placed the paddle ends on my upper body, one at either side of my chest, at opposite sides of—my heart.

I was jerking, rolling, feeling the muscles of my arms and right side blaze with pain, trying to get away, knowing I couldn't, knowing they were going to do it, jerking anyway.

Cimarron, on my left, held his big Magnum by the long barrel and tapped me with its butt in the middle of my forehead. Not hard enough to injure, or knock me out. Just hard enough to hurt, and raise a lump, move part of the ache from the back of my head to the front. It probably didn't even break the skin.

Cimarron said, "Don't be dumb, Scott. I'll *crank* your skull next time. It's gonna happen; let it happen, pal. You got no place to go."

I told him again, in marvelous detail, what to do. But it was pure reflex, just lip movement, no bravado, no smart-mouth, just something that came out with no thought behind it. But I stopped jerking, stopped stretching those already-torn-feeling muscles and tendons.

Bliss moved the paddles an inch or two, saying lightly, "This should be interesting. All right, now, here we go."

And then—

My body exploded, something raced, ripped—

Oh, Jesus God Almighty Christ, oh stop-stop-godalmighty —great knives and hammers tore at me from inside my chest, my head felt as if it was swelling up like a balloon, I thought my eyes were popping out, I could feel a giant heart trembling, swelling and then shrinking, trembling again and wobbling like an out-of-round wheel on a kid's bike, shrinking to a circle, a dot, nothing . . .

A little while ago, or a long while ago, at some unknowable place in rubber-band time, I had heard the breath shriek out of my mouth, all the air in a small universe bursting through my clenched teeth and past my stretching lips. It had sounded like a scream. But it wasn't a scream; no, just air, breath, screaming from my lungs.

I hadn't believed there would be so much pain, hadn't known there *could* be. I hadn't expected pain that was beyond measuring, without a greater agony to compare it with. It had been so intense that I felt emptied, hollowed out. But I was still alive. I guessed I was. My heart was beating. That bruised heart, I thought, that bruised and abused heart . . . keep on going, don't conk out on me now.

Cimarron's beefy face swam in a kind of hazy pink soup above me. His mouth moved and I clearly heard him say, "Michelle Esprit Romanelle. Where is she, Scott?"

Go zonk yourself. Take a sulfuric acid enema. Give me one small chance, Alda baby, and I will slowly squeeze your testicles in a hand-cranked vise and mix what's left of them with liquefied horseflies.

Don't tell the bastard a thing. Don't speak, don't open your mouth. Don't even look at him unless it's to see where to spit. Don't think about pain, *don't* think about the pain. Oh, God. Godalmighty, dammit, dammit! Just don't tell him, don't tell him. Not about Spree. Not Spree.

They were talking. I didn't care what they were saying. But some of it I became aware of, as if by a kind of word osmosis, phrases soaking into me through head or ears or skin. Argument. One more like that might kill him, can't kill the bastard till he tells us where the broad is, what's the matter with the dumb sonofabitch, O.K., do the head, give it a shot, tickle his brains, not too much at first, Doc . . .

Paddles. Those small metal circles pressing, one at each side of my head. Curious name for odd things like surreal twin-handled potato mashers. Something greasy at my temples. Man sliding the paddles. From the corner of my eye I could see a thumb placed on one of those buttonlike projections alongside the dangling black wire. And I could see that little green bulb, glowing now.

"*I'll* handle this, Groder. Don't mess with that dial."

"O.K., O.K., Doc, just wanted to see the big jerk jump a little. He already sapped me a coupla—"

"Move, *move*—there. Here we go." Lightly, lyrically. "Here we go again, boys."

I could feel it starting.

I almost wet my pants. I almost took an involuntary leak right there on the table . . . wherever the table was. I'd known the answer to that a second ago. Or a minute. Or an hour. But I couldn't let that happen, I reminded myself, or reminded that other guy, whichever it was. You take leaks in the toilet, or maybe out in the bushes. Not with your shorts and pants on. At least, not after you've grown up. So just hold it, friend. It was a mildly amusing thought. *Just hold it right there, turkey!* I wanted to laugh. But I couldn't. And I really, really wanted to. I understood then, maybe fully for the first time ever, how wonderful it was to laugh. To feel joy. Joy—not pain. Joy—not the weird, uncomfortable trembling again, different from what I'd felt before.

Somewhere I'd read that there is no sensation of pain in the pinkish-gray matter of the brain itself. That surgeons can slice a scalpel through the jelly, poke it with a probe, spread its convolutions with metal springs—no pain. But maybe . . . maybe there was something worse than pain. The something was growing, filling part of me, encroaching on the rest, dissolving parts of my self like a snake, a shining silver boa constrictor, sucking fragments of me through its mouth and down, and down, into . . .

Panic, sudden uncontrollable panic spilled darkness into my brain, crinkled blackness slashed with pink and gray and green and horror. Billions of razor-edged bits of redness, like impossibly thin cannibal worms, wriggled in squirming bloodiness somewhere behind my eyes—or at least somewhere, in some part of me; another part of me watched. Part of me was unafraid, interested, clinical, even almost amused. But the other part was dying.

Movement on my right, fingers slowly turning a little black dial, sounds not recognizable as words, those metal circles pressing my temples again, then Aaaaahhh . . . no, no, no. It was pain-that-was-not-pain, a spastic puppet-jerk wrenching that slammed and twisted both sides of my brain. Light that wasn't light, darkness that wasn't darkness. I was paralyzed, I couldn't move. Not even a finger or lash of eye. It was like being frozen and warm, then hot, frozen but burning in scalding fire. Slipping, burning, falling, sliding down, down into freezing coils of the snake's smooth gut . . .

It had ended.

I knew the awful pulses and tremors were no longer entering my brain, even though I felt them still. Felt or sensed them, more like memory of a school-prom song than as pressure or physical movement. But the end of the awfulness, the unbearable dissolving of unidentifiable essences, the uncontrollable fear of melting into nowhere —that part had ended.

Cimarron again. The same question. Michelle. Little Spree. Cute-ugly kid with scrunched-up face, chewing on a lemon, belly-flopping into a swimming pool filled with jagged glass.

But I knew Cimarron. Recognized the man, knew who he was. Knew what he was asking. Knew the answer. Knew the answer was: Registry, villa 333. There, there is the lovely, the bright and sweetly burning, the spring flowers and green eyes filled with warm summer rain, Spree, that's where she is, that's where she is, My Spree.

I heard him asking. And I knew, more than I'd ever known a thing in my life before, that if I was ever going to tell him I would tell him now, now, before they did anything to me again, now or not ever. And I didn't.

After that, it didn't matter what they did, what they might do, because they couldn't hurt me anymore, not ever again. I felt wonderful, light, proud—joyous. There were tears in my eyes, I felt the wetness slide down my cheeks, and it was ridiculous, unmanly, feminine weakness in a beat-up and scarred and horny-handed weeping man and I didn't give a good goddamn, I didn't care.

They really did it all then.

After a while I imagined I was up near the ceiling in one corner of the room, looking down at the dummies fooling around with that other guy. He looked like a lump. Looked pretty dead to me. That wasn't right. If he was dead, that wasn't the other guy but just a discarded cocoon; *I* was the butterfly, up here near the ceiling. Down there, Dr. Frankenstein fiddled with dials and switches and potato mashers trying to make thunder and lightning and pour it into the monster strapped to the monster table with weird-looking bolts on his head, wires coming out of them . . .

The castle, the monster, Igor and the doctor, all were gone, left far below, far away, almost farther than memory could reach. Instead, before me, suddenly, was —everything.

Suddenly Everything was transcendentally clear, unimaginably bright and beautiful. Graceful ripples of billowing-blue forever stretched out and on, and on, at every side of . . . of me, I supposed it was. I guessed it was I at the center of all This. This beauty, this star-chiming song, danced and spun around whatever this point of my consciousness was. And I was vast, all-encompassing, endless, and thus hugely satisfied with myself.

I moved, it seemed forward, but in all directions endlessly also, and before me was a great bank of fog, coming nearer, looming larger. I thought—thought with comets and suns and supernovae and coalescing universes forming scintillating synapses in the immensity of my brain—that it was strange there would be fog, like the chill moist grayness over remembered winter beaches, in this bubbling immensity of space. Still nearer . . . and I could see it was not fog but a sea of stars, billions of stars like shining droplets, appearing smaller than grains of sand only because *I* was so vast, all-encompassing, endless.

Why, I had to be a god, I thought, and the thought filled me with forgivable exultations. How grand I was, to fill all of space, breathe stars and suns, drink nebulae and universes, and be a great blistering-shining-majestic *god* of all

I surveyed. *At least* a god, *at least*, and perhaps it was possible that, even more than that, I—

Something monstrously huge, massive, ominous loomed beyond the end of endless space, rose from darkness into darkness and then arced into burning light, moving toward me with dazzling and terrifying speed. It was coming at me, smack at me. Square silver lines of force intersecting within a thick black-hole border; projecting downward from it twin streams of metallic power joining in a loop at its end, like a handle, a handle six times as long as the trembling squareness filled with intersecting vortices and lines forming a magical mesh. It loomed nearer, coming directly toward me, a giant . . . what? Swatter? *Fly* swatter?

A *what*? Coming after *me*, swinging out and down toward *me*—toward this endless Wonder, this star-filled planet-packed asteroid-gathering Superwho? Closer . . . and closer. Yeah. Could it be I was going to get smacked by a giant *fly* swatter?

Ah, come *on*, you've got to be *kiddle*—

Light blinded my eyes.

At first, I assumed it was one more damned supernova. But then I moved.

If I had been a weepy-type girlish fellow, I might have screamed. But I'm made of sterner stuff, very tough stuff, and therefore I merely yelled like a cactus-goosed banshee.

I was back in the room I'd left in order to become an immortal fly-god; the light in my eyes was a frosted-glass-covered bulb in the ceiling; and I yelled because when I moved—tried to move—every muscle and tendon and even piece of fat in my body told me it was at least stretched, probably torn, and possibly snapped.

While not here but out there, I must have jerked and pulled and twitched and strained my body so violently, when Dr. Bliss was turning his little electroshock watt-seconds dial and thumbing his buttons, that the leather straps should have been pulled free from my ankles and wrists. But that hadn't happened. Instead, I had apparently sprained all of myself in new and innovative ways, and, when I moved, every muscle I could identify started silently screaming. So I tried not to move much.

I lay still for long moments, breathing shallowly at first, then more deeply, trying to get my head and my thoughts together, essentially taking a little trip of exploration and discovery through the channels and nooks and crevices of my mind, or at least . . . I made myself form and face the unnerving thought . . . what now remained of my mind, if part remained no longer, thus leaving behind—amusing, but not much—holes in my head.

It was a curious, baffling, frustrating—and at times frightening—exercise. In part because I was sure, without really knowing the source of my certainty, that I'd forgotten some things that had happened and remembered others that had not. Sometimes I recognized the unreal as just that, illusion or error; but at other times I wasn't sure, just knew something was fuzzy, tilted, askew.

And once in a while, when I was following a train of thought or retracing a memory, there would occur a most curious short circuit or glitch, like a trembling deep within the brain, and at the precise moment when that little *zap* zapped, the train would be derailed or the trace lost. Just *zap,* and . . . where'd it go?

And that was scary. Believe me, that sort of thing wiggles the soul. But I remembered—and knew that this I remembered clearly—Claude Romanelle, drooling, vapid, out of it totally, but then one-hundred-percent whole again, right after Dr. . . . Dr. . . .

One of those curiosities. I could see the man's good face, hear his crisp voice, see the brown suit he'd worn. Just couldn't pull in his name. Not yet. Soon, undoubtedly.

It would just take a little time. No problem. Not yet, anyway. I was, in fact, very near normal, not crippled—at least not crippled mentally—in pretty good shape considering the Marquis de Sade games those bastards had played with my head.

So far . . . So far . . . For, throughout all these mental meanderings, I kept wondering when the games would begin again.

I opened my eyes, moved my head gingerly, neck muscles or bones protesting with a kind of *crick* sound. The room appeared to be filled with a thin haze of smoke, pinkish-gray smoke, and all the solid objects looked wavy, like when your TV goes on the blink.

The people were still here, the wavy people. There was the goddamned doctor who'd played with his little black dial and paddles and buttons, Dr. Brass . . . Glass . . . Blass. Dr. Blass. And the big three-hundred-pound sonofa-bitch, Cinnamon Bun, I knew him well. I wanted to kill him. I'd told him I was going to take him out. There, seated, was the thin man in a green robe; middle-aged, good-looking codger . . . Romanelle, Claude Romanelle. My client. I had him pinned down for sure. Then there was the girl, wearing a banana-yellow suit and white blouse, ah, yes, I knew that lovely one well. And the rangy guy slouching against the wall, Cowbody. Couldn't dredge up his real name, but I remembered he was called Cowbody.

It started with a prickling. Like that weird shivering inside my head when the first weak current had started to flow. But there wasn't any current now. It was a different kind of growing panic, swelling like a balloon inside me, tiny at first, getting larger, pressing against my chest, my throat, my heart.

The girl . . . ? She—I knew her, she was dear, she was wondrous, she . . .

It was as though I knew her name very well, but couldn't let it appear, form, become solid as stone. I squinted across the room, concentrated on her face and form. That face was magically beautiful but marked with strain, her pale summer-bright hair in disarray. Her arms were pulled behind her, and eye-jarring bulging breasts pushed almost nakedly against the white cloth of her blouse beneath the yellow jacket.

I knew. Didn't want to know; but knew.

Her eyes were on my face. On me, Shell Scott, her protector, her tight-lipped and tough and invincible and unbreakable go-to-hell hero who—

Slowly, so slowly, realization, never-to-be-forgotten and never-to-be-forgiven realization, swept over me, drowned me, smothered me, stopped my breath. Its implications were worse, more painful, than those agonizing currents that had ripped and roared through my heart and brain.

Spree.

I couldn't remember it at all, not yet. But I knew.

I must have told them.

Chapter Twenty

IT WAS ONLY about five minutes later, only a brief lifetime.

What was happening seemed odd to me, peculiar. I understood part of it, kept straining, reaching, hoping to understand it all because I knew the worst now. It couldn't get any worse than this.

They, Cinnammon and Blass . . . no, not Cinnamon. Cinnarom—Cimarron, Alda Cimarron and Dr. Blass had found Spree, brought her here. She was bound, as was Claude Romanelle. The Cowbody had brought two wheelchairs into the room and both Spree and Romanelle were seated in them now, not only bound but gagged, and with convex white masks, hiding the gags, over their mouths.

The group appeared to be preparing to leave. Without me, of course. Didn't need me any longer; Cimarron had finished with me. Or maybe not, not quite. He was walking this way, toward the table on which I was strapped, beckoning with a finger to Dr. Blass. In a moment they were both looking down at me.

I didn't move, tried not to blink my half-open eyes, kept breathing in the same slow deep rhythm as before.

Softly, his voice rumbling, Cimarron said, "Look at this pile of crap. He ever going to come out of it, or did you screw up and zonk him permanent?"

"I . . . I'm not sure yet," the doctor said apologetically. "He might revive any minute, or possibly in another hour or two."

"And maybe in eight years. Yeah?"

"Yes, that's true, but unlikely. And, Alda, even if he comes around soon, he might be . . . well, nonfunctional."

"You dumb crud, you *dumb* pile of—I ought to break your legs for knocking him into left field. I wanted to show this toughass his broad, let him see her, know *I* got her and he's still the hind-tit sucker. I really did. That would've told him who's down the crapping toilet and who's doing the flushing. This jerk really pissed me off, you know? Just lying there *zonked* he pisses me off. Bullshit about taking me out, telling me to screw myself in every available orifice. Orifice, that's in your ear, isn't it?"

"Not exactly. Alda . . . is *that* why you had Groder bring the woman back here?" The doctor sounded surprised, almost critical.

"Why not? He had to come back here to get Claude, didn't he? We need them both together, don't we? Anyhow, that was before you erased the jerk's brains, or whatever the hell you did. I don't even think *you* know what the hell you were doing."

"Alda . . . if you recall . . . when you insisted on a form of electroshock to soften up Claude, because he felt he was so brilliant the thought of violence to his brain would terrify him, I mentioned that we're not a psychiatric hospital, not equipped for ECT. You remember my saying that, don't you?"

From the corner of my eye I could see Cimarron poking a finger at the gray metal box atop its bright red cart near me on my right. "I remember you saying we could use those goddamn paddles for the same thing."

"I said we'd *try* it, yes, Alda. But . . . if you recall . . . I compared employing a defibrillator for ECT to performing surgery with a hacksaw, which I thought stated my expectations succinctly, and rather well if I do say so my—"

"Oh, shut up, for Christ's sake."

"Well . . . yes. But, Alda, what difference does it make now? We're through with him, aren't we?"

"Well, yeah . . . I guess you're right, Doc. But I wanted to ask him about some other things he probably messed up. Like Foster. I'm not going to let that little black sonofabitch get away with screwing me. I'll give you odds this jerk had something to do with Foster taking a walk. What was it you said Connie told you?"

There was a tickling in my nose. I wanted to sneeze —knew I couldn't. *Must* not sneeze.

"Miss DeFelitta reported that Scott saw Andy leaving Toker's house, but she doesn't know what happened after that. Andy just didn't come back. There's no evidence Scott had anything to do with his disappearance."

"No evidence? The sonofabitch had something to do with everything else, didn't he? Why make an exception? He could tell us plenty, if you hadn't fried—"

"Alda, even if he were functional, I don't believe he'd tell us anything. He's . . . crazy. It's simply ridiculous—"

The tickling kept getting worse, as if the whole inside of my nose were being brushed with tiny feathers.

The rumbling voice was saying, "He'd spill it all if I could show him his big-titted broad, Doc—she's the only reason he stayed clammed for so long. Even you ought to be able to figure that out."

The sneeze was so close to exploding I could feel the involuntary short intakes of breath, the tightening of muscles at the back of my throat and jaw as in the beginning of a yawn. Automatically, I started to move my right arm, rub a finger under my nose—and, of course, felt pain run from wrist up to shoulder as the strap around my wrist resisted movement. But I felt something else . . . I thought.

Cimarron dropped his voice to what might almost have been called a rumbling whisper, and said to Grass, or Blass, to the doctor, "Well, hell, let's get it done. That's the important thing now, finish it with Claude and his kid. Jesus, you ever see such a great pair of tits, Doc?"

The other thing I thought I'd felt was my right arm moving upward toward my chest—and it shouldn't have moved at all. I tried to pull my left wrist upward and sideways but it was almost immobile. The wide leather strap was stretched across my thighs, its ends fastened out of sight beneath the table on which I lay. Two thick leather loops securely affixed to the strap imprisoned my wrists, the loops cinched tight and held snug by three-pronged buckles like the large-size buckle of a man's belt. Those buckles were still tight; they hadn't loosened. But something . . .

"She really is a beautiful woman. Alda, it does seem almost a shame—I mean, perhaps before you dispose of her, of them, it might not hurt if I enjoyed a little time—"

"Knock it off. Don't even mention that kind of crap again or I'll deck you. Jesus, all we've got going here, maybe thirty or forty million bucks, and you're thinking about a piece of ass."

Through slitted eyes I could see the soiled brown strap around my right wrist. Three or four inches of the skin above the leather band was red and raw, already thinly scabbed with dried blood. But I pulled my right hand up, felt it move toward my face, *saw* it move an inch or two, saw the strap slide against the table's edge on my right. In my struggles, jerking and twisting, I must have loosened the strap's concealed end where it was secured beneath the table. Probably one more good yank and it would come free.

Wonderful—and then what? My left wrist and both ankles were still almost immobile. I was unarmed. And, very likely, considering the aches and pains in an infinity of muscles that I had already become painfully aware of, I would not be able to move with more alacrity than an arthritic centenarian.

But it was something. It was a wiggle. Not much, true. But for the first time in quite a while I began to think, not about how or when these bastards were going to kill me, but about living. Maybe. And maybe was good enough.

Cimarron was saying softly, the words barely audible enough for me to hear them, "O.K., let's go, get it done. We'll work on this jerk afterward, one more time. If he's come around by then, he'll spill, believe me. When I tell him they're both dead, he'll cave in and puke everything. You take care of the machinery, Doc, I'll take care of getting guys to spill their guts—"

That's when I sneezed.

The word "sneezed" is entirely inadequate. I'd been trying to suppress the explosion for so long that the last sucking intake of air literally squeaked in my throat, and then all the breath in my lungs shot out through my mouth and nose with the sound of a small hurricane escaping from a foghorn.

The mini-convulsion pulled my head and upper body off the table, and there was no way I could prevent the gobbling howl that followed the sneeze, as sudden movement combined with that pressure from inside me to send saw-toothed and fiery messages to what seemed like every nerve in my arms and legs and torso. If pain was the color black, my entire body would have turned at least blue.

"SHEE-IT!" That was Cimarron.

"Sweet Christ!" That was the Doc. "He must have been just lying there, pretending—Alda, he probably heard everything we said."

"Shee-it. The lousy . . . Hey, so what? You said it yourself. What difference, except . . . yeah. Oh, *yeah*." Cimarron actually sounded pleased, not at all unhappy.

Well, I was in a sweet pickle now. No more playing possum, pretending to be out cold. No way I could even annoy all these guys—five of them, Cimarron and Doc and Derabian and Cowbody plus one other I didn't know, a short husky guy wearing a knee-length white jacket or robe. No way out of the pickle this time . . .

Something stirred up there inside my skull, a lively wormlike wiggle. I followed it with—well, not exactly with full powers of mind, but with a strangely detached attention. At one time I'd wondered, briefly, if these guys might just go away and leave me here alone, knowing I was half dead or at least unconscious. Not much chance of that even when I'd wondered about it; no chance at all now. I knew the defibrillator they'd used on me was exactly where it had been before, black electrical cord running to an outlet in the wall, paddles resting atop the gray metal case, everything the same except that the juice was turned off now. All they had to do was turn it on again and—

No, I wouldn't last through more of that nightmare. Maybe something would survive, but it wouldn't be me.

Cimarron's deep voice was rumbling, "How about that, Michelle, baby? Loverboy's come back. Why don't I just roll you over there, chickie-babe, and let you take a good look at your tough guy . . . and vice versa? You like that, kid?"

I moved back up inside my head to that wormlike wiggle, to a little thought of some kind trying to move around, grow. I followed it along a silvery stream . . . and stopped swallowing. Tried to think of juicy delicious things—rare prime ribs . . . chilled martinis in frosted glasses . . . a full round breast with large areola and prominent nipple . . . a vine-ripened tomato warm in the summer sun.

It was very hard. It wasn't working.

"Here we go, kid. I'll just roll you over next to Loverboy. Scott's his name, right? Shell Scott? Well, from now on we call him Jerk, from the way he jerked and flopped around. Let's go look at the Jerk, Michelle baby."

I could hear strained, muffled noises, probably Spree trying to protest, say something, words stopping behind the gag in her mouth. But I pushed my thoughts away from that, turned again to those images that hadn't worked. I remembered thinking moments ago of the pickle I was in, and put all the mental energy I could gather together into thinking of that: a pickle. Not a sweet pickle but a sour one. I made it as real as I could, concentrated on it, brought it up to my mouth. I felt it crunch between my teeth. And that did it. Finally, it was working.

My eyes were half open, slanted left. Cimarron had pushed Spree in her wheelchair over next to the table, near to me, only three or four feet away now. I could see her eyes, wide, staring at me.

Cimarron took his time, enjoying himself, chuckling about Lover-Jerk and other hilarious inventions. But after a minute or so of that, the miserable sonofabitch said, "Lift his goddamn head up, Doc, so the Jerk can get a real good look"—and ripped Spree's blouse easily in his big hands, split it from top to bottom, then like a man snapping a thread broke her brassiere apart in the middle, pulled it aside, baring—and humiliating—my lovely Spree.

I almost blew it then. Almost; not quite.

I felt the doctor's hands at my head and neck, lifting me. I went along with it, opening my eyes a little wider and starting to moan. Softly at first, then louder, the sound rising in intensity and also rising up the scale, "mmmmMMMMgummMMM," like a mindless humming from behind clenched teeth.

I let my head turn so I was looking at Cimarron, not at Spree, at him. I couldn't let myself look at Spree. She was trying to turn her head away but Cimarron held it solid and still with one big hand. "Take a look, Jerk," he said to me, twisted but real pleasure in the higher than normal pitch of his voice. "Thanks for this gorgeous hunk of broad," he said to me. "No more for you, pal, it's mine now."

I stared at him wide-eyed, trying to focus on a distant horizon, or at the dizziness of swirling space I'd left not long before, and let my lips move, let my teeth unclench. Warm saliva slid over my lower lip, oozed down my chin. I felt it moving slowly, slimily, under my jawbone, onto the curve of my neck.

Saliva, mixed with little-bitty bits of sour pickle.

"SHEE-IT!" Cimarron yelled. "Goddammit." He swung his big head to look at Dr.—something. I'd lost it there for a minute . . . Blass, Dr. Blass. "You dumb sonofabitch!"

The doctor, for a change, ignored him, moved to my side, still holding my head. He turned my face toward him, cool, professional. I moaned a little for him, let my head tilt to one side. Not much spit left, so I slid my tongue around, pushed it against my teeth, managed maybe a quarter teaspoon of yuck.

Dr. Blass remained cool. "So?" he said, looking across my prone body to Cimarron. "It makes a difference?" At which point he simply let go of my head, and allowed it to fall like a loose coconut, clunk against the table. There was some padding to cushion the clunk, but it still jarred my skull and whatever marvelous stuff was still inside it. Suddenly the room was filled with that pinkish-gray fog, or smoke, again. I hadn't been aware that it had cleared up for a while.

* * *

Everyone had left a minute or two ago, except for the short husky guy in the knee-length white robe. He sat in a chair just inside the door, getting out cigarettes, starting to light a smoke.

I'd spent this last minute, and more—while Cowbody and Dr. Blass pushed the two wheelchairs out, Cimarron following the group—pulling with my right hand, trying to get the end of that leather strap even looser. It was difficult, because there was little sensation left now in my hands and wrists, but just as my guard took the first drag on his smoke the strap came free.

I stopped moving, waited for the husky guy to look away, or take another drag. After a minute or so he rested his head on the back of his chair, eyes gazing at the ceiling. I squeezed the fingers of both hands together, released them, kept it up until they started to ache and burn as circulation picked up and blood flowed more freely under the rubbed-raw redness of my wrists.

Husky was looking right at me. I watched him from almost closed eyes, realizing I had to make my move soon whether he was looking at me or not. I didn't know how well, or how fast, I could move if I somehow did get the chance to sit up, or even get onto my feet. But that, too, I would have to discover as it happened. If it happened.

Because Cimarron—and Spree and Romanelle—had been gone for at least ten or fifteen minutes now. I guessed. I wasn't at all clear about how much time had passed. Or much else, for that matter. But I knew there was urgency, a necessity for speed, that I had to hurry. I wasn't entirely sure why, but I felt it had something to do with killing . . .

Husky was looking down, reaching for an ashtray on the floor next to his chair. I pulled my right arm across my body, the loose strap whispering against the table's side, grabbed the tongue of leather at the buckle around my left wrist, yanked. Husky was still looking down, grinding out his cigarette. The three metal prongs slipped from holes in the leather and suddenly my left wrist was free. I clawed at the buckle around my right wrist, at the same time pulling against the strap and levering myself almost to a sitting position, clenching my jaws to avoid letting out an audible grunt or groan. It felt as if knives were twisting inside my stomach and up and down my spine. But I got the buckle open. Both hands were free. The long leather strap, now loose at one end, slid from the table's left side and slapped the floor. One of those buckles hit something metallic with a startlingly loud clanging noise. Husky's head snapped up. His eyes stuck on me as I leaned toward the defibrillator, holding myself partially erect by straining against the straps still around my ankles.

"Hey!" Husky yelled, bending forward. He came up out of his chair fast, took one long leaping step toward me.

Aslant, tilted sideways and with my gut burning, right arm extended and stretching, I twirled the small black dial as far right as it would go, thumb flipping the switch from "Off" to "On." The tiny green light started to glow.

The straps around my ankles helped now, providing leverage as I leaned farther to my right, both hands reaching for those two crazy paddles that not long before had been against my head. Husky loomed on my left, a blur, reaching for me. Each of my hands closed around the twin handles of one of the paddles, thumbs finding those protruding buttons, and I didn't try to hold back the grunts or strangled noises that came out of my mouth as I felt what seemed like muscle and flesh and bones tearing inside me when I moved.

No sound from the gray metal cabinet. Except for that small green light there was no way to tell if it was on or still dead. But I was sitting almost straight up when Husky reached me, thrusting his hands toward my face. I simply moved my right arm hard left, my left arm in a high arc and then down, and managed to slap the two paddles briefly into place at opposite sides of his head as I pressed the buttons with my thumbs.

It was very sloppy. I almost missed him entirely. But for half a second each of the paddles was touching him, and—no question—the gray metal box was turned on.

Half a second was enough. Maybe more than enough. One instant Husky's face was a couple of feet from me, contorted, lips stretched wide, eyes staring. The next instant that face was blank, emptied of expression, as if whatever had animated it was erased and only a plastic mask remained.

He went down loosely and didn't move. He was out cold—maybe dead. I didn't much care which, and I had no time to find out. I was unbuckling the leather straps from my ankles, sliding my legs from the table, getting my feet onto the floor. There was an aching band of muscle and flesh up the back of each calf and thigh. My left ankle felt sprained. But I could walk, if I didn't mind hobbling a little. And I didn't mind.

Before hobbling out I checked Husky, on the floor. Not his pulse; I thought he might have a gun or some kind of weapon on him. But he didn't. So I left him there, moved through the larger office next to this room and on to the door, cracked it and looked out. The long polished corridor stretched away to my right, as it had the last time I'd been here to find Claude Romanelle—months ago, years ago, whenever. The corridor looked endless. I went out, started down the long, long hallway toward the elevator at its end.

I was dizzy, light-headed, getting used to the pain of movement, as much as one can get used to it, but not to the fullness and fuzziness in my head, the feeling that at times I was not walking but swimming through something thick and clinging instead of air, like a man wading neck-deep in quicksand.

I made it into the elevator, down to the main floor, turned left and walked a mile or two, left again for another mile or two, stopped at what looked like the main nurses' station in a large lobby.

A uniformed woman, about fifty, looked at me, stepped closer. I said, "I was just talking to Mr. Cimarron and Dr. Blass. I'd like to know where they are now."

She gave me a strange look. Her eyes dropped to my chest, rose slowly to my face. Oh, yeah, I'd forgotten about that. I wasn't wearing a shirt. They'd stripped me to the waist up there, before playing Ping-Pong with my heart. Odd I remembered that but forgot I wasn't wearing a shirt. Or maybe not so odd; the shirt wasn't all that important.

But finding Cimarron was. So when the nice lady hesitated, I leaned closer to her, as close as I could get, and said, "Alda Cimarron. Dr. Blass. If you know where they are, the wisest thing you could possibly do is tell me. Without one goddamned microsecond of delay."

Something of my sincerity and lack of amusement got through to her. She said rapidly, "Mr. Cimarron and Dr. Bliss—it's not Blass, it's Dr.—"

"O.K. Blass-Bliss, who gives a—go on."

"They left with Mr. Derabian and another man. And two patients. In wheelchairs."

"Where were they going?"

"I have no idea. They just . . . left."

"How long ago?"

She turned to glance at a wall clock, then back at me. "Half an hour ago. Almost."

Then she said, "Sir—wait."

But I was ten yards away by then, huffing and grunting, but slowly picking up speed.

Chapter Twenty-One

WHEN THE NICE nurse told me that Cimarron and company had left Medigenic Hospital half an hour before, the wall clock had showed the time as about a minute after five.

It was now five-forty P.M., and I still didn't know where I would go from here, what I would do. "Here" was the split-level villa Spree and I had briefly enjoyed in the Registry Resort. Only a couple of guests, who gave me curious but not astonished glances, had seen me limp from my parked car to villa 333 and inside. The door had been unlocked, slightly ajar. It didn't occur to me—not until later—that this was undoubtedly how Cimarron had left it when he exited from the room with Spree. I just opened the door and walked in, feeling it was a most natural thing to do.

The latest car on my list of stolen vehicles was parked below—in the Medigenic's parking lot I'd found a year-old Nissan Sentra with the keys in the ignition—and I had a shirt on now. Just a shirt, no jacket; I didn't have any jackets left. But I also had, in the right-hand pocket of my trousers, the Colt .45 automatic I'd left here on the closet shelf. Two fat cartridges in the clip, one in the chamber. That was all, just three; I'd settle for that.

I sat, made myself become still, as relaxed as I could get, roamed through memory and thought. Worthington. Bentley X. Worthington. I couldn't remember his office number. I looked it up, sitting in a chair by the phone, then dialed.

I was remembering the document Worthington had prepared. For Claude Romanelle. That memory had never gone away entirely, it had just been—like many other things—fuzzy, difficult to grasp except by the edges. But I was remembering that Cimarron had to get Romanelle and Spree together in order to win his game, make it work. Worthington, too; Worthington had to be there. Well, Cimarron had Romanelle now, and Spree. I didn't let myself dwell on that, tried to stay halfway relaxed, a little loose.

The phone was answered, a voice said, "Worthington, Kamen, Fisher, Wu, and Hugh. May I help you?"

"Yes. This is Shell. May I speak to . . ."

Damn. I couldn't remember her name. The one who had helped me before.

"Just—Shell?" the voice asked.

"I'm Shell . . ."

Nothing came after that. Just a little *zap* or glitch. It was one of the strangest, and most mind-twitching, moments of my entire life. Also horrible. Maybe it's O.K. to forget a receptionist's name, a lady you've only spoken to once or twice. But—

"Is this Mr. Scott?" the lady asked.

"Yes. Yes. Shell Scott. That's who I am. Ah . . ."

"Oh, I'm so glad you called. This is Lucille. Lucille Weathers. You remember?"

"Yeah, sure. Swell." Lucille? Lucille? "I have to talk to Bentley. It's important."

"I told him you phoned, Mr. Scott, and that I gave you his message."

That I remembered. Ten thousand cops were looking for me.

"He had to leave again. I'm sorry. He didn't get back from court until nearly five. But he left you a message. Again." She laughed lightly. "You do have a difficult time getting together, don't you?"

I thought, You don't know the half of it, lady. But I said, "What's the message?"

"I'll read it to you. Like before."

"Swell. Fine. Let's go."

She read, "Mr. Claude Romanelle phoned me at five P.M. He asked me to come to his home as soon as possible, prepared to witness and notarize certain changes to be made in the document I drew up for him, which document we have discussed. I have certain reservations about this, which you will understand, but must honor the instructions of my client. I expect to be at Mr. Romanelle's home about five-thirty P.M."

I felt sick. That meant he must already be there. Maybe —maybe everything was over. I heard myself saying, "Thank you," hanging up the phone. Then I was out the door, running. Not as speedily or gracefully as I would have liked, but, by God, running.

I swung off Lincoln at the Camelback Inn entrance, skidded into Desert Fairways Drive, slowed as I passed Claude Romanelle's home. Last night when I first came here with Spree, we'd parked in the curving driveway before the house. Now, with the sun on the western horizon, but still bright—and hot—I could see the long strips of yellow plastic tape bearing the bold printed warning: "CRIME SCENE DO NOT ENTER."

I rolled on by, swung into the vacant lot where I'd turned around last night, but this time parked facing the Paradise Valley Country Club's green fairways, with Romanelle's backyard, pool, and landscaped patio on my left. If I was going to get into the house at all, I would probably have a better chance by approaching through the patio to the Arizona Room, rather than from the front. Or so I thought.

And that was about the size of it. No time to sneak up, reconnoiter, take an hour or two to make careful plans. From here on in it was just: do it.

I got out of the car, left the door open. About twenty yards away, near the fairway's edge, a man wearing Bermuda shorts and a purple shirt, plus an oddly shaped golf hat with a brilliant peacock feather stuck into its brim, was addressing a ball with a short iron and looking toward the green about a hundred yards away.

I started toward him, limping, maybe even staggering a mite, but making pretty fair progress. It would be a lot quicker, I thought, if I could get this guy to come to me.

"Hey," I called. "You, there."

He'd somehow gotten himself into a horrible contortion at the top of his backswing, and he just froze in that position for several long seconds, looking very odd indeed. Slowly—without changing the rest of his posture—he cranked his head around toward me. I noticed his mouth was moving, as if he was eating his teeth. But he wasn't saying anything. Just sort of waving his mouth at me.

I kept on a-going, getting closer, first the left leg then the right leg.

"I've got a favor to ask you," I began. Only began.

"You—you—you blithering goddamned idiot!"

He'd finally gotten his mouth to work. Or, rather, to issue intelligible sounds; it had been working for some time. That was right, though. He probably had some reason to be miffed. It is undeniable that golfers are peculiar, and get miffed—sometimes actually homicidal, if the truth be told—should you bug them even a teensy-weensy bit when they are at the top of their backswing.

But, hell, I've played golf a time or two myself, and you can take it from me, that's all a myth. It really doesn't make any difference what happens at the top of one's backswing, because you never know where the ball's going anyway, even if it's quiet as a graveyard.

I couldn't finish my thought. This man was getting *abusive.*

But I kept staggering onward, getting closer. A-one and a-two, and a-one—and by then he was only about three feet away. And he had stopped cursing fluently at me. Indeed, he unwound, or uncoiled, dropped the little club to his side, and sort of smiled unenthusiastically, looking at me intently.

I said, "I'll give you a hundred dollars for that club and one golf ball. And your hat. Yeah, got to cover this hair up."

"What? *What?*"

"*GODDAMMIT—*"

"O.K., O.K.," he said, springing back a foot or so. But

then he said, staring down at me—I was still kind of bent way over—"But this hat *alone* cost me fifty dollars. Sir. I don't mean to be—"

"O.K. Two hundred."

"Well, ah . . . You may not understand this, sir, but I was only thirteen over par through the first nine holes, and—"

"*Three* hundred. O.K.? GODDAMMIT—"

"Of course! You betcha! Here. Would you like the whole bag—?"

"Just the little club and a ball. And the hat."

"Betcha." He dropped a golf ball into my outstretched hand, plopped his gorgeous hat on my white hair, and held the short iron toward me.

I grabbed at it, grunting as I reached out and up.

"Do you . . ." He stopped, started over. "Are you a golfer?" he asked, closely eyeing my spavined posture, bent over, still clawing for his club—an eight iron, I noticed; about right for a hundred-yard pitch, I supposed.

"A golfer?" I repeated. "Yeah, sure. Sort of. But—oh, you mean this?" I tried to look pleasant, indicating with a waggle of my head, or at least my ears, the rest of me. "Nothing," I continued. "A doctor is treating me for a skin rash with some miracle drugs."

"Want me to stick this in your belt?" he asked, moving the eight iron closer.

"Hell, no, I'll get it . . . ah, got it! Nnnguummp." The last was me, straightening up. "O.K., do you have a card?"

"A what? Card?"

"Yeah. With your name on it."

He looked puzzled, but found a business card in his wallet and stuck it into my shirt pocket. "Why . . . do you want my card?"

"So I can pay you. Later. If I live. I'm a little short of cash at the moment. In fact, I don't have any."

He put on one of those frownish smiles again, held it rather rigidly in place, while saying, "Sure. Certainly. Quite all right. Could happen to anybody."

I turned, got one leg going, stayed there grunting for a

couple of seconds until I could get the other leg going. That's it, Scott, I told myself. Now just concentrate on a-one, and a-two—

Behind me the golfer, sounding choked up, called, "Good luck, old man. Hang—hang in there."

The closer I got to Romanelle's patio, which looked out onto the fairway I was just leaving, the more I learned about the condition I was in. What I had was some new kind of disease. I'd started moving slowly, but by the time I reached the fence enclosing the patio I was moving along at a very good clip. The thing was, the more I moved the easier it became, just had to get the oil pumping around and lubricating the parts and I was practically a gazelle. It was when I slowed down, or worst of all stopped, that the oil congealed and everything stiffened and started petrifying. The thing was, then, to keep moving.

I had to slow down a little, unfortunately, before finding a small wooden gate that let me into the back patio. I went through, walked around some oleanders and the base of a palm tree, moving speedily toward the Arizona Room and sliding glass doors in which, only last night, I'd seen the reflection of Romanelle . . . no, of Fred Keats . . . getting ready to kill me.

I remembered vividly the red snake of blood writhing from Keats's throat. But that wasn't the kind of picture to have in mind at this moment. Shove the pictures out; keep it going; just *do* it.

First problem: As I neared the cement deck outside those patio doors I saw a dark swarthy man with a long drooping mustache seated in a canvas-backed chair. I let the golf ball drop from my hand and it rolled past the guy's shoes. He eyed it briefly, then turned, looked up and saw me, and got suddenly to his feet.

"Sorry," I said, "I'm just learning," and really creamed him with the eight iron. It was like a jerky ballet, he looked up, got up, went down. I stepped over him, six feet from the sliding glass door.

At that moment the door slid open. I stopped, grabbing for the gun in its holster at my left armpit. No gun. No holster. I wasn't entirely sure about the armpit. Then I remembered the gun was in my pants pocket. I was trying to get the damned thing out when I realized that the man who'd come outside and was looking back into the room was Bentley X. Worthington.

He said, "I'll be going, then. If there's anything else, call me at my office tomorrow."

Then he slid the door closed, turned around, and saw me. I was moving again—shouldn't have stopped, I *knew* better—in a kind of limping-wobbling-stumbling gait, and Bentley just looked at me and said, "No." That's all he said. Just "No." Over and over.

I brushed past him, leaned forward, got a couple of fingers on the projecting handle of the glass door, pushed at it, pushed again.

"Let me get that for you, old man," Worthington said.

"Thanks. Appreciate it." He pulled the door open, stepped back, saying his word again.

I stepped forward, wobbled determinedly inside, cricking my head around. I knew it was important to figure out who was here, and where who was. The next second, or maybe even minute, was going to be crucial, and it would not do to be wondering about where everyone was at.

I shouldn't have been so worried. All I had to do was listen.

"SHEE-IT!" I knew who that was, way over on my left by a large desk. He was standing in front of the desk, looking quite a bit like an elephant holding a sheaf of white papers in one hoof.

"Scott!"

"Shell—*Shell*!"

That told me one thing: My disguise wasn't working. Those last comments had come from Claude Romanelle, seated behind the desk with a pen still in his hand, and from Spree—lovely Spree—seated next to him, wearing a buttoned-up yellow jacket that covered the torn blouse and bra that must still have been beneath it.

Then, "JESUS H. CHRIST. KILL HIM, SHOOT HIM, SOMEBODY KILL HIM" and "What the gahdamn—" and "Shell!" and "SHEE-IT" and "No."

That's when I got confused.

I knew there was a man leaning against the wall beyond Cimarron—Derabian, it looked like—and another man dropping to the floor, scuttling behind a chair. The scuttler was, I felt pretty sure, Dr. Bliss. At last, I had his name right.

By the time I'd taken all that in on my left, I realized it would be wise to check the remainder of the room on my right. So I started to. I turned that way just in time to see the Cowbody almost against the far wall, right hand moving up fast, and with a gun in it. No, it wasn't Cow*body*, but ... Hell, Cowbody was close enough.

I had the Colt .45 out of my pocket, but Cowbody fired first. He missed me by a mile, or at least a yard, but something jerked me, turned me sideways. I still had my arm extended, gun gripped in my fist, and all I had to do was keep the arm swinging until I saw Cowbody's chest beyond the gun's muzzle and squeeze the trigger.

It was as though the blast of sound, enormous blast in the confined space of the room, hurled him back against the wall, sent him sliding down it. The gun was falling from his fingers as I turned left, holding the Colt shoulder-high. Cimarron had moved from his position before the desk, was jumping toward me. But his hands were empty, and beyond him the man standing there held a gun. He not only held it, he had it pointed at me.

I went into a crouch, not as swift as are my usual crouches, and accompanied by another "nnnguummp," and then the man fired. The slug flicked the hat on my head, even touched the short-cropped hair, snapped by and smacked into something on the wall behind me, something that shattered and fell tinkling.

But even before it tinkled I'd fired at the man and missed, fired one more time and drilled him. As he went down I fired at Cimarron—several times. Silently. The automatic's slide had stayed open after my last shot; clip empty, gun useless now. I remembered: three slugs, three shots I'd fired.

So I threw the empty gun at Cimarron's head, saw it

bounce off his ear as he reached out for me, felt the golf club in my hand—still there, forgotten but tightly clutched all the while—got both hands on the eight iron's grip and pivoted, in reverse, from my left to my right, clubhead accelerating as the wrists pronated—which, according to many PGA instructors, they are supposed to do, whatever that actually means—and the heavy blade glistened through the air like a singing sword and nearly buried itself in Alda Cimarron's jaw, then bounced off, taking a good divot.

But it didn't stop him. It didn't slow him down. That three-hundred-pound body slammed into me like a stampeding elephant and we both lurched and spun, tangled together, all the way to that far wall. I hit the wall with one shoulder, and Cimarron landed hard against it with his big butt and then his head snapped back and thudded with a very meaty sound against the wood.

While he was still splayed out, slightly dazed, I got set and hit him on the chin. Right, left, right again. Three times, three good ones—as good, at least, as I was capable of at the moment. He didn't go down. Yeah, I remembered this guy in the Medigenic hallway, India rubber, a bouncing ball, three hundred pounds of unbelievable.

He shook his head back and forth rapidly, swung his right hand and caught me alongside the head as I ducked and rolled with the blow. Or tried to roll. If it was a glancing blow, it nonetheless was enough to glance me six or seven feet away and start a great silent bell swinging and tolling inside my head. The room got darker briefly, then brightened to normal—what I hoped was normal—once more. I was almost to the patio door again, damn near outside, and I could see Cimarron leaping for me, hands gouging for my chops, his thick round face a twisted mask of rage as he dived at me.

It was a good target, the natural target, that face. And I had time to pull my legs up close to my body and then unwind them with all the strength I had left in me, driving both feet forward through his hands like a bowling ball through glass and solidly against the point of his chin. The shock of that impact, my legs driving forward and Cimarron's awesome bulk descending toward me, slammed all the way through my knees and hips and up to the top of my head. It stunned me temporarily, ripped everything out of my mind except a shifting gray blankness. No thought, no wonder, no sensation at all for . . . Probably for a second or two, no way to tell, no way for me to know.

But I did know that I was still on my back, and Cimarron had fallen sprawling, then slowly pressed the huge arms beneath him and raised his body up off the floor. I knew I had to get up. Get up somehow. But I was tired. I was pooped. I was, in truth, horribly and just about definitively exhausted.

At least Cimarron wasn't leaping lightly to his feet, either. He was still on the floor, on hands and knees, his head hanging down almost loosely from the thick neck. I made myself move, turn, get my hands against the doorframe and pull, getting my feet under me, pushing with trembling muscles of calf and thigh, getting up, getting there. Nothing very speedy about it, and nothing in the least graceful, or dynamic, or efficient. Just slow and sure, functional, a combined pulling and grunting and scrambling that got the job done.

When I was erect, swaying, seeing the whole room and everything in it swimming in ripples and crazy undulations, Cimarron wasn't up off his hands and knees, not quite yet. He turned the big head, bent his neck and looked up, still a picture of fury, hate, murderous intent, a lot of ugly things, which impressed me, again, as a splendid target.

I did it pretty well for a guy about to fall down. I managed not to keel over entirely, planted my left foot solidly, swung my right leg forward, and the toe of my heavy cordovan shoe caught him just at one side of his nose.

I think it overbalanced him more than it stunned him, but the result was that he sprawled flat on the floor. Flat, but still moving, hands clawing, arms pressing down, lifting his bulk maybe an inch. This time I kicked him in the side of the head. It was, in some ways, an easier target, and there was more room, more space somehow. Anyway, I got him good with that kick. Plus the next one or two. I'm not sure how many. All I know is that I jarred him solidly, severely, until the sonofabitch didn't move anymore.

I stood there, muscles quivering, feeling as if I weighed a thousand pounds. I wanted to lie down, sleep, become unconscious. Anything except move. But there was something else I had to do. I wasn't finished. Not yet. Not quite yet.

I walked—staggered, reeled, whatever—walked the length of the room. I knew what I wanted was down there. I couldn't quite remember yet what it was. But it was there. And I was going to get it. I was *really* going to get it—just as soon as I pinned down what the hell it was.

As I neared the desk, people were around me. Voices. People talking to me. A woman talking. "*Shell!*" I couldn't see her yet, but I knew it was . . . zap . . . I knew it was the same woman whose voice I'd heard before. I recognized her conversation.

But it bothered me. I was certain I must know who she was, know her name. Of course I did. I'd known it when I came in here. Just couldn't quite wrap my head around it now. There was a feeling that I knew her well, and had done something terrible, something shameful, and it had much to do with her. It had everything to do with her. I stopped thinking about it. I didn't want to think about it.

A man's voice, "I don't believe it, I still don't believe it." That was Romanelle. Good old Claude.

And there was a brief sight and sound of Worthington X. Bent—no, Bentley. Bentley X. Worthington, looking at my presumably battered face, shaking his head, and saying, "Damnedest, most unbelievable exhibition of . . . of . . . exhibition I ever saw in my life. That was *awesome! Grotesque!* It was *crazy!*"

"Thanks, Bent," I said.

Then the woman was near, close, the perfumed softness of her at my side, fingers touching my face. She was saying, "Oh, Shell, you're hurt. Oh . . . you're *hurt.*"

"Nah," I said. "It only looks that way." I moved my head around, trying to locate her. "Just a minute," I said. "I'll find you."

"Shell, darling, you need a doctor. You need a doctor *right away!*"

That did it. That made me remember, suddenly, what it was I had to do. The last of it. In some ways, maybe, the best of it.

"Thanks, lady," I said, smiling what must have been a most unlovely smile. "That's what I need, all right. And I know the one I want. Now that I've learned how to pronounce his name."

I went looking for him. Didn't have to go very far. He was still where I'd seen him scuttling after diving to the floor, when I'd first come inside. He was behind a large chair covered in shimmering gold cloth, flat on the carpet, hands wrapped over his head.

"Hello there, Dr. Bliss," I said gently. Then I kicked him. Not the way I'd kicked Cimarron. Just a nudge. But not exactly a nudge that could be easily ignored. He looked up at me, eyes wide, frightened.

"Get up, you useless sonofabitch," I said softly. "Get up, and do it now, or I'll pull your guts out right there on the floor."

He got up. Slowly, but he made it all the way. He looked at me as if he thought I was a crazy man about to cook him and eat him alive. The good doctor, who liked to play with electricity, moved away from me until his back was against the wall, arms out at his sides, hands pressed against the wood.

"Bliss," I said, stepping in front of him, "I am going to hit you. I am going to slam you as hard as I can. So don't just stand there. Take a swing at me, do *something.*"

He didn't speak. His knees were visibly shaking. I didn't feel any sympathy for him, none at all. I could still see his fingers turning that little black dial, moving those paddles toward my head.

"Last chance," I said. "Hell, I'm out on my feet, Doc. Feel like I've died and been resurrected twice in the last half hour. Who knows, I may faint if you land a good one on me. Maybe you'll get lucky. No?"

He remained silent. Just stood there shaking.

So I hit him.

I don't know how, with all the aches and creaks and pains and sprains and rips and such in all of my three thousand and ninety-six muscles, I managed to swing so freely and hit him so hard. But I did. I got him solidly in the mouth—the mouth that had said, "I'll handle it" and "Here we go again, boys" as his friendly-family-physician's fingers twirled that little dial—and I almost enjoyed the excruciating catastrophe that shot from my fist through arm to possibly dislocated shoulder, because my ears rejoiced at the meaty SPLAT of the blow landing, and my knuckles felt Dr. Bliss's lips split and splash, felt teeth grittily breaking.

He slammed back against the wall, his head smacking the paneled wood and bouncing forward again. Just in time. It was beautiful. Because, although he was going down he was going down slowly, sliding, slipping slowly down the dark-wood-paneled wall, and as his head bounced forward it carried his face with it, and his face carried that red-smeared torn-flesh-and-streamingred-blood orifice he had so jovially employed for his we're-through-with-him-aren't-we? pleasantries, and that already unrecognizable mouth-mess was still not much below the level of my shoulders, bouncing toward me and descending slowly enough that I had time to hit him again.

So that is what I did. I hit him again. In the mouth.

And that appeared to take care of everything of pressing immediacy. I was suddenly without purpose, without a goal. There wasn't anything left for me to *do*. But as I turned wobbling, staggered to my left, a man put his hand on my arm. It was Romanelle. Claude. The one other man who'd been through what I'd gone through.

He said, "You don't know how Cimarron found Spree, do you?"

"Yeah, I know. I mean, I don't remember, but I can guess—"

"Mr. Scott—Shell. Alda bragged about it to me. I already knew he had Toker's phone tapped. Calls were routed to a voice-actuated transmitter three hundred yards away, in an empty house. Once a day, Andy Foster —before he took off—picked up the tape, took it to Alda. Today, Andy wasn't around to do it. There was a lot of delay. When Alda did finally get the tape, he separately recorded that confession you made. When you phoned Steve Whistler. Remember?"

"Yeah, but . . . I'm starting to . . ."

"He gave that recording to a policeman friend. And then—it took a while—then, when he thought of checking it more carefully, and took the time, he listened closely to the recording of the call you made from Toker's home to Spree. To Spree at the Registry."

"Jesus," I said.

"When they figured out what the number you'd called was, and identified the location, they just went there—"

"My God," I said, interrupting him, not hearing if he said anything else, my head full, spinning. "I didn't tell them," I said. "I really didn't, I didn't tell them."

Suddenly I felt light as air. I could feel the helium gurgling in my veins. Probably, I thought, I could float if I just strained and grunted hard enough. I looked for her, knew she was around here somewhere, creaked my head around with a sound inside my head like *criiickk* . . . and my eyes fell on one of the loveliest sights I'd seen in all of the universes I'd visited not long ago.

For a moment I wasn't *completely* sure . . . ah, then —"Spree?" I said. "Spree, my love. I thought . . ." *zap*, gurgle ". . . I'd lost you, far, far in the dranglows."

She smiled. Full lips curving, soft and sweet as velvet nightsong, warm as longing, lovely as sin. I smiled at her smile, her lips, the white teeth with that slightly too short one there, the great green eyes bright with moonglow and softer than secret whispers, the hair like fairygold spun of honey, and I remembered for sure where I had seen that face before.

Out there, it was, in that far-far place where I'd been, that immensity filled with shouting stars and shining suns and the powers and pleasures of God, and of us.

I held out my arms, reached for and enfolded her, pulled her close, hugged my Spree. "Hey," I said, with my lips against her ear, "I remember you. I really do. I do." And she said, "Me, too," muffled. "Me, too."

But then she was rising, slipping upward. I shook my head back and forth, *cri-ick criiick*, wondering if this was another of those short circuits or *zaps* or glitches. No, not this time. She really *was* up there, way up there, maybe nine, nine and a half feet tall. I looked up at her. She was looking down at me. So I looked down at me, why not? At least, I looked down at my feet. I didn't have any.

That was a crock. How did I get here and do all this if I didn't have any feet? Sure enough, though, all I had was a couple of little short fat legs ending in stumps; no feet at all. "How about that?" I said, to nobody in particular. "Those dirrty bastards."

I recalled all those doctors and Igors clamping machineries on my head and screwing everything on sideways. *They'd* done it. I remembered some of the other stuff, but I sure hadn't noticed them doing anything like this.

"Oh, God . . . Shell—Shell!"

That was Sprue, way up above me there, far-far. "Those dirrty bastards," I repeated. "You know what they did? They shrank me."

"Oh, Shell . . . oh, please."

She was tugging at me, yanking on my coat sleeves or coat shoulders. "Get up off your *knees*," she said in a strangely tortured voice. "Please, *please*."

"Please? Knees?" I said. "Don't be ridic . . . well. Boy. *Oh*, boy. You want to see a relieved ghee, Spry? You want to see a guy who'll never take feet for grunted again as ling as he loves? Langs? Forever?" She was tugging, and the guy, the one with a face like a large imp or reformed devil—Romanoff, Rubadub, something—was tugging also, lifting.

"Hey, thanks," I said.

I was on my *feet*. Feet felt *great*. "Way to go!" I said.

Right in front of me again was—Spree. Had to keep track of that name, Sp and a ree. Her gorgeous face was sort of—lopsided. Twisted. And wet. Wet?

"Hey, what are you *crying* for?" I asked her. "Nothing to cry about *now*. If you want to know the truth, which I picked up in my extensive travels, there's *never* anything to cry about, not really. Not if you'll laugh instead. O.K.? O.K., Sp ree? Spree?"

"Oh, Shell, damn you—damn you—*damn* you, Shell. Are you all right? Are you going to . . . live?"

"What kind of dumb question is that? Can't you tell? Of *course* I'm—"

"But I saw you get hit. By a bullet. Right after you came in. It spun you around, almost knocked you down."

"No. Must've been in a movie I saw. I have *no* recollection—"

"And you just swung your arm around and went bang, and—"

"Did I have a gun in my arm? Or did I just go bang?"

"*Yes*, you had a gun. That's what—oh . . ."

"I was going to say, if I didn't, that's a pretty good trick, or else *pret*-ty stupid—"

"And you're *still* bleeding all over the place."

"No. Why would you say something like that?"

"You are. Look. *Look*, you damn—damn—damn—"

"Don't get lippy with me, kid. O.K., I'll look, just to satisfy the dumb . . . Nguuugh."

After a while I said weakly, "That can't all be from me. I didn't have that much to start with. How many guys got killed in here?"

But there wasn't time for an answer.

Whole bunch of cops. Uniforms, plainclothes, big cops, little cops, nice cops, mean cops—mostly mean—more cops than anybody could possibly desire unless some of them were coroners.

Soon one of them was next to me, tugging at my elbow and saying in a starchy British accent, "Come along quietly now, old man."

That was three times in only . . . whenever . . . that somebody had called me an old man. Wasn't I still thirty? Probably not. I was trying to figure out where all the cops had come from, and why. A mean one who'd just hand-cuffed me and read me a lot of my rights said the paramedics and ambulances would be here practically instantly to resuscitate me, or something to that effect, but then just kept going on and on about my having killed a man named Fred Keats, and killed this one and that one, and hitting several other victims with clubs or guns or bathtubs, I don't remember, and stealing a bunch of cars and guns and people, and operating without a license, and now this thing here, this thing being two or three more dead guys—well, just one of them, Cowbody was dead, the others were only invalids—and unconscious, clearly ruined, barely breathing, respected Alda Cimarron, the president of Golden Phoenix Mines and other financial and charitable institutions, who had been brutally hit and kneed and kicked and presumably pitched into a bunker with an eight iron, and—

I interrupted him. "No problem."

"What? No what?"

"Problem," I said. "Piece of cake."

"Piece of what? What?"

"I find it difficult to understand you, Officer," I said, "when you stammer. I am trying to explain that . . . I can explain all of that."

"All of—what?"

"I wish you wouldn't do that, sir. I am trying to tell you that I can explain . . . everything."

He stood in front of me, smiling. It was an odd smile. Much like the mask of Comedy with thirty-six unfilled cavities in it. Knots of muscle bunched, wiggled, in his jaws, in his cheeks, in his eyes.

He smiled and smiled. "That'll be fun," he said.

Chapter Twenty-Two

SPREE SAID, "AND then what?"

We were no longer in Arizona. We were together in my apartment. In the Spartan Apartment Hotel, Hollywood, California. Back at the place I call home: the tropical fish—which Jimmy, the night man, had taken care of for me while I was away—my bawdy nude, Amelia, the chocolate-brown divan and hassocks and other familiar things. Home. Roots. The place that keeps you anchored to earth when you roam for a while.

So Arizona was behind us; but we had a lot of memories about those days, and nights, some good and some not so good, there in the desert—and we'd been talking about all that, among other things, for hours now.

I said, "And then I hired a Phoenix private detective to locate all the people whose cars I'd . . . borrowed, including Andy Foster, and make sure they were compensated, satisfied, mollified—at least none of them sued me. Plus, he found the guy who sold me the hat and golf club, paid him the three hundred. Unfortunately, he had to go to Michigan to find him. Also, when he gave the man back his eight iron the guy said, Thanks, but he'd given up golf."

"Oh, dear. Because of you, Shell?"

"Oh . . . I think not. Golfers do that all the time."

This morning was the first I'd seen of Spree since her last visit to me at the hospital in Phoenix nearly three weeks ago, and it was almost evening now, dusk softening the city outside. Three weeks; but this morning, when I opened the door and saw her standing there, saw that wonderful face, there was the same magic in that moment as there'd been the first time, more than a month before.

Most of that month had been, for me, recuperation, getting back the old vigor and vitality and then some, more zip and less *zap*, taking lots of powdered vitamin C and little pilules and drops and marvelous glandular and nutritional goodies in unreadable boxes from West Germany and Switzerland and Tijuana, goodies so marvelously virtuous and beneficial for the outer and inner man that it is unlawful to sell them in the U.S. of A. As a result, I had truly never felt better in my life.

Most of my present exuberance and yeastiness was due to the unorthodox ministrations of Dr. Barry Midland. I spent two weeks under his care in a private hospital—not the Medigenic—and I wouldn't let anyone else even take my temperature or prescribe an aspirin. This, needless to say, caused considerable commotion, voluble hueing and crying, virtually a battle-to-the-death upheaval in sacred hospital routine, and thus brought down upon me vast imprecations, condemnations, even questionings of sanity, issuing starchily from numerous doctors, nurses, residents, trainees, and even the guy who cleaned out the toilets, all of whom insisted that *they* were in charge of my life, not I. Or attempted to so insist. Having survived what I had so recently emerged half alive from, it was a piece of cake, no problem, to convince them they were full of it. I won.

My selfish obstinancy and refusal to accept "accepted" medical treatment, added to my natural soon-fed-up-with-it obnoxiousness, also caused Dr. Midland himself some hassle and difficulty. But he assured me that he didn't mind; he was used to it. Besides, he was thinking of establishing a clinic in Tijuana, where he might effectively heal the ailing without going to jail for it.

Ah, yes, jail. I was there for a while, too. Actually, only overnight. The shortness of my stay was mainly because of Bentley X. Worthington, who threw several legal books at police officialdom, threatened numerous private and public bodies with everything except impeachment of the king, and impressed all and sundry with his fearsomeness. We do need friends along the way, caring and capable friends, no doubt about it. Of course, the only people I'd shot or physically devastated one way or another were practicing felons, one of whom was a practicing physician, none of whom were practicing anything anymore. All of which made Worthington's job somewhat less impossible. Interestingly, the taped "confession" I phoned in to Steve Whistler turned out to be one of the most valuable tools Worthington used to pry me out of the can.

"And what about that girl?" Spree asked. "The pretty one."

"*You're* the pretty one."

"Silly boy, you're just trying to turn my head with your flattery."

"That's not all I'm trying—"

"*Tell* me about her. Daddy said something—she wasn't who everyone thought she was? He never finished it."

"Well, that's part of it, all right. I met her as Kay Denver, later learned she was Kay Dark, working for *Exposé*. But the Denver was just for me, the Dark just for Whistler and *Exposé*, and the truth is she's Connie DeFelitta, very expensive call girl—five hundred and up a night—from Chicago. Derabian's part of an organized crime group of financially well-to-do fellows back there—the ones who put up most of the backing, the cash money, to build up Golden Phoenix Mines for the big score, rather the *planned* big score. He, and they, had enough influence and muscle to plant a 'Kay Dark' cover story so convincing that even Steve Whistler checked it out and accepted it. Kay—or Connie—might have had a little something to do with convincing him, too. She's also a very bright and brainy gal, entirely aside from . . ."

"Umm-hmm," she said. "So when she picked you up in Pete's—"

"Spree! Picked me *up*? Picked *me* up? That's not like you—"

"How do you know?" She slitted her eyes, puckered her lips, tried to look mysterious and sultry. "'Ow vud you kanow?" she asked in a really *terrible* accent of some kind, like maybe inner-earth. "Mebbe I gorl zpy vrum eezt, name Myrtle."

"*Myrtle?* Good God—no more—you win. When Kay picked me up in Pete's, she convinced me she had a problem, needed a private investigator—"

"'*Ow* deed zhe gunvinz—"

"Will you stop it? And never mind 'ow. The salient point here, the only item worthy of mention, is that when I traced her to *Exposé* I thought the trail ended there, which is what I—everybody—was supposed to think. Truth is, after being sent out here by Derabian, she reported everything she learned—which, as one on the inside at *Exposé*, was plenty—to Alda Cimarron."

"So . . . when she pic—met you at Pete's, she was really here in Los Angeles digging for Cimarron, *not* for Mr. Whistler."

"Right on. You've got it. You see, everything that *Exposé* knew about the Golden Phoenix, Romanelle, me, you —the ad I ran in an attempt to locate you, for example —Cimarron *also* knew almost immediately. Wheels within wheels, crooks within—"

"I'm glad you *did* run that ad, Shell."

"One of the most memorable things I ever did. I have to thank your dad for that. You know, for a while I thought maybe he was just—using you. But, nope, he wasn't . . . Say, that's right. You're rich now, aren't you?"

"Oh, *poof.* A million or two."

"Last time I looked, Golden Phoenix was bid at two and an eighth, so your half comes to—over two million bucks. When new management comes in, the shares will go higher. But baby, two million isn't *poof.*"

"Well, that's not nearly as important to me as what happens to Dad, Shell. Will he . . . will he have to go to jail?"

"Maybe not. Probably not. He was in on the scam, sure. But he told me the truth, he was about three-fourths blackmailed into it. And there's still his problem back in Chicago, that homicide twenty-odd years ago. But he's got Bentley X. Worthington on his case, plus Kamen, Fisher,

Wu, and Hugh. One thing's for sure, he's getting health-ier."

That much was true. Certainly Romanelle was no longer much worried about his "lethal cancer," which according to Dr. Midland could almost surely be eliminated within a few months. Not surprisingly, Romanelle had opted for Dr. Midland's way, and was growing more vigorous—and possibly more abrasive—every day.

"Yeah," I added to Spree, "I think old Claude is going to be O.K. on all counts."

"I hope so. I like him. I really do, he's a dear old . . . daddy."

She smiled. She smiled a lot, which was good. Still, I was glad she didn't smile *all* the time. That would have been like always having sunrise without a sunset, forever the sun and never the moon. She was so beautiful, and sometimes I looked at her so intently, so lost in simply seeing her, that I forgot I was there. Her face and form just kind of expanded to fill everything there was, no room during those lost moments for anything else. Just Spree.

She said, "Did you go away somewhere, Shell?"

"No," I grinned. "Don't intend to. Well, ah, I think we've uncovered—covered most of the bits and pieces of our recent past. So, about our present . . ."

"Yes?"

"That's what I like to hear. Yes. Yes! It's so much better than no, isn't it? There's a profound lesson for all of us in that simple—"

"What are you getting at, Shell? As if I didn't know."

"That makes it easier. Why don't you?"

"Why don't I what?"

"Take your clothes off again."

"Shell, what is the *matter* with you?"

"Matter? What do you mean, matter? Something's got to be the *matter* with me because I'd like for you to remove the concealing garments from that fabulous, fantastic, gland-exploding bod—?"

"No, I don't mean . . . You know that . . . I mean —Shell, I just put them *on*."

"Yes. That's true. But well, that was, oh, almost ten minutes ago. And I—I miss it. Them. It all."

"You're serious?"

"Serious. Yeah, boy, am I—"

"Well, all right, then. If you insist."

A few minutes later I was sitting on the floor near a hassock, and Spree was sort of dancing over the yellow-gold carpet, going clear around behind me and then back in front of me, close in front of me, thus giving a lot of exercise to my neck, which fortunately had stopped cricking. She had taken my advice, and there was nothing on Spree except Spree. Lovely, it was.

"I'll never get over you," I said. "You're just—hah! —ho!—hoo!—"

"Is that a new language, you dummy? Or are you supposed to be in the darkest jungle—"

"No, no, I just haven't figured out how to pronounce it all yet."

She stopped moving, stood in front of me, maybe a foot, foot and a half away, and she placed one hand under each of those astonishing, magnificent, superabundant breasts, and sort of bounced them up and down a little, or rather a lot, the way one might ride a child giddyap on one's knee . . . no, not like that at all. Forget it.

I watched, fascinated, the rise and fall, the remarkable, the awesome movement, the jiggling and trembling, hardly hearing Spree's words as she said, "Shell, you've been good for me, you really have—you've made me *free*! I'm not ashamed of my great big breasts anymore."

"Hoo—"

"I don't mind letting them be seen now. I really don't. Oh! I feel like just showing them to everybody! Everywhere! All over the place!"

"*Don't you dare!*"

"But you said—"

"Pay no attention to what I said. What do I know? They're mine! Mine!"

She was laughing. In a moment the laughter subsided, but she was still giving me a bright, beaming, wonderful smile. You know, comets and asteroids and all that.

"Oh, Shell. I was just teasing you. You're so much fun when you're crazy."

"Crazy? I'll show you crazy. I'll show you . . . you really don't mind?"

She sat on the floor, snuggled against me. "Not with you, I don't. I don't know why, really." She gave me a sort of mischievous version of that magical smile. "There's certainly nothing very special about *you*, Shell."

"Oh, I don't know," I said.

She gave me an oddly surprised look for a moment, until I finished, "Spree, dear, even counting the bad guys, there's something very special about everybody."